"Ashley's latest flawlessly written historical romance richly rewards romance readers with its multilayered characterization; sexy, secrets-saturated plotting; sharp wit; and enthralling writing." —*Booklist* (starred review)

"Passionate, well-drawn characters, breathless romance, and a memorable love story will leave readers checking out the earlier books in the series and anxiously awaiting the last in the quartet, *The Duke's Perfect Wife*."
—*Library Journal*

"Innovative as ever, Ashley's third novel about the Mackenzie brothers is a beautifully written, tender, touching romance that will leave readers breathless. Her strong characterizations and poignant yet sensual storytelling draw readers into her unforgettable love stories."
—*RT Book Reviews* (Top Pick)

"Readers will love Ainsley, a strong, independent, cake-loving character who takes the time to consider her options rather than just throwing caution to the wind and following Cameron when he arrogantly beckons."   —*Publishers Weekly*

"Ashley simply has a gift with her storytelling. . . . Heart-wrenching romance, balanced with a good amount of steamy sex, and an underlying story line all contribute to the book's enjoyment."   —*Night Owl Reviews*

"Another winner from Jennifer Ashley. . . . It's romantic and heartfelt, steamy and sexy with just the right amount of humor. I absolutely love this book and I cannot get enough of the Mackenzies!"   —*Michelle and Leslie's Book Picks*

continued . . .

THE MADNESS OF LORD IAN MACKENZIE

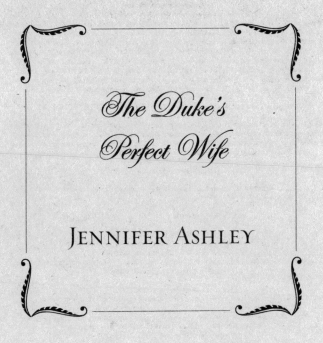

The Duke's Perfect Wife

JENNIFER ASHLEY

BERKLEY SENSATION, NEW YORK

THE BERKLEY PUBLISHING GROUP
Published by the Penguin Group
Penguin Group (USA) Inc.
375 Hudson Street, New York, New York 10014, USA

Penguin Group (Canada), 90 Eglinton Avenue East, Suite 700, Toronto, Ontario M4P 2Y3, Canada
(a division of Pearson Penguin Canada Inc.) • Penguin Books Ltd., 80 Strand, London WC2R 0RL,
England • Penguin Group Ireland, 25 St. Stephen's Green, Dublin 2, Ireland (a division of Penguin
Books Ltd.) • Penguin Group (Australia), 250 Camberwell Road, Camberwell, Victoria 3124, Australia
(a division of Pearson Australia Group Pty. Ltd.) • Penguin Books India Pvt. Ltd., 11 Community
Centre, Panchsheel Park, New Delhi—110 017, India • Penguin Group (NZ), 67 Apollo Drive,
Rosedale, Auckland 0632, New Zealand (a division of Pearson New Zealand Ltd.) • Penguin Books
(South Africa) (Pty.) Ltd., 24 Sturdee Avenue, Rosebank, Johannesburg 2196, South Africa

Penguin Books Ltd., Registered Offices: 80 Strand, London WC2R 0RL, England

THE DUKE'S PERFECT WIFE

A Berkley Sensation Book / published by arrangement with the author

PUBLISHING HISTORY
Berkley Sensation mass-market edition / April 2012

ISBN: 978-0-425-24710-5

BERKLEY SENSATION®
Berkley Sensation Books are published by The Berkley Publishing Group,
a division of Penguin Group (USA) Inc.,
375 Hudson Street, New York, New York 10014.
BERKLEY SENSATION® is a registered trademark of Penguin Group (USA) Inc.
The "B" design is a trademark of Penguin Group (USA) Inc.

PRINTED IN THE UNITED STATES OF AMERICA

10   9   8   7   6   5   4   3   2   1

ALWAYS LEARNING   **PEARSON**

This book is dedicated to my parents: To my father, whom I lost this year, and to my mother, who is stronger than she knows. Thank you for all your encouragement, patience, and love.

Chapter 1

Hart Mackenzie.

It was said that he knew every pleasure a woman desired and exactly how to give it to her. Hart wouldn't ask what the lady wanted, and she might not even know herself, but she would understand once he'd finished. And she'd want it again.

He had power, wealth, skill, and intelligence, and the ability to play upon his fellow man—or woman—to make them do anything he wanted and believe it to be their own idea.

Eleanor Ramsay knew firsthand that all of this was true.

She lurked among a flock of journalists in St. James's Street on an unexpectedly mild February afternoon, waiting for the great Hart Mackenzie, Duke of Kilmorgan, to emerge from his club. In her unfashionable gown and old hat, Lady Eleanor Ramsay looked like any other lady scribbler, as hungry for a story as the rest of them. But while they craved an exclusive story about the famous Scottish duke, Eleanor had come to change his life.

The journalists snapped alert when they spied the tall duke on the threshold, his broad shoulders stretching out a black coat, Mackenzie plaid swathing his hips. He always wore a kilt to remind everyone who set eyes on him that he was, and always would be, Scottish first.

"Your Grace!" the journalists shouted. "Your Grace!"

The sea of male backs surged past Eleanor, shutting her out. She jostled her way forward, using her folded parasol without mercy to open her way to the front of the pack. "Oh, I do beg your pardon," she said, when her bustle shoved aside a man who tried to elbow her in the ribs.

Hart looked neither left nor right as he pulled on his hat and walked the three steps between the club and the door of his open landau. He was master of not acknowledging what he did not wish to.

"Your Grace!" Eleanor shouted. She cupped her hands around her mouth. "Hart!"

Hart stopped, turned. His gaze met hers, his golden stare skewering her across the twenty feet of space between them.

Eleanor's knees went weak. She'd last seen Hart on a train, almost a year ago, when he'd followed her into her compartment, his hand warm on her arm, and made her take a gift of money from him. He'd felt sorry for her, which had rankled. He'd also tucked one of his cards into the collar of her bodice. She remembered the heat of his fingers and the scrape of the card, with his name, against her skin.

Hart said something to one of the pugilist-looking bodyguards who waited next to his carriage. The man gave Hart a nod, then turned and shouldered his way to Eleanor, breaking a path through the frantic journalists.

"This way, your ladyship."

Eleanor clutched her closed parasol, aware of the angry glares around her, and followed. Hart watched her come, his gaze never moving. It had been heady, once upon a time, to be the center of that very studied attention.

When she reached the landau, Hart caught her by the elbows and boosted her up and inside.

Eleanor's breath went out of her at his touch. She landed on the seat, trying to slow her pounding heart, as Hart followed her in, taking the seat opposite, thank heavens. She'd never be able to get through her proposition if he sat too close to her, distracting her with the heat of his very solid body.

The footman slammed the door, and Eleanor grabbed at

her hat as the landau jerked forward. The gentlemen of the press shouted and swore as their prey got away, the landau heading up St. James's Street toward Mayfair.

Eleanor looked back over the seat at them. "Goodness, you've made Fleet Street unhappy today," she said.

"Damn Fleet Street," Hart growled.

Eleanor turned around again to find Hart's gaze hard on her. "What, all of it?"

This close to him, she could see the gold flecks in his hazel eyes that gave him the eagle look, and the red highlights in his dark hair from his Scottish ancestry. He'd cropped his hair shorter since she'd seen him last, which made his face sharper and more forbidding than ever. Eleanor was the only one among the crowd of journalists to have seen that face soften in sleep.

Hart stretched one big arm across the seat, his large legs under the kilt crowding the carriage. The kilt shifted upward a little, letting her glimpse thighs tanned from all the riding, fishing, and tramping about he did on his Scottish estate.

Eleanor opened her parasol, pretending that she was relaxed and happy to be in the same carriage as the man to whom she'd once been engaged. "I apologize for accosting you on the street," she said. "I did go to your house, but you've changed your majordomo. He did not know me, nor was he by any means impressed by the card you gave me. Apparently ladies make a habit of trying to gain your house by false pretenses, and he assumed me one of those. I really cannot blame him. I could have stolen the card, for all he knew, and you have always been quite popular with the ladies."

Hart's gaze didn't soften under her barrage of words as it used to do. "I will speak to him."

"No, no, don't shout at the poor man *too* much. He wasn't to know. I expect you tell him very little, in your maddening way. No, I came all this way from Aberdeen to talk to you. It's really quite important. I called in at Isabella's, but she was not at home, and I knew that this could not wait. I managed to get it out of your footman—dear Franklin, how he's grown—that you'd be at your club, but he was too terrified of the majordomo to let me wait in the house. So I decided to lurk and catch you when you emerged. It was such fun, pretending to be a scribbler. And here I am."

She threw out her hands in that helpless gesture Hart remembered, but woe to any man who thought this woman helpless.

Lady Eleanor Ramsay.

The woman I am going to marry.

Her dark blue serge dress was years out of date, her parasol had one broken spoke, and her hat with faded flowers and short veil perched lopsidedly on her head. The veil did nothing to hide the delphinium blue of her eyes or the spread of sweet freckles that ran together when she wrinkled her nose, all the while smiling her little smile. She was tall for a woman, but filled out with generous curves. She'd been breathtakingly beautiful at age twenty, when he'd first seen her flitting about a ballroom, her voice and laughter like music, and she was beautiful now. Even more so. Hart's hungry gaze feasted on her, he imbibing her like a man who'd gone without sustenance for a very long time.

He forced his voice to remain steady, casual even. "What is this important thing you need to speak to me about?" With Eleanor it could be anything from a lost button to a threat to the British Empire.

She leaned forward a little, the hook at the top of her collar coming loose from the frayed fabric. "Well, I cannot tell you, here, in an open carriage plodding through Mayfair. Wait until we are indoors."

The thought of Eleanor following him into his house, breathing the same air he did, made his chest constrict. He wanted it, he craved it. "Eleanor . . ."

"Goodness, you can spare me a *few* minutes, can't you? Consider it my reward for distracting those rabid journalists. What I have discovered could border on the disastrous. I decided it best I rush down and tell you in person instead of write."

It must be serious to make Eleanor leave her ramshackle house outside Aberdeen, where she lived with her father in genteel poverty. She went few places these days. Then again, she could have some covert motive in that head of hers. Eleanor could do nothing simply.

"If it is that important, El, for God's sake, tell me."

"Goodness, your face looks like granite when you scowl. No wonder everyone in the House of Lords is terrified of you." She tilted back the parasol and smiled at him.

Soft flesh beneath his, her blue eyes half closed in sultry pleasure, Scottish sunshine on her bare skin. The feeling of moving inside her, her smile as she said, "I love you, Hart."

Old emotions rose swiftly. He remembered their last encounter, when he hadn't been able to stop himself touching her face, saying, "Eleanor, whatever am I going to do with you?"

She popping up here before he was ready would force him to alter the timing of his plans, but Hart had the ability to rearrange his schemes with lightning speed. That's what made him so dangerous.

"I will tell you in due time," Eleanor went on. "And give you my business proposition."

"Business proposition?" With Eleanor Ramsay. God help him. "What business proposition?"

Eleanor, in her maddening way, ignored him to look around at the tall houses that lined Grosvenor Street. "It has been so long since I've been to London, and for the Season, no less. I am looking forward to seeing everyone again. Good heavens, is that Lady Mountgrove? It is, indeed. Hello, Margaret!" Eleanor waved heartily to a plump woman who was alighting from a carriage in front of one of the painted doors.

Lady Mountgrove, one of the most gossipy women in England, fixed her mouth in a round O. Her stare took in every detail of Lady Eleanor Ramsay waving at her from the Duke of Kilmorgan's carriage, the duke himself planted opposite her. She gaped a long time before lifting her hand in acknowledgment.

"Goodness, I haven't seen her in donkey's years," Eleanor said, sitting back as they rolled on. "Her daughters must be, oh, quite young ladies now. Have they made their come-outs yet?"

Her mouth was still kissable, closing in a little pucker while she awaited his answer.

"I haven't the faintest bloody idea," Hart said.

"Really, Hart, you must at least *glance* at the society pages. You are the most eligible bachelor in all of Britain. Probably in the entire British Empire. Mamas in India are grooming their girls to sail back to you, telling them, *You never know. He's not married yet.*"

"I'm a widower." Hart never said the word without a pang. "Not a bachelor."

"You're a duke, unmarried, and poised to become the most powerful man in the country. In the world, really. You should give a thought to marrying again."

Her tongue, her lips, moved in such a sultry way. The man who'd walked away from her had to be insane. Hart remembered the day he'd done so, still felt the tiny *smack* of the ring on his chest when she'd thrown it at him, rage and heartbreak in her eyes.

He should have refused to let her go, should have run off with her that very afternoon, bound her to him forever. He'd made mistake after mistake with her. But he'd been young, angry, proud, and . . . embarrassed. The lofty Hart Mackenzie, certain he could do whatever he pleased, had learned differently with Eleanor.

He let his voice soften. "Tell me how you are, El."

"Oh, about the same. You know. Father is always writing his books, which are brilliant, but he couldn't tell you how much a farthing is worth. I left him to amuse himself at the British Museum, where he is poring over the Egyptian collection. I do hope he doesn't start pulling apart the mummies."

He might. Alec Ramsay had an inquisitive mind, and neither God nor all the museum authorities in the land could stop him.

"Ah, here we are." Eleanor craned to look up at Hart's Grosvenor Square mansion as the landau pulled to a halt. "I see your majordomo peering out the window. He looks a bit dismayed. Do not be too angry with the poor man, will you?" She put her fingers lightly on the hand of the footman who'd hurried from Hart's front door to help her down. "Hello again, Franklin. I have found him, as you see. I was remarking upon how tall you've become. And married, I hear. With a son?"

Franklin, who prided himself on his forbidding countenance while guarding the door of the most famous duke in London, melted into a smile. "Yes, your ladyship. He's three now, and the trouble he gets into." He shook his head.

"Means he's robust and healthy." Eleanor patted his arm. "Congratulations to you." She folded her parasol and waltzed into the house while Hart climbed down from the landau behind her. "Mrs. Mayhew, how delightful to see you," he heard her say. He entered his house to see her holding out her hands to Hart's housekeeper.

The two exchanged greetings, and were talking about, of all things, recipes. Eleanor's housekeeper, now retired, apparently had instructed her to obtain Mrs. Mayhew's recipe for lemon cakes.

Eleanor started up the stairs, and Hart nearly threw his hat and coat at Franklin as he followed. He was about to order Eleanor into the front drawing room when a large Scotsman in a threadbare kilt, loose shirt, and paint-spattered boots came barreling down from the top floor.

"Hope you don't mind, Hart," Mac Mackenzie said. "I brought the hellions and fixed myself a place to paint in one of your spare bedrooms. Isabella's got the decorators in, and you wouldn't believe the racket—" Mac broke off, a look of joy spreading across his face. "Eleanor Ramsay, by all that's holy! What the devil are you doing here?" He raced down the last of the stairs to the landing and swept Eleanor off her feet into a bear hug.

Eleanor kissed Mac, second youngest in the Mackenzie family, soundly on the cheek. "Hello, Mac. I've come to irritate your older brother."

"Good. He needs a bit of irritating." Mac set Eleanor down again, eyes glinting with his grin. "Come up and see the babies when you're done, El. I'm not painting them, because they won't hold still; I'm putting finishing touches on a horse picture for Cam. Night-Blooming Jasmine, his new champion."

"Yes, I heard she'd done well." Eleanor rose on her tiptoes and gave Mac another kiss on the cheek. "That's for Isabella. And Aimee, Eileen, and Robert." *Kiss, kiss, kiss.* Mac absorbed it all with an idiotic smile.

Hart leaned on the railing. "Will we get to this proposition sometime today?"

"Proposition?" Mac asked, eyes lighting. "Now, that sounds interesting."

"Shut it, Mac," Hart said.

Screaming erupted from on high—shrill, desperate, Armageddon-has-come screaming. Mac grinned and jogged back up the stairs.

"Papa's coming, hellions," he called. "If you're good, you can have Auntie Eleanor for tea."

The shrieking continued, unabated, until Mac reached the top floor, dodged into the room from whence it issued, and slammed the door. The noise instantly died, though they could still hear Mac's rumbling voice.

Eleanor sighed. "I always knew Mac would make a good father. Shall we?"

She turned and headed up to the next floor and the study without waiting for Hart. At one time, she'd become well acquainted with all the rooms in his house, and she apparently hadn't forgotten her way around.

The study hadn't changed at all, Eleanor noted when she entered. The same dark paneling covered the walls, and bookcases filled with what looked like the same books climbed to the high ceiling. The huge desk that had belonged to Hart's father still reposed in the middle of the room.

The same carpet covered the floor, though a different hound dozed by the fire. This was Ben, if she remembered correctly, a son of Hart's old dog, Beatrix, who'd passed on a few months after her engagement to Hart had ended. The news of Beatrix's death had nearly broken her heart.

Ben didn't open his eyes as they entered, and his gentle snore blended with the crackle of the fire on the hearth.

Hart touched Eleanor's elbow to guide her across the room. She wished he wouldn't, because the steel strength of his fingers made her want to melt, and she needed to maintain her resolve.

If all went well today, she'd not have to be close to him again, but she had to make the first approach in private. A letter could have gone too easily into the wrong hands, or be lost by a careless secretary, or burned unopened by Hart.

Hart dragged an armchair to his desk, moving it as though it weighed nothing. Eleanor knew better, though, as she sat on it. The heavily carved chair was as solid as a boulder.

Hart took the desk chair, his kilt moving as he sat, showing sinewy strength above his knees. Anyone believing a kilt unmanly had never seen Hart Mackenzie in one.

Eleanor touched the desk's smooth top. "You know, Hart,

if you plan to be the first minister of the nation, you might give a thought to changing the furniture. It's a bit out of date."

"Bugger the furniture. What is this problem that made you drag yourself and your father down from the wilds of Scotland?"

"I am worried about you. You've worked so hard for this, and I can't bear to think of what it would do to you if you lost everything. I've lain awake and pondered what to do for a week. I know we parted acrimoniously, but that was a long time ago, and many things have changed, especially for you. I still care about you, Hart, whatever you may believe, and I was distressed to think that you might have to go into hiding if this came out."

"Into hiding?" He stared at her. "What are you talking about? My past is no secret to anyone. I'm a blackguard and a sinner, and everyone knows it. These days, that's almost an asset to being a politician."

"Possibly, but this might humiliate you. You'd be a laughingstock, and that would certainly be a setback."

His gaze became sharp. Gracious, he looked like his father when he did that. The old duke had been handsome, but a monster, with nasty, cold eyes that made you know you were a toad beneath his heel. Hart, in spite of it all, had a warmth that his father had lacked.

"Eleanor, cease babbling and tell me what this is all about."

"Ah, yes. It's time you saw, I think." Eleanor dug into a pocket inside her coat and withdrew a folded piece of pasteboard. She laid this on the desk in front of Hart, and opened it.

Hart went still.

The object inside the folded card was a photograph. It was a full-length picture of a younger Hart, shot in profile. Hart's body had been a little slimmer then but still well muscled. In the photograph, he rested his buttocks against the edge of a desk, his sinewy hand bracing on the desk's top beside his hip. His head was bent as he studied something at his feet, out of the frame.

The pose, though perhaps a bit unusual for a portrait, was not the unique thing about the picture. The most interesting aspect of this photograph was that, in it, Hart Mackenzie was quite, quite naked.

Chapter 2

"Where did you get this?" The question was hard, harsh, demanding. She had Hart's full attention now.

"From a well-wisher," Eleanor said. "At least that is how the letter was signed. *From one as wishes you well.* Grammar indicating the writer is not an educated person—well, at least educated enough to write a letter, but she obviously didn't attend finishing school. I believe it a woman from the hand—"

"Someone sent it to you?" Hart interrupted. "Is that what you are coming around to telling me?"

"Indeed I am. Luckily for you, I was alone at the breakfast table when I opened it. My father was out classifying mushrooms. With the cook, who was not so much classifying mushrooms as choosing them for our supper."

"Where is the envelope?"

Hart obviously expected her to hand the whole thing over to him on the spot. But that would spoil her plans.

"The envelope did not reveal much," Eleanor said. "Hand delivered, not posted, brought to Glenarden from the train station. The stationmaster got it from a train conductor, who said it was passed to *him* by a delivery boy in Edinburgh. One line on the envelope—*To Lady Eleanor Ramsay, Glenarden, near Aberdeen, Scotland.* Everyone knows me and where I live, so in theory, even if the sender had dropped it somewhere between Edinburgh and Aberdeen, it would have reached me. Eventually."

Hart's brows drew down as he listened, again reminding Eleanor of his father. A portrait of the man had hung in this room, in the place of honor above the mantel, but it wasn't there now, thank heavens. Hart must have taken it to the attics, or perhaps burned it. Eleanor would have burned it.

"What about the delivery boy in Edinburgh?" Hart asked.

"I did not have the time or the resources to conduct such an investigation," Eleanor said, drawing her gaze back from the fireplace. A landscape of a kilted man fishing in the Scottish Highlands, painted by Mac, now hung there. "I plunked the last of our money on train tickets to London to come here and tell you that I'd be happy to look into the matter for you. If you will provide the funds and a small salary."

His gaze fixed on her again, sharp and gold. "Salary."

"Yes, indeed. That is the business proposition I mentioned to you. I want you to give me a job."

Hart went silent, the ponderous clock across the room ticking loudly into the stillness.

It unnerved her to be in the same room with him, the world closed out, but not because he watched her with his assessing stare. No, what unnerved her was being alone with Hart, the man with whom she'd once been madly in love.

He'd been devilishly handsome, teasing, and tender, and he'd courted her with a verve that had left her breathless. She'd fallen in love with him quickly, and she wasn't sure she'd ever fallen *out* of love with him.

But the Hart she faced today was a different man from the one she'd been engaged to, and that worried her. The Hart who'd laughed so readily, who'd been animated and excited by life—was gone. In his place was a man even harder and more driven than before. He'd seen too much tragedy, too much death, too much loss. Gossip and newspapers had put it about that Hart had been relieved to be rid of Lady Sarah, his wife, but Eleanor knew differently. The bleak light now in Hart's eyes came from grief.

"A job," Hart was saying. "What are you up to, Eleanor?"

"Up to? Our ears in debt, of course." She smiled at her joke. "Quite seriously, Hart, we need the blunt. Father is dear to me but a wee bit impractical. He believes we still pay the staff wages, but truth to tell, they stay and look after us because they feel sorry for us. Our food comes from their family's gardens or charity from the villagers. They think we don't know. You can call me an assistant to a secretary or some such, if you like. I'm sure you have several of those."

Hart looked into the determined blue eyes that had haunted his dreams for years and felt something break open inside him.

She'd come like an answer to a prayer. Hart had planned to travel to Glenarden soon to convince her to marry him, knowing the pinnacle of his career was nigh. He'd wanted to win everything and present it to her on a platter, so she'd not be able to refuse. He'd make her see that she needed him as much as he needed her.

But perhaps this would be better. If he inserted her into his life now, she'd grow so used to being there that when he put his hand out for her, she'd take it and not say no.

He could find some nominal employment for her, let her track down who had these photographs—she was not wrong that they might help his opposition make a fool of him—while he slowly closed his fist about her. So slowly that she'd not know he had her in his grasp until too late.

Eleanor would be with him, at his side, as she was now, smiling her red-lipped smile. Every day, and every night.

Every night.

"Hart?" Eleanor waved a hand in front of his face. "Wool-gathering, are you?"

Hart snapped his focus back to her, on the kissable curve of her mouth, the little smile that had once made him determined to have her. In all ways.

Eleanor tucked the photograph into her pocket. "Now, as to salary, it needn't be large. Something to get us by, that's all. And accommodations for myself and my father while we're in London. Small rooms will be fine—we are used to scratching for ourselves, as long as the neighborhood is not too seedy. Father *will* walk anywhere alone, and I do not want street toughs bothering him. He'd end up trying to explain to his assailants how knives like the one with which they are trying to stab him first came to be made, and finish with a lecture on the best methods of tempering steel."

"El . . ."

Eleanor went on, ignoring him. "If you do not wish to admit to engaging me for looking into who sent the photograph—and I can see why you'd need to be secretive—you can tell people that you've engaged me to do something else. Typing your letters, perhaps. I did learn to use a typing machine. The postmistress in the village was given one. She offered to teach spinster ladies how to type so that they might be able to find a job in a city instead of waiting in vain for a man to take notice of them and marry them. I, of course, could not move to a city without Father, who will never leave Glenarden for more than a few weeks at a time, but I learned the skill anyway, not knowing when it might become useful. Which it has. And anyway, you must give me a post so that I can earn the money to take us back to Aberdeen."

"*Eleanor!*"

Hart heard his voice fill the room, but sometimes the only way to stop her flow was to boom over it.

She blinked. "What?"

One curl dropped from beneath her hat and snaked down her shoulder, a red gold streak on her serge bodice.

Hart drew a breath. "Give a man a moment to think."

"Yes, I know I can run on. Father never minds. And I am a bit nervous, I must say. I was once betrothed to you, and now here we are, face-to-face, like old friends."

Dear God. "We are *not* friends."

"I know that. I said *like* old friends. One old friend asking another for a job. I've come here in desperation."

She might say that, but her smile, her open look, spoke of eagerness and determination.

Once upon a time Hart had tasted that eagerness, her zest for life, and he longed to taste it again.

. . . *To unbutton the buttons of her bodice, to open them slowly, to lean in and lick her throat. To watch her eyes go soft while he kissed the corner of her mouth.*

Eleanor had been responsive. So loving and strong.

Dark need stirred in the places he'd kept it long buried,

tantalizing and sharp. It told her he could lean down to Eleanor right now, pin her arms behind her on the straight-backed chair, take her mouth in a long, deep kiss . . .

Eleanor sat forward, the collar of her dress brushing her soft chin. "I'll look for the photographs while you tell your staff you've taken me on to help with your pile of correspondence. You know you need everyone you can to help you with your never-ending goal of becoming prime minister. I gather that you are close?"

"Yes," Hart said. Such a short answer to summarize his years of work and diligence, his countless journeys to assess the state of the world, the politicians he'd endlessly courted at endlessly dull gatherings at Kilmorgan Castle. But he felt the need, the *obsession* boil up in his brain. It drove him every day of his life.

Eleanor's gaze had gone soft. "You come alive when you look like that," she said. "Like you used to. Wild and unstoppable. I very much liked that."

His chest felt tight. "Did you now, lass?"

"True, you've become a bit cold these days, but I am quite glad to see that the fire is still within you." Eleanor sat back, practical once more. "Now, then, as to the photographs—how many were there in total?"

Hart felt his fingers press down on the desk, as though they'd go through the wood. "Twenty."

"As many as that? I wonder if the person has them all, or where they obtained them. Who took them? Mrs. Palmer?"

"Yes." He did not want to talk about Mrs. Palmer with her. Not now, not ever.

"I suspected so. Though perhaps whoever is sending them found them in a shop. Shops sell photographs to collectors— of all kinds of people and all kinds of themes. I'd think yours would have come to light long ago if so, but . . ."

"Eleanor."

"What?"

Hart reined in his temper. "If you'll stop talking for the space of a moment, I can tell you that I'll give you the post."

Eleanor's eyes widened. "Well, thank you. I must say, I expected much more of an argument—"

"Shut it. I'm not finished. I won't put you and your father in some crumbling rooms in Bloomsbury. You'll stay here in the house, both of you."

Now trepidation entered her gaze. Good. No more surety that she'd breeze in here and have it all her own way.

"Here? Do not be ridiculous. There's no need."

There was need. She'd walked in here, into his trap, and he'd not open it and let her go. "I'm not fool enough to turn you and your unworldly father loose in London. I have plenty of room here, and I'm rarely home. You'll have the run of the place most of the time. Wilfred is my secretary now, and he will be here to tell you what to do. Take it or throw it away, El."

Eleanor, for possibly the first time in her life, could not think of what to say. Hart was offering her what she wanted, the chance to help him, and—she hadn't exaggerated—to bring home some much-needed money. Her father rarely noticed their poverty, but unfortunately, poverty noticed *them*.

But to live in Hart's house, to breathe the air he breathed every night . . . Eleanor wasn't certain she could do it without going mad. It had been years since their betrothal ended, but in some ways, the time would never be long enough.

Hart had turned the tables on her. He'd give her money to keep her from starving, but on his terms, in his way. She'd been wrong to think he wouldn't.

The silence stretched. Ben rolled his big body over, groaned a little, and settled back into sleep.

"Are we agreed?" Hart spread his hands on the desk. Firm, strong hands with blunt fingers. Hands that worked hard but could be incredibly tender on a lady's body.

"Actually, I'd love to tell you to go to the devil and walk off in a huff. But since I need the blunt, I suppose I must say yes."

"You can say whatever you wish."

They shared another stare, Eleanor looking into hazel eyes that were almost gold. "I do hope you intend to be away quite a lot," she said.

A musele moved in his jaw. "I'll send someone to fetch your father from the museum, and you can move in at once."

Eleanor drew her finger across the smooth surface of the desk. The room was dark with old-fashioned elegance but at the same time unwelcoming.

She moved her hand back to her lap and looked again into Hart's eyes, never an easy thing to do.

"That should be acceptable," she said.

⁓

"He's making you do *what*?" Mac Mackenzie turned from his painting, brush out. A glob of Mackenzie yellow spattered on the polished boards at his feet.

"Papa, do be careful," five-year-old Aimee said to him. "Mrs. Mayhew will scold something rotten if you get paint all over the floor."

Eleanor cradled little Robert Mackenzie in her arms, his small body warm against her chest. Eileen, Mac and Isabella's daughter, lay in a bassinet next to the sofa, but Aimee stood near Mac, hands behind her back while she watched her adopted father paint.

"The idea of the post was mine," Eleanor said. "I can easily type away and earn money for my and my father's keep. Father's books are amazing works, but as you know, no one ever buys them."

Mac listened to her rationale with a stare equal to Hart's in intensity. He wore his usual painting kilt and boots, a red scarf around his head to keep paint out of his hair. Eleanor knew that Mac liked to paint without his shirt, but in deference to his children and Eleanor, he'd donned a loose smock heavily streaked with paint.

"But he expects you to *work* for him?"

"Really, Mac, I do it happily. Hart needs much help if his coalition party is to win. I want to help him."

"So he made you think. My brother does nothing that is not underhanded. What is he playing at?"

"Honestly." The photograph weighed heavily in her pocket, but Hart had asked her—and she agreed with him—to keep it secret from the rest of the family, for now. They'd be outraged that someone might be trying to blackmail Hart, but they'd also laugh. Hart had no wish to be a family joke. "I want the job," Eleanor said. "You know how things are for Father and me, and I refuse to take anyone's charity. Put it down to my Scots stubbornness."

"He's taking advantage of ye, lass."

"He is Hart Mackenzie. He cannot help himself."

Mac stared at her a moment longer, then he thrust his dripping paintbrush into a jar, strode across the room, and slammed open the door. Eleanor jumped to her feet, still holding the baby.

"Mac! There is no need . . ."

Her words were drowned out by Mac's pounding boots on the stairs.

"Papa is angry with Uncle Hart," Aimee said as the door swung slowly shut again. "Papa is often angry with Uncle Hart."

"That is because your Uncle Hart is most maddening," Eleanor said.

Aimee put her head on one side. "What does that mean? Maddening?"

Eleanor shifted Robert, who'd slept soundly through the outburst. Cuddling him filled something empty in her heart. "*Maddening* is when your Uncle Hart looks at you as though he listens to your opinion, then he turns around and does whatever he pleases, no matter what you've said. Your feel your throat closing up, and your mouth tightening, and you want to stamp your feet and shout. And you know that even if you do shout and wave your fists, it will do no good. That is what is meant by *maddening*."

Aimee listened, nodding, as though storing the information for future use. She was Mac and Isabella's adopted daughter, born in France, and hadn't learned English until she was three. Collecting new words was her hobby.

Eleanor pressed a kiss to Robert's head and patted the sofa next to her. "Never mind your uncle Hart. Sit here, Aimee, and tell me all about what you and your mama and papa have been doing in London. And when *my* papa gets here, he'll tell us all about the mummies at the museum."

~~~~~

"I cannae believe you," Mac shouted, his Scots blazing out with his anger.

Hart shut the cabinet that held the portrait he couldn't seem to get rid of and looked around in irritation. Mac was in a fair rage, his clothes and fingers paint-streaked, the gypsy kerchief still on his head. Hart had known this would be coming, but still it irritated him.

"I gave her a nominal post with a salary and a place to live," Hart said. "This is me being kind."

"Kind? I heard you at Ascot, Hart—you said you were prepared to hang out your shingle for a wife. Is this how you're going about it?"

Hart moved back to his desk. "This is my personal life, Mac. Stay out of it."

"*Personal*, is it? When did that keep you out of *my* life? When Isabella left me, you shouted at me something fierce. You all shouted at me—you and Cameron and Ian—"

Mac stopped. "Ian," he said. A grin spread across his face. So like Mac, jumping from emotion to emotion without a pause in between.

"I don't have to shout at you, do I?" Mac asked. "All I have to do is explain things to Ian. And then God have mercy on your soul."

Hart said nothing, but he felt a qualm of disquiet. Ian, the youngest Mackenzie brother, did not understand subtlety. He could spell the word *subtlety* and give a dictionary meaning for it, but Ian couldn't assimilate it, or practice it, or recognize it in others. Once Ian decided on a course of action, not all the devils in hell nor the angels in heaven could sway him from it.

Mac laughed at him. "Poor Hart. I look forward to watching that." He pulled the kerchief from his head, smearing paint through his unruly hair. "I'm glad Eleanor's come to torment you. But she can't tonight. I'm taking her and her father home with me for tea, and Isabella will keep her long after that. You know women when they get to talking. They don't stop for anything but unconsciousness."

Hart hadn't planned to be home that night, but he suddenly disliked the thought of Eleanor leaving the house. If he let her out of his sight, she might vanish, back to Glenarden, her refuge. A place that, despite its crumbling walls, always seemed to shut Hart out.

"I thought you had the decorators in," he growled.

"I do, but we'll squeeze. I only mind them banging while I'm trying to paint. I'll give your best to Isabella." Mac looked pointedly at Hart. "You're not invited."

"I'm going out anyway. See that Eleanor gets home safely, will you? London is a dangerous place."

"Of course I will. I'll escort her and her father myself."

Hart relaxed a little—Mac would do it—but then Mac's smile died. He walked to Hart and stood toe-to-toe with him, looking up the half-inch difference at his older brother.

"Don't break her heart again," Mac said. "If you do, I'll pummel you so hard you'll have to make your speeches to Parliament in a Bath chair."

Hart tried to take the edge from his voice but couldn't quite. "Just see that she gets home."

"We're Mackenzies," Mac said, his gaze steady. "Remember that we break what we touch." He jabbed a finger at Hart. "Don't break this one."

Hart didn't answer, and finally, Mac went away.

Hart took a key from his desk drawer, returned to the cabinet that held his father's picture, and locked it tightly closed.

Living in Hart's house proved to be less distressing than Eleanor had feared, mostly because Hart was rarely in it.

Hart explained Eleanor's presence to London at large by putting about the fiction that Earl Ramsay had come to London to conduct research at the British Museum for his next book. Hart had offered the impoverished Ramsay a room in his house, and naturally, the earl had been accompanied by his daughter-cum-assistant, Lady Eleanor. Mac and Isabella helped keep tongues from wagging by moving in themselves, children and all, a day after Eleanor's arrival, their decorators having started on the bedchambers.

Hart told Wilfred that Eleanor was to type letters on the Remington typing machine he'd bought for Wilfred from America. She would also open and sort Hart's social correspondence, help Wilfred arrange Hart's social calendar, and assist Isabella in setting up Hart's lavish entertainments. Wilfred nodded without much change of expression—he was used to Hart's arbitrary and sometimes bizarre orders.

Lord Ramsay took living in Hart's Grosvenor Square mansion in stride, but Eleanor found it difficult to get used to all the splendor. In Glenarden, the Ramsay house near Aberdeen, one never knew when a brick would tumble from a wall or rainwater would flood a passage. Here, no bricks were allowed to fall, no water to drip. Quiet, well-trained maids hovered at Eleanor's beck and call, and footmen jumped to open every door Eleanor walked toward.

Lord Ramsay, on the other hand, enjoyed himself hugely. Ignoring the household's usual hours, Lord Ramsay rose whenever he wanted to, invaded the kitchen for repast when he was hungry, then packed his notebooks and pencils in a little knapsack and strode off alone into London. The majordomo tried to explain that Hart kept the carriage standing by to take Lord Ramsay wherever he wished, but Lord Ramsay ignored him and walked to the museum every day or took an omnibus. He discovered that he loved the omnibus.

"Just imagine, Eleanor," Ramsay said when he arrived home very late the second night of their stay. "You can go anywhere you wish for a penny. And see so many people. It's quite entertaining after the isolation of home."

"For heaven's sake, Father, don't tell Hart," Eleanor said. "He expects you to behave like a peer of the realm and travel about in luxury."

"Whatever for? I see much more of the city this way. Do you know, someone in Covent Garden tried to pick my pocket? No one's picked my pocket before. The thief was only a child, can you believe it? A little girl. I apologized to her for my pocket's being so empty, and then I gave her the penny I was holding for the omnibus."

"What on earth were you doing in Covent Garden?" Eleanor asked worriedly. "That's nowhere near the museum."

"I know, my dear. I took a wrong turning and wandered quite a long way. That is why I am so late getting home. I had to ask many a policeman for directions before I found the way."

"If you took the carriage, you wouldn't get lost," Eleanor said, putting her arms around her father. "Or have your pockets picked. And I wouldn't worry so."

"Nonsense, my dear, the policemen are most helpful. You have no reason to fret about your old papa. You just get on."

He had a gleam in his eyes, the maddening one that told Eleanor that her father knew full well what he was doing but would play the absentminded old man as much as he liked.

While her father busied himself at his museum or riding the omnibus, Eleanor worked on her ostensible duties. She found that she enjoyed typing the letters Wilfred gave her, because they allowed her a glimpse into Hart's life, albeit his formal one.

The duke is pleased to accept the ambassador's invitation to the garden party on Tuesday next.

Or,

The duke regrets that his attendance at the gathering on Friday night will not be possible.

Or,

His Grace thanks his lordship for the loan of the book and returns it with gratitude.

Polite nothings and very unlike Hart's style of delivery. But Hart didn't actually write the responses—he scrawled *yes* or *no* on letters that Wilfred vetted, and shoved them back at him. Wilfred drafted the replies, and Eleanor typed them.

Eleanor could just as soon have made up the words herself, but Wilfred, proud old soul, thought this duty was one of his raisons d'être, so Eleanor never offered to take over.

Just as well. She'd be tempted to type such things as: *His Grace regrets he will be unable to attend your charity ball. Of course he won't come, you silly cow, not after you called him a Scots turd. Yes, I heard you say that in Edinburgh last summer, and it got back to him. You really ought to guard your tongue.*

No, better that Wilfred drafted the letters.

As for the photographs, Eleanor pondered what to do. Hart had said there'd been twenty photographs in all. Eleanor had been sent the one—she had no way of knowing whether the well-wisher had them all or only this one. And if only the one, where were the others? At night, alone in her bedchamber, she would take out the photograph and study it.

The pose showed Hart in perfect profile. The hand that leaned on the lip of the desk tightened all the muscles in his arm, his shoulder round and tight. Hart's naked thighs held sinewy strength, and the head bowed in contemplation was by no means weak.

This was the Hart Eleanor had known years ago, the one she'd agreed without hesitation to marry. He'd had the body of a god, a smile that melted her heart, a sinful glint in his eyes that had been for her and her alone.

He'd always prided himself on his physique, kept fit by plenty of riding and walking, boxing, rowing, or whatever sport took his fancy at the moment. From what she'd glimpsed behind his kilt and coat, Hart had grown even more muscular and solid since this photograph. She toyed with the fantasy of snapping a photograph of him in this pose as he was now, and comparing the two.

Eleanor's gaze finally roved to the thing for which she pretended she had no interest. In the picture, Hart's phallus was partially hidden by his thigh, but Eleanor could see it—not erect, but full and large.

She remembered the first time she'd seen Hart bare—up in the summerhouse on Kilmorgan land, the folly that perched on a cliff with a wide view of the sea. Hart had removed his kilt last thing, his smile wicked when Eleanor realized he wore nothing under it. He'd laughed when her gaze couldn't help but slide down his body to him erect and wanting her. She'd never seen a man unclothed before, let alone *such* a man.

She remembered the thump of her heart, the flush of her skin, the triumphant warmth to know that the elusive Lord Hart Mackenzie belonged to *her*. He'd laid Eleanor down on the blanket he'd thoughtfully packed for their outing and let her explore his body. He'd taught Eleanor all about what *she* liked that afternoon. He'd been right about everything.

Hart's smile, his low laughter, the incredibly tender way he'd touched her had made her fall madly in love with him. Eleanor believed herself the most blessed of women, and she had been.

Eleanor sighed and tucked the photograph and her memories away, back into their hiding places.

She'd been living in Hart's house three days when the second photograph came, this one hand delivered directly to her.

Chapter 3

"For you, my lady," Hart's perfect parlor maid said, executing a perfect curtsey.

The envelope read: *Lady Eleanor Ramsay, staying at number 8, Grosvenor Square.* Same printing in the same careful style, but no seal, no indication from whence the letter had originated. The envelope was stiff and heavy, and Eleanor knew what must be inside.

"Who brought this?" Eleanor asked the maid.

"The boy, my lady. The one who usually brings messages to His Grace."

"Where is this boy now?"

"Gone, my lady. He delivers all over the square and up to Oxford Street."

"I see. Well, thank you."

Eleanor would have to find the boy and put him to the question. She went back upstairs, shut herself in her bedchamber, drew a chair to the window for the light, and opened the envelope.

Inside was a piece of cheap paper sold by the hundredweight at any stationery shop, and a piece of folded pasteboard. Inside the pasteboard card lay another photograph.

In this one, Hart was standing at a wide window, but what showed outside was rolling landscape, not city. His back was to the photographer, his hands on the windowsill, and again, he wore not a stitch.

A broad back replete with muscle slimmed to a backside as firm as firm could be. Hart's arms were tight, taking his weight as he leaned on the windowsill.

The photograph was printed on stiff paper, much like a carte de visite, but without the mark of a photographer's studio. Hart had likely had his own apparatus for taking portraits, and his former mistress, Mrs. Palmer, had taken them. Eleanor could not imagine Hart trusting such things to anyone else.

Mrs. Palmer herself had told Eleanor what sort of man Hart Mackenzie truly was. A sexual rogue. Unpredictable. Demanding. Thought it all an adventure, *his* adventure. The woman in the equation was simply means to his pleasure. She had not gone into detail, but what she'd hinted had been enough to shock Eleanor out of her complacency.

Mrs. Palmer had died two and a half years ago. Who, then, possessed these damning photographs, why was he or she sending them to Eleanor, and why had they waited until now? Ah, but now Hart was poised to push Gladstone out of his seat and take over the government.

The note was the same as the first. *From one as wishes you well.* No threats of blackmail, no promises to betray Hart, no demand for payment.

Eleanor held the letter up to the light, but she saw no sign of secret messages or clues in the thin watermark, no cleverly hidden code around the edges of the words. Nothing but the one sentence printed in pencil.

The back of the picture held no clues, and neither did the front. Eleanor fetched a magnifying glass and studied the grains of the photograph, on the off chance that someone had printed tiny messages there.

Nothing.

The enlarged view of Hart's backside was fine, though. Eleanor studied that through the glass for a good long time.

The only way to speak to Hart alone—indeed, at all—was to ambush him. That night, Eleanor waited until her father had retired to his bedchamber, then she went to the hall outside Hart's bedroom, one floor below hers. She dragged two chairs from the other side of the hall to the bedchamber door, one chair for Eleanor to sit on and one for her feet.

Hart's house was larger and grander than most in Mayfair. *Naturally.* Many London town houses were two rooms deep and one room wide, with a staircase hall opening from the front door and running up through the entire house. Larger houses had rooms tucked behind the staircase and perhaps a second room in front of the staircase on the upper floors.

Hart's mansion was wide and deep, having rooms on either side of the staircase as well as behind it. The ground floor held the public rooms—a double sitting room on one side, a grand dining room on the other, and a fairly large ballroom running across the back of the house.

The open staircase wound upward through the house in a large, elegant rectangle, the landings forming a gallery around each floor. The first floor above the ground floor held more drawing rooms, a two-room deep library, and another private dining room for the family. The next floor contained Hart's large study, the smaller study in which Eleanor and Wilfred worked, and Hart's bedchamber across the back of the house, where Eleanor waited now. She, her father, and Mac and Isabella, occupied rooms above that, with the top floor now holding a makeshift nursery and studio.

Eleanor sat with her back against Hart's bedchamber door and stretched her feet across to the other chair. A gaslight hissed above her, and she opened a novel from the lending library and started to read.

The novel was a thrilling one, with a blackhearted villain determined to bring down the innocent heroine, the hero always stuck in a jungle fighting tigers or some such thing whenever the heroine was in trouble. Never around when you needed them, heroes. The hiss of the gaslight was soothing, the air warm, and her eyes drifted shut.

She jumped awake, her book falling with a crash, to find Hart Mackenzie standing over her.

Eleanor scrambled to her feet. Hart remained where he was, unmoving, his cravat off and dangling from one hand. He was waiting for her to explain herself—typical.

He was dressed in Mackenzie plaid and formal coat, his shirt open to reveal the damp hollow of his throat. His eyes were red-tinged with drink, his face dark with whiskers. He smelled heavily of cheroot smoke, night air, and a woman's perfume.

Eleanor hid her dart of dismay at the perfume, and cleared her throat. "I'm afraid that the only way I can speak to you, Hart, is to lie in wait like a tiger . . . in a jungle. I wish to discuss the photographs with you."

"Not now," Hart said.

He shoved aside the chair and made to open his bedchamber door, but Eleanor stepped in front of him. "My, you are in a temper. You'd never speak to me about them, if you had your way. The house is asleep. We can be private. I have things to ask you."

"Tell Wilfred. He'll set an appointment with me."

Hart opened the door and moved past her into his room. Eleanor marched in right after him before he could shut the door.

"I'm not afraid of your bedchamber, Hart Mackenzie. I've been in it before."

Hart gave Eleanor a look that made her heart pound. He tossed the cravat and collar onto a chair and moved to a table and a decanter of brandy. "If you want it all over Mayfair that you chased me into my bedroom, by all means, stay and close the door."

Eleanor left the door open.

"You haven't changed the furniture in here either," she said, keeping her voice light. "The bed is positively medieval. And quite uncomfortable as I recall."

Hart slanted her another glance as he sloshed whiskey into a glass and clinked the stopper back to the decanter. "What do you want, Eleanor?" he asked, an edge to his voice. "I've had a hell of a night."

"To talk about the photographs, as I said. If I'm to find them, or discover what this person means by sending them to me, I need to know more."

"Well, I dinnae want to talk about the be-damned things *right now*."

She started to answer, then stopped, taking in his dishevelment, his angry frown. "You are very cross tonight, Hart. Perhaps the lady disappointed you."

Hart stared at her over the glass he'd started to raise. "What lady?"

"The one whose perfume you positively reek of."

His brows went up. "You mean the Countess von Hohenstahlen? She's eighty-two and drenches herself in scents that would make a tart blush."

"Oh."

Hart drank down the whiskey in one swallow. His face changed as the smooth Mackenzie malt did its work.

He clunked the glass to the table. "I'm tired, and I want to go to bed. We'll speak in the morning. Ask Wilfred to make an appointment with me."

Humph. As Eleanor turned to the door, she sensed Hart's relief behind her that she was leaving. That relief made her angry.

Eleanor went on to the door, but at the last minute, she closed it and turned around. "I do not wish to wait," she said.

Hart had thrown off his coat, and now, caught unawares, his eyes betrayed his exhaustion. "Christ, Eleanor."

"Why are you so reluctant to speak of the photographs? They could damage you."

Hart let himself collapse into a chair, kilt draping over his legs, and reached again for the decanter. A gentleman should never sit in a lady's presence without asking her to sit first. But Hart simply poured himself more whiskey and rested his elbows on the chair's arms as he lifted the glass.

"I would have thought you'd like to see me damaged."

"Not like this. You don't deserve to be laughed at. The queen would be quite disparaging, and she has much influence—although she and the Prince Consort used to collect photographs of nudes, did you know that? Not many have seen them, but she once showed them to me. She loves to talk about Albert. She rather worshiped him."

Her words ran out as Hart watched her, his golden gaze hard on her.

"What do I deserve, then, lass?" His words slurred the slightest bit, which meant he was well on the way to being thoroughly drunk. Hart rarely showed any effect of drink, so when he did, he was already far past inebriation. "What do I deserve, Eleanor?"

She shrugged. "You deserved me to break the engagement. At the time. Perhaps you didn't deserve me not forgiving you for as long as I did, or me being too proud to even speak to you. But it's done. We both have gone on with our lives. Apart. As it was meant to be."

"Was it meant to be?" His voice was low, soft, a Mackenzie man's bedroom voice.

"We'd not have rubbed on well, and you know it, Hart." She circled her thumb and fingertips together. "Too many sparks."

"Aye, you've got fire in you, lass, that is true. A temper." The delicious Highland accent broadened as more whiskey went into him. "And fire of another kind. I've not forgotten that."

Eleanor had not forgotten either. Hart had known exactly how to warm her, how to run his hands down her body and draw her to him, how to make her instigate the first kisses. Hart had known how to touch her, what to whisper into her ear, how to let his breath linger on her skin.

A lady should know nothing of men before her wedding night, but Eleanor had known everything about Hart Mackenzie. His well-muscled, hard body, the old scars that crisscrossed his back, the fire of his mouth on hers, the skill of his hands as he'd unbuttoned and unlaced her clothes.

Thrice he'd seduced her, and thrice she'd let him. Once at the summerhouse, once in this bedroom, and once in his bedchamber at Kilmorgan. They were betrothed, she'd reasoned. Where was the harm?

Hart sat in the chair across the room, drinking whiskey, but he might as well have been next to her, drawing his fingers down her spine again, making her shiver like he used to.

Eleanor forced the pleasant memories away. She needed to stay focused, or she'd fall at his feet and beg him to make her shiver again. "About these photographs," she said. "I saw nothing in either of them to give me a clue as to who sent them."

He came alert. "*Either* of them? There's another?"

"I received it this afternoon. Hand delivered to me here.

I haven't had the chance to question your delivery boy as to who gave it to him."

Hart sat up in the chair, no longer looking inebriated. "Then that person knows you are here."

"Gracious, the whole of England must know. Lady Mountgrove will have told everyone in it by now. She saw you bring me here, remember? To be sure, she'll have been watching this house to see whether I left it again. Which I have, of course, but then I come right back. And stay."

"I'll question the delivery boy."

Eleanor shook her head. "No need. The photographs are being sent to me. I'll question him."

Hart set the glass on the arm of the chair. "This person knows who you are and where you are, and I don't like that." He held out his hand. "Let me see the photograph."

"Don't be silly, I don't carry it about *with* me. It's upstairs in my chamber, hidden with the other. I can tell you that the picture is much the same as the first, except that you are looking out a window. From what I could see through said window, I believe you were at Kilmorgan Castle."

He nodded. "Busy proving that the house was mine, I suppose. Showing myself that I wasn't afraid to do anything in it."

"The house wasn't precisely yours at the time," Eleanor said. "Your father must still have been alive then."

"Alive, but away. A good time to do as I pleased."

"The photographs are very well done, you know. Quite artistic. The pictures the queen and Prince Albert collected are also very tasteful, though it's not the same thing. You posed for yours, yourself. The queen would never forgive that—a duke acting as a common artist's model? Did Mrs. Palmer take all of them?"

"Yes." The word was terse.

Eleanor opened her hands. "You see? This is exactly the sort of information I need. Mrs. Palmer might have left the collection to someone, or someone might have found them after her death. You really ought to let me into that house in High Holborn where she lived to look around."

"No." A loud, blunt, final syllable.

"But it's not a bawdy house anymore, is it?" Eleanor asked. "Just a property you own. You sold the house to Mrs. Palmer, and she willed it back to you. I looked that up. Wills are public records, you know."

Hart's hand clenched around his glass. "El, you are not going to that house."

"You ought to have put up my father and me there, you know. It would be much handier for the British Museum, and I could search it from top to bottom for more photographs."

"Leave it alone, Eleanor." His voice was rising, the fury unmistakable.

"But it's just a house," she said. "Nothing wrong with it now, and it might hold a vital clue."

"You know good and well that it's not just a house." The anger climbed. "And stop giving me that innocent look. You're not innocent at all. I know you."

"Yes, I am afraid you know me a bit *too* well. Makes talking to you dashed difficult sometimes."

Eleanor had a little smile on her face, making a joke of it, and Hart couldn't breathe. She always did this, walked into a room and took the air out of it.

She stood primly before him in her blue dress that was out of fashion and simply made, her eyes ingenuous as she announced she should look through the house in High Holborn, the existence of which had wedged them apart.

No, not wedged. Batted Hart aside like a cricketer whacking one all the way into the tea tents.

Eleanor had been quite decorous about it after her initial outburst, she with all the right on her side. She could have sued Hart for taking her to his bed, for ruining her, for violating any of the numerous terms in their complicated betrothal contract.

Instead, she'd said good-bye and walked out of his life. Leaving a great, gaping hole in it that had never been filled.

Hart had forgotten all about the pictures until Eleanor turned up a few days ago to slide one across his desk to him.

"If this person is a blackmailer, El, I want you to have nothing more to do with it. Blackmailers are dangerous."

Her brows rose. "You've had dealings with them before, have you?"

Too bloody many times. "Attempting to blackmail the Mackenzie family is a popular pastime," Hart said.

"Hmm, yes, I can see that. I suppose there are those who believe you'll pay to keep your secrets out of the newspapers or from being whispered into the wrong ears. You and your brothers have so many secrets."

And Eleanor knew every single one of them. She knew things no one else in the world did.

"All these blackmailers have one thing in common," Hart said. "They fail."

"Good. Then if this is a blackmailer, we will see him off as well."

"Not *we*," he said firmly.

"Be reasonable, Hart. Someone sent the photos to *me*. Not to you, not to your enemies, not to your brothers, but to me. I think that has some significance. Besides, why send them at all, free and clear, with no demands for money?"

"To show you that they have them and make demands for the rest."

She nibbled her lip. "Perhaps."

Hart did not give a damn about the bloody photographs right now. Not with Eleanor rolling her red lip under her teeth and making Hart want to bite it for her.

"You are cruel, El." His voice went quiet again.

Her brows drew together into a delicious little frown. "Cruel? Why on earth do you say that?"

"You haven't spoken to me for years. Suddenly you gallop down to London declaring you're here to save me like some benevolent angel. Did you turn around one day last week and decide that you'd forgiven me?" He could hope.

"Of course not. I began to forgive you years ago. After Sarah died. I felt so horrible for you, Hart."

He stopped, cold working its way through the whiskey. "That was nearly eight years ago."

"Yes, I know that."

"I never noticed you forgiving me," he said, his voice tight. "No letters, no visits, no telegrams, no declaration to my brothers or Isabella."

"I said that's when I *began* to forgive you. It took much longer than that to make all the anger go away. Besides, you were Duke of Kilmorgan by then, well ensconced behind ducal barriers, and quite on your way to wresting power from anyone who had it. You also returned to Mrs. Palmer—I may live in a backwater, but trust me, I am well informed of all you do. And the third reason I never made indication is because I had no idea whether you'd care for my forgiveness or not."

"Why would I *not* care?"

The empty look in his eyes made Eleanor go soft. Going soft was dangerous around Hart Mackenzie, but drink had erased his hardness, letting her glimpse inside his shell.

She found it alarmingly blank. What had happened to him?

"You courted me to gain influence over my father's connections and cronies," she said. "I knew that. It is the same reason you married Sarah, and I imagine the same reason you'll take your next wife. Whether or not I forgave you all your past sins might not have held the remotest interest for you."

Hart came out of the chair. Eleanor backed away. She wasn't afraid of him, but he was drunk, she knew she easily angered him, and Hart was a very large man.

"I told you," he said. "Nothing I said to you while I was courting you was a lie. I liked you, I wanted you . . ."

"Yes, I did rather enjoy being seduced by you." Eleanor held up her hand, palm out, and unbelievably, he stopped. "I forgave you, because we were both very young, very arrogant, and a bit stupid. But life moves on. I am likely one of the only people to know how much of a blow Sarah's death was to you. And your son's death. And, indeed, Mrs. Palmer's. She was rather awful, and I am *very* angry with her for what she did to Beth and Ian, but I know you cared for her. Losing someone you've cared about for a very long time is quite painful. I do feel sorry for you."

"Mrs. Palmer died two years ago," he said rigidly. "We are still not up to the present day."

"I am trying to explain. Why on earth would I think you would be pleased for me to turn up on your doorstep, bleating that I'd forgiven you? The photograph was a godsend, because it gave me the excuse to come here. I did not lie when I said money was a bit tight, so I thought I might as well ask you for a job to go with it. You gave me that hundred pounds last year, but such things don't last forever, and the house needed many repairs. Going hungry so that your loved ones can eat sounds romantic, but I assure you, it quickly becomes tiresome. Your cook is quite gifted. I've feasted well these last few days."

"Eleanor. Stop."

"But you did ask me . . ."

"For God's sake, will you *stop*?"

Eleanor blinked at him, but when he only closed his mouth, she drew a breath.

"Very well," she said. "If you'd prefer me to be succinct, I am here because: item one, I need the position; item two, I'm annoyed that someone would try to hurt you by means of the photographs; item three, I would like us to be friends, with no hard feelings between us."

Hart clutched the empty glass until the facets pressed into his fingers. Her eyes were enormous, blue like delphiniums in the sunshine.

Friends, no hard feelings.

She held out a salve, with a smile, offering peace. She knew more about him than anyone else in the world, including his brothers, and she'd just said she was sorry for him. Here he was, then, the beast in the tower with the princess petting his head.

"As for the photographs." Eleanor's voice cut through his drink-soaked brain. "Who knew about them besides you and Mrs. Palmer? I still think I ought to go to the house in High Holborn and look about, or talk to some of the ladies who used to live there—"

"No, you will bloody well leave it alone!"

Eleanor looked at him, her lips parted, surprise in her eyes, but no fear. Eleanor had never feared him, something that had amazed and intrigued the young Hart. The entire world thought him dangerous, unpredictable, terrifying, but not Eleanor Ramsay.

Now she was ripping the bandages off his wounds, making the blood flow anew, when Hart didn't want to feel anything ever again.

"Eleanor, why are you in here, making me talk about all this? Making me *think* about it?" And he was too drunk to stop the whirling memories.

"Oh, dear." She took a step toward him. "Hart, I *am* sorry."

Eleanor reached for his hand. Hart felt the air between her

fingers and his warm, as though they touched before the contact. Anticipation. He needed her touch.

Eleanor stopped the movement and let her hand fall, and something inside him screamed.

His idea that he could coolly court her again was insane. Hart could never be cool with her, never.

Eleanor said nothing. One red gold curl drooped over her forehead, the only strand not tightly braided in place.

Hart wanted to thread his fingers through her hair and pull it loose, feel it tumbling over his hands. He'd scoop her to him and stop her words with kisses. Not tender, sweet kisses but needy, demanding ones.

He needed to taste her, to find her fire, to not let her leave this room tonight. He wanted to loosen the prim bodice and scrape his teeth across her bare shoulder, wanted to leave his mark on her white throat.

He imagined the salt scent of her skin, her pleasant moan as he licked her, the dark jolt in his heart as she put her hands up to protest.

If he kissed her, he'd make her stay, have her bodice crumpled around her waist, her corset unlaced. He'd touch her in slow strokes, hands on her body, relearning her heat.

He'd held back with her when they'd been engaged, but Hart knew that if took her this night, he'd not hold back. He was drunk, frustrated, and in deep pain. He'd teach her things that would shock her, and he'd not let her go until she'd done them back to him.

His need tightened like a net around him, a need he'd not felt in years. His wild sexual yearnings had vanished into the vast emptiness that was Hart Mackenzie, or so he'd believed. That need snaked through him now and mocked his self-control.

The yearnings didn't go away, he realized. *They only went dormant.* Until tonight when they were kicked into roaring by black-lashed eyes and a curl against a sweetly freckled forehead.

"Get out," Hart said in a harsh voice.

Eleanor's red lips popped open. "What?"

"I said, *get out!*"

If she stayed, Hart wouldn't be able to stop himself. He was too drunk for control, and God only knew what he'd do to her.

"Gracious, Hart, you have turned hard."

She didn't understand how hard. Picturing himself pinning Eleanor on the bed, holding her by her wrists drawn over her head, feeling her soft breath while she moaned in pleasure—had him hard as granite.

"Get out, and leave me alone."

Eleanor didn't move.

Hart snarled, turned, and hurled his crystal goblet into the fireplace. Glass shattered and leftover droplets of whiskey sprayed, the fire catching them and bursting into tiny blue flames.

Hart heard Eleanor's swift footsteps behind him, felt the draft as the door was flung open, heard the click of her heels in the gallery. Running. Away from him.

Thank God.

Hart let out his breath, closed the door, and turned the key in the lock. He moved back to the decanter and poured another large measure of whiskey into a clean glass. His hands were shaking so he could barely raise the glass to his lips to drink.

Hart opened his eyes to sunshine pounding through the window and a sound in his head like a saw scraping granite.

He was facedown on the bed, still in shirt and kilt, a whiskey glass an inch from his outstretched hand. The last swallow had spilled from it, leaving a sharp-smelling spot on his coverlet.

Hart's mouth felt as though it had been stuffed with cotton, and his eyes weren't focusing. He made the supreme effort of raising his head, and discovered that the sawing sound came from his valet, a young smooth-mannered Frenchman he'd hired when he'd promoted Wilfred, stropping a razor over a steaming bowl of water.

"What the devil time is it?" Hart managed to croak.

"Ten o'clock in the morning, Your Grace." Marcel prided himself on speaking English with no trace of accent. "The young lady and her father are packed and ready. They're downstairs waiting for the carriage to take them to the station."

Chapter 4

Half of Hart's staff looked utterly shocked to see His Grace charge down the stairs in kilt and open shirt, his face dark with beard and his eyes bloodshot.

They must not know him well, Eleanor thought. Hart and his bachelor brothers used to get falling-down drunk in this house, sleeping wherever they dropped. The servants either became used to it or found a calmer place of employment.

The servants who'd been with him a long time barely glanced at Hart, going on about their business without breaking stride. They were the ones who'd become inured to working for Mackenzies.

Hart pushed past Eleanor, his clothes smelling of stale smoke and whiskey. His hair was a mess, his throat damp with sweat. He turned in the foyer and slammed his hands to either side of the door frame, blocking Eleanor's way out.

Eleanor had seen Hart this disheveled and hung over after a night of revelry before, but in the past, he'd maintained his wicked sense of humor, his charm, no matter how rotten he felt. Not this time. She remembered the emptiness she'd seen in him last night, no trace of the sinfully smiling Mackenzie who'd chased twenty-year-old Eleanor. That man had gone.

No. He was still in there. Somewhere.

Lord Ramsay said from behind Eleanor, "Eleanor has decided we should return to Scotland."

The new, cold Hart fixed his gaze on Eleanor. "To Scotland? What for?"

Eleanor simply looked at him. The splintering of glass, the *Get out!* still rang in her ears. The words had cut her, not frightened her. Hart had been working through pain, and the whiskey had sharpened it.

Please, something in his eyes whispered to her now. *Please, don't go.*

"I asked you, why?" Hart repeated.

"She hasn't given a reason," Lord Ramsay answered. "But you know how Eleanor is when she is determined."

"Forbid her," Hart said, words clipped.

Her father chuckled. "Forbid? Eleanor? The words do not belong in the same sentence."

It hung there. Hart's muscles tightened as he held on to the door frame. Eleanor remained ramrod straight, looking into the hazel eyes that were now red-rimmed and haggard.

He will never ask, she realized. *Hart Mackenzie commands. He does not beg. He has no idea how to.*

And there they always battled. Eleanor was not meek and obedient, and Hart meant to dominate every person in his path.

"Sparks," Eleanor said.

Heat flared in Hart's eyes. Hunger and anger.

They would have stood there all day, Hart and Eleanor facing each other, except that a large carriage rattled up to the front door. Franklin the footman, in his post outside, said something in greeting to the guest who stepped down from the carriage. Hart didn't move.

He was still standing there, facing Eleanor in tableau, when his youngest brother, Ian Mackenzie, ran into the back of him.

Hart jerked around, and Ian stopped in impatience. "Hart, you are blocking the way."

"Oh, hello, Ian," Eleanor said around Hart. "How lovely to see you. Have you brought Beth with you?"

Ian prodded Hart's shoulder with a large hand in a leather glove. "Move."

Hart pushed away from the door frame. "Ian, what are you doing here? You're supposed to be at Kilmorgan."

Ian came all the way in, swept a gaze over Eleanor, ignored Hart, and focused his whiskey-colored eyes on a point between Eleanor and Lord Ramsay.

"Beth told me to send her love," he said in his quick monotone. "You'll see her at Cameron's house when we go to Berkshire. Franklin, take the valises upstairs to my room."

Eleanor could feel the fury rolling off Hart, but he would not shout at her with Ian standing between them.

Trust Ian to diffuse a situation, she thought. Ian might not understand what was going on, might not be able to sense the emotional strain of those around him, but he had an uncanny knack for controlling any room he walked into. He did it even better than Hart did.

Earl Ramsay was another who could diffuse tension. "So glad to see you, Ian. I'd be interested to hear what you have to say about some Ming dynasty pottery I've found. I'm a bit stuck on the markings—can't make them out. I'm a botanist, a naturalist, and a historian, not a linguist."

"You read thirteen languages, Father," Eleanor said, never taking her gaze from Hart.

"Yes, but I'm more of a generalist. Never learned some of the specifics of the ancient languages, especially the Asian ones."

"But we are going to Scotland," Eleanor said. "On the moment. Remember?"

Ian started for the staircase. "No, you will stay here in London until we journey to Berkshire. All of us. We go every year."

Hart, breathing hard, watched his brother go up. "This year is different, Ian. I'm trying to force an election."

"Do it from Berkshire," Ian said, and then he was gone.

"It sounds the best arrangement," Alec Ramsay said with his usual cheerfulness. "Franklin, take our baggage back upstairs as well, there's a good fellow."

Franklin murmured, "Yes, your lordship," scooped up as many bags as his young arms could carry, and hurried up the stairs.

"My lady?" One of the housemaids came in from the vestibule, looking calm, as though Eleanor and Hart hadn't started a row in the middle of the front hall. "Letter's come for you. Delivery boy gave it to me."

Eleanor thanked her and took it, making herself not snatch it out of the maid's hand. Aware of Hart's breath on her cheek, Eleanor turned over the envelope.

For Lady Eleanor Ramsay, staying at number 8, Grosvenor Square. Same handwriting, same paper.

Eleanor burst past Hart and through the vestibule before he could stop her, and ran outside into a cold wind. She looked frantically up and down the street for a sign of the delivery boy, but he had already disappeared into the traffic of the morning.

~~~

Eleanor sought Ian an hour later and found him in Hart's study. Hart had left the house already, bellowing at Marcel to make him decent before he'd banged out to his club or to Whitehall, or wherever he'd gone. Hart never bothered telling anybody.

Ian sat at the desk, writing, and did not look up as Eleanor entered. His large frame filled the chair, his kilt flowing over his big legs. Across the room, his valet, Curry, stretched across a divan, snoring.

Ian did not look up when Eleanor approached the desk. His pen went on moving, swiftly, evenly, ceaselessly. Eleanor saw as she reached him that he wrote not words, but strings of numbers in long columns. He'd already covered two sheets with these numbers, and as Eleanor watched, Ian finished a third paper and started a fourth.

"Ian," Eleanor said. "I beg pardon for interrupting . . ."

Ian continued to write, his lips moving as his hand roved down the page.

"Ian?"

Curry yawned, moved his arm from over his eyes, and sat up. "Give up, yer ladyship. When 'e starts with the numbers, there's no talking to 'im until 'e's finished. Fibrichi's sequences or something."

"Fibonacci numbers," Ian corrected him without looking up. "That is a recurrence sequence, and I do those in my head. This is not one."

Eleanor pulled a straight-backed chair to the desk. "Ian, I very much need to ask you a favor."

Ian wrote more numbers, pen moving steadily, without pause. "Beth isn't here."

"I know that. She couldn't help me with this anyway. I need the favor from *you*."

Ian glanced up, brows drawing together. "I am writing Beth a letter, because she isn't here." He spoke carefully, a man explaining the obvious to those too slow to keep up with him. "I'm telling her I arrived safely and that my brother is still an ass."

Eleanor hid her smile at the last statement and touched the paper. "A letter? But this is all numbers."

"I know."

Ian redipped his pen, bent his head, and went back to writing. Eleanor waited, hoping he'd finish, look up again, and explain, but he did not.

Curry cleared his throat. "Beggin' your pardon, your ladyship. When 'e's at it like that, you'll not get much more from 'im."

Ian didn't stop writing. "Shut it, Curry."

Curry chuckled. "Except for that."

Eleanor drew one of the finished pages to her. Ian had written the numbers in an even, careful hand, each two and five and six formed in an identical manner to all the other twos and fives and sixes, the rows marching in exactitude down the page.

"How will Beth know what the numbers mean?" Eleanor asked.

"Don't get the pages out of order," Ian said without looking up. "She has the key to decipher it at the other end."

Eleanor slid the paper back where she found it. "But why are you writing to her in code? No one will read these letters but you and Beth, surely."

Ian gave Eleanor a swift glance, his eyes a flash of gold. His lips twitched into one of his rare smiles, which vanished as he bent over the numbers again. "Beth likes it."

The smile, the look, tugged at Eleanor's heart. Even in the fleeting glance, she'd seen great love in Ian's eyes, his determination to finish this letter and send it to Beth so she could enjoy decoding it. A way to tell her sweet nothings that no one else could understand. Private thoughts, shared between husband and wife.

Eleanor thought back to the day she'd first met Ian, when Hart had taken her to the asylum to see him. She'd found there a scared, lonely boy, arms and legs too large for his body, Ian enraged and frustrated because he could not make the world understand him.

Hart had been amazed that Ian had actually talked to Eleanor, had even let her slide an arm around his shoulders—briefly. Unheard of, because Ian hated to be touched.

That terrified youth was a far cry from the quiet man who sat here composing letters for his wife's delight. This Ian could meet Eleanor's eyes, if only for a moment, could let Eleanor in on a secret and smile about it. The change in him, the deep well of happiness he'd tapped, made her heart swell.

She also remembered the time that she and Hart had worked out a secret code between themselves. Nothing as elaborate as Ian's number sequences, but a way for Hart to send Eleanor a message when he would be too busy to meet her that day. In whatever city they happened to be in, he'd leave a hothouse flower—usually a rose—lying in the corner of a garden where it would not be seen by the casual passerby. In London, it would be in Hyde Park at a certain crossing of paths, or in the garden in the middle of Grosvenor Square, under a tree nearest the center of it—Hart had made certain Eleanor had been given a key to the gardens very early in their courtship. In Edinburgh, he left them at their meeting spot in Holyrood Park.

Hart could have sent a note, of course, when he had to back out of an appointment with her, but he said he liked knowing she'd walk by their meeting spot and see the signal that he was thinking of her. Eleanor realized, of course, that he must have sent someone, an errand boy perhaps, to leave the rose for her, but it had never failed to melt her heart. She'd pick up the flower and take it home, keeping it to remind her of him until they met again.

The charmer, Eleanor thought. *A way to disarm my anger whenever he had to put business first.* The little flower with its hidden meaning had warmed her heart more than any apologetic note could have done, and he'd known that.

Even nowadays, the rare times she found herself in Edinburgh or London, she'd glance to that spot in Hyde Park or Holyrood, still looking for the sign. The pang when she did not see it always surprised her.

Eleanor sat for a time, letting the lump in her throat work out, while Ian went on writing, oblivious to her thoughts.

"I don't see your key," Eleanor said when she could speak again. "How do you know what numbers to write down?"

Ian shrugged. "I remember."

Curry chuckled again. "Don't look so amazed, your ladyship. 'E's got a mind like a gearbox, and 'e knows every click it makes. It's right frightening sometimes."

"I can hear you, Curry," Ian said, pen moving.

"Aye, and you know I don't tell lies about you. Best just ask 'im, yer ladyship. 'E'll be here awhile."

Eleanor yielded to Curry's wisdom. "The thing is, Ian, I want you to help me do something, and I don't want you to tell Hart. I must ask that you promise to keep it from him. Will you?"

Ian said nothing, his pen scratching in the stillness.

"I'll tell 'im to come ask you what you need," Curry said. "When 'e's come out of it."

Eleanor rose. "Thank you, Curry. But not a word to His Grace, please. Hart can be . . . well, you know how he can be."

Curry got himself to his feet and straightened his shirt. He cleared his throat. "A bit of advice, your ladyship," he said. "Begging your pardon, and your pardon too, your lordship." He turned his full gaze on Eleanor. "'Is Grace is a 'ard man, and 'e gets 'arder by the year. If 'e gets the prime minister–ship, the victory will make 'im like steel. I don't think anyone will soften 'im then, not even you, your ladyship."

Curry's dark eyes held truth. He was not a finely trained servant from an agency, but a pickpocket Cameron had rescued from the streets years ago. Curry got away with his rudeness and outspokenness because he looked after Ian with as much tenderness as a father would a son. The brothers believed that Ian had survived the asylum because Cameron had sent Curry to him.

Ian finally set down his pen. "Curry doesn't want to lose forty guineas."

Eleanor stared at him. "Forty guineas?"

Curry turned brick red and didn't answer. Ian said, "The wager that Hart will marry you. We made it at Ascot in June. Curry wagered forty guineas that you will say no. Ainsley wagered twenty on yes, and I wagered thirty. Mac said he bet thirty-five that you'd plant your heel in his backside. Daniel said . . ."

"Stop!" Eleanor's hands went up. "Are you telling me, Ian Mackenzie, that there's a wager going around about whether I will marry Hart?"

"Sorry, your ladyship," Curry said. "You wasn't supposed to know." He shot Ian a glare.

Eleanor curled her hands to fists. "Is Hart in on this?"

"'Is Grace declined to participate," Curry said. "So I'm told. I wasn't there at the original wager. I came in after, like, when it went 'round the servants. But what I heard was that 'Is Grace mentioned the possibility of marrying, and your name came up."

Eleanor lifted her chin, her heart pounding. "Absolute nonsense. What was between me and Hart was long ago. Finished."

Curry looked embarrassed but not ashamed. *Sorry he's been caught, but not sorry he made the wager.* "As you say, your ladyship."

Eleanor made herself march to the door. "Please send word when you're finished, Ian, and we'll talk then."

Ian had gone back to writing. Whether he'd heard Eleanor, she couldn't be certain.

Curry made a perfect butler's bow to her. "I'll tell 'im, your ladyship. Leave it to me."

"Thank you, Curry. And I will see to it that you win your wager." With another glare at the small man, Eleanor lifted her chin, swept out of the room, and closed the door with a decided click.

⁓

Blast you, Hart Mackenzie, Eleanor thought as she strode down the Strand, the maid assigned to look after her hurrying in her wake. *Starting a wager that you'll marry me.* She gathered from Curry's explanation that Hart had thrown out the announcement like a fizzing bomb and stood back to watch what happened. That would be just like him.

She stopped and looked into a shopwindow, trying to catch her breath. She'd hopped out of the landau near St. Martin's Lane, to the maid's dismay, hoping a brisk walk would soothe her temper. It hadn't quite worked.

As she looked at the secondhand clocks displayed, Curry's exact words came back to her—*'Is Grace mentioned the possibility of marrying, and your name came up.*

The Mackenzie brothers had been quite keen that Eleanor should marry Hart when Hart first courted her, had rejoiced when Eleanor had accepted him. They'd been vastly sorry when Hart and Eleanor had parted, but Mac and Cam had told her, privately, that though they were unhappy about her decision, they completely understood. Hart was an arrogant bully and an idiot, and Eleanor was an angel for putting up with him as long as she had.

Perhaps the brothers had taken Hart's suggestion that it was time he married again to mean he'd set his sights on Eleanor. Wishful thinking and high hopes. Hart, she was certain, had never mentioned a name. He'd have been too careful for that.

She would have to quiz Isabella closely about it. Isabella had much to answer for over this wager, and so did Ainsley, Cameron's wife. Ainsley was one of Eleanor's oldest friends, but neither she nor Isabella had bothered to mention this family betting pool to Eleanor.

Eleanor walked on, her anger somewhat lessened but not quite. She decided to push her troubling thoughts aside and focus on her errand at hand.

She'd decided to follow up on her idea that the photographs might have been found in a shop. People sold off photographs all the time to collectors or photography enthusiasts either privately or through shops dedicated to photos or photographic equipment. The Strand had several such places. Eleanor decided it worth her while to find out, subtly, whether any of them had acquired a collection of photographs of Hart Mackenzie in his altogether, and if so, to whom they'd sold them on to.

The first two shops Eleanor entered turned up nothing,

though she found a landscape photograph she bought for a tuppence to put in a little frame for her desk.

A bell tinkled as Eleanor pushed open the door of the third shop, which was dusty and dim. Her maid, a young Scotswoman called Maigdlin, plopped herself down on a chair just inside the door, sighing in relief. She was a bit plump and disapproved of tramping through streets when there was a perfectly good landau handy.

Eleanor seemed to be the shop's only customer. The sign on the window announced that the proprietor specialized in photographs and other ephemera of actors and famous aristocrats. Boxes upon boxes stood on long tables, and Eleanor started patiently looking through them.

Stage actors were popular here, with entire boxes devoted to Sarah Bernhardt and Lillie Langtry. Photographs of Wild West traveling shows livened up one corner, with Buffalo Bill Cody and a string of dancing girls and trick ropers filling one box, another holding American Indians of various tribes in exotic costume.

Eleanor found pictures of prominent Englishmen on a table against the far wall—an old one of the Duke of Wellington with his characteristic nose, quite a few of Mr. Gladstone and the now-deceased Benjamin Disraeli. Pictures of Queen Victoria and the Prince Consort were popular, along with photographs of the Princess Royal, the Prince of Wales, and other members of the queen's large family. Another box was filled with photographs from The Great Exhibition.

Eleanor found several of Hart Mackenzie, Duke of Kilmorgan, but they were formal portraits. One was fairly recent—Hart standing tall in full Scottish dress, old Ben at his feet. One was a picture of him from the chest up, his broad shoulders filling the frame. The last was of Hart seated regally on a chair, his arm resting on the table beside him. He focused his eagle stare on the camera, eyes catching anyone who looked at him.

"Duke of Kilmorgan, miss? He's very popular with our customers."

Eleanor jumped as a tall, narrow-limbed young man with a pointed face and dark eyes looked at the photographs in her hand. She couldn't help noticing that the angle of his glance took in the curve of her bodice and lingered there.

Eleanor took a step to the side. "You don't have many of him."

"Because his photographs sell as quick as we get them in. The young ladies, they find him handsome."

Of course they did. How could they not? Even the stiff poses didn't mar the attractiveness of Hart Mackenzie.

"I have others if you want to see them." The clerk winked. "More *discreet* photographs, as they say. In the French style."

Eleanor's heart beat faster. The clerk was a bit repulsive, but Eleanor could not afford not to check what he had. She pulled the veil of her hat over her eyes and tried to appear shy. "Perhaps I ought to have a look at them."

"In the back." The clerk gestured toward a curtained doorway. "This way, miss."

Eleanor looked at the heavy velvet draperies that blocked all view of the back room. "Can you not bring the photographs out to me?"

"Sorry, miss. Shopkeeper would have my head. He sells the things, but they stay in the back."

He kept his arm out, pointing at the curtain. Eleanor drew a breath. She needed to know. "Very well. Lead on."

The shopkeeper grinned, charged over to the doorway, and held the curtain up for her. Eleanor made a staying gesture to the maid and ducked into the back room, trying not to sneeze at the dust when the clerk let the drape fall.

The dim room looked innocuous—nothing more than a jumble of tables and boxes and much dust. Eleanor tried, and failed, to stop another sneeze.

"Sorry, miss. Here we are."

The clerk pulled a pasteboard box out from the bottom of a haphazard stack and opened the lid. Inside lay a cluster of photographs, all of Hart, all showing much skin. Eleanor shook the box, scattering the photographs across its bottom and counted about a dozen of them.

Eleanor looked up and found the clerk standing an inch from her. He was breathing hard, his face perspiring.

"Are there any more?" she asked him in a businesslike tone.

"No, miss, that's all."

"Did you have more before? I mean, has someone else bought any others?"

The clerk shrugged. "Don't think so. Shopkeeper bought these a while ago."

"Who sold them to him?" Eleanor tried to keep the excitement from her voice, not wanting to arouse his suspicions. Or arouse anything else for that matter.

"Don't know. I wasn't here then."

Of course not. That would have been too helpful.

Why no one had found or purchased these since their arrival was explained by the chaos of the room. The photographs would have been difficult to chance upon in this jumble, and if the proprietor refused to bring them to the front, a person would have to ask for them specifically.

"I'll take them all," Eleanor said. "These and the three I found in front. How much?"

"A guinea for the lot."

Her eyes widened. "A *guinea*?"

"Told you, His Grace of Kilmorgan is popular. Now if I could find some of the Prince of Wales in his altogether, I could fund my retirement." He chuckled.

"Very well. A guinea." Hart had already started giving her wages for typing, but Hart could pay her back for this.

The clerk reached for the box. "I'll just wrap that up for you."

Eleanor reluctantly put the box into his hands and stood by while he folded brown paper around it and secured it with twine. She took the package he handed her and headed for the curtain, but the clerk stepped in front of her.

"The shop shuts for tea, miss." His gaze roved down her primly buttoned bodice. "Perhaps you could stay and share it with me. We could look at more photographs together."

Most decidedly not. Eleanor gave him a sunny smile. "A kind offer, but, no. I have many errands to attend to."

He put his arm across the curtained door. "Think about it, miss."

The clerk's arm was thin, but Eleanor sensed a wiry strength in this young man. She was highly aware that only she and

Maigdlin were in the shop, aware that she'd voluntarily gone alone into the back room with him. If Eleanor screamed for help, passersby were as likely to condemn her as to help her.

But for years, Eleanor had dealt with the inappropriate advances of gentlemen who thought her fair game. After all, she'd been engaged to the notorious Hart Mackenzie and afterward had retreated home to look after her father, never to marry anyone else. Had Mackenzie ruined her? Not a few people speculated on this. On occasion, a gentleman would do his best to find out.

Eleanor smiled up at the clerk, putting on her best innocent expression. He started to bend to her, lips puckered in a ridiculous way. He even closed his eyes, the silly man.

Eleanor ducked under his rather musty-smelling arm, spun herself out the doorway, and slammed the heavy velvet drape back into him. The clerk shouted and fought the dusty folds. By the time he'd untangled himself, Eleanor had slapped her coins onto the counter and was heading out the front door.

"Come along, Maigdlin," she said as she hurried to the street. "We'll go and have some tea."

"My name's Mary, my lady," the maid said, panting behind her. "Housekeeper should have told you."

Eleanor set a brisk pace west along the Strand. "No, it isn't, Maigdlin Harper. I know your mother."

"But Mrs. Mayhew says I should go by Mary. So the English can pronounce it."

"Absolute nonsense. Your name is your name, and I'm not English. I'll speak to Mrs. Mayhew."

The maid's disapproving look softened. "Yes, my lady."

"Now, let us find some tea and sandwiches. And heaps of seedcake. His Grace will pay for it all, and I intend to enjoy myself."

~───⌣

The house in High Holborn looked the same as it had the night Angelina Palmer had died, the night Hart had walked out of it forever.

The house was to let, but none had taken it this Season, perhaps because it lay too far from fashionable quarters for the rent Hart was asking. Or maybe he'd set it so high because he truly did not want anyone here. The house should sit empty until its ghosts died.

Hart told his coachman to return for him in an hour. The town coach rumbled away, and Hart opened the front door with his key.

Silence met him. And emptiness. The downstairs rooms had been cleared of furniture, save for a stray piece or two. Dust hung in the air, the cold heavy.

He'd not wanted to come here. But Eleanor's assertion that a clue to the photographs might be found in the house made sense. Hart did not trust anyone in his employ enough to confide in them about the photographs, and he certainly didn't want Eleanor there, so he'd come himself.

As he climbed the staircase he'd lightly run up as a younger man, he fancied he heard whispers of laughter, the trickle of whiskey, deep voices of his male friends, the high-pitched chatter of ladies.

The house had at first been a nest for Angelina Palmer, when Hart had been proud to be only twenty and yet to have caught such a ladybird. The house had then become his refuge. Here, Hart had been master, his brutal father far from it. The old duke hadn't even known of the existence of the place.

The house had also become a point of contact during Hart's rising political career. Hart had hosted gatherings here in which alliances had been formed and plans made, which resulted in Hart now being at the head of his coalition party. Here, Hart had celebrated his first election to Commons at the tender age of twenty-two, he unwilling to wait until he inherited his seat in the Lords to start telling Parliament what to do.

Here, also, Angelina Palmer had lived to please Hart. When Hart's friends had gone, and he and Mrs. Palmer were alone, Hart had explored the darker side of his needs. He'd been unafraid to experiment, and Angelina had been unafraid to let him.

Angelina at first had assumed that Hart, still at university, would be too young and inexperienced to prevent her from straying with whatever gentleman she wished. But when Hart discovered her transgressions, Angelina for the first time had seen Hart change from laughing, devilish rogue to the hard, controlling man he would become. Hart had looked her in the eye and said, "You are with me, and no other, whether I see you every night or once a year. If you cannot obey that simple stricture, then you will go, and I will advertise the vacancy of your position."

He remembered Angelina's reaction—irritation, then surprise, then shock when she realized he meant it. She'd humbled herself, begged his forgiveness, and Hart had taken his time about granting it. Angelina might be the older of the pair, but Hart held the power. Angelina was never to forget that.

Later, when Angelina had sensed that Hart was growing bored and restless, she'd brought in other ladies to keep him entertained. Anything, Hart realized now, to prevent him from leaving her.

Hart reached the first floor of the house, fingers skimming the banisters. The day Angelina had ruined his betrothal to Eleanor, Hart had quit the house and never lived there again. He'd sold it to Angelina—through his man of business—telling her to do whatever she liked with the place.

Angelina had turned it into an exclusive bawdy house that accepted only the best clientele, and had done very well out of it. Hart had returned for the first time five years later, right after Sarah's death, seeking refuge from his grief.

Hart walked down the hall toward the bedroom where one of Angelina's girls had died, his footsteps reluctant. Behind that door, he'd found Ian asleep and smeared with the young woman's blood. He remembered his dry-mouthed terror, his fear that Ian had committed murder. Hart had done everything in his power to protect Ian from the police, but he'd let his deep-seated fear blind him for years as to what really had happened in that bedroom.

He shouldn't have come here. The house held too many memories.

Hart opened the door to the bedroom, and stopped.

Ian Mackenzie stood in the middle of the carpet, gazing up at the ceiling, which was painted with nymphs and cavorting gods. A mirror hung on the ceiling, right over the place the bed used to be.

Ian stared up into the mirror, studying his own reflection. He must have heard Hart come in, because he said, "I hate this room."

"Then why the devil are you standing in it?" Hart asked.

Ian didn't answer directly, but then, Ian never did. "She hurt my Beth."

Hart walked into the room and dared put his hand on his brother's shoulder. He remembered finding Angelina with Beth, Beth barely alive. Angelina, dying, had told Hart what she'd done, and that she'd done it all for Hart. The declaration still left a bitter taste in his mouth.

"I am sorry, Ian," Hart said. "You know I am."

Eye contact was still a bit difficult for Ian with anyone but Beth, but Ian took his gaze from the mirror and directed it at Hart. Hart saw in Ian's eyes remembered fear, worry, and anguish. They'd almost lost Beth that night.

Hart squeezed Ian's shoulder. "But Beth's all right now. She's at your house in Scotland, safe and sound. With your son and baby daughter." Isabella Elizabeth Mackenzie had been born late last summer. They called her Belle.

Ian ducked out from under Hart's hand. "Jamie walks everywhere now. And he talks. He knows so many words. He's nothing like me." His voice rang with pride.

"Why aren't you in Scotland with your beloved wife and children, then?" Hart asked.

Ian's gaze drifted to the ceiling again. "Beth thought I should come down."

"Why? Because Eleanor was here?"

"Yes."

Dear God, this family. "I wager Mac rushed out and sent Beth a wire as soon as Eleanor turned up," Hart said.

Ian didn't answer, but Hart knew the truth of it.

"But why have you come *here*, today?" Hart went on. "To this house, I mean?" Ian was sometimes pulled to places that had frightened or upset him, such as his father's private study at Kilmorgan, where he'd witnessed their father kill their mother in a fit of rage. After Ian's release from the asylum, Hart had found him in that room many times, Ian sitting huddled behind the desk where he'd hidden that fateful day.

Ian kept his gaze on the mirror as though it fascinated him. Hart also remembered that, because Ian had trouble with lies, he'd learned to be very good at simply not answering questions.

Oh, bloody hell. "Ian," Hart said, his rage boiling up with nightmare force. "Tell me you didn't bring her here."

Ian finally looked away from the mirror, but he never looked at Hart. He wandered across the room to the window and peered out at the fog, his back firmly to his brother.

Hart swung away and strode into the hall. He cupped his hands around his mouth and shouted. *"Eleanor!"*

Chapter 5

The word echoed up and down the staircase, soaring to the painted cherubs that lurked at the very top of the house.

Silence.

Silence meant nothing. Hart took the stairs to the next floor two at a time.

One of the doors on the landing stood ajar. Hart shoved it open with such force that the door banged into the heavy bureau that partially blocked it.

Someone had moved excess furniture up here, and now the chamber was a jumble of bookcases, dressing tables, chests of drawers, and armoires. A velvet sofa, coated with dust, canted at an odd angle in the middle of the room.

Eleanor Ramsay looked up from where she'd been searching the sofa cushions, a cloud of dust around her.

"Good heavens, Hart," she said. "You do make a lot of noise."

Hart's world took on sharp edges. Eleanor Ramsay could not be here, in this place with its horrible memories of anger, greed, jealousy, and fear. Eleanor here was like a daffodil in a quagmire, a fragile blossom all too easily pulled to its doom.

He did not want this world, this part of his life, so much as touching her.

"Eleanor," he said, voice tight with fury, "I told you not to come here."

Eleanor shook out a cushion and plopped it back onto the sofa. "Yes, I know you did. But I thought I should get on looking for the photographs, and I knew that if I asked you for the key, you'd never give it to me."

"So you went behind my back and asked Ian?"

"Well, of course. Ian is much more logical than you, and he does not bother me with pesky questions. I did not tell him about the photographs, if you are worried about that. They are quite personal, after all. It did not matter anyway, because Ian never asked me why I wanted to come."

Hart gave Eleanor a look that had made Angelina Palmer drop her poised courtesan smile and whiten in fear. Eleanor merely stared at him.

On her head perched a pillbox hat with an absurd little veil. She'd pulled the dotted veil up out of her eyes, but not completely—it hung lopsidedly, dangling over her right brow. Her dark brown dress was filmed with dust she'd raised, and dust caught on her damp cheeks. One lock of hair had escaped her coiffure, a red snake dancing down her bodice. She was delightfully mussed, and dear God, he wanted her.

"I told you, I do not want you in this place," he said. "Not now. Not ever."

"I know." Eleanor moved, calm as she pleased, to the bureau that blocked the door and leaned to open the bottom drawer. "I wasn't silly enough to rush here by myself, if that is what is bothering you. I met my father and Ian at the museum, sent my father and Maigdlin home in your landau, and had Ian walk with me here. I've been watched over every step of the way."

"What is bothering me is that I asked you not to come here at all and you flagrantly disobeyed my wishes." His voice rang through the room.

"Disobeyed your wishes? Dear, oh, dear, Your High and Mighty Grace. I ought to have mentioned that I've always had trouble with obedience, but then, you knew that. If I sat quietly and waited to obey my father, I would long ago have become a dried-up skeleton on a chair. Father is very bad at making any sort of little decision, even including how much sugar he wants in his tea. And he never can remember whether he likes cream. I learned at an early age to not wait upon anyone's permission, but simply to do."

"And now you work for me."

She rummaged in the drawer, not looking at him. "I'm hardly your servant, but the same principle applies. Were I to wait for your commands, I'd be in that little study with Wilfred, tapping my fingers on the desk, wondering when you would bother to appear. Even Wilfred wonders at your absences, and he is a man of few words."

"In that study is exactly where I want you to be!"

"I don't see why. Wilfred doesn't *really* need me to type your correspondence. He gives it to me for something to do, because he feels sorry for me. My time is much better spent trying to discover who is sending the pictures and what they mean by it. And you could help me search instead of standing in the doorway shouting at me."

She made his blood boil. "Eleanor, I want you out of this house."

Eleanor blithely ignored him to open the next drawer. "Not until I've finished looking. There are many nooks and crannies and much furniture."

Hart pushed his way around the bureau, seized Eleanor by her shoulders, and pulled her upright. She came up swiftly, one blue eye now completely shielded by the veil.

Before Hart registered that he did it, he skimmed his hands down her arms to her wrists and pulled them behind her back. He knew how to lock a woman's hands, knew how to hold her still. Eleanor stared up at him, red lips parted.

Need streaked through him, a craving that closed him in razor-sharp claws. Hart studied the red lips that beckoned him, breasts rising against her tightly buttoned bodice, the lock of hair, fallen, gold red against her cheek.

He leaned and took the curl in his mouth. Eleanor drew a breath, and Hart turned his head and caught her lip between his teeth.

Eleanor's eyes were enormous this close to his. Gone was her defiance, her stubborn obliviousness. She focused on Hart and Hart alone, as he bit down on her lip, not brutally, but enough to trap her. Her breath was hot on his cheek, and her wrists were quiet under his hands.

Tamed? No. Never Eleanor. If she quieted in his skilled grasp, it was her choice to.

Hart could easily take her, now, perhaps across the top of the chest behind her. It would be quick and intense—a few thrusts, and Hart would be spent. They wouldn't even have to undress. Eleanor would be his, again, inescapably.

Hart pressed a soft kiss where his teeth had scraped. Her lips were slightly salty with perspiration, silken soft, the warm tang of her mouth satisfying. He nipped her again, pulling her lip with his teeth, again gentling the movement by kissing where he'd bitten.

Eleanor moved her lips to kiss him back, her eyes closing to slits while her pink, soft mouth found his. Hart slanted across it, ready to lick inside, but Eleanor pulled back.

"Don't." Her whisper was quiet, and he wouldn't have heard it had they not been this close. But no fear rested in Eleanor's eyes. He saw sorrow and heartache instead. "It's not fair."

"Not fair?"

"To me." Her lashes were wet.

Dark need tore at him. Hart gripped her wrists, but Eleanor didn't flinch, didn't move.

He was Hart Mackenzie, the Duke of Kilmorgan, one of the most powerful men in Britain, and Eleanor Ramsay had put herself into his power. Hart could do anything he wanted to her, up here, alone in this room.

Anything at all.

Eleanor's eyes, one behind the pin-dot veil, one visible, stared into his. Hart dragged in a breath that burned fire, and made himself let her go.

His body fought him releasing her, and he backed a step before he turned away and leaned on the bureau. He pressed his fists to the wood, his lungs hurting, blood pounding through his body.

"Hart, are you all right?"

Eleanor looked up at him in concern. Still, she had no fear. Only worry—for him.

"Yes, I am all right. Why the hell wouldn't I be?"

"Because you look very red and will break the wood if you're not careful."

"I'll be better the minute you are out of this house!"

Eleanor spread her hands in her dove-colored gloves. "When I'm finished searching."

Hart roared. He grabbed the chest of drawers and overturned it, the thing crashing to the floor. At the same time, the doorway darkened and Ian strode in, his Mackenzie scowl all for Hart.

Eleanor turned to Ian, giving him a bright smile. "There you are, Ian. Will you please take Hart downstairs? I will finish much more quickly if he's not up here throwing the furniture about."

Hart went for her. Ian tried to stop him, but Hart shoved Ian out of the way and lunged at Eleanor.

She shrieked. Hart didn't care. He lifted her and tucked her over his shoulder, then he pushed past Ian—who had decided to step back and let this happen—and carried Eleanor bodily down the stairs.

"Ian, bring my package!" Eleanor shouted back over his shoulder. "Hart, put me down. This is absurd."

Hart's town coach was pulling to a halt under the gaslights, which were turning the now-misty air a sickly yellow. Hart at least set Eleanor on her feet before he guided her down the steps to the street, hand on her elbow, pushing her at the carriage.

Instead of fighting him, Eleanor subsided after one "Really, Hart." He saw her glance at the passersby and decide not to make a scene.

Hart shoved her into the coach that his footmen hastily opened. He climbed up beside her and directed his coachman to Grosvenor Square, knowing good and well that Eleanor would never stay in the carriage if he didn't hold her there all the way home.

~~~~~

The pictures Eleanor had found at the shop were breathtaking. Hart in all his glory.

Eleanor sat alone at the table in her bedchamber that evening, the photographs spread before her. She was in her dressing gown, the new ball gown she'd wear tonight lying in emerald delight across the bed.

Ian, bless him, had brought the brown-paper package to her when he'd returned to Hart's, again never asking what was in it. Eleanor waited for Maigdlin to go down to her supper before she cut the twine and unwrapped the box, laying out the photographs one by one.

There were twelve in all, six taken in the same room as the one in which he'd been looking out the window. The other six had been done in a smaller bedroom, the décor of which reminded her of the house in High Holborn.

Eleanor put her finger on one photograph and drew it to her. This one was different from the others, because in it, Hart wasn't naked. Facing the camera full on, he wore only a kilt of Mackenzie plaid that sagged low across his hips. This photograph was also different, because here, Hart was laughing.

His smile lit his eyes and softened his face. One hand was on his waistband, and the other came up, palm forward, as though telling the cameraman—or woman, in this case—not to take the picture. The shutter had gone off anyway.

The result showed Hart as he truly was. Correction, Hart as he used to be—a devilish rogue with a charming smile. The man who'd teased Eleanor and winked at her, who'd called her wicked for wanting to be anywhere near a notorious Mackenzie.

Hart had laughed at her and made Eleanor laugh back. Hart had not been afraid to tell her anything—his ambitions, his dreams, his worries for his brothers, his rage at his father. He would come to her at Glenarden and lie with his head on her lap amidst the summer roses, and pour out his heart. Then he'd kiss her, lover's kisses, not chaste courtship kisses. To this day, when Eleanor smelled red roses, she felt the smooth pressure of his lips on hers, remembered the dark taste of his mouth.

Memories flooded her, and her eyes filled. Hart had been such a devil, but full of life and hope, laughter and energy, and she'd loved him.

The man Hart had become no longer had the hope and the laughter, though he still had the obsession. Hart was driven—she'd read in the newspapers how he won gentleman after political gentleman to his side, making them *want* to follow him. Hart never had anything good to say about Bonnie Prince Charlie—*the arrogant bastard who beggared the Highlanders*—but Bonnie Prince Charlie must have had the same ability to make the skeptical believe in him.

But with Hart's rise to power, more warmth had left him. Eleanor thought about what she'd seen in his eyes, both in the vestibule this morning when Hart had blocked her way out of his house, and this afternoon when he'd found her in the High Holborn house. He was a hard and lonely man, driven by anger and determination, no more smiling excitement, no more laughter.

Eleanor slid that photograph aside and drew the next one toward her. Hart still smiled at the camera, but with practiced deviltry. The kilt was off now, trailing to the ground from his hand.

He was a beautiful, beautiful man. Eleanor traced his chest, remembering what it had been to touch him. She'd gotten a taste of it this afternoon, when he'd held her arms behind her, his strength pinning her. She'd been at his mercy—she knew she'd not be able to walk away until he released her. Instead of growing afraid, Eleanor had felt dark excitement beat through her veins.

"Eleanor, aren't you ready?"

Eleanor jumped as Isabella's voice sounded outside her bedchamber door. Eleanor swept the photographs back into the box and was shoving the box into the bottom drawer of her dresser when Isabella Mackenzie entered in a swish of silver satin and taffeta.

Eleanor locked the drawer and dropped the key into the top of her corset. "Sorry, Izzy," she said. "I was just finishing something. Will you help me dress?"

～

Hart knew full well the moment Eleanor joined the throng that filled his ballroom.

Eleanor wore green—a dark, bottle green gown with a neckline that plunged down her breasts and bared her shoulders. A bustle, more restrained than the gigantic ones worn by the other ladies, drew her overskirt back before spilling it to the floor in a soft wave of satin.

The style drew attention to her waist hugged by a small, tight bodice, and that in turn drew attention to the décolletage framing her full breasts. A necklace, a simple chain with an emerald drop, pointed to her cleavage. Emerald earrings dangled from her ears, as green as the dress.

Hart had been thinking about David Fleming, the MP who was Hart's eyes and ears in Commons, and wondering how the man was getting on. Fleming tonight was using his art of persuasion to sway to Hart's side one or two men on the fence about pushing a vote of no confidence on Gladstone. Hart knew the time was near when he could force Gladstone to resign, and either concede that Hart's coalition had the majority, or call for elections, which Hart would make bloody sure he and his party won.

Get them over by any means necessary, Hart had told Fleming. Fleming, debauched but charming and devious as a snake, had assured Hart of his victory.

But once Eleanor entered the room, worry about Gladstone, votes, and victory dissolved to nothing.

Eleanor was radiant. Tonight was the first Hart had seen her in anything but the ugly cotton or serge dresses Eleanor wore buttoned up to tomorrow. The gown let her glow. Isabella must have either lent Eleanor the dress or bought it for her, but either way, the result was breathtaking.

A little too breathtaking. Hart couldn't take his eyes off her.

"Very tired of you borrowing my wife to hostess your boring parties," Mac said, stopping next to Hart in a rare moment of empty space around him. "Between these blasted balls and musicales, *and* the decorators underfoot, I never see her."

Hart didn't pull his gaze from Eleanor as he took a sip of malt whiskey. "What you mean is you don't have as much time to bed her as you'd like."

"Can you blame me? Look at her. I want to kill any man who so much as speaks to her."

Hart had difficulty dragging his gaze from Eleanor, but he conceded that Isabella, in a dress of silver and green that rested like a whisper on her slim figure, looked fine. Isabella always did.

Mac had fallen madly in love with the woman the moment

he'd set eyes on her. It had taken his idiotic brother six years to learn *how* to love her, but thank God, that storm was over, their marriage now in a safe harbor. Isabella and Mac were radiantly happy, with Isabella busily taking care of Mac so Hart no longer had to.

Mac waved off a waiter who stopped with champagne, Mac now a teetotaler after years of nearly killing himself with drink. "What happened to your declaration that you'd be looking for your own wife?" he asked Hart after the waiter had whisked himself away.

Hart's gaze slid back to Eleanor, who was greeting a marquis and marchioness like the old friends they were. Her eyes glowed as she talked, her gloved hands moving as she used them to emphasize her words. Her laughter pealed, and she turned to greet another, rather shy lady and draw her into the group, putting said lady at instant ease. That was one thing about Eleanor—she could charm the hide off Attila the Hun.

"Did you hear me?" Mac growled.

"I did hear you, and I told you to leave it alone."

"You have Eleanor right in front of you. For God's sake, kiss her senseless and send for the vicar. Then she can hostess your fêtes, and Isabella can stay home with me."

"Not for much longer," Hart said mildly, still watching Eleanor. "You and Isabella will be running off to Berkshire, where the two of you can stay in bed all day and all night."

"Because then you'll turn Ainsley and Beth into your hostesses. You do know that your brothers are ready to lynch you, don't you?"

"Having a lovely woman greet my guests is part of the plan," Hart said. "Isabella understands that."

Mac did not look impressed. "Hart, you'd schedule Christ's second coming and have Wilfred send him an itinerary. You must learn to let things happen."

Without waiting for an answer, Mac swung around and shouldered his way through the crowd, drawn back to Isabella.

Learn to let things happen. Hart took a sip of whiskey to hide his cynical laugh. What Mac did not understand was that Mac, Cam, and Ian led the lives they did now because Hart had refused to stand back and let things happen.

If Hart hadn't orchestrated every detail of their lives, Cam and Mac might even now be trying to scratch out a living in some malaria-infested jungle or up in frozen Scotland farming the tough soil. Racehorses, art, women, and fine whiskey would be unheard-of luxuries.

And Ian? Ian would be dead.

No, Hart's brothers did not know the extent of what he'd done, and Hart prayed they never would know. The only person who had any inkling was the lady in the bottle green gown smiling and talking with the guests, engaging them with her radiance. She was the only one in the wide world who knew the truth of Hart Mackenzie.

~~~

Eleanor watched Mac stride away from Hart, and Hart's admirers surge around him to fill the space.

This ball was all about rewarding Hart's staunch supporters and drawing more into the coalition party he'd formed, taking gentlemen away from Gladstone on one side, and from the Tories on the other.

The two ladies who slithered up on either side of Hart had no interest in politics, Eleanor was certain. The lady on Hart's left was Lady Murchison, a viscount's wife, the one on his right, the wife of a navy commander. The commander's wife had her fingers firmly in the crook of Hart's arm, and Lady Murchison skimmed her gloved hand surreptitiously down Hart's back.

She wants to go to bed with him.

Of course she did. Who could resist Hart in his black coat and Mackenzie kilt, wool socks on his finely shaped calves? Hart went on speaking to the small group gathered around him, as though he never noticed the two ladies squeezing closer and closer to him.

Eleanor made herself turn away and beam smiles on the other guests. She was good at this—putting people at their ease, making certain everyone who wished to dance found the right partner, that the elderly guests weren't set against the wall and forgotten. The turnout was quite a crush, though Eleanor knew the guest list was limited enough that those not on it would move heaven and earth to *be* on it. All part of the game to make Hart's light shine the brightest.

Ian was absent tonight, but this was not to be wondered at. Ian hated crowds. Isabella said that when Beth was with him, Ian would walk through fire—or even a crowd—as long as his wife was by his side.

I cannot blame him, Eleanor thought as she moved about, chatting to all and sundry. People liked to stare and point at Ian. *The Mad Mackenzie,* they called him, a bit unfairly. *He married that little half-French nobody,* they'd whisper. *The poor woman must have been desperate for a husband.*

Not so poor, and not so desperate. Beth had inherited a large fortune before she'd married Ian. But Eleanor knew the way of the world—some whispered out of annoyance that Beth hadn't married into *their* family, thus bringing them all that lovely money.

Eleanor did enjoy the chance tonight to catch up with some of her girlhood friends. These ladies were married now and preoccupied with worries about finding good nursemaids or their sons' first ventures into public school. And, of course, because Eleanor was still unmarried, they wanted to matchmake.

"You must join us for our boating party, dear El," one lady said with undisguised fervor. "My brother and his closest friend have just returned from Egypt. Baked quite brown—you'd hardly know them. What stories they tell! Quite fascinating. I'm sure they would be interested to see you."

"My father would enjoy hearing their stories," Eleanor said. "He loves travel, as long as he's not required to move far from his armchair."

The lady laughed, but her eyes were bright with determination. "Well then, you must bring your dear father along. We've missed him so."

More such offers were forthcoming, all couched as outings that wouldn't be the same without Eleanor. And, of course, a bachelor brother, male cousin, and even a widowed uncle would make up the party. Eleanor's acquaintances, it seemed, had decided that their goal before the Season ended was to Get Poor Eleanor Married Off.

Through it all, Viscountess Murchison clung to Hart's side. Mr. Charles Darwin might have claimed that human beings had descended from apes, but Lady Murchison's ancestors must have been barnacles.

As Eleanor watched, Lady Murchison let her hand inch down until it rested on Hart's plaid-covered backside. Hart was too savvy to jump, but he turned a hint to his left, which forced Lady Murchison's hand to slide away.

Did the lady look disappointed? Not at all. She laughed and sent him a merry glance, looking all the more resolute.

Wretched cow.

Eleanor made her way toward Hart, pausing in each cluster of guests to chat and listen, admire and congratulate, advise and console. The ballroom floor was full of whirling couples, but Hart remained firmly on the sidelines, the duke famous for never dancing at his own balls.

Bustles were such cumbersome things, Eleanor thought as she pressed her skirts to slide between bedecked ladies. Fashion this year seemed to dictate that the female of the species should strap long shelves to their backsides and fill them with giant bows and large velvet roses. *Perhaps we should add tea things or a row of books,* Eleanor mused as she squeezed through yet one more clump of ladies.

She popped out between the group tight around Hart and people clustered next to it, trying to get close to him. Somehow, she managed to jostle the arm of a tall gentleman who held a full glass of bloodred claret. He lost his hold on the goblet, which teetered and danced on his fingertips.

And then, disaster. The glass tumbled from his hand and flipped end over end on its way to the floor. Ruby liquid arced through the air and came down all over the front of Lady Murchison's silver satin bodice.

Lady Murchison shrieked. The gentleman with the claret gasped and started babbling shocked apologies. Eleanor pushed through, gloved hands pressed to her cheeks. "Oh, *dear.* You poor, poor thing."

Lady Murchison's face went ugly green as she let go of Hart, who'd taken a large handkerchief from his pocket and held it out to her. The bodice was ruined, a bright red blotch spreading on it like blood from a wound.

Eleanor seized Lady Murchison's hand as she lifted the handkerchief. "No, no, don't brush it—it will set the stain. We will find a withdrawing room and send for your maid and some soda water."

So speaking, she dragged Lady Murchison away, the tall gentleman still apologizing in anguish. Lady Murchison had no choice but to go with Eleanor. Everyone was staring, exclaiming, giving Lady Murchison murmurs of sympathy.

Everyone, that is, except Hart. He sent Eleanor a penetrating look even as he snapped his fingers for a footman to run for the soda. Hart's look told Eleanor that he knew exactly what Eleanor had just done and exactly why she'd done it.

Chapter 6

"El."

Eleanor stopped at Hart's voice from the landing below her. It was an hour since the mishap with Lady Murchison, and Eleanor had gone upstairs to find a shawl for a lady who complained of cold. Dancing and drinking continued in the ballroom below, a Scottish reel filling the hall with its happy strains.

The gaslights were low, Hart a bulk of shadow against deeper darkness. He looked like a Highlander lurking to strike down his enemies—the only thing missing was his claymore. Eleanor had seen a painting of Hart's great-great-grandfather, Malcolm Mackenzie, complete with sword and haughty sneer, and she decided that Hart resembled him greatly. Malcolm had been a madman, legends went, a ruthless fighter none could defeat, the only of five Mackenzie brothers to survive Culloden field. If Old Malcolm had possessed even an ounce of the same determined focus as Hart, then Malcolm had been dangerous indeed.

Eleanor pasted on a smile and went down the stairs to him, arms filled with the shawl. "What are you doing up here, Hart? The ball isn't over, yet."

Hart stepped in her way as she tried to flow past him. "You are the very devil, Eleanor Ramsay."

"For fetching a shawl for a chilly lady? I thought I was being kind."

Hart gave her a look that held some of his old fire. "I had Wilfred write Lady Murchison a cheque for the dress."

Of course, he would not have forgotten the little incident in the ballroom. "How thoughtful you are," Eleanor said. "Wine does make a deplorable stain. Too bad, really—it was a lovely gown."

Eleanor tried to duck around him again, but Hart caught her arm. "El."

"What?"

She couldn't read what was in his eyes, a stillness behind the gold. She thought he might harangue her about deliberately ruining Lady Murchison's gown—the lady had conceded defeat when the soda wouldn't wash out the stain, and had gone home. But Hart said nothing about that.

Instead he touched the emeralds dangling from her ear. "These were my mother's."

Hart's voice went soft, his finger brushing Eleanor's earlobe with equal softness. This is what Lady Murchison had longed for, Hart's skilled touch, the way his voice could drop to gentleness, curling heat through the lucky lady's body.

"Isabella insisted, I'm afraid," Eleanor said quickly. "I wanted to refuse—they having belonged to your mother and all—but you know Isabella. She fixes on a thing, and she hears no argument. I would have asked you about it, but it was rather last minute, and you were already receiving guests. I can remove them if you like."

"No." Hart's fingers closed on the earring, but gently, not pulling. "Isabella was right. They look well on you."

"Even so, it was rather audacious of her."

"My mother would have wanted you to wear them." His voice went softer still. "She would have liked you, I think."

"I did meet her, once," Eleanor said. "I was only a child—eight years old, not long after my own mother passed—but we did get on rather well. She said she wished she had a daughter."

Eleanor remembered the duchess's sweet perfume, the way she'd pulled Eleanor into an impulsive embrace and hadn't wanted to let her go. Hart's mother, Elspeth, had been a beautiful woman, but with haunted eyes.

Hart looked a little like her, although Ian and Mac resembled her most. Hart and Cam had the look of their father, a big brute of a man who hadn't liked Eleanor, but that had been fine with her.

Hart released the earring and raised Eleanor's hand to his lips. He kissed the backs of her fingers, the heat of his mouth searing through the thin fabric of her gloves.

Eleanor stood very still, clutching the slippery folds of the shawl, heart hammering. Hart closed his eyes as he kissed her glove again, as though trying to absorb her warmth through his lips.

This afternoon, Hart had seized her in a forceful embrace, had pinned her wrists behind her in an impossible grip. He'd bitten down on her lip, but he hadn't been teasing or playful. He'd had raw need in his eyes.

And Eleanor hadn't been afraid. She'd known that Hart wouldn't hurt her. Break her heart, yes; hurt her, no.

Tonight he was everything that was gentle. Hart touched her lip in the place he'd bruised it. Eleanor had covered the tiny bruise with a subtle amount of lip paint, but Hart knew exactly where he'd marked her.

"Did I hurt you?" he whispered, brows drawing together.

Eleanor couldn't stop her tongue darting out to touch her lip. "No."

"Don't ever let me hurt you," he said. "If I do anything you don't like, you say, *Stop, Hart,* and I will. I promise you that."

She shook her head. "You've never done anything I didn't like." She blushed as she said it.

Hart touched her upper lip. "I'm a wicked man. You know that. You know all my secrets."

"Not really. I know that you like . . . games. I've come to understand that. Like the photographs. Though exactly what sort of games, I have always been curious to know."

If she thought he'd tell her, here in the stairwell, she was disappointed.

"Not games," he said. "Not with you. What I want with you . . ." His eyes glittered. "I want things I shouldn't want."

He cupped her cheek. She saw the pulse throb in his throat, his face suffuse with color.

Hart was holding himself back. Whatever thoughts were in his mind, whatever he wanted that he couldn't say, he was stopping himself. The shaking of his fingers, the rigidity of his body, the way his eyes darkened in the shadows told her that.

He bent closer. Eleanor smelled his shaving soap, the whiskey he'd drunk, and faintly behind that, Lady Murchison's rather dreadful perfume.

Closer still. Hart's eyes closed as he touched his lips to the place he'd bitten her.

Eleanor's chest hurt, and she stood still, astonished that she ached this much. Hart's lips caressed, thumb at the corner of her mouth.

Eleanor raised herself up to him, tasting the bite of his tongue as it swept into her mouth. Gently, gently, Hart still holding back. His lips were smooth, dry where his mouth was wet. The wild taste of him was still familiar. The years fell away, and they *fit*.

Hart's fingers were strong, hot points, his mouth even stronger. Eleanor melted against him, her body too warm, hungry for him.

Say, Stop, Hart, *and I will.* He meant she should say it if he locked her in place as he'd done this afternoon, rendering her helpless against him.

She was helpless now, and she had no intention of telling him to stop.

The shawl slid from Eleanor's nerveless grip and pooled at their feet. Hart moved closer, his thighs pressing her skirt, his arm firm around her waist. Eleanor felt the hardness of him through layers of fabric, his wanting obvious. Her thoughts flashed back to the photograph of him laughing in nothing but his kilt, then his smile when he'd let the kilt drop.

He'd been beautiful. She wanted him to bare his body for her again—for *her*, and for no one else.

Eleanor knew exactly why Lady Murchison had let her hand wander to his backside. Eleanor slid her fingers there now, brushing past the formal frock coat and finding the finely spun wool of the plaid. Hart must be wearing something under it, but if so, it was something rather thin. Eleanor cupped the firmness of his buttocks, agreeable warmth shooting through her as she felt strong muscle beneath the wool.

Hart raised his head. His gentle look fled, and the sinful smile of the young Hart Mackenzie spread across his face.

"Devil," he said.

"You are still rather attractive, Hart."

"And you still have fire in you." Hart brushed a fingertip over her lashes. "I see it."

"On the contrary. Things have been rather chilly in Aberdeen."

"And you came to London to warm yourself? Wicked lass."

Eleanor squeezed his buttocks again, unable to help herself. "Why do *you* think I came to London?"

Uncertainty sparkled in his eyes, and his brows came down. Eleanor remembered the heady power she'd felt when turning his teasing back on him. Hart wasn't used to that—he wanted to be master of all situations. When he didn't know what Eleanor was thinking, it made him wild.

"Because of the photographs, you said. And you told me you wanted a job."

"I could have taken a typing post in Aberdeen. I didn't have to come all the way to London for it."

Hart touched his forehead to hers. "Don't do this to me, El. Don't tempt me with what I can't have."

"I have no intention of tempting you. But you wonder why, don't you? I see it every time you look at me."

Hart's hand came around her jaw again. "You disregard your danger. I'm a dangerous man. When I know what I want, I take it."

"You didn't want Lady Murchison?" Eleanor let her eyes go wide.

"She's a harpy. The wine wasn't necessary."

"I disliked watching her touch you."

Hart squeezed Eleanor's mouth the slightest bit, making a pucker, which he kissed. "I like that you disliked that. Saving me for you to touch?"

Eleanor pressed his backside again. "It seems that you don't mind."

"Of course I don't mind. I never minded." Another soft kiss. "You have clever fingers, El. I remember."

Eleanor wanted to collapse, like the shawl around her feet. Hart Mackenzie was expert at teasing—but what they'd shared in the past made this real. If she asked him, would he accompany her to her room on the upper floor, would he spend the rest of the night in her bed, while they remembered how they'd enjoyed learning each other's bodies?

Before she could speak, Hart lifted her from her feet and sat her on the landing's railing. Eleanor gasped, feeling empty air behind her back, but Hart's strong arms held her safely. He pressed aside her skirts as he stepped between her legs, the shawl forgotten behind him on the floor.

"You make me come alive," Hart said.

Eleanor's voice shook. "Is that so bad a thing?"

"Yes." His jaw tightened. "I succeed because I focus. I fix on one thing and do anything to obtain that thing. Come hell or high water. You . . ." He held her with one arm while he touched a finger to her lips. "You make me break that focus. You did it before, and you're doing it now. I should send you back down to the ballroom and out of my sight, but right now, all I want to do is count your freckles. And kiss them. And lick them . . ."

Hart brushed a kiss to her cheekbone, and another, and another. He was doing it, kissing every one of her freckles. Eleanor leaned back in his arms a little, knowing he wouldn't let her fall.

She felt hot, wild, as he always had made her. Eleanor the prim and proper spinster, helper to her widowed father, paragon of Glenarden, knew she'd let Hart do to her anything he wanted, and worry about consequences when it was time for consequences.

His lips found hers again, his strong, mastering mouth caressing. Eleanor wound her arms around him and let herself kiss him back. Their mouths met, and met again, the soft noise of kisses drifting through the stairwell. Eleanor twined one leg around his and slid a slippered foot up his hard, hard thigh.

He drew back a little, eyes glinting with his smile. "There's my wicked lass," he whispered. "I've never forgotten you, El. Never."

Eleanor felt as wanton as he called her. But what of it? They were rather elderly, weren't they? A widower and a spinster, past the age of scandal. What harm was a little kissing on the staircase?

But this was not harmless, and Eleanor knew it. Her twining leg opened her to him, and Hart knew how to step between her so that his hardness wedged exactly to the right place . . .

"Mackenzie?" A voice drifted upward through the banisters, one slurred but holding a note of surprise.

Eleanor gasped and jumped, and would have fallen but for Hart's iron-strong arms around her. The real world swirled back at her like a cold wind, but Hart merely raised his head and looked down the stairs in impatience.

"Fleming," he said. "What do you want?"

"Many apologies for interrupting," came the sardonic reply. "Put it down to my remarkably bad timing."

Eleanor recognized the voice. He was David Fleming, one of Hart's oldest friends and political cronies. When Hart had begun courting Eleanor, David had declared himself in love with Eleanor as well—openly and without shame. To his credit, he'd never tried to interfere with the courtship or steal Eleanor from Hart, but after Eleanor had broken the engagement, David had rushed to Glenarden and asked Eleanor to marry him. Eleanor had given him a polite, but firm, no.

She liked David, and she'd continued on friendly terms with him, but he enjoyed drinking and dicing to the point of debauchery. His love of the political game was the only thing that kept him from pursuing his vices into oblivion, and Eleanor feared what would happen to him when the political game no longer held his interest.

"If you can tear yourself away, Mackenzie," Fleming drawled, "I have Neely in my coach. I've done as much as I can, but I need your touch to bring him in. Shall I tell him to return at a better time?"

Eleanor watched Hart change from the wicked young man she'd been in love with to the hard, passionless politico Hart had become.

"No," he said. "I'll be right down."

David took a few steps forward, face coming into the light. "Good God, that's Eleanor."

Hart scooped Eleanor from the railing, and she landed on her slippered feet, skirts falling decorously back into place.

"I know who I am, Mr. Fleming," she said as she snatched up the fallen shawl.

David leaned against the wall below, brought out a silver flask, and took a drink. "Want me to beat on him for you, El? After we land Neely, of course. I need Hart for that. I've had a devil of a time getting him this far."

"No need," Eleanor said. "All is well."

She felt David's keen, dark stare on her all the way from the ground floor. "I love to hate him," he said, gesturing at Hart with his flask. "And hate to love him. But I need him, and he needs me, and therefore, I will have to wait before I kill him."

"So you've said," Eleanor answered.

Eleanor did not look at Hart as she went down the stairs, but she felt his heat behind her. David put away the flask, took Eleanor's elbow when she reached the last stairs, and guided her the rest of the way down.

"Honestly, El," he said. "If you need protection from him, you tell me."

Eleanor stepped off the final stair and withdrew from his grasp. "Do not bother about me, Mr. Fleming," she said, flashing him a smile. "I am my own woman, and always have been."

"Do I not know it." David heaved an unhappy sigh and lifted Eleanor's hand to his lips.

Eleanor gave him another smile, withdrew, and hurried back to the ballroom with the shawl, never looking back at Hart. But she felt Hart's gaze on her, felt the anger in his stare, and hoped he would not take out that anger on poor Mr. Fleming.

~~~~~

David Fleming's coach was ostentatious, like himself. The prim Mr. Neely, a bachelor of Spartan habits, looked out of place in it. He sat upright, his hat on his rather bony knees.

"Forgive the coach," Fleming said from the opposite seat as Mr. Neely glanced about in distaste. "My father was avaricious and flamboyant at the same time, and I inherited his fruits."

Hart, for his part, couldn't catch his breath. Having Eleanor warm in his arms, she looking up at him with absolute trust, had crashed into him and made everything else as nothing. If Fleming hadn't interrupted, Hart would have taken her tonight. Perhaps there on the stairs, with the possibility of one of the guests looking up and seeing them rendering it doubly exciting.

His hardness had deflated a bit when David had called up the stairs, but thinking about Eleanor on the railing, her foot sliding up to his backside, was making it rise again.

Pay attention. We throw the net over Neely, and he brings in his dozen staunch followers, wrenching them away from Gladstone. We need him. Fleming was right to fetch me—he's too decadent for Neely's taste.

The reformed Hart Mackenzie, on the other hand, who rarely touched a woman these days, could win over a prudish bachelor. Nothing like a rake who's seen the error of his ways to excite a puritan.

Neely gave David a disapproving look as David lit a cigar, leaned back, and inhaled the smoke with pleasure. David rarely bothered controlling his appetites, but Hart knew that David had a razorlike mind behind his seeming depravity.

"Mr. Fleming believes he can purchase my loyalty," Neely said. He made a face at the smoke and coughed into a small fist.

David had nicely primed the target, Hart saw. "Mr. Fleming can be crude," he said. "Put it down to his upbringing."

Neely gave Fleming an unfriendly look. "What do you want?" he asked Hart.

"Your help." Hart spread his hands, the words coming easily to his lips while his body sat back and craved Eleanor. "My reforms, Neely, will strike to the heart of matters dear to you. I hate corruption, hate looking the other way while human beings are exploited in the name of enriching the nation. I'll stop such things, but I need your help to do it. I can't work alone."

Neely looked slightly mollified. Hart knew better than to appeal to him by promising gains of power or wealth—Neely was a well-off, upper-middle-class English gentleman with strong ideas about one's place in society. He disapproved of David's wild lifestyle and Hart's vast estate, but he didn't condemn the two men entirely. Not their fault. Hart was a duke,

David the grandson of a peer. They belonged to the aristocratic classes and couldn't help their excesses.

Neely also believed that the duty of the higher classes was to better the lot of the lower classes. He wanted them to remain peasants, of course, but happy and well-cared-for peasants, to show the world at large that the English, at least, still practiced noblesse oblige. Neely would never dream of drinking a pint "down at the pub" with a coal miner or hiring a Cockney pickpocket to be a valet to his brother. But he'd certainly fight for better wages, lower bread prices, and less dangerous working conditions.

"Yes, well," Neely said. "You have put forth some excellent ideas for reforms, Your Grace." He wet his lips, gaze darting first to David, then Hart.

David caught the look and shot Hart a glance. "Perhaps we can sweeten the pot, eh?" David asked. "I sense that you wish to ask us something. You're in confidence here. Words will go no further than the three of us and these walls." He patted the cushioned velvet beside his head.

Hart expected Neely to ask for another tax on the aristocracy or their help on a pet project, or some such, but he surprised them by saying, "I wish to marry."

Hart raised his brows. "Do you? My felicitations."

"No, no. I mean, I *wish* to marry, but I am afraid that I am acquainted with no eligible, unmarried ladies. Perhaps, Your Grace, with your wide circle, you could introduce me to someone suitable?"

While Hart hid his annoyance, David took a pull of his cigar, removed it, and looked through the smoke at Hart. "Perhaps Lady Eleanor could help? She knows everyone in the country."

Neely perked up at the mention of a title. "If this lady would be so kind?"

David stuck his cigar back into his mouth, and Hart gave him an irritated glance. While Eleanor acknowledged that many women of her class married to make social or financial connections, she might not be best pleased at being asked to introduce the prissy and snobbish Neely to one of her friends.

"I have to caution you," Hart said to Neely, "that even were Lady Eleanor to agree to help, whether the young lady in question accepted your offer of marriage would be entirely up to her. A marriage is too nebulous a thing to guarantee."

Neely thought about this, and nodded. "Yes, I see. Well, gentlemen, I will consider things."

Hart felt the fish slipping away. But he had no interest in scouring England to find this man a bride. He'd have to resort to threats, not exactly what he wanted to do this night either.

Before he could speak, David blew out smoke and said, "Tell us what you really want, Neely."

Hart glanced at David in surprise, then he wondered how he'd missed the signs. Neely was nervous, far more than a man wishing to be introduced to the right woman.

Hart's head was not in this game tonight. Of course not. His thoughts were on the stairwell with Eleanor, her instant but innocent response, the taste of her mouth, the scent of her skin . . .

"You were about to ask for something else, before you settled on the safe topic of marriage," David said, dragging back Hart's attention. "Confess. You're among friends. Worldly friends, at that."

In other words, *you can be honest with us, because we're as bad as any gentlemen could be. You cannot possibly shock us.*

Neely cleared his throat. He started to smile, and Hart relaxed. David had found a point of comradeship with him. Now to bring the fish into the boat.

Neely looked at Hart. "I want to do what you do."

Hart frowned, not understanding. "What I do?"

"With women." Neely's eyes took on a hopeful light. "You know."

Oh, dear God. "That was in the past, Mr. Neely," Hart said coolly. "I've reformed."

"Yes. Very admirable of you." Neely drew a breath. "But you'd know where I can find such things. I like the ladies. I like them very much, but I'm a bit shy. And I have no idea which ones to approach for . . . certain things. I met a fellow in France who told me he put a halter on one and rode her like a horse. I'd like . . . I'd like very much to try something like that."

Hart struggled to hide his disgust. What Neely asked for was nothing like the exotic pleasures Hart had learned and enjoyed. Neely asked for what he *thought* Hart enjoyed—using women, perhaps hurting them, for his pleasure. What Neely meant was a perversity, and not at all the art Hart practiced.

What Hart did was about trust, not pain—Hart promising the most exquisite joy to the woman who surrendered to him absolutely. He'd schooled himself to understand exactly what each woman wanted and exactly how to give it to her, and how to ease her back safely in the end. A lady never needed to fear when she was in Hart's care.

However, the art could be dangerous, and an inexperienced pervert like Neely could truly hurt someone. The thought that Neely assumed Hart enjoyed handing out pain annoyed him. The man was an idiot.

But Hart needed the man's votes. He swallowed his anger and said, "Mrs. Whitaker."

"Ah." David smiled and gestured with the cigar. "Excellent choice."

"Who is Mrs. Whitaker?" Neely asked.

"A woman who will take good care of you," Hart said. Mrs. Whitaker was a courtesan who knew how to contain overexcited men like Neely. "David will see you to her house."

Neely looked eager and fearful at the same time. "Do you mean on the moment?"

"No time like the present," Hart said. "I will leave you in Mr. Fleming's hands. Good evening, Mr. Neely. I must return to my guests."

"Quite." Neely made a bow in his seat but did not extend a hand. He'd never think it proper to offer to shake hands with a duke. "I thank you, Your Grace."

David and Hart shared another glance, and Hart opened the door. He climbed with relief out of the smoky carriage as David stretched his legs across the seat Hart had vacated and crossed his ankles, the very picture of decadence. A footman shut the door and the carriage rolled away.

Hart's breath steamed in the chill of the night, but his house glowed with light and warmth. Music, voices, and laughter poured out the front door.

Hart strode into the house much more willingly than he'd walked out of it. He wanted to see Eleanor. Needed to see her. Needed her warm blue eyes and her wide smile, her effusive chatter like sudden rain on a dry, hot day. He wanted her beauty to cancel out the ugliness of Neely, wanted to return to the innocent pleasure of kissing her freckles, which had tasted honey sweet.

There she was, in the bottle green that for some reason brought out the blue of her eyes, the emerald earrings that had belonged to his mother dangling from her ears. A strange relief wafted over Hart when he looked at her, as though the ball, the meeting with Neely—all of it—was nothing, and only Eleanor was real.

She was chatting animatedly—nothing shy about Eleanor— to ladies and to gentlemen, gesturing with a furled fan she seemed to have acquired. Or perhaps it had dangled from her wrist the entire night; Hart couldn't remember. The closed fan became a perfect horizontal as she moved her hand to make a point, then the fan came up to touch her lips.

Hart went rock hard. He stopped in the doorway to the ballroom, one hand on the door frame to keep himself from falling over.

He wanted Eleanor for all those dark pleasures he'd scorned Neely for not understanding. He wanted her surrendering to his hands, trusting him with everything she had, while he took the fan and touched her with it. He wanted to see her astonishment when she discovered how profound the pleasure of simple touching could be, the depth and breadth of it.

He wanted it now.

Hart pushed himself away from the door frame, giving cursory nods to those who tried to gain his attention, and made his way to Eleanor.

Chapter 7

Eleanor saw him coming out of the corner of her eye. Hart looked like an enraged bull, or at least an enraged Highlander in a kilt. His short hair was rumpled, the light in his eyes was harsh, and those who attempted to speak to him melted out of his way.

Things with this Mr. Neely must not have gone well.

Hart kept barreling toward her, as though he meant to sweep her over his shoulder, as he had at the High Holborn house, and carry her off. The strength of him when he'd done that had thrilled her at the same time it had infuriated her.

Hart stopped in front of her, doing nothing so scandalous, but the tension in his body spilled to hers. He fixed Eleanor with his eagle stare and stuck out one large, gloved hand. "Dance with me, El."

The command jerked out of him, and Eleanor knew he did not really want to dance. But they were at a ball full of people, in a place where Hart could not voice what he truly wanted.

Eleanor glanced at his offered hand. "Hart Mackenzie never dances at balls. Known for it, you are."

"I'm prepared to give everyone a shock."

Eleanor wasn't certain what she saw in his eyes—rage, need, and again that bleak emptiness. Something was hurting him. She had the feeling that if she refused this simple request, the blow would erase every bit of new understanding they'd achieved.

"Very well," she said, placing her hand in his. "Let us shock the world."

Hart's smile blazed out, the dangerous man back. "Your words." He nearly crushed Eleanor's hand as he pulled her onto the ballroom floor. "Let us waltz, Lady El."

"It's a Scottish reel," she said. The fiddles and drums were around playing a raucous beat.

"Not for long."

Mac and Isabella were leading the reel, ladies and gentlemen romping around and around the circles with them. Hart walked with Eleanor straight to the orchestra leader and snapped his fingers at the man. The fiddles stuttered to a halt as Hart spoke to the conductor in a low voice, then the man nodded and raised his baton again. The opening strains of a Strauss waltz filled the room, and the dancers looked about in confusion.

Hart guided Eleanor to the middle of the room with his hand on the small of her back. The orchestra gained strength, and the bewildered ladies and gentlemen started forming couples.

Hart stepped into the waltz with the downbeat of the main theme, pulling Eleanor effortlessly with him. They swirled past Mac and Isabella, who remained where they'd been for the reel.

"What the blazes are you up to, Hart?" Mac asked him.

"Dance with your wife," Hart returned.

"Delighted to." Mac, grinning, clasped Isabella in his arms and whirled her away.

"You're getting yourself talked about," Eleanor said as Hart swung her to the center of the ballroom.

"I need to be talked about. Stop looking at me as though you're afraid I'll tread all over your feet. Do you think I never dance because I've forgotten how?"

"I believe you do whatever you please for your own reasons, Hart Mackenzie."

No, Hart hadn't forgotten how to dance. The floor was crowded, yet Hart whirled her through the other dancers without danger, propelling her with strength. His hand was strong on her waist, the other firmly holding her gloved hand. His muscular shoulder moved under Eleanor's touch, and the contact electrified her.

Hart took her across the ballroom floor, spinning her and spinning her. The vast and opulent room whirled past, and she saw the blur of his guests staring in astonishment.

Hart Mackenzie never danced, and now he danced with Lady Eleanor Ramsay, the very-much-on-the-shelf spinster who'd turned him down years before. And *how* he danced. Not with polite boredom, but with energy and fervor.

Hart's look said he didn't give a damn what anyone thought. He'd dance with Eleanor tonight, and the world could go hang. Eleanor's feet felt light, her heart lighter still. She wanted to lean back in his arms and laugh and laugh.

"We waltzed the first night we met," she said over the music. "Remember? We were the talk of the town—decadent Lord Hart singling out young Eleanor Ramsay. So delicious."

The raw look in Hart's eyes didn't lessen. "That wasn't the first time we met. You were nine and I was sixteen. You were at Kilmorgan, trying to play a tune on our grand piano."

"And you sat down next to me to teach me how to play it." Eleanor smiled at the memory, the tall Hart, already handsome in his frock coat and kilt, with an air of arrogant confidence. "In the most condescending way possible, of course. A young man from Harrow deigning to notice a child."

"You were a devilish brat, El. You and Mac dropped mice into my pockets."

Eleanor laughed as the ballroom spun around her. "Yes, that was quite enjoyable. I don't believe I've ever run quite so fast before or since."

Her eyes were beautiful when she laughed, sparkling and blue like the sun on a Scottish loch.

Hart had wanted to discipline Mac himself for the mice, but their father had discovered the prank and tried to beat Mac senseless. Hart had stopped him and had later taken a beating on his brother's behalf.

Eleanor's smile wiped out the cloud of memory. Bless her, she could always do that.

"I meant that we waltzed the first night we met *properly*," she was saying.

"You wore your hair in ringlets." Hart pulled her closer, the space between their bodies diminishing. "I saw you sitting with the matrons, looking prim and respectable, and *I wanted you so much.*"

Hart felt the supple bend of her waist under his hand, her body warm as a flush colored her face. Nothing had changed. Hart still wanted her.

Eleanor smiled as she'd smiled that long-ago night, unafraid and daring him. "And then you didn't do anything very wicked at all. I confessed myself disappointed."

"That is because I do my wickedness in private. As I did on the terrace, and in the boathouse, and in the summerhouse."

Eleanor's cheeks went delightfully pink. "Thank heavens we are so public here."

Hart stopped. Couples nearly collided with them but carried on dancing, saying nothing. Hart Mackenzie was the eccentric Duke of Kilmorgan, they were his guests, and anything he did in his own house was to be tolerated.

Hart led Eleanor quickly from the floor. "I take that as a challenge," he said when they reached a quieter corner. "Meet me on the terrace in ten minutes."

Eleanor, being Eleanor, opened her mouth to ask why, but Hart gave her a formal bow and walked away from her.

⁓

Ten excruciating minutes later, Hart strode through a servants' back hallway in his vast house, startling a footman and a maid who were also stealing a private moment, and walked out through a side door to the terrace.

It was empty. Hart stopped, his breath steaming. Cold and disappointment hit him like a slap.

"Hart?"

A whisper came from the shadows, and then Eleanor stepped out from behind a pillar. "If you wanted a secret meeting, could you not have chosen a drawing room? It's bloody freezing out here."

The relief that swept over him threatened to drown him. Hart tugged Eleanor against him, gave her one swift, fierce kiss, and then pulled her rapidly down the terrace steps, out of the garden, around the side of the house, and through a gate that led to a stairway. Down these stairs they went and back inside the house, into a long, white-painted hall. This hall was empty of servants, the staff engaged in Hart's private supper ball for three hundred upstairs.

Hart towed Eleanor through another door into the warm steam of the laundry room. There was no light in there, but plenty of lamplight streamed through windows that looked back out to the gaslit passage.

A huge sink stood at one end of the room, with taps to pour out hot water from the boiler on the other side of the wall. Ironing boards were folded in the corner, and irons waited patiently on shelves to be heated on the small stove. A long table was covered with clean, folded laundry, snowy white linen ready to be carried to the bedrooms above.

Hart shut the door, enclosing them in humid warmth. He slid his hands to Eleanor's bare shoulders, not liking how cold she was.

The conversation with Neely had left a bad taste in his mouth. Hart had been aware that people believed he was like Neely, a seeker of questionable pleasures at others' expense. Hart had never cared what people thought of him before. Why Neely's rather disgusting eagerness should bother him tonight, he didn't know.

No, he did know. He didn't want Eleanor thinking that he was a man like Neely.

"What did you wish to speak to me about so privately?" Eleanor asked. "May I assume you did not win over Mr. Neely, hence your mood?"

"No, Neely capitulated," Hart said. "David is seeing to him."

"Congratulations. Do victories always make you this cross?"

"No." Hart caressed her shoulders. "I don't want to talk about Neely or victories."

"Then what did you wish to speak about?" She gave him one of her coyly innocent looks. "The flower arrangements? Not enough vol-au-vent at supper?"

For answer, Hart hooked his fingers into the top of her long glove, the buttons popping as he drew the glove down, down, down. He kissed the bared inside of her wrist, then kissed it again. Warm, sweet Eleanor.

He wanted to bathe in her and cleanse himself of all the things he'd done and all the things he would do in the name of making himself prime minister. He'd begun the supper ball as the duke trying to win over those who would help bring him power. He'd segued into the man who'd make a bargain with the devil himself if it would win him his vote.

He did not want to be that person anymore. At this moment, he wanted to be with Eleanor and shut out the world.

Eleanor's eyes softened as he drew her up to him and kissed her parted lips.

Something jolted between them. *Sparks*. Always sparks.

Hart kissed across her lower lip, lingering on the place where he'd bitten her. A tendril of darkness danced somewhere inside him, but he wouldn't let himself ruin this. Not with Eleanor's lips soft under his, her mouth warm and responding.

Sweet and tender, that was Eleanor, and yet she had a core of steel. Hart kissed her throat and then her shoulder, her skin damp with their wild dancing.

Not enough. It wasn't enough.

Hart swept her into his arms and deposited her on the low table heaped with laundry. Before Eleanor could protest, he was over her on hands and knees as he laid her back.

"You'll ruin the linens," she struggled to say. "They worked so hard on them."

"I pay my servants the highest wages in London."

"For putting up with you."

"For letting me ravish my love on a pile of clean laundry." Hart plucked a pair of drawers from behind her shoulder, a lady's drawers, made of thin linen and trimmed with lace. "Your laundry, I believe."

Eleanor tried to snatch them. "Hart, for heaven's sake, you can't be waving my knickers about."

Hart held them out of her reach. "Why are they so worn out?" The place that cupped her bottom was threadbare, and the lace on the leg openings had been mended many times. He picked up the companion camisole, again of fine fabric but carefully mended over the years. "Isabella needs to outfit you from the skin out."

"I can do it myself," proud Eleanor said. "I'll buy some new smalls out of my wages."

"You should have a roomful of new ones. Throw these away."

"I shall have to if you rip them."

"Don't tempt me." Hart drew the camisole across her cheek. "These are linen. I want to see you in silk."

"Silk is expensive. Lawn is more practical. And you shouldn't see me in either."

Hart lifted the drawers again. "When you put them on tomorrow, think of me." He pressed a kiss to the worn fabric that would go over the round of her buttocks.

Eleanor's eyes widened. "Cheek."

"Cheek? Was that a pun?"

"You're horrible."

"I never pretended to be anything else." Hart dropped the drawers on the pile and lost his smile. "You make me wicked, El. When I walk into a room with you in it, everything and everyone goes to hang."

"Then you shouldn't walk into rooms with me in them. You have so much responsibility now."

"And you danced back into my life just as I'm poised to grab my greatest success. Why?"

"To help you. I told you."

Hart leaned to her, looking into her blue eyes. "I think God is playing games with me. Having his vengeance."

Eleanor frowned. "I'm not sure God works quite like that."

"He does with me, but then I've always had the devil in me. Maybe you were sent to save me."

"I highly doubt that. No one could save *you*, Hart Mackenzie."

"Good. I don't want you to save me. Not right now."

"Then what do you want?" she asked.

"I want you to kiss me."

Eleanor's eyes softened. She wound her arms around his neck, and Hart forgot about darkness, forgot about Neely, forgot about everything but Eleanor.

Their mouths met in the silence of the room, Eleanor's a

point of warmth. The laundry slipped and slid beneath them as Hart laid her down all the way and pressed his knee between her skirts.

He longed to wrest off the skirts and the cage of the bustle that kept him from her. From there, it would be easy to remove her drawers and be inside her in one swift thrust. And then he could be with her, complete. Finding her heat, becoming one with the woman he'd always wanted. Craved. For years.

If he asked politely, she'd say no. So, he'd have to be impolite.

Hart tugged her glove the rest of the way off and pressed a hard kiss to her palm. He wrapped the glove once around her wrist and then around his.

Eleanor watched, startled, not sure what he meant by it. Hart wasn't certain either. He only wanted her close, and to stay.

The strange binding of the glove licked heat through Eleanor's body. Hart was heavy on top of her, and the glove around both wrists bound him to her, she to him.

He'd taught Eleanor to kiss long ago. Showed her how to part her lips, how to let him inside her mouth. She'd let this man slowly, slowly take all her innocence. Seducing her, teaching her to give in to her desires and not be afraid.

"El," he whispered.

Breathing hurt. Hart had said her name like that on the day in the summerhouse in Scotland when he'd laid her down and kissed her in the sunshine. He'd told her that he wanted her and exactly how he'd wanted her. Eleanor had laughed, pleased with her power. Eleanor Ramsay, bringing the great Hart Mackenzie to his knees.

Foolish, foolish Eleanor. She'd never had power over Hart, and that very day, he'd proved it.

He was proving it again. He kissed down to her décolletage, his breath heating her bare skin, his hair like rough silk. She found her unbound hand coming up to stroke his hair— she hadn't told it to do that.

He would unmake her. Again.

Hart, no. Let me go.

The words wouldn't come. Hart kissed her throat, lips lingering, searing like a brand. She was hot from dancing, cold from their brief moment on the terrace, and burning inside.

Hart's body fitted against hers. Hart Mackenzie, again in her arms, where he belonged.

He raised his head, his golden eyes dark. "I've missed you, El."

I've missed you. I've missed you so much it's breaking my heart.

Hart kissed her again, and Eleanor knew she'd surrender. Tonight, she'd let him have her, never mind the cost. It frightened her how easily she was going to succumb.

The glove wrapped around their wrists made her shiver. More so when Hart lifted her bound hand and pressed a kiss to the inside of her wrist.

He followed that with a lick and then a gentle bite. He nipped her again, then he raised his head. "El, I want . . ."

"I know."

"No, you don't. You can't." He shook his head. "You are innocence itself, and I am evil incarnate."

She smiled, her heart beating faster. "You are a bit devilish, I admit."

"You have no idea what a man like me wants."

"I have *some* idea. I remember the summerhouse. And your bedroom upstairs, and at Kilmorgan." Three times she'd been Hart Mackenzie's lover; three times in her life she thought she'd die of happiness.

"That was innocent. I was holding myself back, because I didn't want to hurt you."

Hart was holding himself back now. Eleanor saw something desperate in his eyes that she didn't understand. She longed to reach it but couldn't.

"I tell myself that you're precious and breakable," he said. "But you have a fire in you I want to touch. I want to show you my evil games and bring that fire to life, to teach you what that fire can be."

"That does not sound like so bad a thing."

"It could be, El. I can be *very* bad."

"I'm not afraid," she said, still smiling.

Hart's laugh was laced with heat. "That is because you don't truly know me."

"I know more than you think."

"You tempt me every time you look at me. You with that

fan." Hart picked it up from the laundry table and threw it across the room.

Eleanor put her hand out in protest. "Good heavens, Hart, if you've broken that . . . Fans are expensive."

"I'll buy you a new one. I'll buy you a cart full, if you promise me never to use it like you did tonight—telling me and every man in the room that you wanted to be kissed."

Her eyes widened. "I did no such thing."

"You kept tapping the confounded thing to your lips and looking coy over it."

"I did not."

"It made me want to take you, right there in the ballroom. I want to take you now. I want you bare on this table, and I want . . ."

He checked his words, and Eleanor's pulse raced. "You want what?"

Hart looked at her with eyes that were molten. "I want everything. To be your lover in all ways. I want to come to your bedroom every night and teach you things that will shock you. Best lock your door, El, because I don't know how long I can stay away."

His smile held sin, the man she'd known before finally shining out. But he was right; even all those years ago, Hart had held himself back. Eleanor had sometimes caught a glimpse of intense hunger when he looked at her, which he'd quickly mask.

"I told you, I'm not afraid," she said. "I'm not a virginal young lady, needing shelter and protection. After all, I'm the one who told Ainsley she should run away with Cameron."

"Did you, minx?"

"She came to me for advice, since I had experience with a Mackenzie."

Hart smoothed Eleanor's hair, his touch becoming tender. "I want you. It's what I've wanted every day since I met you. It's always been *you*. And that's why you need to get off this table and get away from me. Now."

"But . . ."

Hart dragged her up to him for another kiss that forced her mouth to open to his. His teeth scraped her lips, but her body rose to his, and her mouth responded, tangling and stroking with his.

He released her suddenly, and she fell back onto the soft laundry, breathless, her lip throbbing where he'd bruised it.

He made her feel loosened, freed. She drew her hand down his arm, thrilling to feel the muscles like steel beneath his coat.

Hart leaned to whisper into her ear. "You need to stay far away from me, Eleanor Ramsay. You say you don't need protection, but that is exactly what you do need. From me."

He kissed her again, a hard kiss, demanding. All at once, she felt him free her wrist, the glove sliding away to land on her chest. Hart kissed her lips one more time as he lifted himself away from her and got to his feet.

Eleanor sat up, clutching the glove, trying to catch her breath. Hart ran his hand through her curls, then bent down for one more kiss.

Hunger blazed in his eyes, one so fierce Eleanor knew she should be frightened, but she wasn't. Hart wanted her, even after all these years, and that made her warm and excited.

She saw him fight the hunger, watched him tuck it away beneath his iron self-control.

He touched an emerald dangling from her ear with fingers that shook. "Keep the earrings," he said. "They suit you."

Then Hart walked away, without apology, without good-byes. He slammed the door open and strode out into the bright corridor, leaving Eleanor alone and shivering on a table filled with crumpled laundry.

Hart walked into his private dining room the next morning, out of temper, and found it full of people.

He'd tried to snatch a few minutes' sleep after the ball had ended but had given up, because Eleanor had invaded his dreams. In them they'd been dancing, dancing, but her green dress had slid down with every turn, revealing her beautiful and most distracting breasts. At the same time, she'd danced away, just out of reach. Eleanor had smiled at him, knowing his wanting, knowing he couldn't have her.

Hart looked irritably around the room as he made for the sideboard, ravenously hungry. "Do none of you have homes?"

Mac glanced up from the foot of the table, where he was spreading marmalade on toast for Isabella next to him. Isabella paid no attention to Hart, continuing to scribble in the little notebook she always carried with her. Mac had accused Hart of organizing things to death, but Isabella and her lists could defeat Hart every time.

Ian sat halfway down the table, a newspaper spread wide in front of him. Ian could read extraordinarily quickly if he didn't get fixed on something, and he turned two pages in the space of time that Hart lifted lids from serving platters and shoveled eggs and sausages onto his plate. Lord Ramsay sat opposite Ian, also reading a newspaper, but far more slowly, absorbed in each page.

Eleanor was the only person missing, and her absence made Hart all the more irritable.

Lord Ramsay said, without looking up, "I do have a home, but I thought I was your guest."

"I did not mean you, Ramsay. I meant my brothers, who both have perfectly good houses and servants of their own."

Isabella gave Hart an unworried look from her green eyes. "The decorators have torn up the bedrooms. I told you."

Yes, Hart knew that. Ian, on the other hand, had a large house on Belgrave Square, which Beth had inherited from the fussy old lady to whom she'd been a companion. Hart knew that Ian and Beth kept the house in good working order for whenever they might take an impulsive trip to town.

Ian, of course, said nothing, turning another page of the newspaper. He wouldn't explain, even if he did pretend to listen.

Hart thunked his plate to his place at the head of the table. "Where is Eleanor?"

"Sleeping, poor thing," Isabella said. "She worked like a drudge all day and all night and waved off the last guests with me a few hours ago. Likely she's also exhausted from the way you pulled her around the dance floor. You know *everyone* is talking about that, Hart. What do you intend to do about it?"

Chapter 8

"Do?" Hart shoveled up a forkful of eggs and thrust them into his mouth. They were cool and congealing, but he chewed and swallowed the mess. "Why should I do anything?"

"My dear Hart, you have the reputation of never taking a lady to a ballroom floor, under any circumstance," Isabella said.

"I know that."

Hart had learned a long time ago that singling out this young lady or that one to dance led to expectations. The girls and their mothers started believing he'd propose, or their fathers would use the indication of interest to try to finagle favors. Hart did not have time to dance with all ladies at any given event, and the families of those left out would take it as a slight. Hart had decided early on in his career that if he wanted to keep people dangling on his string, it was best to appear to favor no young ladies at all. He'd danced with Eleanor, and he'd danced with Sarah, and that was all.

"I know you know that," Isabella said. "Mamas have learned *not* to push their daughters in front of you at supper balls because the effort is wasted. And then, last night, you pluck out Eleanor and waltz her about with great fervor. You have ripped the lid off the powder keg. Some speculate you did it as vengeance for her jilting you—because now she'll be talked about. Others speculate that it means you are once again on the marriage mart."

Hart abandoned the eggs and sliced the sausage. It looked greasy. What had happened to his celebrated cook?

"It is my own business with whom I dance or don't dance."

Lord Ramsay looked up from his newspaper, putting his finger on the column where he'd stopped. "Not when you're famous, Mackenzie. When you are a famous person, everything you do is well picked over. Debated. Discussed. Speculated on."

Hart did know that, having seen his life and that of his brothers spilled out in newspapers all the years of their lives, but he was too out of sorts to be reasonable.

"Do people not have anything better to talk about?" he grumbled.

"No," Lord Ramsay said. "They don't." He went back to his paper, lifting his finger from the words as he resumed reading.

Isabella rested her arms on the table. Mac kept spreading marmalade, his grin at Hart's discomfiture irritating.

"I mentioned a powder keg," Isabella said. "Your dance means that mamas all over London and far beyond are going to assume you fair game. They will try to throw their daughters between you and Eleanor, claiming they have the better match for you. In that case, Hart, we should get you married off quickly and avoid the battles to come."

"No," Hart said.

Mac broke in. "Your own fault, my brother. You raised Isabella's expectations at Ascot last year, declaring you were thinking about taking a wife. She grew quite excited, but since then, you've done nothing about it."

In the box at Ascot, Hart had known exactly what he was doing. He supposed his brothers had come up with the romantic idea that he'd ride up to Eleanor's dilapidated estate, beating his way through the overgrown garden to find her, and carry her off. Never mind how much she protested—and Eleanor would protest.

No, he would go about taking her as wife as thoroughly and deliberately as he ran one of his political campaigns.

Overt courting would come later, but it would come. For now, having her live in his house and help Wilfred and Isabella organize his life was getting her used to the demands of it. He'd have Isabella coax her to a dressmaker's so that Eleanor would grow used to pretty things and find it too much of a wrench to give them up. He would indulge her father in all the books, museums, and conversation with experts he could want, so that Eleanor would not have the heart to take it all away from him again. After a time, Eleanor would find herself so entrenched in Hart's life that she'd not be able to walk away.

The dance last night had been a whim—*no, not a whim,* a voice said inside him. *A burning hunger.*

Whatever Hart's reasoning had been, he'd use the dance to indicate to the world that he had set his sights again on Eleanor. Hart's party would take the country by storm soon, the queen would ask Hart to form a government, and Hart would lay his victory at Eleanor's feet.

"I told you, Mac," Hart said. "That is my own business."

"Marrying quickly will also save Eleanor from scandal," Isabella said, ignoring both of them. "Attention will focus on your new bride-to-be, and the impromptu dance with Eleanor will be forgotten."

No, it wouldn't. Hart would make certain that it wouldn't.

Isabella turned a page in her notebook and applied her pencil. "Let me see. The lady must be, first, Scottish. No English roses for Hart Mackenzie. Second, of the right lineage. I'd say earl's daughter or above, don't you agree? Third, she must be beyond reproach. No scandals attached to her name. Fourth, not a widow—that way you avoid her former husband's family suddenly wanting favors or making trouble for you. Fifth, she should be well liked, able to smooth people over after you irritate them to death. Sixth, a good hostess for the many soirees, fêtes, and balls you will have to host. Knowing who should not sit by whom, and so forth. Seventh, she must be well liked by the queen. The queen is not fond of Mackenzies, and a wife she likes will help things along for you when you become prime minister. Eighth, the young lady ought to be fine-looking enough to draw admiration, but not so showy as to incite jealousy." Isabella lifted her pencil from the page. "Do I have everything? Mac?"

"Nine: Able to put up with Hart Mackenzie," Mac said.

"Ah, yes." Isabella wrote. "And I'll add strong-minded and resolute. That will be number ten, a nice round number."

"Isabella, please stop," Hart said.

Isabella, amazingly, ceased writing. "I am finished for now. I'll draw up a list of names of young ladies who fit the criteria, and then you can begin courting them."

"The devil I will." Hart felt something cold and wet bump his knee. He looked down to see Ben looking up at him, heard his tail thump the floor. "Why is the dog under the table?"

"He followed Ian," Isabella said.

"Who followed Ian?" Eleanor's voice preceded her into the room.

Did Eleanor look exhausted from her long night, from her exuberant dance with Hart, from Hart kissing her first in the stairwell and then on the pile of laundry? No, she looked fresh and clean, and smelled of the lavender soap she liked as she went around Hart to the sideboard. Lavender—the scent always meant Eleanor to him.

Eleanor filled her plate, then brought it back to the table, kissed her father's cheek, and sat down between him and Hart.

"Old Ben," Isabella said. "He likes Ian."

Eleanor peeped under the table. "Ah. Good morning, Ben."

She says good morning to the dog, Hart thought irritably. *No words for me.*

"Eleanor, what do you think of Constance McDonald?" Isabella asked.

Eleanor began eating the cold eggs and greasy sausage as though they were the headiest ambrosia. "What do I think of her? Why?"

"As a potential wife for Hart. We are making a list."

"Are we?" Eleanor ate, her gaze on Ian and his newspaper. "Yes, I think Constance McDonald would make him a fine wife. Twenty-five, quite lovely, rides well, knows how to wrap stuffy Englishmen around her finger, is good with people."

"Her father's Old John McDonald, remember," Mac said. "Head of the McDonald clan and a right ogre. Many people are afraid of him. Including me. He nearly thrashed the life out of me when I was a callow youth."

"That's because you got drunk and half trampled one of his fields," Isabella said.

Mac shrugged. "That's a truth."

"Do not worry about Old John," Eleanor said. "He's a sweetie if handled correctly."

"Very well," Isabella said. "On the list Miss McDonald goes. What about Honoria Butterworth?"

"For God's sake!" Hart sprang to his feet.

Everyone at the table stopped and stared at him, including Ian. "Do I have to be made a mockery of in my own house?"

Mac leaned back in his chair, his hands behind his head. "Would you prefer we made a mockery of you in the street? In Hyde Park, maybe? In the middle of Pall Mall? The card room at your club?"

"Mac, shut it!"

A faint laugh escaped Lord Ramsay's mouth, which he covered with a cough. Hart looked down at his plate and noticed the sausage he'd taken a bite from now missing. He hadn't eaten it.

The sound of breathy chewing came from under the table, and Eleanor looked suddenly innocent.

A shout worked its way up through Hart's throat, and he couldn't stop it coming out of his mouth. His voice rang against the crystals of the chandeliers, and Ben stopped crunching.

Hart slammed away from the table, his chair falling over behind him. Somehow he got himself out of the room, walking as swiftly as he could down the hall and toward the stairs. Behind him, he heard Eleanor say, "Goodness, what is the matter with *him* this morning?"

～

Just as well Hart had gone, Eleanor thought, lifting her fork in an unsteady hand. She felt quite shy with him this morning, after the heady kisses in the laundry room and him holding her on the railing in the upstairs hall. She was wearing the very drawers he'd pulled out of the laundry pile last night, Maigdlin having brought them upstairs this morning.

Maigdlin had said nothing about servants finding the laundry in a sad state, because they hadn't. Eleanor had stayed behind and refolded every single garment before rejoining Isabella to help her through the rest of the ball.

When Eleanor had slid on the drawers this morning, she'd remembered Hart pressing a kiss to the fabric and telling her to think of him. Eleanor had, and now she swore she could feel the imprint of his lips on her backside.

Eleanor lifted the remaining sausage from Hart's plate and fed it to Ben. "Why are you writing out potential brides for Hart?"

Isabella laid down her pencil. "I am not. This is all flummery, Eleanor. We all know that *you* are his perfect match; he just needs a push to get there."

Eleanor felt chilled. "I believe he is right about one thing, Izzy. This is his business, and mine."

"Now, don't go all haughty on me. You know I am right. Am I not right, Lord Ramsay?"

Lord Ramsay folded his paper and laid it on the table, the last page ready to read. "It would not be so bad a thing for you to marry him, El."

Eleanor stared at him in surprise. "I thought you were happy when I broke the engagement. You stood up to Hart with me."

"Yes, indeed, I agreed at the time. Hart was arrogant and even dangerous, and you were not well suited. But now, things are different. I am growing old, my dear, and when I die I will leave you penniless. Destitute. I'd rest much easier knowing you had all this." He waved his hand at the grand dining room.

Eleanor stabbed her fork into her eggs. "Well, it doesn't matter what you all want, or even what I want. It isn't up to us, is it?"

Across the table, Ian had fixed his attention on the pot of honey. As though he didn't realize he was doing it, he reached for it, lifted the dripper, and let the golden stream of honey fall back into the pot.

"What do you think, Ian?" Eleanor asked. At least from Ian, she'd get honesty. Brutal honesty, but that's what she needed.

Ian didn't answer. He lifted the dripper again, swirling the sticky honey, watching it fall in a sunlit swath.

"Leave him alone," Mac said. "He's thinking of Beth."

"Is he?" Eleanor asked. "How do you know?"

Mac winked at her. "Trust me. An excellent idea you had with the honey, Ian. You may trust me on that too."

Isabella flushed, but she did not look unhappy. "I believe Cameron started that bit of nonsense."

"Not nonsense." Mac licked his finger and bent to Isabella. "Tasty."

Lord Ramsay smiled and took his attention back to his paper. Eleanor watched Ian.

"You miss her," she said to him.

Ian dragged his gaze from the honey and fixed it on Eleanor, eyes as golden as the liquid he stirred. "Yes."

"You'll see her soon enough," Mac said. "We're off to Berkshire next week."

Ian didn't answer, but Eleanor saw in Ian's fleeting glance that next week would not be soon enough. She set down her fork, pushed back her chair, and went around the table to him.

Mac and Isabella watched in surprise as Eleanor put her arms around Ian and bent down to kiss his cheek. They tensed, waiting to see what Ian would do. Ian did not like being touched by anyone except Beth or his children.

But Ian had looked so lonely sitting there that Eleanor felt compelled to comfort him. Ian had left his beloved Beth to travel to London to ensure that his oldest brother didn't break Eleanor's heart. A noble and generous deed.

"I will be all right," Eleanor said to him. "Go back to her."

Ian remained still while Mac and Isabella held their breaths and pretended not to. Even Eleanor's father glanced up, concerned.

Ian slowly lifted his hand and gave Eleanor's wrist a warm squeeze. "Beth has already left for Berkshire," he said. "I will meet her there."

"You'll go today?" Eleanor said.

"Today. Curry will pack for me."

"Good. Give her my love." Eleanor pressed another kiss to his cheek and rose.

Isabella and Mac let out their breaths and went back to the remains of their breakfasts, carefully not looking at Ian. Eleanor walked back to her place, wiping away the tears that had started in her eyes.

"Wilfred," Eleanor said several hours later, looking up from her Remington. "This letter has nothing in it. You've written a name and an address, and that is all."

Wilfred removed his spectacles and looked across his desk at her. "No letter, my lady," he said. "Just enclose the cheque inside the blank paper and address the envelope."

To Mrs. Whitaker, Eleanor typed on the envelope. "That is all? No note saying, *Here is payment for . . .* or *Please accept this contribution to your charitable works . . . ?*"

"No, my lady." Wilfred said.

"Who is this Mrs. Whitaker?" Eleanor asked as she rolled the platen to type the address. "And why is Hart sending her . . ." She turned over the cheque Wilfred had placed face-down on her desk. *"One thousand guineas?"*

"His Grace can be generous," Wilfred said.

Eleanor stared at him, but Wilfred only bent his head and went back to writing.

Eleanor had learned that Wilfred was a poor source of information about the Mackenzie family. The man refused to gossip about anything or anyone. This quality was likely why Hart had promoted him from valet to private secretary, but Eleanor found it quite inconvenient. Wilfred was discretion made man.

Wilfred was a human being some of the time, Eleanor knew. He had a daughter and a granddaughter in Kent and doted on them both. He kept their photos in his desk drawer, bought them chocolates and little gifts, and boasted of their accomplishments to Eleanor, in his quiet way.

However, Wilfred never spoke about his shady past when he'd been an embezzler; never mentioned a *Mrs.* Wilfred; and never, *ever* told tales about Hart. If Wilfred did not want Eleanor to know why Hart was sending one thousand guineas to this Mrs. Whitaker, Wilfred would take the secret to his grave.

Eleanor gave up, typed the address on the envelope—George Street, near Portman Square—and neatly folded the cheque inside the paper.

Perhaps Hart had found the source of the photographs. Perhaps he was paying the woman to destroy them or to keep quiet about them, or perhaps to persuade her to send him the rest.

Or Mrs. Whitaker might have absolutely nothing to do with the photographs.

Eleanor tucked the cheque into the envelope, closed it, and added the envelope to her stack of finished correspondence.

The house near Portman Square where Mrs. Whitaker lived was ordinary-looking enough. Eleanor studied it carefully as she strolled past for the third time.

Eleanor had used the pretense of doing some shopping to journey to Portman Square, timing the outing to coincide with Isabella returning to her own house to argue with the decorators. In order to lend verisimilitude, Eleanor wandered the shops on the square and nearby streets, buying little gifts for the Mackenzie children and their mothers. Maigdlin trailed her, carrying packages.

Eleanor had seen no activity at all in or around Mrs. Whitaker's house in the hour or so she'd drifted up and down George Street. No maids cleaning the stoop or footmen walking out to pass the time of day with the maids next door. The blinds remained closed, the door firmly shut.

In order to linger on the street a little longer, Eleanor started browsing the carts of the street vendors, deciding to buy a present for Cameron's son Daniel. That Daniel was now eighteen was difficult for Eleanor to swallow. He'd been a wild and unhappy child when Eleanor had first met him, always in some scrape or another, earning Cameron's wrath. He'd resisted Eleanor's attempts to be motherly, but he had shown Eleanor his collection of live beetles, which Hart had told her was an honor.

Daniel had turned out all right, she'd seen, despite growing up in a houseful of Mackenzie bachelors. He was settled at the university in Edinburgh now, and seemed happy enough.

Eleanor was startled out of thoughts of Daniel by the door of Mrs. Whitaker's house opening. A footman, a large, beefy lad like Hart's footmen, came out of it. At the same time a carriage pulled up, and the footman hurried the few steps across the pavement to open the coach's door.

Eleanor stepped to a street vendor who sold little cakes and watched as a quick-walking maid emerged from the house, followed by a woman who must be Mrs. Whitaker.

The lady was not very tall, but she was voluptuous, a trait she did not bother to hide. Even her fur wrap, pulled on against the chill, was draped to show off her large bosom. She painted—she had deeply rouged cheeks and red lip color— and the hair under her highly fashionable hat was very black.

Mrs. Whitaker adjusted her skintight leather gloves, gave her footman a kind enough nod of thanks, and let him hand her into the carriage. Eleanor stared openly as the carriage moved off, bearing mistress and maid. The footman, looking neither right nor left, strode back into the house and shut the door.

"Good heavens," Eleanor said to the man selling cakes. "Who was that?"

The vendor glanced at the retreating carriage. "Not the sort of woman I should be talking about to a lady, miss."

"Truly?" Eleanor slid a coin to him, and the vendor put a warm, wrapped seedcake into her hand. "Now you do have me curious. Do not worry—I am quite long in the tooth and not easily shocked."

"No better than she ought to be, and that's the truth, miss. And the gentlemen what go in and out at all hours . . . Some of the highest in the land, would you believe?"

Yes, Eleanor would believe it. That Mrs. Whitaker was a courtesan did not surprise her in the least. That she was a very successful one showed in her expensive furs, elegant carriage, and high-stepping horses.

Eleanor hid her dismay by unfolding the paper that wrapped the cake and nibbling a corner. "Gracious," she said.

"I do mean the highest," the vendor said. "The things I could tell you. Princes go in there. And dukes, like that Scots one, what always wears his kilt. Why a man wants to wear a skirt, I couldn't say. I'd think the cold would go right up his jacksie, wouldn't you? Oh, begging your pardon, miss. I forget my tongue."

"Not at all." Eleanor smiled at him and took another bite of cake.

Curiosity certainly killed the cat. Mrs. Whitaker was a

courtesan, and Hart Mackenzie had sent her a thousand guineas. For the photographs? Or for the usual reason a gentleman paid a courtesan?

Well, Hart was a man, his longtime mistress was dead, and gentlemen did have bodily needs. That was a scientific fact. Their gently born wives could neither understand these bodily needs nor were able to endure them, the scientists went on to say, because gently born ladies did not have the same needs.

Absolute nonsense. Eleanor scoffed at this fiction, and so did her father. The truth was that gentlemen visited courtesans because they enjoyed it. Ladies stayed home and endured their husbands straying because they had no choice.

Hart had never been a saint, and he was dedicated to no one at the moment. Eleanor should not condemn him.

And yet. Eleanor's heart burned, and for a moment, the street blurred. Another conveyance came toward her while she stood unable to move, a dark square in her clouded vision.

The carriage solidified as it pulled to a stop in front of the house. "Speak of the devil," the vendor said. "That's his crest. The Scots duke's, I mean."

Eleanor's vision cleared. There was no time to run and nowhere to hide. Eleanor scuttled to the nearest lamppost and put her shoulder against it, hiding her face to eat another bite of seedcake.

She saw square, polished boots stop in front of her, saw the hem of blue and green Mackenzie plaid above them. Her gaze moved from the kilt that hugged his hips to his crisp shirt under his open greatcoat to Hart's granite face under the brim of his hat.

Hart said not one word. He'd know perfectly well why Eleanor lurked outside the house of a courtesan called Mrs. Whitaker—he had no need to ask. Eleanor could claim it coincidence that she'd chosen to purchase a seedcake three feet from the woman's door, but Hart would know better.

Eleanor met his gaze and refused to feel remorse. After all, *she* wasn't the one visiting a courtesan or paying her a thousand guineas.

They might have stood on the cold street, staring at one another the rest of the day, if the door of the house hadn't burst open again. The same beefy footman emerged, this time carrying a man out over his shoulder. Hart barely paid any mind as the footman made straight for Hart's carriage and put the man inside.

Eleanor's astonishment mounted as David Fleming came out of the house, looked up at the cloudy sky, put on his hat, and climbed into Hart's carriage as well.

Eleanor swung back to Hart, questions on her lips.

Hart pointed at the carriage. "Get in."

Eleanor started, and the cake vendor, who'd been watching with evident enjoyment, looked worried. "No need," Eleanor said to Hart. "I'll find a hansom. I've brought Maigdlin, and I have so many parcels."

"Get into the carriage, El, or I'll strap you to the top of it."

Eleanor rolled her eyes and took another bite of seedcake. She waved at Maigdlin, who was at another vendor's cart a little way down the street. "Come along, Maigdlin. We're going."

The maid, looking relieved, trotted back toward Eleanor and the familiar coach, set down the parcels, and let Mrs. Whitaker's footman boost her up beside the coachman. The cake vendor watched the proceedings, arrested in the act of lifting another cake off his tiny coal stove.

"It is quite all right," Eleanor told the cake seller. "His Grace can't help being rude." She turned and made for the carriage. "Hart, give the man a crown for his trouble, won't you?"

Chapter 9

Inside the coach, Eleanor sank onto the seat opposite the two gentlemen already there—David Fleming and an unconscious, white-faced Englishman Eleanor had never seen before.

"Who is that?" she asked. The footman started handing in her parcels, and Eleanor leaned to tuck them beneath David's seat. "Excuse me. Could you just push that under? Be careful; it's breakable."

David obeyed, regarding Eleanor with bloodshot eyes. He was in evening dress and smelled strongly of cigar smoke, brandy, perfume, and something else it took Eleanor a moment to identify. It had been a very long time since she'd encountered such a scent, but she soon realized what it was—that of a man who has been with a woman.

David saw Eleanor's assessment, grew red in the face, jerked out his flask, and took a long drink.

"Hart, don't sit on that," Eleanor said as Hart hauled himself into the carriage. "It's for Beth. Could you, please . . . ?"

Hart growled, took the parcel, and shoved it onto the shelf above the seat. "Couldn't you have put these in the back?"

"Good heavens, no. Some of the things are fragile, and

I don't want to give a lucky thief the chance to relieve me of them. Thieves climb onto the backboards and rifle the baggage, you know."

"No one robs *this* coach," Hart said.

"There's always a first time. I spent my week's wages on these gifts."

The carriage jerked forward, David still staring in shock. "Mackenzie, what are you doing? This is *Eleanor*."

"Mr. Fleming is awake," Eleanor said. "He can recognize ladies he's known for years." She studied the other man, who snored against the wall. "Who is he?"

David kept staring at Hart and didn't answer. "That is Mr. Neely," Hart said.

"Ah," Eleanor said, understanding. "I see. You sent him to Mrs. Whitaker in return for whatever he promised you."

"I need his backing and that of his friends when we go after Gladstone," Hart said.

"Hart." David was anguished.

"I keep no secrets from Eleanor."

No?

"There is no point," Hart went on. "As you can see."

"Well, if you had let Wilfred tell me why you sent her a thousand guineas, I would not have had to try to find out for myself," Eleanor said. "Although I did need to do the shopping."

"A thousand?" David glanced down at the sleeping man. Mr. Neely looked innocuous, like a clerk or a banker, with well-kept hands. "Then again, he was a lot of trouble."

"I assumed he would be," Hart said.

"What did he do?" Eleanor asked, her curiosity rising.

David shot Hart a worried look. "You brought her into the coach to make me look a dissipate rake in front of her, didn't you?"

"I already know you are a dissipate rake, Mr. Fleming," Eleanor said. "You've never made a secret of it. He seems very small and fragile. What on earth sort of trouble could he cause?"

"He refused to leave," Hart said. "So I was told. How did you finally manage it?" he asked David.

"The liberal application of whiskey. On top of what he'd

already had. Whenever the puritanical decide to indulge themselves, it's a sight to behold. I doubt he'll remember much of it."

"Good," Hart said. "I do not need him to have a day of remorse that sends him running back to my rivals. You'll take care of him?"

"Yes, yes. Sober him up, lessen the agony as much as I can, tell him he thoroughly enjoyed himself."

Eleanor studied Mr. Neely, childlike in his sleep. "You bribed him with a courtesan to obtain his vote," she said.

David winced. "*Bribe* is such an unkind word."

"No, she is right," Hart said. "It was a bribe, El, pure and simple. But I need him, and his friends."

He met her gaze without blinking. Hart knew exactly what he'd done and how bad such an action made him, and he'd weighed the consequences of it before he'd done it. The balance had come out on the side of bringing Neely into his fold. Hart had known how to play the man, and he'd played him.

"You are awful," Eleanor said.

"Yes."

He was ruthless, driven, and determined to win no matter what it took. The look in his eyes told her that.

Eleanor glanced at Mr. Neely again. "I suppose his support is terribly important?"

"It's twenty more seats behind me."

"And you need as many backsides as possible, do you?" Eleanor asked.

David barked a laugh. Hart kept his gaze on Eleanor, never wavering. He was not asking for her understanding or forgiveness. He was simply showing her what he did and what he was.

"I do," he said.

Eleanor let out her breath. "Well, then. Let us hope the thousand guineas was worth it."

~

Hart descended at Grosvenor Square, telling David to continue to Neely's home and get the man to bed—and resisted the urge to drag Eleanor into the house. He did tell her he wanted to speak to her in his study, but it took a long time for her to extricate herself and all her parcels from the carriage.

David helped her with a look of idiotic surrender. The man was still in love with her.

Then Eleanor had to instruct Maigdlin and Franklin to take her parcels to her room, told them to split the seedcake she'd bought from the vendor, and at last headed up the stairs.

Even with all that, Eleanor made it to Hart's study before he did, because Wilfred waylaid him to sign things. Hart entered to find Eleanor standing in front of the polished Queen Anne cabinet, both doors open, as she gazed at the painting inside.

Hart came up behind her and closed the doors, shutting out the face of his father. "I locked that."

"I know. I found the key in your desk."

Hart locked the cabinet again, strode to the desk, and put the key back into its place. "I keep the key here because I don't want anyone opening the cabinet."

She shrugged. "I was curious."

"You are avoiding my true question. What possessed you to take a hansom to Portman Square and stand outside Mrs. Whitaker's?"

"Why do you keep it?"

Eleanor had removed her pillbox hat with its veil, and he got the full force of her blue eyes. "Keep what?" he growled.

"The portrait of your horrible father. Why not put it on the fire?"

"Édouard Manet painted it. It's valuable."

"Monsieur Manet was one of Mac's teachers, was he not?"

Hart had told Eleanor the story long ago. When the old duke had condescended to have his portrait painted while in Paris, Mac had met Manet, and ran away to take lessons with him.

"Mac can paint something else equally as valuable for you," Eleanor said. "Get rid of the thing."

Hart loved Eleanor's clear-eyed way of looking at the world. The portrait of his father grated on him, but for some reason Hart kept it, perhaps believing that through it his father would see that Hart had grown beyond the scared youth he'd been. Hart wanted the old duke to see that he'd surpassed him, had become something more than a rakehell and a bully. *You beat me until I couldn't stand, but I've beaten* you, *you bastard.*

Eleanor, on the other hand, simply looked at the picture and said, *Get rid of the thing.*

"I keep it locked inside the cabinet so I don't have to look at it," Hart said. "My great-grandchildren can sell it for a profit."

"I hate to think of it in there, haunting you."

"It isn't haunting me. Stop changing the subject and tell me why you went to Mrs. Whitaker's."

Eleanor came to the desk, rested her hands on it, and looked across it at Hart. "Because I thought she might have something to do with the photographs, of course. I thought you might be paying her blackmail money—a thousand is a fortune. I had to find out why."

Hart saw nothing but inquisitiveness in Eleanor's eyes. No anger, no jealousy. But then, the greatest part of Eleanor's anger when she'd learned about Mrs. Palmer had not come from jealousy.

"I sent Neely to Mrs. Whitaker, because I knew she could manage someone like him."

Her brow puckered. "What do you mean *someone like him*? Like him in what way?"

"I mean an unworldly man pretending to be worldly. They are the most unruly when they finally let themselves off the lead."

"And apparently he had to be carried out again by Mr. Fleming. Mrs. Whitaker did not mind doing you this favor?"

"I paid her a thousand guineas. Of course she did not mind."

"Was Mrs. Whitaker educated? Finished, I mean?"

Hart's patience thinned. "I have no bloody idea."

"I ask because the notes are badly spelled, which points more to a servant. However, if Mrs. Whitaker came from a poor background, she might still not write well, despite her big house and her furs. Have you asked her about them?"

"No!"

"Goodness, you do like to shout. I am trying to solve your problem, Hart, but a little assistance would be welcome. Mrs. Whitaker might have known Mrs. Palmer—Mrs. Palmer might have given her some of the photographs. Were Mrs. Whitaker and Mrs. Palmer friends?"

"Friends? God, no. Angelina had no friends."

"That sounds lonely. You should ask Mrs. Whitaker anyway, though if she truly has no knowledge of the photographs, you will have to ask discreetly so she does not find out about them. Difficult, but I think you can do it."

Eleanor's eyes narrowed in thought, and she touched her finger to her lip, unconsciously rubbing it over the little bruise Hart had made. His entire body went hot and hard.

It would be so easy to go around the desk to her, to unbutton the ugly gown she wore, to strip her to her corset. He'd nip her neck as he unfastened her, leaving a love bite while he drank her in.

Eleanor drew a breath, her breasts lifting under her primly buttoned bodice. "Perhaps if I . . ."

"No," Hart said abruptly.

Eleanor's eyes widened. "You do not even know what I was about to suggest."

"No, you will not go back to Mrs. Whitaker's or try to speak to her yourself. And you will *not* return to the house in High Holborn."

She gave him a look of exasperation, which told him he'd guessed correctly about the last part. "Be reasonable, Hart. I never finished searching the house, because, as you recall, you removed me—forcibly. I do not expect to find the photographs there, but there might be some clue as to where they've gone. If you are worried for my safety, I'll have one of your pugilists accompany me."

His impatience became full-blown anger. "*No.* And don't you dare cajole Ian into taking you back there." Hart thought of Ian standing in the room in which the woman had been killed, gaze fixed on the ceiling, and he let out his breath. "It upsets him."

"I know. He told me, but he also said he ought to see the place once more himself. To allay the ghosts, as it were."

Ghosts. That whole house was full of ghosts. Hart wanted to burn the place to the ground.

"Ian can't take me anyway," Eleanor tripped on. "He's not here. He left this morning."

Hart stopped. "Left? What do you mean, he *left*? Where the devil did he go?"

"To Berkshire. He was missing Beth, and I told him to go to her. She's already on her way to Berkshire, to help Ainsley prepare, so off he went. They won't mind Ian arriving early."

"When did this happen? He never said a word to me." Not a word. Not a good-bye. But that wasn't unusual for Ian. When Ian decided to do a thing, there was no stopping him.

"You were off playing your political games," Eleanor said. "Ian said good-bye to me, but he did not want to wait about for your return."

When had Hart lost control in his own house? The last time he'd seen Ian, his brother had been quietly reading the paper in the dining room at breakfast. As far as Hart knew, Ian hadn't had any plans to rush off to Berkshire within the hour.

Hart thought of the congealing eggs and greasy sausage on his plate this morning, and his fists tightened. "Eleanor, what did you do with my cook?"

"Hmm?" Her brows rose. "Oh, Mrs. Thomas. She got word that her sister was ill, and I told her she should take a week and visit her. She's in Kent. The sister, I mean, although by now, Mrs. Thomas will be there too, of course. There wasn't time to find a replacement before this morning, but I imagine one will be here by tonight. Mrs. Mayhew is seeing to it."

When had he lost control? The day Eleanor Ramsay had lurked in a crowd of journalists in St. James's and Hart had been foolish enough to scoop her up and bring her home.

Only this morning he'd thought himself clever for keeping her close, drawing her into his life, netting her until she would think that staying was her own idea.

He had to be insane. Not only was Eleanor turning his house upside down, he couldn't stop his visions of her, ones that continued what he'd started with her last night. He looked across the desk and wanted her—now. He could unwind his cravat and use it to gently tie her wrists. Or maybe to blindfold her so that she wouldn't know where he was, or what pleasure he intended for her, until he touched her skin, kissed her neck, nipped the skin of her shoulder . . .

He wanted to strip everything from her—gown, corset, combinations, lift her to the desk, spread her across it, and lick from her throat to the glory between her legs. Her hair was golden red there, he remembered.

He wanted to wrap her hands, perhaps in a pair of soft, silk stockings, to hold her thus while he feasted on her. She'd wriggle in joy, and he'd murmur, *Eleanor, do you trust me?*

Yes, she'd whisper.

He'd bring her to pleasure again and again, and when she was warm and smiling, he'd climb onto her and inside her. He'd have her in this room, and banish *his* ghosts.

The vision gave him hard, aching pleasure. Hart knew he was standing in the study, the desk between himself and Eleanor, she fully dressed, but he could feel every touch, every kiss, every breath.

"Hart?" she asked. "Are you all right?"

The tug of concern in her voice undid him. Hart stood up and removed his fists from the desk. It hurt, his whole body hurt to leave while Eleanor watched with worry in her blue eyes, but he knew he had to get out of this room.

Hart made himself go to the door, open it, and walk out, without stopping to look back at her. He walked around the landing, sidestepping Ben in the middle of it. He continued to his own bedroom, entering it by nearly ripping open the door.

Marcel, who was brushing one of Hart's coats, looked up in surprise.

"Draw me a bath, Marcel," Hart growled as he tore off his cravat and opened his shirt. "Make it a cold one."

⁓

Hart managed to keep himself away from Eleanor for three days. He rose and left the house before she awakened and returned when he was certain she'd be in bed.

Hart filled his days with meetings and debates, arguments and committees. He tried to plunge himself into the troubles of the country and the empire, to wipe away any thought of his domestic life. It worked when he was in a shouting match with his opposition, when he tried to persuade yet another MP to lean to his side, and when he adjourned with Fleming to their club or a gaming hell to continue the battle for political domination there.

But as soon as Hart descended at his doorstep in Grosvenor Square, knowing Eleanor was in the room above, her body damp with sleep, the visions of her returned and would not be banished.

He spent more and more time away from home, staying very late at meetings and creating meetings so that he could stay late. It was after one very late evening that the assassination attempt was made.

Chapter 10

It was inky dark, Hart emerging from the Parliament buildings in the wee hours, still arguing with David Fleming about some point.

Hart heard a loud *bang*, then shards of stone flew from the wall beside him. Instinct made him drop and pull David down with him. Hart heard the bull-voiced shouting of his coachman and the running footsteps of his large footmen.

David got to his hands and knees, eyes wide. "*Hart!* Are you all right?"

Hart felt a sting on his face from the stone and tasted blood. "I'm fine. Who fired that shot? Did you grab him?"

One of Hart's former prizefighters panted up to him. "Got away in the dark, sir. You're bleeding, Your Grace. Were you hit?"

"No, the wall was hit and the stone lashed out at me," Hart said with grim humor. "You all right, Fleming?"

Fleming ran his hand through his hair and reached for his flask. "Fine. Fine. What the devil? I told you the Fenians would be hot to kill you."

Hart dabbed at the blood with a handkerchief, heart hammering in reaction, and didn't answer.

Fenians were Irish who'd emigrated to America, formed the group dedicated to freeing the Irish from the English, and sent the members off to do their worst. A newspaper had proclaimed this morning that Hart would try to defeat the Irish Home Rule bill in order to push out Gladstone, and the Fenians had reacted strongly.

Hart's action did not mean he was against Irish independence—in fact, he wanted Ireland completely free of the English yoke, because this would pave the way for Scottish independence. He simply thought Gladstone's version of the bill was ineffectual. Under Gladstone's bill, Ireland's independence would be marginal—they'd be allowed to form a parliament to settle Irish matters but it would still be answerable to the English government.

Hart knew that if he forced Gladstone to call a vote on the bill, the man would not have enough support to pass it, which would then lead to a vote of no confidence, and Gladstone's resignation.

Once Hart was in power, he'd put forth ideas to free Ireland completely. He would do all it took to shove Irish Home Rule down Englishmen's throats and then shove Scottish independence—his true goal—down their gullets as well.

But the newspapers printed what they wanted, and angry Irishmen, not knowing what was in Hart's head, had started making threats.

Hart sent his footmen to search the area and round up any passing policeman, then got into his coach with David, David imbibing heavily from his flask.

When Hart reached the house after depositing David at his flat, he told his footmen and coachman not to gossip about the shooting and upset Eleanor and her father with it. Hart had experienced assassination attempts several times in his career, with the same lack of marksmanship—someone was always angry at him. He'd have policemen try to find the shooter and watch the house, but the routine wasn't to be disrupted. However, if his household guests went anywhere, they were never to be without at least two bodyguards to protect them, and never without the carriage. His men agreed, shaken themselves.

Irish separatists were not the only possible assassins. Hart wondered, as he entered his quiet house, whether the person sending Eleanor the photographs had any connection with this shooting. The letters hadn't seemed threatening, and there might be no connection at all. However, Hart had a renewed desire to look at the photographs and letters Eleanor had collected.

The thought of leaning over the evidence side by side with Eleanor, her sweet breath touching his skin, made his heart pump faster than it had when the bullet had sailed past him. Best not to risk it.

Hart could demand that Eleanor bring him the photographs so he could look at them alone, but he immediately dismissed the idea. Eleanor would never agree. She'd become extremely proprietary about the photographs—why, Hart couldn't imagine. But, no matter; he'd acquire them by stealth.

The next day, Hart waited until Eleanor and Isabella were ensconced in the downstairs drawing room, planning Hart's next lavish entertainment, Mac safely in his studio, and the earl writing in the small study, before he quietly mounted the stairs to the floor above his study and entered Eleanor's room.

Eleanor's bedchamber was empty, as Hart knew it would be, the maids already finished there. Hart strode to Eleanor's small writing table and began opening drawers.

He did not find the photographs. He found that Eleanor kept writing paper neatly in one drawer, envelopes in another, pens and pencils, separate from each other, in yet another. Letters she'd received from friends—Eleanor had many friends—were bundled in the fourth drawer. Hart leafed quickly through the letters, but none contained the photographs.

Where had she put the bloody things? He knew he had only a few minutes before Eleanor or Isabella would want to dash up here for something or other.

With mounting frustration, Hart searched the tables on either side of the bed, but she hadn't tucked the pictures into either of them. Her armoire revealed garments neatly hung or folded—plain gowns in drab colors, and not many of them.

The deep drawer beneath held a bustle encased in tissue and that was all.

The chest of drawers on the other side of the room was more of a lingerie chest—the top drawers held stockings and garters; the next, camisoles and knickers; then came a drawer with a corset made of plain lawn, well mended.

Hart made himself cease lingering to imagine Eleanor in the underwear and concentrate on searching. He was rewarded when, under the corset, he found a book.

The book was large and long, the kind in which ladies pasted mementos of special occasions or memorable outings. This particular book was fat, plumped out with whatever Eleanor had thought worth preserving. Hart pulled it out of the drawer, set it on her writing table, and opened it.

The book was all about him.

Every page had been covered with a chronology of Hart Mackenzie. Newspaper and magazine articles provided the text and photographs of Hart the businessman, Hart the politician, Hart the duke's son, and then Hart the duke. Society pages showed Hart at gatherings hosted by the Prince of Wales, at charity banquets, at clan gatherings where he reproclaimed his loyalty to the leader of clan Mackenzie.

She'd pasted in newspaper photographs of Hart speaking with the queen, with various prime ministers, and with dignitaries from around the world. The story about Hart becoming Duke of Kilmorgan and taking his seat in the House of Lords was here, including a history of the dukes of Kilmorgan back to the 1300s.

Eleanor Ramsay had collected Hart Mackenzie's entire life and pasted it into a memory book. She'd carried the book down here from Scotland and kept it hidden like a treasure.

The announcement of Hart's marriage to Lady Sarah Graham in 1875 occupied its own page. Eleanor had written in colored pencil next to a newspaper drawing of Hart and Sarah in their wedding finery: *It is done.*

The rest of that page was blank, as though Eleanor had meant to stop the book there. But Hart turned the page and found more articles about his burgeoning political career, about the festivities he and his new wife hosted both in London and at Kilmorgan.

The announcement of Sarah's death and the death of baby Hart Graham Mackenzie was surrounded by a wreath of flowers cut from a card. Eleanor had written next to it: *My heart is heavy for him.*

More articles followed about Hart coming out of mourning to pursue his career even more obsessively than before. *He means to be prime minister,* one journalist wrote. *England will tremble under this Scottish invasion.*

On the page after the last article, Hart found his photographs.

Eleanor had collected fifteen so far. She'd pasted each carefully into the book and outlined them in colored pencil—red, blue, green, yellow—she'd chosen arbitrarily. Notes appeared under each: *Received by hand February 1, 1884,* or *Found in Strand shop, February 18, 1884.*

There were photos of Hart facing the camera, or with his back to the camera, or in profile; Hart in only a kilt, Hart naked, Hart smiling, Hart trying to give the camera an arrogant Highland sneer. The one of Hart in his kilt, laughing, telling Angelina not to close the shutter, had been surrounded by curlicues. *The best,* Eleanor had written.

Hart turned the last few pages, which were blank, ready for more photographs. He started to close the book but noticed that the back cover itself bulged. Investigating, he found that something had been slid behind the endpaper and the cover, the endpaper carefully pasted back into place. It did not take Hart long to peel the black paper down, and behind it, he found the letters.

There weren't many, perhaps a dozen in all, but when Hart unfolded one, his own handwriting stared back up at him.

Eleanor had kept every letter Hart had ever written to her.

Hart sank into a chair as he leafed through them. He saw that she'd even kept his first stiff missive, sent to her the day after he'd contrived his initial meeting with her:

Lord Hart Mackenzie requests the pleasure of Lady Eleanor Ramsay's company for a boating party and picnic on August 20th, below the grounds of Kilmorgan Castle. Please respond to my messenger, but don't give him a tip, because he's already gouged me extra for carrying this to you, as well as using it as an excuse to visit his mother.

Your servant,
Hart Mackenzie

He remembered clearly every word of her written reply.

To my mere acquaintance, Lord Hart Mackenzie:

A gentleman does not write to a lady to whom he is not related or betrothed. Kissing me at the ball is hardly the same thing. I think that our shocking enjoyment of said kiss should not be repeated on the riverbank below Kilmorgan, no matter how idyllic the setting, as I believe there is a rather public view of it from the house. Add to that, a gentleman should not invite a lady to a boating party himself. A maiden aunt or some such should pen the letter for him and assure the young lady that said maiden aunt will be there to chaperone. I will instead invite you to take tea here at Glenarden; however, by the same rules, I cannot properly ask an unrelated gentleman to take tea with me, so I will have my father write you a letter. Do not be alarmed if this invitation wanders off into the medicinal properties of blue fungus or whatever has taken his interest by then. That is his way, and I will endeavor to keep him to the point.

Hart had laughed loudly over the charming letter, and responded.

A lady does not write to a gentleman either, bold minx. Bring your father to the boating party, if you please, and he can root around in all the fungi he wants. My brothers will be there, along with neighbors, which include a pack of society matrons, so your virtue will be well guarded from me. I promise I have no intention of kissing you on the riverbank—I will take you deeper into the woods for that.

Your servant and much more than mere acquaintance,
Hart Mackenzie

Hart folded the letter, remembering the joy of the boating party. Eleanor had come with Earl Ramsay, and then driven Hart insane by planting herself in the middle of the matrons, flirting with Mac and Cameron, and daring Hart to try to get anywhere near her.

She'd carefully not let him corner her until she'd gone back to the boathouse to fetch an elderly woman's forgotten walking stick. Being kind had been her downfall, because Hart had caught her alone in the boathouse.

Eleanor had given him a wide smile and said, "Not fair. This isn't the woods," before Hart had kissed her.

The walking stick had fallen from Eleanor's hands as her head went back, her eyes drifted closed, and Hart opened her lips. He'd tasted every corner of her mouth, let his hand rove until it cupped her breast through the thick fabric of her bodice.

When she'd tried to step away in weak protest, Hart had given her a wicked smile and told her he would leave her the second she told him to. Forever, if she wished it.

Eleanor had met his gaze with her very blue eyes and said, "You're right, I *am* a bold minx," and pulled him down for another kiss.

Hart had lifted her onto a workman's bench and hooked one arm under her knee, showing her how to twine her leg around his. As Eleanor had stared up at him, he'd seen it dawn on her that whatever relations she had with Hart Mackenzie would not be conventional. He saw her desire ignite, saw her decide that she would allow herself to enjoy whatever he intended to show her.

That tiny moment of surrender had made his heart—and other parts of him—swell. Hart had thought, at that moment, that he'd caught her, but he'd been a fool.

The next letter was full of teasing by Hart about their brief moment in the boating house, with some inane innuendo about the walking stick. Eleanor had written him a saucy letter back, which had heated Hart's blood and made him wild to see her again.

He found the letter he'd written after she'd accepted his proposal, made in the summerhouse at Kilmorgan.

Seeing you bare in the sunshine, with the Scottish wind in your hair, sent all my tactics for winning you to the devil. I knew that if I asked you then, your answer would be final. No going back. I knew I should leave it alone, but I went ahead and asked the foolish question anyway. Lucky man that I am, you gave me the answer I longed to hear. And so, as promised, you will have everything you ever wanted.

Young and arrogant, Hart had thought that if he offered Eleanor riches on a silver platter, she would fall at his feet and be his forever. He'd read her very wrong.

The next letter, written after Hart had taken Eleanor to meet Ian when Ian had been living at the asylum, was evidence that Eleanor was nothing less than extraordinary.

I bless you a thousand times over, Eleanor Ramsay. I do not know what you did, but Ian responded to you. Sometimes he doesn't speak at all, not for days or weeks. On some of my visits to him, he's only stared out the window or worked on blasted mathematics equations without looking at me, no matter how much I try to get him to acknowledge that I'm there. He's locked in that world of his, in a place where I can't go. I long to open the door and let him out, and I do not know how.

But Ian looked at you, El, he talked to you, and he asked me, when I went back to see him today, when you and I would marry. Ian said that he wanted us to marry, because once I am safe with you, he can stop worrying about me.

He broke my heart. I pretend to be a strong man, my love, but when I'm with Ian, I know how very weak I am.

Subdued, Hart leafed through the remaining letters. There were not many, because once his engagement with Eleanor had been made official, she and he had been together quite a lot. The few letters written when he'd been detained in London or Paris or Edinburgh without her were filled with praises to her beauty and to her body, her laughter and her warmth. He found the letter he'd written her telling her with eagerness that he'd come to Glenarden when he was finished with business in Edinburgh, the fateful visit when Eleanor had waited for him in the garden and given him back the ring.

The last two letters had been written several years after the engagement ended. Hart opened them, numbly surprised that Eleanor had kept them at all. He read them out of order, the first telling Eleanor of Ian's return to the family after their father's death:

> *He is still Ian, and he isn't. He sits in silence, not answering when we speak to him, not even looking around when we address him. He is somewhere inside, trapped by years of pain, frustration, and out-and-out torture. I do not know if he resents me for not helping him sooner, or if he is grateful to me for bringing him home— or if he even knows he's home. Curry, Ian's valet, says he behaves no differently here as he had there. Ian eats, dresses, and sleeps without prodding and without help, but it's as though he's an automaton taught the motions of living as a human being, with no real knowledge of it.*
>
> *I try to reach him, I truly try. And I can't. I've brought home a shell of my brother, and it's killing me.*

Hart folded that letter and opened the last with slow fingers. This one was dated 1874, a month or so before the letter about Ian. The pages were still crisp, the ink black, and he knew every word of it by heart.

> *My dearest El,*
>
> *My father is dead. You will have heard of his death already, but the rest of it I must confess or go mad. You are the only one I can think to tell, the only one I can trust to keep my secrets.*
>
> *I will deliver this by my most trusted messenger into your hands alone. I urge you to burn it after reading—*

that is if your unshakable curiosity makes you open a letter from the hated Hart at all, instead of putting it straight into the fire.

I shot him, El.

I had to. He was going to kill Ian.

You once asked me why I let Ian live in that asylum, where doctors paraded him like a trained dog or used him for their strange experiments. I let him stay because, in spite of it all, he was safer there than he could be anywhere. Safe from my father. Whatever they did to him at the asylum is nothing compared to what my father could have done. I've long known that if I managed to talk Father into taking Ian out of it, Ian would only end up in a worse place, perhaps entirely out of my reach and at my father's mercy.

Thank God the Kilmorgan servants are more loyal to me than they were to Father. Our majordomo approached me one day with what a housemaid had told him—that she'd overheard my father whispering to a man that he would pay him to slip into the asylum and kill Ian, by whatever quiet method the man chose.

As I listened to the majordomo report this horror, I realized that I could no longer wait to act.

I believed the truth of what the housemaid had overheard, because I knew that my father was capable of such a thing. It was nothing to do with Ian's madness. You see, Ian witnessed my father commit a crime.

Ian told me about it in bits and pieces over the years, until I finally put together the entire truth. What Ian saw was my father killing my mother.

The way Ian described the incident, I don't believe Father intended to kill her, but his violence certainly caused her death. He grabbed my mother and shook her by her neck, until that neck snapped.

Father found Ian crouched behind the desk and knew he'd seen it all. The next day Ian was hauled to London to sit before a commission for lunacy. Ian had always been half mad, but facing the commission was beyond him, and of course, they declared him insane. The action saved my father—if Ian were declared mad by a commission, then whatever story Ian told about my mother's death would likely not be believed.

At the time, I had no idea of any of this, but I fought my father's decision. In vain—Ian was taken straight to the asylum, where my father had prepared a place for him in advance by paying them an obscene amount of money. I wasn't yet old enough or experienced enough to know how to defeat him. I simply did all I could to make Ian comfortable where he was, as did Mac and Cam.

Of late, for some reason, Father began to believe that Ian was going to expose him. Perhaps Ian had grown more coherent about the incident, perhaps one of the doctors reported to my father that Ian was talking about his mother's death—I never learned. In the end, I assume that my father feared someone at last believing Ian's words and investigating. So he set his plan in motion.

I stopped that plan; I stopped it dead in its tracks. I found the men in my father's pay, and I paid them to go far away. I sent my own people to guard Ian and had all missives from the asylum waylaid and passed to me.

My father found out and raged at me, but I knew he would try again. And again. My father was a ruthless man, as you know, selfish to the point of madness. I started proceedings to release Ian from the asylum into my guardianship, but the process was slow, and I feared my father would find a way around me before Ian was safe.

I knew I had to confront my father, to stop him for good.

One evening, two weeks ago, I went to his study at Kilmorgan. Father was well drunk, which was nothing unusual for that time of day. I told him that Ian had confided the story of our mother's death to me and that I believed it. I told him that I was perfectly willing to testify to the truth of it, and I told him that I had put plans in motion to get Ian's commission of lunacy reversed.

My father listened as one stunned, then he tried to attack me. But I am no longer a terrified little boy or a fearful youth, he was drunk, and I easily bested him.

He was surprised when I punched him full in the face. He'd trained me to be his obedient slave, to let him beat me any time he wished and to not shed a tear over the pain. He said he'd done it to make me strong. He'd made me strong all right, and now he was understanding how strong.

At the same time I started proceedings to have Ian's commission reversed, I'd had my man of business draw up documents for a trust, one that divided the current wealth of the dukedom and the Mackenzie family into four equal pieces, one for each son, Ian included. The documents also give me custody of Ian, making Ian's fate mine to decide.

Father railed against me, of course, but my man of business had done a thorough job. With one stroke of a pen, my brothers would be free, and Father's money would be given to the sons he despised.

He shouted at me and told me he'd kill me, told me he'd kill my brothers and see us in hell. I had to threaten him with violence, and I do not want to tell you about what I had to do. It is enough to say that, in the end, he signed the document and regarded me in stark fear. I'd become a monster, in his eyes, but I am only the monster he created.

I gave the papers at once to my man of business's courier, who was waiting outside. He took one copy to Edinburgh and one copy to London, and there they both reside.

My father raged until he fell into a stupor and was put to bed. The next day, he strode out with his shotgun, saying he was going after a buck. He took the ghillie along, but I didn't trust him not to double back, get himself and the shotgun onto a horse, and ride across country to the asylum where Ian still resided.

My father must have known I would come after him, because he sent our ghillie ahead and waited for me in an isolated spot. Sure enough, the moment I caught up to him, Father had that shotgun in my face, his finger on the trigger.

I fought him. It was a mad struggle for the gun there in the woods. The barrel seemed to be pointed at me forever, and I knew that if I died this day, my brothers wouldn't have a chance against him, even with the documents he'd signed. He'd find a way to annul the agreement and make their lives an even greater misery than he had before. And Ian would be dead.

I finally got the shotgun turned around, and now the barrel faced him.

I can lie and tell myself that it was an accident. That I was fighting for the gun and it went off. But I had it in my hands, El. I saw in my mind's eye, in the split second before I pulled the trigger, the years of terror we'd have to endure if he went on living. Our father was a devious and insane man, and God help us, we inherited our bits of insanity from him. I saw that Ian would never be safe from him, no matter how diligent I was, if I did nothing.

I ended that hell in the woods. I pulled the trigger and shot him in the face.

The ghillie came running, of course. I was holding the gun by the barrel, looking horrified. It had jammed, I said. Backfired when it had gone off.

The ghillie knew, I know he did, but he said that, aye, His Grace must have failed to check that the barrel was clear before he fired at a stray bird. Accidents happened.

And so, the thirteenth Duke of Kilmorgan is gone. My brothers suspect the truth, just as the ghillie did, but they have said nothing, and I have not enlightened them. I vowed in that woods that they would never have to pay for what I've done.

Tonight, I confess my sins to you, Eleanor, and to you alone. Tomorrow, Ian comes home. Perhaps the Mackenzies can find some peace, though I doubt it, dear El, because we are so very bad at peace!

Thank you for listening. I can almost hear you saying, in that clearheaded way of yours: "You did what you have done. Let that be an end to it."

I wish I could hear you say it, in your voice like a soothing stream, but do not worry. I will not rush to Glenarden and throw myself at your feet. You deserve peace as well.

God bless you.

Hart heard a faint sound. He looked up from the letter, tears in his eyes, to see Eleanor standing in the doorway, prim and proper in a dress buttoned to her chin, her lips parted as she stared back at him.

Chapter 11

"You were supposed to burn this," Hart said. He couldn't get up, could not move, drained from what he'd just read.

Eleanor closed the door and came to the table littered with the letters. "I couldn't, somehow."

He noticed that she did not need to ask which letter he meant. "Why not?"

"I don't know, really. I suppose, because, of all the people you could have told, you chose to tell me."

"There was no other person," Hart said. "No one in the world."

It hung there. Hart closed the book and stood up, his feet heavy. He needed to touch her. She watched him come to her, said not a word when he cupped her face in his hands and leaned to kiss her.

She tasted of sunshine. Hart didn't pause to wonder why she'd come upstairs, whether Isabella expected her to rush right back down. Hart only cared that Eleanor was here, that he had the warmth of her under his hands, the woman who knew his direst secrets and had never told a soul.

He felt strong again in her embrace, his hurts flowing away

under Eleanor's caress. He waited for dark needs to grip him, to ruin this moment, but they didn't come.

He feathered kisses across her cheek, catching the freckles that he held so dear. "El . . ."

"Shh." Eleanor pulled him all the way into her arms and rested her head on his shoulder. "Say nothing. There's nothing to be said."

Hart pressed a kiss to the top of her head, loving the satin warmth of her hair. His heart was sore, but Eleanor was soothing away the hurt.

"You pasted the photographs into a book," he said. "A book about me."

Eleanor raised her head. She caught the look in his eye, and her face flamed as red as her hair. "Well, I . . ."

Hart felt light as he watched her struggle for an explanation. He saw her go through several, then she grew redder still, and said in a tiny voice, "You are very fine to look at."

Hart wanted to laugh, mirth being all the brighter after the memories the letters had forced upon him.

Eleanor frowned suddenly, touching his face where the chipped stone had cut him. "What happened?"

"Nothing important. Don't change the subject."

Her fingers were soft. "Even marred, you are a handsome man. You must know that."

Many women had told Hart so, but he'd never let himself wallow in their praise. Riches and position could tinge the perspective, rendering the unpleasant beautiful.

"I don't want you to keep the photographs Mrs. Palmer took," he said. "Burn them."

"Don't be daft. They're finely done. And besides, if I grow angry enough at you, I'm sure I could sell them for quite a lot of money."

Hart lost his smile. "You would do that?"

She pretended to consider. "Perhaps, if you keep telling me not to search certain places for who sent them—or to do anything I please, for that matter."

Her teasing melted him. "I was right. You are a bold lady. You haven't changed since you lured me into that boating house."

"*Lured* you? I believe I was minding my own business, and you stalked me there."

"An argument that could last ages. But no matter." He snatched up the book. "I'll just burn the entire thing."

Eleanor lunged for it. "Don't you dare."

Hart swung around and headed for the coal stove, its warm glow and Eleanor pumping life back into him.

Eleanor ran after him and grabbed the book, and Hart pretended to wrestle her for it. She knew he pretended, because Hart could have snatched the book out of her hands any moment he wanted to. She yanked, and he released it suddenly, sending her a few scuttling steps back.

She didn't fall, because Hart steadied her as she teetered on her heels. He ripped the book out of her hands, dumped it to the writing table, and then caught her around the waist and lifted her with ease onto the bed.

Eleanor squirmed against him as he came with her onto the mattress. But she didn't struggle as much as she perhaps should have, because Hart was laughing.

Hart, who never laughed these days, was doing it now as he lowered her onto her back, his kilt spilling over her skirts. His eyes sparked with deviltry, and he laughed.

Eleanor sank beneath him with pleasure but discovered an impediment. "Ow, oh. Dratted *bustle*."

Hart locked his feet around hers and rolled over with her in the big bed. Eleanor landed on top of him, the bustle creaking as it righted itself like a ship from stormy water.

Eleanor looked down at him, her laughing, teasing Highlander, and fell in love all over again.

Hart skimmed his hands along her back, palms warm even through her clothes. She tried not to feel a tingle of excitement to feel his hardness obvious through his kilt.

She bent her knees and waved her feet in her high-heeled, buttoned boots. "I must get up. My governess taught me never to lie on a bed in my shoes."

His smile turned wicked. "I'll teach you to lie on it in nothing *but* your shoes."

Pleasant heat spun through her. "That would be . . . very naughty."

"Of course it would be. That is the point."

Eleanor tapped the end of his nose. "I admit that when I am with you, I find myself becoming naughty indeed."

"Good."

"I must be a very bad woman, mustn't I, to let you take such liberties?"

He grinned, his eyes alight. "El, your innocence rings to the skies."

"Not so innocent." She gave him a mock frown. "Remember that I grew up with a father who thought nothing of discussing the reproductive habits of every living creature—including human ones—over the soup."

"Your mother must have been a patient woman."

"My mother loved him to pieces." Eleanor felt a bite of sadness as she always did when her mother came into her thoughts, the woman dying, ill, when Eleanor had been eight years old.

Hart's eyes darkened. "I always envied you that. Your father and mother actually loving each other. Your happy childhood home."

"Yes, it was happy," Eleanor said. "And then sorrowful."

Hart wrapped his arms around her. "I know."

"At least Father and I have rubbed along well all this time. Which brings me around again to my knowledge of mating habits. You may think me innocent, but I am quite worldly, in my own way."

"I know that. You keep nude photographs of a man hidden in your corset drawer."

"Which you snooped through, drat you."

"Giving me some idea of the state of your wardrobe. You have not instructed Isabella to dress you as I asked. Your gowns are horrible."

"Well, thank you very much."

He touched the pad of her lower lip. "Nip your pride in the bud, lassie. If you're to parade about with this family, you'll need decent clothes or you'll stand out like a beacon. Isabella will outfit you and send me the bill."

"Indeed, no. People will say I'm your fancy woman."

He chuckled. "What an expression. I pay you wages."

"For typing. An honest wage for an honest job."

"Consider it a clothing allowance. I'll not have my employees looking drab. My housekeeper dresses better than you do."

"Insult heaped on top of insult."

"Truth. Now I want truth from you—why did you keep all that trash about me?"

"To feed your pride, obviously."

Hart laughed again. It felt good to have him shaking under her, true mirth in his eyes, not the bleakness she'd seen when she'd walked into the room. As though reading his letters had ripped the dressing from a wound, he'd bled, and now, she hoped to God, he could let himself heal.

Or at least lie on the bed with her and tease her as though they were dear friends or casual lovers. He'd been like this when he'd courted her, laughing, teasing, goading her into admissions one moment, becoming incredibly tender the next.

At *this* moment, he tickled her.

"Stop." Eleanor drummed her hands on his chest. "No wonder people fear the great Hart Mackenzie—vote for me, or I'll tickle you to death."

"I'd do it, if it worked." His smile faded. "Burn those photos, El. They're terrible."

On the contrary, they were beautiful. She did not at all like the fact that Mrs. Palmer had taken them, but Eleanor could find no fault with the results.

"No, indeed," she said. "The well-wisher sent the photographs to me, not you, and I paid a solid guinea for the others. I'll not burn them. They're *mine*."

Hart tried the scowl, the Mackenzie glare, the little growl. Heaps more effective if he hadn't been flat on his back, his kilt spread, his hair a mess. As it was, Eleanor kissed the bridge of his nose.

"I'll only get rid of them if they are replaced," she said. "Use my clothing allowance to buy me photographing apparatus and have more photos done, ones only for me."

Hart's scowl died, and his eyes took on, of all things, embarrassment. "Who would take these photographs?"

"Me, of course. I know how to work photographing apparatus. My father hired a camera once, and all the chemicals and machines for a darkroom, so we could make plates of local flora for one of his books. I quite enjoyed it. I'm a dab hand, I must say."

"You can type, you can photograph. What can't you do, paragon?"

"Embroider." Eleanor wrinkled her nose. "I'm very bad at it. And I never did learn to play the piano. In the maidenly pursuits, I'm not much good. I seem to do better at masculine pursuits."

Hart's smile reappeared. "I'd say you were excellent at pursuing the masculine."

"Oh, very funny, Your Grace. What about the camera?"

"You truly want to take photographs of me?" He sounded . . . shy.

"I do indeed," she said. "Is that so difficult to believe?"

"I'm much older now."

Eleanor let her smile grow. She moved her gaze over his face with its healing cuts, his throat damp behind his pulled-askew cravat, his broad chest under shirt and waistcoat, his flat abdomen. She knelt back to continue looking at him, taking in his tight hips and thighs outlined by the crumpled kilt. The plaid had dragged a little above his knees to show her brawny muscle above his thick wool socks.

She heaved a pleased little sigh. "I don't see that there's much wrong with you, Hart Mackenzie."

"Because I'm fully dressed. Fine feathers."

An intense and uncontrollable daring gripped her. Before Eleanor could stop herself, she grasped the hem of the kilt and inched it upward until it bared his thighs. Hart lay very still, one arm behind his head, as she looked him over.

"Nothing wrong there either," she said.

"I ride every day."

"Very commendable. A sound mind in a sound body. I think these will look quite nice in a photograph."

Heaven help us, he was blushing.

"Are you that worried?" she asked.

"I was a young man when I was courting you."

"And I was a very young woman. Although, you do have wrinkles." Eleanor touched spiderweb lines at the edges of his eyes. She liked them, because it meant he smiled a little, at least.

"You don't," he said.

"Because I'm a bit plump. Were I a slender woman, I'd be an old stick by now."

Hart touched her face with gentle fingers. "I've never seen you more gloriously beautiful."

Eleanor's heart sped, but she knelt back before the treacherous warmth he stirred might make her say something she'd regret. Slanting him a smile, Eleanor flipped the kilt up past his hips.

She stilled. "Oh."

Hart's eyes went dark. "What's the matter, love?"

"I thought you would be wearing flannels. It's rather cold."

"I haven't gone out this morning," he said.

Hart's shyness was gone, he once again turning the tables. He rested his head in his cupped hands and waited to see what she'd do.

Between his thighs lay the tight spheres of his balls, and above those, the length of him arced back against his abdomen, cradled by plaid.

"I wish I had the photographing apparatus now," Eleanor said.

"Do you, naughty woman?"

Oh, yes. Hart would make a heady portrait—him lying back, his kilt crumpled around his hips to reveal his wanting while he watched her with warm eyes.

She'd learned his body a long time ago, becoming familiar with the scar that snaked up the inside of his right thigh, the way his hair curled along his legs, how one knee was not the perfect mirror of the other. The photographs didn't show these small details; they were known only to the woman who had the privilege of gazing at him this close.

Hart said nothing, did nothing.

Eleanor touched the scar, finding the little ridge smooth and cool. Something sparked in Hart's eyes as she traced the scar upward, but he remained still.

His skin was warmer closer to the join of his legs. His scar ended halfway up the inside of his leg, but Eleanor let her finger continue along the trail until she found the crease between ball and thigh. She caressed there a moment, the last safe place, and then moved her fingers to the shaft.

Hart's body jerked the slightest bit. His gaze fixed on her, waiting.

Eleanor's smile widened as she drew her finger up the length of him to his tip. His skin was smooth, hot, and at the same time, silken soft. Strength encased in a firm package.

"The male's organ stiffens," she said. "So that he might penetrate the female's softest place and enter her for his purpose."

"Bawd," Hart said, voice rough. "Who taught you such talk?"

"A scientific journal."

Hart's laughter shook him, but not enough to make Eleanor's fingers slide away. "I hope you damn well don't whisper such things to any other man, especially not in that sweet voice."

"Only to you, Hart. Only ever to you."

He stilled. "Eleanor, you are killing me."

She lifted her hand away. "Shall I stop?"

"No!" Hart grasped her wrist, grip biting down, then he stopped himself, deliberately uncurling his fingers. He tucked his hand behind his head again, but she saw it shaking. "I don't want you to stop," he said. "Please."

It was very difficult for this man to say *please*. Eleanor put her finger to her lips, hesitating as though pondering what to do. Hart watched her, his entire body tense.

Eleanor rested her hand on him again. Again he jerked, Hart trying to contain his reaction.

She glided her palm up the length of him, exactly as he'd showed her that long-ago day in the summerhouse. Hart sucked in a breath, body rigid. Eleanor brushed her palm over his tip and then slid her hand back down.

"Oh, God, Eleanor . . . *lass*."

The groan nearly undid her. Eleanor stroked him again, this time a little faster. Hart grew even harder under her touch, and Eleanor warmed with the power of it.

"El. Sweet El. Holy Christ."

Hart's hands tightened to fists, as though he stopped himself, with great effort, from reaching for her.

In the summerhouse and the bedchambers, they'd undressed before intimate touching had commenced. Eleanor had not known how exciting things could be when they both remained fully clothed. *What a delicious discovery.*

Hart, for his part, was making all kinds of discoveries. That Eleanor was more beautiful than ever, that he wasn't quite dead, that her touch was incredible. Despite Eleanor's assertions, she *was* innocent, and her little smile opened up every devilish part of him.

The wild feeling in his cock spread down his body and up again into his heart. Hart was going to die of this. Hart the master, the all-powerful, surrendered to his lady's touch.

God, it was glorious.

"Eleanor," he said breathlessly. "You undo me. You always have."

"Shall I stop?"

Look at her, playful and challenging, utterly innocent and wicked at the same time. He'd let her walk away from him, because he'd been stupid, and young, and too bloody arrogant. He'd never let her walk away again. Even if he had to lock her into this chamber with him for the rest of their lives, he'd keep her with him, always.

It would not be so bad an existence. His servants could cut a hole in the door to pass them food and drink, and maybe Hart would remember to eat it.

"Never stop," Hart heard himself say. "Never. Please. Oh, dear God."

He rose on his elbows, unable to stay flat against the pillow. He watched the hand that pleasured him, with small, feminine fingers that were proving to be very, very clever.

"Take me all the way, El. Please, or you'll kill me."

Eleanor knew what he meant. She did have knowledge, because Hart had taught it to her a long time ago.

Eleanor lay down at his side as she kept up the beautiful friction, and Hart wrapped his arm around her. Her head rested on his chest, and strands of red gold hair snaked across his black coat. Hart stroked her, keeping his touch gentle.

Darkness rose, but Hart fought it down. He wanted this to be simple, light, a woman pleasuring him because she wanted to pleasure him.

Basic physical need took over. His mind blanked to all but the scent of Eleanor's hair, the glorious feeling of her fingers, her warmth at his side. Nothing but her and him, sensation, wanting.

His hips moved. *"Eleanor."*

He scooped her up to him and thrust his mouth over hers just as it ended. Heat scalded his thighs, but the sensation went on and on. Hart kissed Eleanor's mouth, and she moved her lips in greedy response.

"Lass, what you do to me."

Eleanor's eyes were half closed, lovely blue between black lashes. Hart's words ran out, and he simply kissed her.

It was peaceful here. The house was quiet, he and she close, Hart kissing Eleanor on her bed on a rainy London morning.

She touched his face as they kissed, saying nothing. Sweet kisses. No hurry.

"You soothe me," he whispered.

Her eyes softened. "I'm glad."

Time flowed by. Hart and Eleanor were nose-to-nose, kissing, touching, enjoying the silence.

They lay together in quiet enjoyment, until Wilfred's dry cough in the hall invaded the peace, reminding Hart of the real world waiting for him. He wanted to tell the real world to go hang.

Eleanor, sensibly, fetched a towel from her washstand and brought it back to the bed. Hart wiped her hands and himself with the linen, then kissed her as he slid from the bed, the heavy folds of his kilt once more falling to cover him.

When he married her, they would have many more days like this. No matter how busy their lives became, no matter how many people vied for their attention, Hart would make certain that the duke and duchess often retired from the public eye to lie together in joyful silence.

It was all he could do to make himself leave the room, and her, his heart full.

~

Eleanor blew out her breath as Hart closed the door. She went to her washbasin and bathed her hands and face in cool water, fetching yet another towel from her cupboard.

She was still shaking. What had possessed her? But it had been beautiful.

She went to the writing table, where Hart had left the book, and began gathering up the letters to return to their hiding place. Not many seconds later, she found herself sitting down to flip through the pages of the memory book, back to the photographs.

She smiled. Hart might insist he was past his first youth now, but he'd looked quite fine on her bed with his kilt bunched around his hips. Better even, than he had years ago. He'd filled out, his body reaching the potential his younger features had promised.

She sighed and began gathering the letters again. She unfolded the letter she'd found Hart reading and skimmed through it, her heart aching for him all over again.

Hart was right; she ought to have burned it. But Eleanor had reasoned the likelihood small that anyone would find the hidden letter in her out-of-the-way abode on the Scottish coast. The servants never touched her belongings, and her father went rarely to her bedchamber. She'd not thought about the letters tucked into the book as she'd packed for London; she'd simply not wanted to leave the book behind.

But Eleanor understood the danger of keeping the letter. Hart shooting his father had been an accident, she was certain—they had wrestled for the shotgun, and it had gone off. What had been in Hart's mind the split second between the gun landing in his hands and the shot flying out of it was between Hart and God.

Whatever had happened, the duke's death had brought Ian home to safety. But if Hart's enemies ever got hold of the letter, it could spell disaster for Hart.

Eleanor marched to the stove and opened its door. "Let that be an end to it," she said, using the words Hart predicted she would, and consigned the letter to the flames.

～

The shooting attempt made Hart rethink the travel arrangements to Berkshire. Hart would not be staying at Cameron's the entire month anyway, as he usually did, but traveling back and forth to London as he could.

Train stations were extremely public places, full of opportunities for crazed assassins to fire at people. Hart agonized over the decision but concluded that Eleanor and her father well might be safer in public, with Mac to guard them, than they would alone in a coach on some empty stretch of country road. Hart would keep them safe by not traveling with them at all.

He climbed to the top of the house the day before they were to depart, having been told that the entire family and

Eleanor were taking nursery tea in the room that had been set aside for the children.

When he entered, Eleanor looked up from sinking her teeth into a cream-slathered scone. Hart stopped. The sudden vision of him licking the cream from her lips made him dizzy for a moment.

When he could see again, he took in Mac sitting at a table with Eileen, Isabella next to him, Robert in a baby chair. Eleanor crammed in beside them at the table, while the nanny, Miss Westlock, supervised from a bench on the other side of the room. Aimee sat on a window seat with Lord Ramsay, the earl showing Aimee fossils he'd brought with him from Scotland.

Hart dragged his gaze again from the smear of cream on Eleanor's lips and addressed Mac. "I'm leaving for Berkshire this morning. I have errands to run along the way, so I'll take the coach. The rest of you will travel down by train tomorrow afternoon."

"Coach?" Mac said. He licked clotted cream from his thumb and shook his head at his daughter. "Eileen, please don't put butter in your brother's hair." He looked back at Hart. "Hadn't you better come with us?"

"I told you, I have errands . . ."

Eleanor glared at him. "Hart, we *know*." She lifted a copy of a gossipy newspaper from the chair beside her and held it up to him.

Duke of Kilmorgan narrowly escapes with his life!
Shots fired outside Parliament. Have the Fenians found
a new target?

"How the devil did that rag get into the house?" Hart growled. "Mac?"

Mac looked innocent, but Eleanor's face was bright with rage. "You lied to me when I asked how you hurt yourself. You said it wasn't important. How could you? You were nearly *killed*."

Hart touched his face where the cuts were fading. "It *isn't* important. The man was a terrible shot, and I wasn't paying attention. I didn't tell you because I don't want the lot of you fussing."

"Fussing? Hart, this is dangerous. This is something you tell your family. And your friends."

"Which is exactly why I don't want any of you with me!" Hart's voice rang as he lost hold of his patience. "If the man is such a bad shot, I don't want my family and friends to become accidental victims when he misses me. Eleanor, you and your father will travel with Isabella and Mac, and I will go with my bodyguards and Wilfred. Wilfred used to be in the army. He knows how to duck."

Eleanor's stare turned icy. "Do not try to make a joke of this. I suppose you did not even talk to the police."

"I did, as a matter of fact. I asked Inspector Fellows to look into it, because if anyone can scare up a culprit, it is our favorite Scotland Yard detective. But he doesn't have much to go on, only a few chipped bricks. And the man might not have been shooting at me in particular, but at anyone coming out of the building."

Lord Ramsay broke in. "You must understand that the thought of you traveling alone makes us uneasy, don't you, Mackenzie? You in a coach? On an empty road between Reading and Hungerford?"

"I will not *be* alone. I hire former pugilists as footmen for their large bodies and quick reflexes."

"Which did not help you the night you were shot," Eleanor pointed out.

"Because that night I was not paying attention." He'd been thinking about Eleanor in a corset, her hair up, high-heeled ankle boots on her feet. "Now I've been warned," he said.

"Hardly reassuring." Eleanor's eyes still held anger. "But I suppose we'll never talk you out of it. You will send a telegram the moment you arrive, won't you?"

"El," Hart said.

"No, never mind. Ainsley will do it. Please make certain you inform Cameron of the problem. Or Cameron might take umbrage, and he's larger than you."

Hart didn't bother to keep the irritation from his voice. "Leave it, Eleanor. I will see you in Berkshire."

She scowled at him, but Hart only saw her in his heady vision of the corset and boots, made more erotic by a liberal addition of clotted cream. He turned away and made himself walk out the door.

Eleanor had always loved Waterbury Grange, Cameron's Berkshire estate, though she'd not visited it in ages. Cameron, second-oldest brother of the Mackenzie family, had purchased it shortly after his first wife had died, saying he wanted somewhere far from the place in which he'd spent his unhappy marriage.

Green fields stretched to wooded hills, and the Kennet and Avon Canal drifted lazily along the edge of the property. Spring meant lambs staggering after mothers across the field, and foals keeping close to the mares that wandered the pastures.

Mackenzie family tradition brought them to Waterbury every March. There the brothers, and now their wives and children, would watch Cameron train his racers while they withdrew from the eyes of the world. Here was their chance to be a private family for a short time before Cameron took his three-year-olds to Newmarket.

The house was old, a shapeless pile of golden brick, but from what Ainsley said in her letters, she'd been busily redecorating the inside. Eleanor looked forward to seeing her progress.

But when Eleanor, her father, Isabella, Mac, the exuberant children, their robust nanny, and old Ben climbed down from the carriages that brought them from the train, it was for Hart to meet them at the front door of Waterbury Grange and tell them that Ian had gone missing.

Chapter 12

"You know Ian does this all the time," Beth said. She looked worriedly at Hart, and Eleanor sensed that Beth's anxiousness was more for Hart than for her absent husband.

Beth stood in the breezy front hall with a child on each arm—son Jamie and tiny daughter Belle. The Mackenzie dogs, all five of them, wandered among the new arrivals, tails waving.

"Ian likes to be alone sometimes," Beth said. "He doesn't like crowds."

"We aren't a crowd," Hart snapped. "We're family. You should have told me at once that he'd gone."

At the note in Hart's voice, Eleanor looked up from kissing the two babies. Hart's hands were clenched in his gloves, his jaw tight. He had a right to be worried after the shooting by the Parliament buildings, but his alarm seemed to go beyond that.

"I didn't know," Beth said. "Ian's gotten better about telling me when he's going on one of his long walks, but he was already up and out when I woke this morning."

"And you didn't bother to tell me," Hart repeated.

"You were at Hungerford all morning, sending telegrams to London," Beth said. "And I did not think it was any of your business."

Hart went still at her words, and his look turned dangerous. Beth lifted her chin and met his gaze.

Eleanor understood perfectly well why Beth hadn't mentioned Ian's absence to Hart. Hart had the habit of walking into his brothers' houses and attempting to take over their lives. Sometimes Ian felt the need to slip away, out from under Hart's heavy-handedness. Cameron and Mac could shout at Hart when they grew angry at his interfering, but Ian's defense was to disappear. Ian sometimes needed to be alone, to find rest from his overwhelming family before he faced them again. Eleanor had heard about the battle Beth had fought with Hart to let Ian live as he needed.

Beth spoke calmly. "I've been married to Ian for nearly three years now, and I know what he does. A stay in London always unnerves him, you know that. I imagine he went out today to enjoy *not* having people surrounding him. He'll return when he's ready."

Hart tried to pin Beth with his stare, but Jamie squirmed to get down from Beth's arms, and Beth turned her full attention to her son. Hart's jaw went tighter as Beth blatantly ignored him, and he turned and strode out of the house. Two of the dogs broke free and followed him.

Eleanor caught up to Hart in the drive. She dodged in front of him to make him stop, and Ruby and Ben roamed around them, tails moving.

"I know you're worried about the shooting," she said. "But Ian's not a fool. He's more careful than you are, in many ways. I telegraphed Ainsley about the incident in case you didn't bother telling anybody, so Ian would have known to take precaution. I'm certain he only went fishing. You know how he loves to fish."

The terrible worry did not leave Hart's eyes. "He does. Says the water calms him." He scanned the empty fields. "I'm going to look for him."

He started to walk on, but Eleanor got in front of him again. "I believe you are the one in the most danger, Hart Mackenzie. Whoever it was shot at *you*."

"I won't go alone. I have my own men, and Cameron employs a horde."

"Ian will be distressed if a horde comes upon him," Eleanor pointed out.

"Better he's distressed than dead."

Hart's words were quiet, but Eleanor read profound fear in his eyes. She knew he'd never admit to that fear outside of being tortured, but Hart was deeply afraid, and Eleanor knew why.

Protection of Ian had been Hart's driving force for three decades. Eleanor had first seen that drive when Hart had taken Eleanor to meet Ian in the asylum. She remembered Hart questioning and bullying the doctors about Ian's care, his routine, his accommodations. Whatever Hart Mackenzie had done for the last thirty years of his life, good or ill, he'd done most of it for Ian.

Eleanor touched Hart's chest, feeling his heart hammering beneath her palm. "I do agree with you, Hart. If people are shooting, then you need to keep an eye on Ian. But even so, we must be calm. We'll find him."

His focus switched sharply to her, anything but calm. "There is no *we*. *You* need to stay here."

"I can help look, you know. We all can."

"*No.*" The word was fierce. "Finding Ian will be difficult enough. I do not want to have to scour the countryside for you and all my sisters-in-law at the same time. If Ian returns on his own, I need you here to help Beth keep him home."

"You mean you don't want me underfoot."

"I don't. You'll distract me. I can't afford to be distracted just now."

"I distract you. How flattering."

Hart leaned to her. "Which means I'm having difficulty thinking of anything but you. That is your fault. You seduced me like the siren you are. Now stay here and let me look for my brother."

He needed to search, Eleanor saw that. Ian would be annoyed at Hart when Hart interrupted his fishing trip, but Ian knew how to put Hart in his place. The world thought that the "slow" Ian obeyed Hart, but the family knew differently.

"Godspeed," Eleanor said softly.

Hart cupped her cheek and brushed a sudden, hot kiss to her lips. Then he strode away from her and made for the paddocks, where the huge forms of his brother Cameron and Cameron's equally tall son, Daniel, waited for him.

Hart knew that Beth and Eleanor were right—in all likelihood, Ian had gone off on one of his rambles to collect himself before the rest of the family arrived. Ian had difficulty responding to people, or at least understanding how they wanted him to respond to them.

Ian said what he thought, not the expected or polite thing. From brutal experience, he'd learned to keep quiet and withdraw when he was with too many people, but sometimes he had to turn his back on the world altogether until he felt better able to cope with it.

Hart kept up his conviction that Ian would be fine, but as the hours passed, his worry settled in and stayed. He found no sign of him, no Ian fishing on the banks of the canal, no tall man in a kilt wandering across fields.

When the sun went down, Hart met Cameron, Mac, and Daniel in Hungerford, the three reporting they'd still not seen Ian nor found anyone who'd seen him.

Hart's worry turned to crawling fear. He could not banish the picture of Ian lying facedown in a field, shot, bleeding, dying, or already dead. Either that or tied and blindfolded in some filthy room, his enemies refusing to let him go until they had Hart.

Cameron's and Mac's eyes reflected Hart's uneasiness. Daniel, who'd initially scoffed at the idea that Ian of all people could be lost and hurt, now worried too.

"Daniel, go south to Coomb," Hart said. "He likes to climb the hill to the old gibbet and watch the world go by. Cameron, search the canal east to Newbury. If Ian has spent all day studying a lock, I'll pummel him. Mac, I want you to go back to the house and make sure the ladies don't get the idea to go searching as well. I told Eleanor not to, but you know the Mackenzie females."

Mac scowled. "Hell, Hart, can't you find something easier for me to do? Go up against an army of assassins in my underwear, maybe?"

"I am not letting any of them wander the countryside to be a target. Keep them home and protect them."

Mac raised his hands in surrender, but Hart knew his brother agreed with him. Mac would keep the ladies safe. "Fine," Mac said. "But I'm stuffing my ears with cotton wool."

Hart and his brothers and nephew separated, each taking a few men with him, and Hart resumed his search.

He walked his horse along the dark towpath, heading west along the canal. *Blast you, Ian. Why did you choose* now *to go roaming?*

It was too dark to go very fast, and a misstep could send Hart or his horse or the men following him into the canal. He tried to take care, but everything in him was urging, *hurry, hurry, hurry.*

They clopped down through Little Bedwyn, then Great Bedwyn and on toward Wilton and Crofton. No Ian Mackenzie. No tall Scotsman staring at water moving through the locks, or idly fishing, or walking restlessly up and down the banks.

Ian could be anywhere. Holed up in a barn to sleep or climbing aboard a train to who-knew-where. Ian followed no rules but his own, and he might not bother to buy a ticket for the train until he was on it. He would eventually wire Beth to tell her where he was, but it might be some time before he did. *Ian* would know he was all right, but he did not always remember to reassure others or even understand why he should. Ian was better about all this now that he was with Beth, but he still liked to sometimes disappear on his own.

As a child, Ian had bolted from crowds that frightened him or even from the supper table at Kilmorgan, running, running to rid himself of terrors he didn't understand. Hart would follow him, find him, and sit with him in silence until Ian calmed down. Only Hart had been able to stop Ian's frightened tears and intense rages. Only Hart had been able to put a comforting arm around Ian's shoulders—for the brief moment Ian allowed it—to reassure him that he was not alone.

When Ian had first come home from the asylum, he often would walk away from the house and stay away for days. Hart had gone insane with worry, but Ian always returned, in his own time. Hart would shout at Ian and command him not to do it again. Ian would listen in silence, gaze averted, but when Ian decided he needed to be on his own again, he simply went. All the shouting in the world could not change his mind.

Things were different now. Ian had Beth, and his need to withdraw had dwindled. Ian did not like to spend too much time away from Beth and his children, in any case, and he mostly stayed home, drawing comfort from them.

So, why had he gone this time?

I will never let anything happen to you, Ian Mackenzie, Hart vowed as he rode through yet another village. *I promised you that, and I'll keep the promise until I die.*

Hart became separated from his men. He wasn't certain when it happened, but in the dark, with Hart well in the lead, he must have ridden over a canal bridge they hadn't seen him take, or perhaps they'd ridden over one, assuming Hart had crossed it.

Hart debated doubling back but decided against it. He'd not seen anything today to indicate assassins lurking behind every bush, and no one he'd spoken to had noticed strangers in the area. His men would catch up to him when they could.

The lack of obviously dangerous people did not alleviate Hart's anxiousness for Ian. He kept searching.

He clattered into quiet villages, inquired in the local pubs, asked at farms if a gentleman had put up with them for the night. Most of the people around here knew Ian or had at least heard of him, but none could help.

A church clock was striking four when Hart rode over yet another canal bridge. He was exhausted, and his men were long gone, probably returned to Waterbury by now. Hart's muscles ached from the long day in the saddle, and his eyes kept drooping in spite of his efforts to keep them open.

He should stop and rest, then resume looking again at sunup. His worry wanted him to keep going, but his reason told him he'd be sharper if he broke for a few hours and waited for daylight.

Hart unsaddled his horse, pulled off the bridle, and slid the halter he'd brought with him over the horse's head. He tied the horse to a sturdy sapling, giving the beast enough rope so it could graze, then Hart lay down with his head on the saddle, his cloak wrapped tightly around him.

He woke on a sudden to the same church clock striking eight, the sun in his eyes, and the bulk of Ian Mackenzie looming over him.

Chapter 13

"Damn you, Ian," Hart said.

He sat up, rubbing his neck, stiff from lying against the saddle. The horse had broken free and now wandered a little way from them, head down, cropping grass.

Ian said nothing. He didn't ask what Hart was doing here or why he'd been sleeping on the ground in the middle of nowhere beside the canal. In continued silence, Ian turned away and caught the horse.

The horse shoved his face against Ian's side as Ian removed the halter and buckled on the bridle. Animals liked Ian—Cameron's horses and the Mackenzie dogs followed him about with affection.

Hart rubbed his jaw, feeling the scratch of whiskers as he climbed painfully to his feet. He lifted the saddle that had served as his pillow and carried it to the horse. "What are you doing out here, Ian?"

Ian took the saddle from Hart and set it on the horse's back, then reached beneath the horse and caught the girth, tightening it with the expertise of a long-experienced rider.

"Looking for you," Ian said.

"I thought I was looking for you."

Ian gave Hart a you-are-hopelessly-behind-in-this-conversation look. "They said you were trying to find me."

"Who did?" Hart scanned the empty countryside beyond the line of trees that bordered the canal. "Did you find my bodyguards? How did you even know I was back here?"

Ian took up the horse's reins, then he stopped and looked at Hart, straight into his eyes. "I can always find you."

They stood like that for the barest moment, brother staring at brother, until Ian broke the contact and turned away, leading the horse back to the towpath.

~~~~~

I can always find you.

The words echoed in Hart's head as he watched his brother walk away, kilt stirring in the wind. No boats moved on the quiet canal in the dawn, and mist curled under the overhanging trees and the bridges.

I can always find you. Knowing Ian, he'd simply been stating a fact and not implying that he had a special connection to Hart.

But Hart felt the connection to Ian, the tether that had stretched between himself and his brother from the moment Hart had realized that Ian was different, special, and that Hart had to protect him. He'd sensed the connection through the years Ian had spent at the asylum and every year since Ian's release. Hart felt it so strongly that when Ian had been accused of harming someone eight years ago, Hart had done everything in his power to shield Ian from the consequences and had been prepared to take the blame on himself.

Not that Ian would bother talking such matters through. He continued leading the horse westward along the path without waiting to see whether Hart followed.

Hart caught up to him. "Cameron's house is the other direction."

Ian kept walking. He did not look at Hart, only watched the canal or nudged stray branches out of the way so the horse would not trip on them. Hart gave up and walked in silence beside him.

Ian's destination became clear when, after about a mile, he led the horse over a narrow bridge and down to a long canal boat moored on the far bank. The boat's foredeck contained several children, two goats, three dogs, and a man dangling his feet over the bow and smoking a pipe. The large horse that pulled the boat grazed, untethered, along the side of the canal.

Without a word, Ian dropped the reins of Hart's horse and stepped onto the deck of the boat. One of the children, a girl, climbed off at the same time to catch Hart's horse. She stroked the horse and crooned to it, and the horse seemed happy to let her.

Hart went on board after Ian, because Ian clearly expected him to. The pipe-smoking man nodded once at Hart but didn't bother to get up. The children stared, as did the dogs. The goats didn't care one way or the other.

An older woman came out of the cabin. She was shrunken to almost the size of the children, and she was dressed all in black with a black scarf over her hair. Her eyes were as black as her clothes and alert and sparkling.

She pointed at a wooden crate next to the rail. "You," she said to Hart. "Sit there."

London society might be surprised to see His Grace of Kilmorgan quietly and obediently take the seat. Ian sat down next to Hart, still without speaking.

The girl on the bank fixed Hart's horse with the halter, took off its saddle and bridle, and piled the tack on the deck. She walked to the tow horse, who looked up patiently, and put a halter on it as well.

All unhurried. No one on the boat got off to help the little girl, who didn't wait for them to. The older woman, once she'd seen Hart and Ian sit, disappeared below.

Hart had met these Romany before, although he'd never been on their boat. He'd stood on a bank of the canal near Cameron's estate fifteen years ago, while the same woman in black had told Hart in heavily accented English that because Cameron had saved her son Angelo from arrest and death, her family would look after Cameron now. Angelo had become Cameron's servant, assistant trainer, and close friend.

The girl got the tow horse harnessed and its ropes attached to the boat. She clucked to the large horse and guided it forward, leading Hart's horse on her other side. Hart's well-trained and spirited stallion quieted under the girl's touch, content to follow her and the tow horse like a docile pony.

The pipe smoker went back to studying the water ahead of them, and Angelo's mother returned with two chipped mugs filled with coffee. Hart thanked her and drank deeply. The coffee was rich and dark, no cream or sugar to cut the thick taste.

The boat headed into the rising sun. The Romany were the only ones moving on the canal so far. Thick mist floated under the trees along the towpath, and beyond the trees, fields opened out. Lambs followed their mothers on the damp green, the lambs and ewes looking like mobile clumps of mist in the gloom.

There was silence here, and peace. Hart closed his eyes.

He awoke to find the day brightening and that Ian now leaned on the bow. The pipe-smoking man had taken over steering the horse, while the little girl and the other children had gone inside. The goats and dogs remained on deck.

Hart moved to stand next to Ian. "You still haven't told me why you came out here."

Ian gazed down at the water, watching the boat's bow breaking the glasslike canal. It wasn't unusual for Ian not to respond to a question, or to wait until a day or two after a question was put to him before he answered. Sometimes he never answered at all.

"I told Angelo's people about the shooting," Ian said. He closed his mouth after he spoke the words, and Hart knew nothing more would be forthcoming.

He filled in the rest himself. The Romany roamed up and down these canals and across the fields, despite the farmers' and villagers' attempts to keep them out. The Romany would know the instant someone out of the ordinary appeared in the area, and they would keep a sharp eye out for danger. Angelo was much beloved by his family and so, by extension, were Angelo's friends. When Ian had learned of the assassination attempt, he'd decided it was a good idea to find and inform the Romany.

"Wise of you," Hart said. "But you didn't bother to tell Beth where you were going, or Curry. We have the entire estate out searching for you. Can't you learn to leave a *note*?"

Ian didn't react to Hart's anger. "Beth knows where I go."

"Well, she didn't this time. And I sure as hell didn't."

Ian rested his arm on the railing and looked at Hart, sweeping his gaze over Hart's open greatcoat, mussed hair, unshaven jaw. Whatever Ian was thinking or feeling, Hart didn't know. He never knew.

"Ian," he said, exasperated.

Ian still didn't answer. Hart heaved a sigh and rubbed his bristly face again. "Fine, have it your way."

Ian went back to studying the water.

Hart used to believe himself the only person who truly understood Ian, but he'd learned, painfully, that despite the connection he felt with him, he'd barely penetrated his brother's shell. The moment Ian had met Beth, however, Ian had responded to her, emerging from his private place of silence and rage. Ian had started engaging with the world through the conduit of Beth.

What Hart had tried, and failed, to do for years, Beth Ackerley, widow of a poor parish vicar, had done in a matter of days.

Hart at first had been angry with Beth, envious of her bond with Ian, fearful that she would exploit him for her own ends. But Beth had proved her deep devotion to Ian, and Hart now loved her for what she'd done.

Hart leaned on the railing and let out a heavy breath. "How do you do it, Ian? How do you deal with the madness?"

He'd been speaking generally, thinking of his own struggles. He didn't expect Ian to respond, but Ian said, "I have Beth."

I have no one.

The words came out of nowhere. They were not true. Hart had his brothers, his interfering sisters-in-law, Daniel, and now his small nieces and nephews, who could be adorable—especially when they wanted something. He had Wilfred and his handpicked staff who were loyal to him to a fault. He even had David Fleming, a friend he'd been with through thick and thin over many years.

But no one gets close to Hart Mackenzie the man.

Hart had given up mistresses after Angelina Palmer's death, forgoing even casual encounters for satiation. He'd been living like a monk. No wonder the merest whisper of Eleanor's scent made him as randy as an eighteen-year-old. Eleanor had laughed at him, but her laughter hadn't stopped Hart from wanting her touch.

"How do I deal with *my* madness?" Hart's words sounded hollow against the water.

This time, Ian didn't look at him and didn't answer.

"You once said that we were all mad," Hart said after a time. "Remember? On the day we found out about Inspector Fellows, you said that Mac was a genius with painting, Cameron with horses, me with money and politics, and Fellows with solving crimes. You were right. And Father, of course, had the same madness. I think he saw much of himself in you, and that scared him."

"Father is dead. And I said Mac painted like a god."

Hart gave him a wry smile. "Sorry, I don't have your gift for precise memory. But I think my madness is growing. What do I do if I can't stop it?"

Ian didn't look at him. "You will."

"Thank you for your confidence."

"You need to show Eleanor the house," Ian said after another silence.

Hart started. "House? What house?"

"In High Holborn. Mrs. Palmer's house."

Hart gripped the boat's rail. "The devil I do. I never want Eleanor in there again. I'm still angry at you for taking her there. Why did you?"

"Because Eleanor needs to know all about it," Ian said.

"Bloody hell, Ian. Why?"

"The house is you."

What on earth did he mean by that? "No, Ian. No. The house might have been a large part of my life once, but that era is over."

Ian shook his head and kept shaking it. "You need to show Eleanor the house. Once you tell her everything about it, you will know."

"*I* will know?"

"Yes."

"I will know what?" Hart's exasperation grew. "Whether Eleanor can run at double speed to get away from me again?

Whether she'll stop to kick me in the backside before she goes?"

"Yes."

Hart let out his breath again. It didn't steam as much, the morning having grown warmer. "I can't take her there. There are things I still don't want her to know."

"You have to. Eleanor needs to understand you, as Beth understands me."

Ian's jaw tightened as he spoke, his hand as tight on the railing. At least he'd stopped shaking his head like a stubborn mule.

"You're a hard man, Ian Mackenzie."

Ian did not answer.

Tell Eleanor everything.

Angelina Palmer had taken it upon herself to visit Eleanor Ramsay in Scotland a few months into their engagement and tell her about Hart. That he owned the High Holborn house, that he entertained ladies there, that he'd pleasured them in ways well-bred young women could not imagine. Angelina hadn't described things in detail to Eleanor, thank God; but the hinting had been enough.

Hart had deliberately not visited the house and Angelina while he was courting Eleanor, not wanting to be that sort of liar. Feeling virtuous because of this, he'd coaxed Eleanor to surrender her virginity to him.

But Eleanor had awakened something inside Hart, an excitement he'd not felt before or since. He'd wanted to explore it, had explored it as much as he possibly could.

Angelina's motives for revealing her existence had not been to make Eleanor jealous or to convince Hart to return to her. No. Angelina had known as soon as she'd made the decision that her actions would lose her Hart forever. The marriage to Eleanor had been important to Hart, and Hart was not the forgiving sort. But Angelina had done it anyway.

She hadn't gone to Eleanor to reveal Hart's sexual exploits. She'd gone to warn Eleanor of her danger, because Angelina knew exactly what sort of man Hart was on his way to becoming.

And Angelina had been right.

Eleanor's rejection had taken the arrogant Hart unawares.

Astonished and furious, Hart had threatened both Eleanor and her father with dire consequences if Eleanor broke the engagement, because that was the brutal sort of man Hart was learning to be. His father had beaten his lessons into Hart very well.

Hart had never learned how to mitigate his anger or even speak to someone without immediately deciding how to manipulate him. Hart had hated his father but had become much like him, having had no other example to follow.

And so, Hart had no idea how to simply be with a person and, as Mac had admonished him, let things happen. He could have had the chance to learn with Eleanor, but he'd thrown that chance away.

A beam of sun dazzled the water and stabbed into Hart's eyes. When he raised his head, he saw that they were drawing near a lock, the lockkeeper ambling out of his house toward the pumps at the gate.

"I can't tell Eleanor the things I did, Ian," he said.

Ian shot him an impatient look. The approaching lock was far more interesting than complicated conversations with Hart. "You had two sets of rules," Ian said. "One for Mrs. Palmer and one for Eleanor. You think that if you follow the wrong set of rules with Eleanor, it means you don't love her."

Hart opened his mouth to hotly deny this, but the words stuck in his throat. Thoughts he reached for—things he'd been certain of—shattered like glass at his touch.

Ian pushed himself from the gunwale, finished with worrying about Hart's problems. "How many gallons fill the lock per minute, do you think?" he asked.

Without waiting for an answer, Ian turned from Hart and jumped from the boat to the bank. Ian caught up to the man guiding the horse and walked with him in silence, probably busy calculating the depth of the pond and the time the water in it would take to fill the lock.

~

A spring rain began, pouring down in earnest as the canal boat pulled over to the bank. The Romany had steered through the last lock below Hungerford, and now they'd reached the part of the canal that marked the boundary of Cameron's property.

Hart looked up the green field that ran from canal to the

house on the rise and saw that it was full of people. Annoyed, dripping people with umbrellas, most of them Mackenzies.

Not all of them. A tall Scotsman who was *not* a Mackenzie stood very close to Eleanor, holding an umbrella over her head. Hart recognized him—Sinclair McBride, one of Ainsley's many brothers, the one who was the barrister. Hart felt his rage begin to boil as Sinclair bent down to Eleanor to shelter her with the umbrella, and Eleanor smiled serenely up at him.

～

Eleanor watched Hart standing on the deck like a king about to address his subjects. *Bloody man.* She'd been terrified when his lackeys had returned in the middle of the night, saying they'd lost him along the woods by the canal. Only early that morning, when Angelo had ridden up to say that Ian and Hart were safe with his family, had the panic lessened. Now Eleanor was simply angry.

She started forward, but Ainsley's brother Sinclair touched her shoulder. "Best not. It's muddy and you might have a fall."

He was sweet, really. Sinclair McBride, a widower, had arrived with his two children this morning to further fill the nursery. Ainsley had invited him and the rest of her brothers to stay at Waterbury this spring, but thus far, only Sinclair had been able to turn up.

Ian had stepped off the boat. Beth ran to him, despite the mud, and Ian swept her up into a warm embrace. Everyone surrounded them and began talking at once. Demanding to know where Ian had run off to. Why had he worried everyone so? Thank God Hart had found him.

The Romany piled off the boat, children, goats, dogs, men, and women, and trudged to the middle of the rainy field to start setting up tents. Cameron seemed to find this in no way unusual. He began talking to a man with a pipe, and Daniel and Angelo joined them, along with Eleanor's father. Daniel started helping the Romany men stretch canvas over the tents, and the children ran inside them. Sinclair handed Eleanor the umbrella and moved to assist.

Last to leave the boat was a black-clad older lady. Hart assisted her across to the bank, but he did not get off with her.

What was he doing? Hart stood back, like the king Eleanor

had thought of, or better still, a general, watching everyone, waiting to direct them if necessary. He kept his eyes on his brothers, formidable giants with their wives never far from their sides. They all looked happy—Beth, Isabella, and Ainsley laughing at their Mackenzie men but gazing at said men with deep love.

"He needs you."

Eleanor jumped at Ian's voice in her ear. He was beside her, his keen gaze on her, while Beth stood not far away chattering with the older Romany woman.

"Who does?" Eleanor asked Ian. "Hart?" She peered through the rain at the stubborn duke leaning on the rail of the tied-up boat. "Hart Mackenzie needs no one."

Ian's whiskey-colored eyes were dark under the umbrella's shadow. "You're wrong," he said. He turned and trudged away, back through the rain to Beth.

He needs you.

Hart did look so alone. He was watching the family he'd done everything in the world to keep safe, but watching. Not part of them.

Eleanor lifted her already muddy skirt and picked her way down the slope to the bank, mindful of Sinclair's words about slipping. Hart watched her come—she could feel his gaze on her all the way down the field—but he didn't leave the boat to meet her.

Not until she'd reached the canal boat did Hart step to the rail, snatch the umbrella that threatened to turn inside out in the wind, toss it aside, and haul Eleanor across the foot of water between them.

Eleanor landed against him. Hart was soaking wet, his coat open, wet strands of hair against his unshaven face. From behind those strands, his eyes were amber and sharp, alive.

"What are you doing?" Eleanor asked, still angry. "Are you going to weigh anchor and float us away?"

"Angelo's mother asked me to look after the boat. They've come to watch Cameron and Angelo train the horses."

"She meant for you to have one of the staff do it, surely."

"No, she meant me." Hart gazed into the strengthening rain, which obscured the tents on the hill. "Dukes and errand boys are all the same to her. But it doesn't matter. It's quiet here."

Quiet was one thing Hart Mackenzie did not have an abundance of, and Eleanor knew that when he returned to London, he'd have even less.

"Shall I go, then? Leave you in peace looking after your canal boat?"

"No." The answer was abrupt, swift. Hart's hand, heavy and strong, landed on hers. "You're all wet. Let's go inside. I want to show you the boat."

He half guided, half pulled her down the few stairs to the cabin door. Hart wrenched open the swollen wooden door, towed Eleanor through, and shut it again.

The sound of rain turned to a hollow drumming on the roof and a pattering against the windowpanes. This, coupled with the quiet hiss of coals in the little corner stove, was soothing. Eleanor understood Hart's reluctance to leave.

"I've never been on a canal boat before," she said, looking around in delight.

The Romany might be itinerants, but their home was cozy. The tiny stove gave off good heat. Pots and pans hung above the stove, scrubbed gleaming clean, and bunks at the far end were piled with colorful quilts and blankets. The bench that ran along one wall under the windows held embroidered cushions she recognized as Ainsley's work.

"I thought you'd like it," Hart said.

"I take it you had no run-ins with assassins on your jaunt?"

"No."

Just the one word, when she'd been worried to death. "I am speaking lightly of it, because, Hart, I was so scared . . ." She trailed off, her hands balling. She wanted to fling her arms around him, and at the same time, she wanted to beat her fists against his chest. To stop herself from doing either, she folded her arms across her stomach.

She felt Hart's warmth as he came to her, smelled the wet linen of his shirt and damp wool of his coat. Hart slid off the coat and set it aside, then he cupped her elbows with his big hands and drew her against him.

The kiss, when it came, was hungry. No teasing, no playing, no cajoling. A desperate kiss that wanted her.

He needs you.

Eleanor pressed her hands against his wet shirt, feeling his heart racing beneath her touch. His skin was too cold, his mouth, hot as flame.

She pushed at his shirt, the buttons already loose. "You need this off. You'll catch your death."

Hart impatiently shrugged off the shirt and let it fall to the floor. He was bare beneath, no flannels covering his bronzed, tight skin.

He pulled her into the circle of warmth near the stove and drew her up to him again, thumbs opening her mouth. His next kiss was even more fierce, more desperate.

Eleanor's fingers curled into his shoulders as she kissed him back. He kissed her harder, tasting her mouth, licking the rain from her lips. Eleanor ran her hands down his naked back, feeling hot, smooth skin.

Her body was on fire. Eleanor kissed his warm lips, chasing his tongue with her own. She felt the top buttons of her bodice open, then Hart's fingers, easing the placket apart. His palm slid behind her bared neck, strong and warm, holding her.

He broke the kiss to swiftly unbutton the rest of her bodice and peel it down her arms. He didn't pull off the bodice entirely—his eyes darkened as her arms were pinned to her sides by the fabric. Hart growled softly and kissed her again, she lifting her hands as much as she could to place them at his waist. She felt the in and out movement of his breath, the warm wool waistband of his kilt, the hotter skin of the man inside it.

"Eleanor. El." He raised his head, eyes dark in the shadows of his damp hair. The smile, when it came, was sinful. "I keep having visions of you in nothing but your corset."

Eleanor's heart beat faster, a tingle of heat racing through her. "I've been having visions of you in nothing but your kilt. In fact, I have photographs to pore over if necessary."

His smile went wider, and the Hart Mackenzie she'd fallen in love with years ago shone through. "What am I going to do with you, minx?"

"My father sent for some photographic apparatus so he can take pictures of the Berkshire flora. Perhaps he will let me borrow the camera."

Hart stopped, and then his wicked grin returned. "Do your worst. But only . . ." He pulled her bodice all the way off, then slid his hand behind her back and smoothly untied the cord that closed her corset. The laces loosened and spread under his fingers. "Only if you do the same for me."

"Pose for pictures for you? Good heavens, no. I'm far too modest."

The laces came undone, the little straps that held the corset over her shoulders sliding off under Hart's large hands. He leaned close.

"These will be private photographs. Very private. Only you and only I will see them."

"Hmm," she said. "I will think on it."

Hart smiled against her mouth, followed by a lick across her lips. "If you want me in only my kilt, you must agree to the terms."

Eleanor's face heated. "I told you I'd think on it."

"I knew the moment I kissed you in that boathouse that you were a wicked lass. Prim and proper for the world, wild with passion behind closed doors. The perfect lady for me."

"I've only ever been wild with you, Hart. You taught me."

"Did I?" Hart was laughing, hands on her back, nothing between him and her but the thin linen of her camisole. "You were eager to learn."

"You were an interesting . . . instructor."

He smiled, his forehead against hers. "El, you make me young again. You make me . . ."

His smile died with his words. Hart's hands went to her waist, fingers unfastening her skirt and the petticoat beneath. Eleanor's skirts fell—she'd donned no bustle to wander the rainy meadow this morning.

"I make you what?" she whispered.

Hart's warm hands glided to her buttocks, his laughter completely gone. She saw stark need in his eyes, and loneliness, and fear. Fear of many things, all complicated, all too real.

"I can't do this alone," he said. "I need you, El."

She knew he didn't mean for ravishing in a canal boat while the Romany raced off to see Cameron work the horses.

"I . . . *need* . . . you." The words tore from him, this man who never dared voice weakness to anyone.

Eleanor slid off her camisole and twined her arms around Hart's neck.

"I'm here," she said.

~~~

Hart slid his thumb across Eleanor's lower lip, in wonder, as always, at her softness. He was a hard, hard man, and Eleanor was all things warmth and comfort. He'd been a fool to let her walk away.

He drew her up to him and sank himself into another kiss. She tasted like rainwater, heat, and desire.

He'd taught her, yes, he'd taught her. Not everything—not by a long way—but he'd taught her.

Eleanor looked up at him with her warm blue eyes, her passion shining unashamed. He loved that about her—Eleanor had never seen any shame in her need.

Her skirts were on the floor, she standing in nothing but her drawers. Hart smoothed the fabric that cupped her buttocks, linen so fine it was almost silk. She'd obeyed him and gotten new ones.

He ached for her, his cockstand berating him to get on with it. But he did not want to go too fast, did not want to rush. The Romany and Ian had given Hart this gift—a gift of time with Eleanor.

More than that. Eleanor might consider this a stolen moment, but Hart was not going to keep it to a moment. He had to keep her safe from the world, and now from Sinclair bloody McBride. McBride was a handsome Scot with two small children and badly in need of a wife, and here was Eleanor ripe for the plucking. He saw what Ainsley was up to, asking him here.

Hart had to move swiftly, never mind his plans. No more waiting.

He untied the tapes that held her drawers closed and slid his hands inside them. Softness met his fingers, the silk of Eleanor. He circled his thumbs on her skin as he kissed her, then moved one hand to the warmth between her thighs.

She was hot, wet, ready, as needy as Hart was. He moved his fingers, rewarded by her little noise of pleasure as her body loosened. Anything maidenly and resistant in her dissolved and floated away. The prim young spinster vanished, and Eleanor the passionate woman filled her place.

Her breasts were soft, fuller now than when she'd been twenty. Hart leaned down and licked between them, tasting warm, salty skin.

The cabin was narrow and low. Hart didn't have room to sweep Eleanor into his arms and carry her to the nearest bunk, but he guided her back to it, kissing her and touching her all the way.

He lifted her and rested her buttocks on the bunk, stepping between her thighs as he parted them, and slipped her drawers the rest of the way off. Eleanor cupped his face in her hands, her eyes half closed as she waited for what was to come.

Hart unfastened the pin that held his kilt closed and caught the folds as they fell. He pulled the plaid up and draped it across the bunk behind Eleanor.

The bunk was too narrow. It would never hold them. Hart lifted Eleanor again, and their bodies came together, both damp from the rain and slick from the stove's heat.

Hart moved his hands down her spine to her buttocks, smoothing, soothing. He lifted her a little more, and then he was gliding into her, her slick depths welcoming him.

Inside her. *His Eleanor.*

Hart stilled, the sensation of her surrounding him filling him with joy.

"Hart." Her warm breath feathered over his damp skin. She touched his face, smiling a little as she rubbed fingers over his rough whiskers.

Eleanor's red hair was dark with rain, the ringlets soft under his lips. She'd rushed out into the wet without a hat. Typical Eleanor. Impetuous, impatient.

Her nose was gloriously dusted with freckles. Hart kissed one, then another, then another, all the while feeling the sharp joy of being *inside* her. Part of her. She was his.

Hart braced his hand against the cabin wall and thrust up into her. It was awkward in this space, but he did it. *"El."*

His voice grew more grating with each thrust, her body

welcoming him. Hart's fist grew tight against the wall, his head bowing to her neck. Eleanor was pressed firmly against him, her skin to his. Water from his hair trickled down on both of them.

More, *more*. Never stop. Never.

Eleanor let her hands rove his back, gliding down to his buttocks, touching every inch of him. She'd always loved to explore his body, and Hart willingly let her.

He nipped her earlobe where the emeralds had dangled, licked the shell of her ear. His mouth moved to her neck, lips closing to leave a love bite.

El, I've missed you. I've died a little every day without you.

Eleanor tilted her head, letting him taste her. When he raised up again, she lowered her mouth to *his* neck, and he felt the small bite of her teeth, her mouth leaving its mark.

A wave of need rushed at him, slamming into him to carry him away. He knew he was coming, finishing, but he stayed hard inside her, his hand braced on the wall to keep him on his feet. Eleanor's little moans became cries of delight as she reached her own peak.

"Eleanor." Hart closed his eyes and tried to slow himself. Climax meant that it was over, that he'd have to let her go.

No. No. Never.

Hart held on to her, feeling the last of it, the mixture of excitement and lassitude that meant he'd reached a perfect moment.

"I can't do this without you, El." He opened his eyes, hearing the catch in his voice. "I need you."

"Hart . . ."

"Don't go away from me again." The note in his voice was desperation. "I'll never bear it if you go away again."

Tell her everything, Ian had admonished.

I can't. Not until she's mine, not until she can't ever leave me.

Eleanor looked at him with her beautiful blue eyes, her brows together, Eleanor assessing him.

"Please," he said. Dear God, he almost sobbed it. But his heart was hurting. She'd go again, and that would be the end of him.

Eleanor touched his face with gentle fingers. She looked

into his eyes as though she could see into his soul. Eleanor was the only one who could.

"Yes," she said, her voice so soft he almost didn't hear her. "I'll stay."

Hart swallowed, the breath he let out almost a sob. "Thank you," he whispered. "Thank you."

Chapter 14

The boat had drifted. Eleanor emerged from the cabin to find that they were floating in the middle of the wide canal.

"Hart," she called in alarm.

Hart came out, devastatingly handsome in his shirt and kilt, his coat still somewhere below.

A rope stretched through the water between the bow and the bank. When Hart tugged at it, it came loose.

Eleanor put her hands on her hips. "I suppose the great Duke of Kilmorgan couldn't remember to tie up the boat?"

Hart didn't look the least bit ashamed. "My mind was on other things."

Arrogant, sinful, smiling once more. The lonely, terrified man who'd said to her inside the cabin, *I'll never bear it if you go away again,* had vanished. Hart Mackenzie had gotten his own way once more.

A lone rider came along the towpath, the man huddled in a greatcoat against the wind and rain. Hart cupped his hands around his mouth and shouted, "You there! Grab the rope!"

The man looked up, started, and slid off his horse. "Mackenzie? What the blazes are you doing in the middle of the canal?"

"Balls," Hart said. "It's Fleming."

Eleanor peered through the rain and waved. "Please do pull us in, dear Mr. Fleming."

"Don't humor him," Hart growled.

"We need his help, unless you want to float sideways all the way to Hungerford lock. The lockkeeper would laugh at us."

Fleming moved to the rope and pulled it from the water, then started to reel them in, hand over hand. Hart lifted an oar that had been lashed to the cabin and used it to guide the canal boat back to the bank. The boat bumped gently, the canal water still. Hart tied the oar back in place as Fleming fastened the line to a tree stump.

Fleming had his hands out, helping Eleanor to damp land before Hart could reach her. Fleming looked from her to Hart, his dark brows lowering. "What the devil is this, Mackenzie? If you've despoiled her, I'll shoot you like the mangy dog I know you to be."

Hart stepped off the boat behind Eleanor and slid his arm around Eleanor's waist. "Congratulate me, Fleming. Eleanor has just agreed to be my wife."

Eleanor's mouth popped open. Not *exactly* what she'd said. She'd agreed to stay when he'd given her that heartbreaking look and begged her to. In what capacity, they hadn't yet discussed.

Fleming didn't believe it either. His hand went to his pocket, drawing out the silver flask he always seemed to have on hand.

Eleanor knew that David realized quite well what they'd been doing on the boat. Eleanor and Hart were out here alone, the boat drifting. Eleanor had dressed with Hart's help, but her collar was not all the way buttoned, her skirts still crinkled from lying on the floor. Hart was entirely in dishabille. When the wind opened Hart's shirt, the tiny love bites Eleanor had given him were plain to be seen.

Hart did not bother to pull his shirt closed. "What are you doing in Berkshire, Fleming? You're supposed to be minding the store in London."

"I sent you a telegram," David said. "But Wilfred telegraphed back that you'd vanished without a trace, so I thought I'd better come up and help look for you. The vote is tomorrow. Am I right to think that you want to be there for it?"

David spoke almost offhandedly, but there was a sparkle in his eyes. Hart's answering smile bore an animation Eleanor hadn't seen in him in a long time. "And do we have them?"

David's smile was just as triumphant. "Oh, yes. Unless half decide at the last minute to betray us, we do."

"You have what?" Eleanor asked.

She'd always liked that David didn't insist that such discussions were not meant for ladies. He answered readily. "Bums on seats, my dear El. Bums on seats that will vote our way. Enough to overturn Gladstone's bill and wipe him away with a vote of no confidence. It's all over. He'll have to call elections, our party will win a majority, and Hart Mackenzie will be prime minister of Britain, God help us all."

Eleanor's excitement rose. "Good heavens, Hart."

"It has been a long time coming," Hart said. The fire in his eyes belied the calm in his voice.

"But if Mr. Gladstone knows you will defeat him, why would he let it come to the vote?" Eleanor asked.

David answered before Hart could. "Because any more delay at this point makes our victory more certain. If he calls an election tomorrow, he might have a chance to return, although we don't intend to let that happen." David rubbed his hands together. "Hart Mackenzie will be back in Commons, to lead it this time. There are those still stinging from his whiplike wit from back when he was an MP. They breathed a sigh of relief when he took his title and went to the Lords. And now he's returning. Ah, the delight."

"I imagine it will be quite entertaining," Eleanor said. "My father will be certain to watch from the gallery."

"David." Hart said the word without inflection, but Fleming seemed to understand.

"Right. I'll be up at the house, warming away the rain with some of your single malt. I intend to drink large quantities." David caught his horse, mounted, and rode on up the towpath.

"You'll be off to London with him, then," Eleanor said, her voice too bright.

Hart cupped her shoulders, hands warm through her damp bodice. "Yes."

"It's everything you've worked for," she said.

"Yes." He circled his thumbs on her collarbone. "We'll have

the wedding at Kilmorgan. A large, showy affair to satisfy the general public. No eloping for the new prime minister."

Eleanor found it hard to meet his gaze. His eyes blazed hot, determined, Hart the controlling master once again. "You'll be far too busy to have anything to do with weddings at the moment, surely," she tried.

"I'll buy you the most ostentatious wedding jewels I can find and let the newspapers go insane. They can make our reconciliation a grand romance if they want, and we'll give it to them."

"Make a good show of it, you mean," Eleanor said tightly. "It will help you with the election."

"I don't care about that. You'll have to marry me this time, Eleanor. David will be telling the family any moment how he found us, and then we'll never have any peace. They'll know exactly what you and I were doing out here on this boat."

"That's Ian's fault. He sent me to you when he knew you were alone."

"Yes, my devious little brother manipulated things to his satisfaction. But we are stuck with it."

"So, I must marry you to save my reputation?"

Hart stepped close to her. "Your reputation won't be harmed. I'll make certain the knowledge does not go outside the family. But I want you to marry me regardless. I need to take care of you."

"You need to . . ."

"I will take care of you whether you marry me or not, but things will be easier if you are my wife. You need a husband, Eleanor, as much as I need a wife. When your father passes, you'll have nothing. Glenarden will go to a cousin you barely know, and you'll be turned out. What will you do then?"

"I'm proving to be very good at the typing machine." Eleanor tried to make a joke, but Hart did not laugh.

"You will end up in a cheap boardinghouse full of dreary old women," he said. "Prey for any man who decides that a lovely spinster is fair game. Or you'll pass from country house to country house, living with friends, but I know you—you'll feel horribly ashamed and believe you're taking advantage of them."

"When you put it like that, things do sound rather bleak."

"They don't have to be. Once you're a Mackenzie, no one can touch you. Even being betrothed to me will have weight. You'll never have to worry again, El. Neither will your father. And who knows, I might have given you a child today."

Eleanor shook her head. "I did not conceive when we were lovers before, and I am rather long in the tooth now . . ."

"You never know, El. Today was an impulse, but you shouldn't pay for it. Neither should a child. I'd want him to have a name."

Eleanor heard the fervor in his voice. *Hart wants a baby,* she realized in surprise. Her heart warmed.

Hart's hands were firm points on her shoulders, hot in the cold rain. "I will take care of you and any child—my name will take care of you."

Eleanor's mouth was dry, thoughts rising and dying in her head. "Any woman marrying you will have to become a grand society lady, the other half of your political career."

"I know. I know that, El. But I can't imagine anyone who would do better."

A more skeptical woman might think Hart had seduced her today so he could have a hostess to entertain wives of the political gentlemen he needed to woo. But Eleanor hadn't imagined the catch in his voice when he'd said, *I'll never bear it if you go away again,* or the spark in his eyes when he'd a moment ago spoken of the possibility of a child.

She wet her lips. "It is much to ask."

"Yes, it is." Hart cradled her face in his hands, his thumb smoothing across her lower lip. "And I will do everything in my power to make sure you do not regret it."

Eleanor looked into his eyes. She read the certainty of victory in the amber depths, surety that he'd win everything he wanted. And yet, behind it, she saw fear. Hart was poised at a crossroads—from this day forward, his life could go in any direction. And he was afraid.

He was not alone in his fear. Eleanor's throat was tight, her knees weak, her limbs trembling as *her* entire life was swept away by the utterance of a few words.

"I suppose this means Curry has lost his forty guineas," she said.

"Damn his forty guineas." Hart pulled her to him and

kissed her. His hard embrace told Eleanor she'd never get away from him again, and Eleanor, sinking into Hart's wonderful warmth, was unsure she wanted to go.

When Eleanor and Hart reached the house, all was chaos. Romany children ran around the field, in spite of the rain, chasing or being chased by Mackenzie and McBride children. The Mackenzie dogs joined the Romany goats and dogs in the romping, barking or bleating nonstop. The children screamed with a sound that could peel paint from walls.

Fleming came to meet Hart and Eleanor, leading his horse, his flask still out. "Good God, it's a massacre," he said, taking a drink. Hart agreed with him.

The running children saw them and streamed their way, Aimee shouting at the top of her lungs. "Uncle Hart! Aunt Eleanor! Come and see our tent. It's a real Romany tent." The Romany children piled around her, some understanding her English, some not. They smiled up at Hart, black eyes dancing.

Adults came after the children—Mac, Daniel, Ian, Ainsley stopping to lift and cradle her crawling daughter, Gavina, named for the child Ainsley had lost. Ian's son, Jamie, saw his father, waddled determinedly toward him, and threw his arms around Ian's leg.

Ian's eyes softened from his usual distant stare to focus on his son. He smoothed the boy's hair, then let Jamie hang on to his boot as he walked, slowly, toward Hart. Jamie laughed, loving the game.

"What's happened?" Ainsley asked, shielding Gavina from the rain. "Something's happened, Eleanor. Tell."

Ian stopped next to David and lifted Jamie, both to keep him away from Fleming's horse's hooves and to let Jamie pet the beast's nose.

"Eleanor will marry Hart," Ian said.

A huge smile blossomed on Ainsley's face as Eleanor's mouth popped open. "How on earth do you know that, Ian Mackenzie?" Eleanor asked.

Ian didn't answer. Jamie went on petting the horse with his tiny hand.

"True?" Daniel demanded.

"Sadly," Fleming answered. "I'm an unfortunate witness."

"Next month," Hart said in clipped tones. "At Kilmorgan." He was very aware of Eleanor's hand in the crook of his arm, her grip tightening as he spoke.

"Next *month*?" Ainsley said, eyes wide. "That's very little time. Isabella will be incensed. She'll want a grand wedding."

Mac laughed out loud. "Good on you, Eleanor. You fixed him at last."

"That's twenty pounds you owe me, Uncle Mac," Daniel said.

"And me, Mac Mackenzie." Ainsley hoisted her daughter and made to turn away. "And twenty you owe Ian, and Beth. Teach you to bet against Eleanor."

Mac kept laughing. "I am happy to lose. But I truly thought you'd give him the boot, El. He is such a bastard, after all."

"She's not at the altar yet," Fleming said. "Double or nothing she comes to her senses before then?"

Mac waved him away, still grinning. "Learned my lesson. Never wager against anything that depends on Hart Mackenzie. He's devious and underhanded, and he gets his way every time."

"I say he won't," Fleming said in his lazy drawl.

Daniel pointed at him. "Done. I'll take that wager. I say Eleanor gets him to the altar."

Hart ignored them all. He turned Eleanor to him and pressed a casual kiss to her lips. Marking her as his in front of family, friends, and rivals.

Ian alone stayed quiet. But the look he sent Hart—one of determined satisfaction—unnerved Hart a bit. Ian Mackenzie was a man who always got what he wanted, and sometimes Hart wasn't entirely sure *what* Ian wanted. But he knew he'd find out, and that Ian would win, whatever it was.

⁂

Gladstone lost his control of the government. In a loud victory, Hart's coalition, led by David Fleming in Commons, defeated Gladstone's weakly supported bill wholeheartedly. Gladstone, frowning his formidable frown, saw nothing for it but to dissolve Parliament and call for elections.

That same night, a brick crashed through Hart's front room window in his Grosvenor Square house. That brick had a note wrapped around it, which proclaimed that the Duke of Kilmorgan was a marked man to the Fenians.

Hart tossed the paper into his desk drawer and told his majordomo to order the window repaired.

He was not so foolish as to dismiss the threat, however. He took double the guards when he went out anywhere in London and sent for Inspector Fellows. Eleanor, at least, was safely in Berkshire.

"Sit down," Hart said irritably when Fellows arrived in Hart's study in answer to his summons. "Don't stand there as though you have a policeman's baton shoved up your backside. You make me nervous."

"Good," Lloyd Fellows said. He took the chair but sat with his back upright, looking in no way obedient.

While Cameron, Mac, and Ian had accepted Fellows as one of their own without much fuss, Hart and Fellows still circled each other warily. They were about the same age, resembled each other, and both had worked very hard to get where they were in their own worlds.

"I understand that felicitations are in order," Fellows said. The newspapers had blared it, even though the official announcement had not yet appeared. *The Duke of K—will wed the daughter of a scholarly peer and take over England at the same time,* one newspaper declared. Another said, *The Scottish duke will marry his first sweetheart after waiting more than a decade. To be sure, one will never be able to say that they married in haste, repented at leisure.* And other nonsense.

"Which means I am too busy to deal with these kinds of threats." Hart handed Fellows the paper that had come through his window the night before.

Fellows took it gingerly and read it, brows rising. "Not much to go on. No one's made much headway on the shooter either, I regret to say."

"Doesn't matter. It's Irishmen angry at a Scotsman, and I know finding them is a long shot. What I want is for you to keep them away from me. And on no account let them, or anyone else for that matter, touch my family."

"A tall order. You mean you want a bodyguard."

"I have bodyguards. I've left three to watch over Eleanor, and she's with my brothers, who will take care of her for now. But I need to go about my business without hindrance. You're canny, Fellows, and resourceful. You'll do it."

"You have a high regard for my ability," Fellows said dryly.

"You pursued Ian and me for five years with a ruthlessness that would have made our father proud."

"But I was wrong," Fellows pointed out.

"So was I, in that case. This is where we are alike. When we are clearheaded, nothing can stop us. When we let emotion overcome us, we see nothing. I was blinded by worry for Ian and could not see the truth." Hart stopped. "I still am."

Fellows studied the paper again. "I take your point. I will see what I can do."

Hart leaned back in his chair, lacing his hands behind his head. "You're invited to the wedding, by the way. Isabella will send you a formal invitation."

Fellows tucked the note into his pocket. "Are you certain you want me there?"

"It matters not what I want, or what you want. If you don't come, Beth and Isabella, Ainsley and Eleanor will be most displeased. They will tell me so. Repeatedly."

Fellows relaxed enough to laugh. "The great duke made nervous by his sisters-in-law and wife-to-be?"

"You've met them. Only very strong women can take living with Mackenzies, and so when one of us finds one . . ." He pretended to shudder.

"Your brothers seem pleased with themselves," Fellows said. "And you are to wed your former fiancée. You should be the happiest man in the world."

"I am." Hart ignored the tightening in his chest as he said this. He'd coerced Eleanor into agreeing the same way he'd cornered Gladstone into a fight before the man was ready.

"You look it," Fellows said without inflection. "I will be the only bachelor left. No wife to greet me on my return home, no sons to guide my doddering footsteps when I'm gray."

"That is up to you. I imagine one of my sisters-in-law could find you a match if they put their minds to it."

Fellows raised his hand. "No, no."

"Be careful. They are determined women."

Fellows nodded, then they both fell silent, uncertain how to end the conversation. They had once been enemies, they'd not yet become friends, and they were still not entirely comfortable with each other.

"You know, Fellows . . ." Hart began.

"No." Fellows stood up, and Hart got to his feet with him. "I know what you are going to say. Do not offer me a post in the great Mackenzie empire. I am happy with the job I have."

Hart didn't ask how Fellows knew he'd been about to propose that Fellows work for Hart personally, to be in charge of keeping the Mackenzie family safe. The two men thought too much alike.

"I'll help you, for Lady Eleanor's sake," Fellows went on. "But understand this—I worked a long time to become an inspector, I enjoy being a policeman, and I'll not give up my career because you beckon."

Hart raised his hands. "Well and good. But, if ever you need it, the offer stands."

"Thank you." Fellows nodded once and turned to leave.

"Wait, Fellows. I need to ask you a question."

Fellows turned back, trepidation in his stance. He wanted to be elsewhere, that stance said, but he waited politely.

"How would you trace a letter?" Hart asked. "Find out who sent it to you, I mean?"

Fellows blinked at the question, then considered. "I'd have a look at the envelope. Find the postman who delivered it, trace the letter's steps backward. Why? Have you been receiving threatening letters in the post?"

"No," Hart said quickly. Fellows's eyes narrowed, scenting the half lie. "Suppose I know the city from which the letter originated? Edinburgh, say?"

"Ask questions at the post office there. Station yourself outside said post office and watch to see if that person returns to send another."

"Sounds tedious."

"Most policing is tedious, Your Grace. Tedious, hard work."

"So it seems. Thank you for your help, Fellows. And when you receive Isabella's invitation to my wedding, for God's sake, answer that you'll attend."

Fellows gave him a mirthless smile. "I long to say no, and watch the fireworks go off around you."

"They'd go off around you too. Don't think they wouldn't. The ladies would be disappointed, and you'd never hear the end of it."

"Hmm. Then I'll respond correctly."

"See that you do."

Fellows nodded again, and took his leave.

The High Holborn house was as quiet and dusty as it had been a few weeks ago when Hart had found Eleanor there. He conceded that Eleanor was right about the fact that the house might hold a clue to whoever was sending the photographs. That did not mean, however, that he'd let her back in here.

Hart stole a few hours away from election hysteria a few days after his meeting with Fellows to take his coach to High Holborn and enter the house alone.

Ian wanted Hart to tell Eleanor all about his life here. Hart realized that was why Ian had let her come here in the first place. She should know all of Hart, Ian had intimated, down to the bottom of his grimy soul.

Hart stood in the bedroom filled with jumbled furniture, where Eleanor had busily searched. He remembered her red gold hair under the pillbox hat, the veil that drooped over her eye, her maddening but warm smile.

"I can't do it, Ian," he said out loud.

Hart was not ashamed of his proclivities, or what he'd done in games of pleasure. But he thought of how Eleanor had looked at him on the canal boat, with desire in her eyes, and trust, and languid delight. He needed nothing more, he thought.

Why shouldn't that be enough, Ian Mackenzie?

You need to show Eleanor the house. Once you tell her everything about it, you will know.

No. Ian was wrong. Some things were better left buried.

He quickly made his search, discovered nothing, quit the house for Bond Street, and bought Eleanor the largest diamond necklace he could find.

～～⌒

Eleanor's wedding day dawned fair and clear, a soft Scottish April morning, the only clouds well beyond the hills surrounding the Kilmorgan estate.

Eleanor stood in her room while Isabella, Beth, and Ainsley dressed her from the skin out in wedding finery. Silk camisole and drawers, new corset with pretty pink bows down the front, a long bustle to hold the many yards of wedding satin, a silk bodice that hugged Eleanor's shoulders and buttoned snugly up the back. Seed pearls and lace adorned the bodice, and yards and yards of cascading ruffles and lace spilled down the front of the skirt. The skirt caught in a gentle pouf over the bustle, with roses, both silk and real, adorning it. From there the fabric flowed to the ground, ending in a three-foot train covered with seed pearls and lace.

Maigdlin smiled as she put another pin into Eleanor's glossy red hair. "You're pretty as a picture, lass—my lady. Pretty as a picture."

"Absolutely beautiful." Isabella stood back, hands clasped, and surveyed her work. "I want to throw my arms around you and eat you up, but I spent two hours getting you to look like this, El, so I will refrain."

"Hugs afterward," Ainsley said cheerfully. She sat on the bed, doing last-minute sewing on Eleanor's veil. "And wedding cake—a nice, tasty one with plenty of currants and candied orange. On the happiest day of your life, you should enjoy your cake."

The happiest day of her life. Eleanor's throat was dry, and a cold pain had formed in her stomach.

She'd barely seen Hart since the heartbreaking morning in the canal boat, and the happy celebration with the family and the Romany later.

Hart had returned to London immediately with David to overturn Parliament while Isabella had swept Eleanor, Beth, and Ainsley into the most hurried, intense, and agitated planning Eleanor had encountered in her life. No expense to be spared, nothing too extravagant—but tasteful, everything had to be perfectly tasteful. Nothing ostentatious or vulgar for the new Duchess of Kilmorgan.

Eleanor had seen Hart alone only once since then, when he'd returned to Berkshire for a day and given her the ring. Eleanor twisted it on her finger now, the diamonds and sapphires catching the light, the same ring he'd given her the first time. She'd thrown this at him in the garden of Glenarden the day Eleanor had sent him packing.

"I thought you'd given this to Sarah," she'd said as Hart slid the cool band onto her finger.

Hart's voice had gone quiet, his warm hand cradling hers. "I only ever gave it to you. I bought a new one for Sarah. This ring belonged to my mother."

"Like the earrings." Those reposed in Eleanor's jewel box, wrapped carefully in tissue.

"Exactly. She'd be pleased with you."

Eleanor thought of the gentlewoman who must have felt lost and alone in the family of unruly boys and men. At least the duchess would have had no shame in her sons, had she lived to see them grow up.

"I'm happy to wear it for her," Eleanor said.

"Wear it for me too, damn it." Hart turned her hand over and kissed her fingertips. "Try to look happy that we're marrying at last."

"I *am* happy." And she was. But . . .

Hart had grown so *distant*. He was busy and preoccupied, true, because of everything happening in London. But she'd thought, that rainy morning on the bank of the canal, that she'd at last reached the real Hart buried under layers of pain and heartache.

She had found him, she knew it. But then he'd gone again.

Eleanor had looked over their clasped hands and the sparkling ring, straight into his eyes. *I'll not be your perfect wife, Hart Mackenzie, obeying you because it's my duty. I'll search until I find you, and I'll make you stay this time. I swear this.*

The wedding took place in the ballroom. Isabella had not wanted to take a chance with the changeable weather to have the ceremony in the garden, and the family chapel was too small. But as the weather had stayed clement, she'd ordered all the doors opened, and a breeze from the famous Kilmorgan gardens wafted up and into the house.

The Scottish minister waited at one end of the room, and the rest of the ballroom overflowed with guests. Isabella, happy that at least one of the Mackenzie brothers was having a proper wedding, had invited the world. Peers of the realm, ambassadors, minor royalty, and aristocrats from every European country, Highland lairds and heads of clans, and The Mackenzie himself with his wife, sons, daughters, and grandchildren.

Local people and friends of the family filled out the rest: David Fleming, Ainsley's brothers, Isabella's sister and mother, Lloyd Fellows. Lord Ramsay's friends and colleagues, who ranged from Scottish ghillies to learned professors and the head of the British Museum. Rounding them out were Eleanor's girlhood friends with their husbands. The Mackenzie children and the two McBride children had been allowed to come, supervised by Miss Westlock and Scottish nannies in the back.

The front corner of the room had been partitioned off with chairs and velvet ropes. Behind this barricade sat the Queen of England herself. She was in black, as usual, but wore a plaid ribbon pinned to her veil, and her daughter Beatrice was in Scots plaid.

In deference to the queen, everyone stood.

Every person in the room, including the queen, turned to stare as Eleanor entered on her father's arm. Eleanor halted for an instant, all those eyes on her unnerving.

They were speculating—why had Eleanor Ramsay changed her mind after so many years and agreed to marry Hart Mackenzie? And why had he decided that a spinster of thirty-odd years, daughter of an impoverished and absentminded earl, was a better match than the quantity of eligible ladies in Britain? A marriage of convenience—it had to be.

"The best thing is to ignore them," Earl Ramsay whispered to Eleanor. "Let them think what they want and pay no attention. I've been doing that for years."

Eleanor dissolved into laughter and kissed the earl on the cheek. "Dear Father. Whatever would I do without you?"

"Muddle along, I expect. Now let's get you married off so I can go home in peace."

Thinking of her father returning to Glenarden alone—with Eleanor not there to take tea with him, to listen to him read from the newspapers, to discuss bizarre and esoteric topics with him—made her eyes fill. Though she reminded herself that her marriage ensured that her father could go on writing his obscure books and eating scones with his tea in a well-repaired house, saying good-bye to him would hurt.

Eleanor lifted her chin, following her father's advice about ignoring everyone, and she and her father walked forward.

Eleanor swished past them all in her glorious dress, following Aimee, who scattered rose petals along the way. There was no music, Isabella declaring that it was not in the best of taste. The orchestra would play afterward.

Isabella, Beth, and Ainsley stood in the front row near the queen, all three radiant and smiling at Eleanor. On the other side of the aisle, mirroring them, stood Mac, Cameron, and Daniel, tall and formidable in kilts and black coats, the plaid of the Mackenzies swathing their shoulders. They were proud and handsome, with eyes of various shades of amber—Daniel and Cameron, the same height now, looked heartbreakingly alike. Mac reached around the earl and clasped Eleanor's shoulder, gladness and strength pouring through his touch.

At the very front of the room, standing to one side of the minister, stood Ian Mackenzie, Hart's second, also dressed in kilt and plaid. Ian glanced once at Eleanor before his gaze was pulled back to that which he liked to look at most: his wife.

Next to Ian, Hart. Hart's gaze fell on Eleanor, and the world went away.

He wore his kilt and plaid, the ducal sash of the Kilmorgans across his chest. He'd brushed back his dark red hair, which emphasized his hard, handsome face, honed with time and the brutal decisions he'd had to make. Ian at Hart's side was as handsome as his brother, but Hart commanded the room.

Hart had won. Everything. The dukedom, the nation, his wife.

Eleanor curtseyed to the queen, and her father bowed, then the earl relinquished Eleanor, looking quite cheerful about it, to Hart.

She whispered to Hart as he took her hand, "Don't look so bloody pleased with yourself."

Hart's answer was a smile, wicked and swift.

The ceremony began. Hart stood like a rock at Eleanor's side as the minister droned the service in a thick Scots accent. The room was warm from the heat of pressing bodies, and droplets of perspiration slid from under Eleanor's veil and down her cheek.

When the minister asked whether anyone knew of a reason why Eleanor and Hart could not marry, Hart turned and glared down the room so intensely that Daniel and Mac both chuckled. No one answered.

The ceremony was far too short. Eleanor found herself saying her vows, promising to give herself entirely to Hart and to let him worship her body, in sickness and health, in good times and terrible ones, through thick and thin, forever and ever, amen. Hart's smile when he cupped her face in his hands to kiss her was triumphant.

Eleanor Ramsay was married, and now the Duchess of Kilmorgan. The orchestra played, and over it, Eleanor heard Daniel shout, "That's forty guineas you owe me, Fleming."

David shrugged, looking none too worried, and pulled out a sheaf of banknotes.

Quite a lot of money seemed to be changing hands. The three Mackenzie men were the worst, but even Patrick Mc-Bride, Ainsley's oldest brother, was collecting banknotes, and so—the cheek of her—was Ainsley. Daniel seemed to have placed the most bets, followed by Mac, who had switched sides and wagered that Eleanor would see Hart fairly married.

"I ought to have formed a pool," Eleanor said to Hart. "I might have won a bundle."

Before Hart could turn Eleanor and parade her back down the room, Ian stepped close and touched Eleanor's elbow. "Thank you," he whispered, and then he was gone, back to Beth and to scoop up his children.

Hart propelled Eleanor through the parted crowd, his arm around her as though he'd never let go of her. His pace was animated, his eyes sparkling.

As they cleared the crowd at the back of the room, a youth darted in through the open French windows. Eleanor saw everything in slow motion, as the lad, perhaps twelve or so and wearing horse boy's livery that looked too large for him, stared at Hart in rage and then absolute terror. The boy reached a hand into his open coat, brought out a revolver, and fired it straight at Hart.

Chapter 15

Eleanor screamed and shoved Hart out of the way, hard enough to make him let go of her. She heard the roar of the pistol, smelled the acrid scent of gunpowder, felt herself falling, heard Hart swearing. His voice was the last thing she remembered as she succumbed to pain, then numbness.

When she swam to consciousness again, she found herself on the floor, Hart on top of her, Daniel and Cameron on top of *him*. There was shouting, crying, cursing.

Hart cupped Eleanor's face in his hands, gaze searching, eyes filled with fear. "El."

I'm perfectly all right, Eleanor tried to say. She had no energy to form the words. She looked down at her beautiful wedding gown and saw that it was scarlet with blood. *Oh, dear. Isabella will be so annoyed.*

"Eleanor, stay still." Hart's voice was harsh.

Cam and Daniel got to their feet. Cameron bellowed orders at the top of his lungs, the sound hurting her head, and Daniel dashed away.

Eleanor touched Hart's chest—whole, no blood. Thank God.

"I thought he hit you." Eleanor's words came out a slur. She tried to push Hart away, but her hands were too weak.

"Don't move." Hart lifted her and cradled her against his chest. "El, I'm so sorry."

But Hart hadn't had the revolver. That boy had fired the shot. *So young, so young . . . Poor lad.*

Lord Ramsay flung himself on his knees on her other side, his faced creased with terrible worry. "Eleanor. My sweet little Eleanor."

Hart looked up at the ring of faces surrounding them, singling out Cameron, who'd returned, it seemed. "Tell me you have him. Tell me you got the bastard."

Cameron nodded grimly. "Fellows is on him. He and the constable are taking him to the village lockup."

"No, I want him here." Hart's voice cut through the noise. "Put him in my study and hold him there."

Cameron didn't argue. He nodded once and pushed away, his big body parting the crowd.

"How did he get past you?" Hart was bellowing to his men, and really, Eleanor did have a headache.

He was just a boy. Who notices a boy sent to hold the horses?

Eleanor heard them answering Hart, but dizziness spun the room about her, and she had to close her eyes. The next time she opened them, Isabella, Beth, and Ainsley hovered over her.

"Let us take her, Hart," Beth was saying. "She needs looking after."

Hart didn't want to let Eleanor go. He held Eleanor on his lap, against his chest, great rage on his face. His eyes were wet, though, making the golden light in them glitter.

Eleanor tried to reach for him, to comfort him, but her hand fell back. *Don't worry, Hart. They simply need to help me fix my dress. It will be all right.*

Her words came out a mumble, which worried her. Beth shoved a glass under her nose. "Drink this."

Eleanor obeyed because she was suddenly very thirsty. The water tasted wrong, but she drank. It slid down her throat, and her limbs went limp.

We should go and greet our guests now, she tried to say. *Isabella's planned everything so carefully . . .*

When Eleanor woke again, she was lying flat on her back in bed, her left arm stiff and hot. Her fine wedding dress was gone, and she was in her nightgown. From the way the light slanted through the windows, it was late afternoon.

She threw the covers off in panic. Today was her wedding day. Why hadn't Maigdlin or Isabella woken her? She had dreamed of the wedding—the crowd, the queen, Hart fine in his plaids, his eyes holding triumph.

Eleanor sat up, but her head spun so much that she fell back to the pillow. After taking a few deep breaths, she lifted her head again, carefully this time.

She discovered that her left arm was wrapped, wrist to shoulder, in a tight bandage. Eleanor stared at it in surprise. No wonder it felt so odd.

The arm's soreness cleared the fog of sleep, and Eleanor remembered. She'd been walking back down the aisle with Hart, a married lady, when the lad in a horse boy's livery had darted through the windows, aimed the pistol, and fired. In panic, she'd shoved Hart aside. The bullet must have hit her as she and Hart tumbled to the floor.

She lifted her arm, and pain rippled through it like fire.

Her cry brought hurrying footsteps, then Maigdlin. "My lady, are you all right? Do you need more laudanum? I'll fetch it."

"No." Eleanor lay down again, being careful not to move too quickly. "I don't want to sleep. Where is Hart? Is he all right?"

"His Grace is in his study, my lady. I mean, Your Grace. He's been shouting something fierce. The constable took that boy with the pistol away, even though His Grace told him not to, and now His Grace is threatening to sack him if he don't get the boy back here. But the constable says he answers to the magistrate, and now His Grace wants the magistrate here too. And the guests don't know what to do—about half have left, but the others are staying the night here, and it's a right mess." Maigdlin related the tale with relish. "His Grace is torn up about the bullet hitting you. Right off his head, he is."

"It grazed my arm. I remember now."

Maigdlin's eyes rounded. "No, Your Grace. It went right through. Doctor says it's a mercy it didn't lodge in the bone or rip open all your blood vessels. Went clean through and out the other side. He says if you hadn't dodged just right, it would have gone straight through your heart."

"Oh." Eleanor looked at her arm again. The revolver had been much too heavy for the boy's thin hands. He must not have been able to aim it properly. "What about my dress?" Eleanor bit her lip. She thought of its froths of lace and roses, and felt a pang of loss. It had been beautiful, and she and Hart hadn't yet posed for the wedding photograph.

"Their ladyships are working on it now. Lady Cameron says you'll want the gown, but she keeps crying over it. So do the other two."

"Tell their ladyships I will be perfectly fine, and that they must save that dress. Now, help me into my dressing gown. I'm going downstairs to speak to my husband."

My husband. How readily the words came to her tongue.

"His Grace says you're not to get out of bed. Not for any reason."

"His Grace is too certain that I will obey his orders. Now, help me."

Maigdlin's worried face creased with a sunny smile. "Yes, Your Grace."

~

The magistrate finally crumbled under Hart's commands. Hart's pugilist footmen and the constable dragged the young man back to Kilmorgan, with Fellows accompanying them, and brought the culprit to Hart's study.

The constable dropped the lad into the chair in front of Hart's desk. It was a comfortable, padded chair, reserved for Hart's important guests. Mackenzie ancestors glared down from the walls in the huge room, the deceased Mackenzies all swathed in the same dark blue and green plaid as Hart. Their gazes seemed to fix on the young man cringing before them.

Hart leaned back against his desk and looked at him too. Hart was still tight with rage, the bile of it in his mouth. When he'd seen the blood, and Eleanor falling, he'd experienced a horrible helplessness he never wanted to feel again, a knowledge that, no matter how hard he fought, he would lose her. Now, this instant. As he had Sarah, as he had Graham.

The assassin was a child. He couldn't be more than thirteen, fourteen at most. He had a clear white face, his skin almost translucent, the hue of Celtic tribes from northern Ireland or the Hebrides. He had black hair badly hacked short, eyes like blue glass, ruddy cheeks, and an expression of abject terror.

Hart said nothing. He'd discovered long ago that silence made a fine weapon. Forcing someone to wait and wonder what Hart was thinking gave him the upper hand from the outset. The youth stared back at him, his defiance and bravado evaporating under Hart's gaze.

"What's your name?" Hart asked.

"He won't give it," the constable said from the far end of the room. "Not even when we hit him."

Hart ignored him. "What is your name, lad?"

"Darragh." His voice was faint, scratchy, but with an unmistakable lilt.

"Irish, are you?"

"Erin go bragh."

Hart left the desk and moved to a chair that stood against a window, the plainest seat in the room. He carried the chair back to the desk, set it down, and sat on it himself, leaning forward, arms on thighs.

"There are no Fenians in this room," he said. "None of your mates, or the boys you grew up with, or the men who took you in and gave you the gun." A new, American-made Smith and Wesson revolver, which must have cost a pretty penny. "Right now the only thing between yourself and the constable—and my men, who I guarantee are itching to beat you into oblivion—is me."

Some of Darragh's bravado returned. "I'm not afraid of them."

"I would be. My men used to be prizefighters, some of the finest Britain has produced. Most are bare-knucklers, and they aren't worried about following rules. The matches they fought weren't always legal."

Darragh looked more uncertain, but his chin stayed up. "Ye deserve to die."

Hart nodded. "Many people think so. Some people want me dead because they've hated my family so long that it's tradition, but I admit I have more enemies than friends. Why do *you* think I deserve to die?"

"All th' stinkin' English deserve to die until the Irish are free."

"I'm not English, and I happen to agree."

"Ye don't. You threw out th' only Englishman who was pulling for us, tore Irish Home Rule to pieces."

"Is that so, lad? Tell me what the Irish Home Rule bill is."

The boy wet his lips and flicked his gaze away. "English words. They don't mean nothing now."

"No one bothered to explain it to you, did they? They shoved a gun at you and told you that you'd fight for the glory of Ireland. The gist of Home Rule has been in every newspaper every day for the last few years. All you need to know about it has been there." Hart waited until Darragh's gaze swiveled to his again. "But you can't read, can you?"

"Ye deserve to die," Darragh repeated.

"Your friends sent you on a fool's errand. They knew you'd get caught, whether you succeeded in shooting me or not, and probably killed. Here is another English word for you. *Expendable*."

"They didn't send me! I was honored to come."

"Did you know the Queen of England would be here?"

A mute shake of the head.

"Your friends would have known. You'd never have made it out of this village alive, Darragh. You still might not. People are very touchy about those who put the queen in danger. Me—I'm just a politician and a right bastard. No one would miss me. But though the queen might be the devil to you, plenty in England, and even Scotland, love her and are very protective of her. If they thought for one moment that you'd come here to shoot the *queen*, they'd have ripped you apart on the spot. You'd never have made it to trial, let alone the gallows."

"I'd have died with honor." It was a whisper.

"No, you'd have died in terror and humiliation. You are finished. Your friends will find the next eager young man ready to do their bidding and buy another pistol for him. Your sacrifice has been for nothing."

"That's not true. Ye don't know 'em!"

"I might not know their names, but I know men like them. I used to be the same, once. I thought the Scots could arm themselves—with me to lead them—and wrestle Scotland back from the English. Then I realized that the power of words was much stronger. I put away my sword, and here I am."

"You're a lying bastard. Ye joined them."

"No, I didn't. They only think I did." Hart allowed himself a smile, then he wiped away the smile and sat forward again. "The trouble is, I can forgive you for shooting at me, Darragh. Both times. That was you in London, wasn't it?"

Darragh nodded, and swallowed.

"I understand why you did it. Once upon a time, I might have tried the same. But what I can't forgive you for is shooting my wife."

At the change in tenor of Hart's voice, Darragh's look of fear returned. Hart saw him understand that now Hart's rage was personal.

"It wasn't meant to happen—"

"Tell me who your friends are, Darragh. They're the ones to blame for my wife lying on the floor in a pool of blood, in her wedding dress, no less. They won't escape my wrath."

Darragh gasped for breath. "I'll never tell ye—"

The lad's words were cut off by a commotion outside the study's back door. The study had a grand entrance for intimidating guests and then a smaller door behind the desk, which led to an anteroom and back halls. Someone was arguing with the guard Hart had stationed at the rear door, someone female, with a very determined voice.

"Excuse me," Hart said and rose.

Darragh stayed in his chair, clutching its arms, while Hart walked to the door.

"You jolly well will let me in," came Eleanor's voice. "He is my husband, and he's in there with a killer. Stand aside at once."

The guard mumbled something, and Hart yanked open the door.

Eleanor, standing a foot away, transferred her glare to Hart. She wore a thick brocade dressing gown, her arm in a sling, with her hair hanging in a fat red gold braid over her shoulder. Though her face was white with pain, she tried to walk past Hart and into the study.

Hart put his arm across the door. "Eleanor, go back to bed."

"No, indeed, Hart Mackenzie. I want to know what is going on in there."

"I have the matter well in hand." He gave her a severe look, but his heart beat swiftly with worry. Eleanor's color was high, her eyes too bright. She might recover from the wound, but he could still lose her to fever, as he'd lost Sarah and his son. "Go back upstairs. I will tell you about it later."

Eleanor returned his stare for a few more seconds, then with a speed an injured woman should not have possessed, Eleanor ducked under his arm and hurried into the study. Hart stifled a curse and went after her.

"Good heavens." Eleanor regarded Darragh in surprise. "How old are you, lad?"

"This is Darragh," Hart said, coming to stand by her side. "He was telling me how he didn't mean to shoot you."

Eleanor ignored him. "Darragh what? Surely you have a surname."

Darragh gazed at her in defiance, but under Eleanor's unwavering stare, he wilted. "Fitzgerald, ma'am."

"Where are you from?"

"Ballymartin. Near Cork."

"Gracious. You are a long way from home."

"Yes, ma'am."

"Does your mum know about the Fenians? And the revolver?"

"Me mum's dead."

Eleanor sank down into the chair Hart had vacated. Hart had chosen it because the seat was a little higher than that of the soft chair in which Darragh sat. He found the setup perfect for keeping himself a little above whatever person he questioned, perfect for implying that personal comfort was of no concern to him. He could interrogate whoever he needed to all night, the hard chair said.

Eleanor cared nothing for any of that. She simply saw a chair and sat upon it.

"I'm sorry, lad," she said. "Do you have other family?"

"Me sister. She married and went to America."

"Why didn't you go to America with her?" She sounded interested.

"Not enough money, ma'am."

"I see. I do understand what happened, Darragh. You were trying to shoot Hart, and you hit me by mistake. I imagine it was difficult to aim in all the confusion, and I tried to push Hart away. I don't much blame you for wanting to shoot Hart, because he can be devilishly irritating, but I am a bit put out with you for ruining my wedding, not to mention my wedding gown. My sisters-in-law worked their fingers off to make everything perfect, and they are quite distressed."

Darragh's anger returned. "Do ye think that matters to me?"

"It matters, lad," Eleanor said, skimming her fingers over her bandage. "Everything matters. Everything you do touches someone in some way, even though you might not understand that until later. You raised a pistol, but even before you fired it, you changed the life of every person in the room. You introduced them to fear, to uncertainty, to the fact that in a place they felt safe, there was sudden danger. There were children in that room, babies. By the bye, you should be glad that Ian Mackenzie has been restrained by his brothers, because he was ready to tear your head off for endangering his little boy and girl. You'd better hope he doesn't get out of his room."

Darragh swallowed. "Ian Mackenzie. He's th' crazy one?"

"Everyone should want to be mad like Ian. But even Ian would see—if he stopped trying to kill you long enough to notice—that you are a child yourself."

"I'm no child! Fucking English."

"Watch your mouth, boy," Hart growled.

"Yes, you are a child," Eleanor said, undisturbed by the interruption. "And, by the way, I'm not English at all. I'm Highland Scots through and through." She flowed into the broadest Highland accent Hart had ever heard. "Me family hasnae one drop o' English blood in it."

"You're a liar, then." Darragh's eyes glittered. "I was told all about *you*. Your great-grandmother made a whore of herself to an Englishman so they'd drop a title on her get. That's why your dad's an earl. You're as English as they are."

To Darragh's surprise—and Hart's too—Eleanor burst into laughter.

"Oh, my, is *that* story still in circulation? People believe anything, don't they? Let me tell you the true story, laddie."

She leaned forward, catching and holding Darragh's attention, her red braid swinging.

"First, it was my great-*great*-grandmother. Her husband, her brothers, her father, and her husband's brothers all went off to fight the Butcher at Culloden. There, her family died to the last man."

The Scots accent smoothed out, though a trace of it lingered.

"All that was left was my great-great-grandmother, Finella, alone in that big house. Well, the English saw the fine landholding of Glenarden and claimed that since all the menfolk were dead, it was unoccupied, ripe for plucking. My great-great-grandmother said it wasnae empty at all—Scots land can be passed to the women, and since her husband had been laird, *she* was now laird, and the land was hers.

"The English didn't like that, I can tell you. Highlanders were a conquered people and should bow down. And here was this lass, younger than I am now, defying the English and saying the place belonged to her and her heirs. Well, one English colonel said, *Marry me, and I'll live here, you can stay, and our children will inherit the land.* My great-great-grandmother, she thought about this, then she said *all right,* and the man moved in. The English were pleased with this colonel for making Finella do their bidding, and they made him an earl, calling him Earl Ramsay, which had been Finella's surname from her father. But very soon after the wedding, the man died, and my great-great-grandmother had a baby, a son, and that son became earl."

Darragh opened his mouth, but Eleanor held up her hand. All the men in the room, including Inspector Fellows, were hanging on Eleanor's words, Hart saw, waiting for the end of the story.

"What Finella didn't say—the secret she kept to her grave, telling only her son when he was old enough to understand—was that she'd felt the baby quicken in her after his father went off to war. He was her Scottish husband's son, and Finella saw a way to save him by marrying the Englishman. She beguiled all the English into thinking that the child was the colonel's, and so by English law should inherit Glenarden. The English never knew her son wasn't the true child of the Englishman.

But no, he was pure Highland Scots, of the Ramsay clan on his mother's side, the McCain clan on his father's. My father is the direct descendant of that brave woman and her little boy, and I am too. So, don't lump me in with the bloody Sassenachs, Darragh Fitzgerald."

Hart hadn't heard that version of the tale, but if Eleanor's great-great-grandmother had been anything like Eleanor, Hart believed it. Hart could imagine the woman—with her red gold hair and plaid skirts billowing in the wind—telling the English bastards that the land was hers and that was that. *But, yes, I can be persuaded to do things your way if you like*, she'd say, blinking those cornflower blue eyes at them, and then proceed to do whatever she pleased.

"Tell me," Hart said to Eleanor. "How was it that the English colonel died so soon?"

"Oh, great-great-grandmother pushed him off the roof," Eleanor said. "From that corner just above my bedroom. It's a nasty drop there. He was simply awful to her, according to the stories, so I can hardly blame her."

Chapter 16

Hart looked at Darragh, who was listening, openmouthed. "Remind me, Darragh, not to go up onto the roof with my wife."

"Best not," Eleanor agreed. "You can be rather aggravating." She turned her smile on Darragh. "So you see, lad, I have no more love for the English than you do. That colonel muscled his way into Great-Great-Grandmother Finella's home and had his way with her, which is why I do not blame her one whit for the roof. I myself would love to see England become detached from Scotland and drift off into the sea—except that two of my sisters-in-law are Sassenachs, and I'd want them safely here first. Along Lord Cameron's Romany friends. And Mrs. Mayhew and Franklin and all the servants from Hart's London house. Not to mention my English friends, and my father's cronies at all those universities and the British Museum." She made a helpless gesture with her good hand. "So, you see, it is not such a simple thing, is it? To say all people labeled *this* should live, and all labeled *that* should die? Neat and tidy, you don't have to think about it. But alas, the world is much more complicated than that."

Darragh was clearly out of his depth. He looked to Hart for support.

"She's asking you to think about what you're doing, lad," Hart said. "To use your intellect, not your emotion."

"I suppose he's not been told he has an intellect," Eleanor said sadly. "My father says that is the trouble with so many. They're told they'll never amount to much, and so they believe it, and so it becomes true. But the human mind is quite intricate, no matter what body it is born into." Eleanor gently tapped Darragh above his left ear. "So many thoughts in there, all of them with great potential. They simply need to be pursued."

There it was—Eleanor smiling at the lad, her fingertips soft on his hair. Darragh looked into her blue, blue eyes, and was smitten.

Eleanor smoothed Darragh's hair, a motherly gesture. "What do you intend to do with him, Hart?"

"Send him to America to his sister," Hart said.

Fellows came alert on the other end of the room. "No, you don't. He shot at you and hit your wife. He needs to be arrested and stand trial for that."

"His colleagues will never let him live that long," Hart said. "He stays with me, I protect him, and he tells me every last detail about his friends and where I can find them."

"I'll not betray them," Darragh said quickly.

Hart bent him a severe look. "You will. In exchange, you go to America and forget about secret organizations. Get an honest job and live a long and healthy life."

Fellows strode to them. "Mackenzie, the law isn't for you to take into your hands. *I* need to know these contacts. I can't go back to my chief inspector and tell him that I let you send a violent criminal off to America with a slap on the hand."

"You know that once he tells us what we need to know, his life won't be worth anything," Hart said. "If his colleagues don't come for him, he'll go to Newgate and be hung or shot for treason."

"Rewarding him by sending him to America to live with his sister won't exactly reform him, will it?"

Eleanor broke in before Hart could answer. "Neither will hanging him, Mr. Fellows. He's only a boy. He's nothing more than a trigger, like an extension of the pistol. I'm willing to give him a chance, if he helps you find those who want Hart dead."

Darragh sat silently through the exchange, fear large in his eyes. It was beginning to dawn on him, Hart saw, how he'd been used. "I'm not a trigger," he said in a small voice.

Eleanor smoothed his hair again. "Best you keep your head down and mouth shut, lad. Or Inspector Fellows will be driving you away in a cart with bars on it. Your only chance is to do what His Grace tells you."

Darragh blinked back tears. "But I can't . . . tell."

"Mackenzie," Fellows said, voice strained, "I understand your tactics. I even admire you for them, but you'll cost me my job."

"Hart will never let it come to that." Eleanor smiled sweetly at Fellows, then Hart. "Will he?"

"No," Hart said. "The Home Office will answer to me soon enough, Fellows. You'll keep your job. Especially if you are instrumental in rooting out a cache of Fenians."

"Then that's settled," Eleanor said. "Perhaps you should give Darragh some tea before you start with the questions. He looks all in."

Hart put his hand under Eleanor's arm and lifted her from the chair. "You are the one who is all in. The boy will be fine. You are going back to bed."

"I am rather tired." She sagged, and Hart slid his arm around her waist. "You must give me your word you won't hurt him," she said.

"He'll stay intact. Fellows, keep the boy here while I take Eleanor upstairs."

Fellows glared at him. He looked so much like their father when he did that.

Eleanor's legs buckled, and Hart swept her into his arms and carried her out. The anteroom and halls beyond were empty, Isabella having the sense to herd the remaining guests into the garden for an alfresco dinner.

Hart carried Eleanor through the enormous front hall, still decorated with swags for the wedding, and up the stairs. The giant vase that always stood on the hall table today was filled with pink roses and lily of the valley.

Eleanor smiled at Hart as he carried her upward, her eyes

sleepy blue slits. She touched his chest, the diamond and sapphire engagement ring glittering next to the plain gold of the wedding band. Eleanor Ramsay. *His wife.*

"Don't be too long," she murmured. "It's our wedding night, remember."

Eleanor rested her head on Hart's shoulder and went sweetly to sleep.

Hart Mackenzie was an arrogant son of a bitch who would never change.

Lloyd Fellows stormed away from Hart's study several hours later. Hart had carried his wife to her bedchamber—what a tender husband—and then returned to put Darragh through it. Hart was expert at twisting information out of anyone, and he'd twisted it out of Darragh. He'd never even touched the lad. Darragh had given up the names of the leaders and where they met in London and in Liverpool.

Fellows doubted they'd still be there. They'd have heard from one of their own that the assassination attempt was a failure and that Darragh had been taken. They'd still be in the area, though, and now Fellows knew their names. It would not be long before he found them.

He admired Hart and at the same time wanted to strangle him. Hart Mackenzie had grown up with every privilege, while Lloyd Fellows had grubbed for himself. Fellows had worked hard all his life to take care of his mother in the back streets of London while Hart had slept between soft linen sheets and eaten food prepared by celebrated chefs.

Now Mackenzie, instead of staying at his injured wife's bedside, had sat in his opulent study and done Fellows's job. Better, probably, than Fellows could have.

It rankled. Never mind that Hart had given Fellows enough information with which to return to London and start rooting out the madmen who thought nothing of shooting into crowds and blowing up railway lines. Fellows would nab them and get all the glory. Hart would let him. That rankled too.

To relieve his feelings, Fellows stormed into a room at the end of the hall, unaware even of where he was going in this colossal house.

"Oh," said a female voice.

Fellows stopped, his hand on the door handle, and saw a young lady standing unsteadily on a ladder, her hands full of garlands. She was definitely teetering, the garlands rendering her unable to steady herself. Fellows hurried to her and kept her from falling by putting strong hands on her hips.

"Thank you," she said. "You did make me jump."

She was Lady Louisa Scranton, Isabella Mackenzie's younger sister. The dress beneath Fellows's hands was a dark blue silk, the hips beneath that supple.

Fellows had met Lady Louisa on several occasions at Mackenzie gatherings but had done no more than exchange polite pleasantries with her. Louisa much resembled her sister, Isabella, with brilliant red hair, green eyes, a curving figure, and a red-lipped smile.

Fellows wanted to let his hands linger. She smelled of roses, and her flesh beneath the fabric was warm.

He made himself ease his hands away. "Are you all right?"

She blushed. "Yes, yes. I was taking down these garlands and became careless. I thought they should come down, under the circumstances. The guests won't be using this room."

It was a drawing room, one whose ceilings were a mere fifteen feet high rather than the twenty to thirty usual in this house.

"They have servants to do this."

Her skirts made an enticing rustle as she reached for more garlands, rising on tiptoe in slender ankle boots.

"Yes, but truth to tell, I felt rather underfoot and wanted to be useful. Isabella can grow quite agitated when she's upset, and rather bossy, poor lamb."

Fellows couldn't think of a thing to say. He was a policeman. Polished manners were beyond him.

"Lady Eleanor will recover, I think," he said stiffly.

"I know. I looked in on her not long ago. She's sleeping like a baby." Louisa's green eyes scrutinized him, and Fellows suddenly felt hot. "You are very tall. Would you help me reach that?" Louisa pointed to a garland fastened to a sculpted frieze out of her reach.

"Of course."

Fellows thought she'd descend, and he held out his hand to

help her, but she shook her head. "You need to come up here, silly. We both must grab it or the whole thing will be ruined."

Silly. No woman in Lloyd Fellows's life had dared to tell him he was silly.

He put his foot on the bottom rung of the stepladder. Another two steps, and he was level with her.

He found it difficult to breathe. This close to her, he was sharply aware of her scent, the curve of her cheek, how her red hair darkened at the temples.

"There we are," Louisa said softly, and she kissed him.

A light touch, a virgin's kiss, but the cushion of her red lips ignited fires throughout his body. Fellows slid his hand to the nape of her neck and scooped her up to him. He did not open her lips, but brushed them again and again, taking in the warm softness of her. He ended with a kiss to the corner of her mouth, which he savored for a time.

"I shouldn't have done that," she whispered, breath gentle on his skin. "But I've been wanting to kiss you."

"Why?" His throat was dry.

Her lips curved into a smile. "Because you're a handsome gentleman, and I like you. Besides, you once saved Mac's life."

"And this is gratitude?"

Her smile widened. "No, this is me being dreadfully forward. I would not blame you one whit for being disgusted."

Disgusted? Was she mad?

"You should have told me." His voice still wasn't working.

"It is not something easily worked into conversation." Louisa reached for the garland. "Anyway, now I have told you. And I truly need help with this garland."

Fellows put a firm arm around her and reached up beside her. He was not quite sure what had just changed in his life, but the world felt different, and he would make certain that he and Louisa continued to explore what had begun in this room.

Eleanor slept. She dreamed dark dreams that slipped away when she swam to wakefulness and pain. Then she was restless, the injury keeping her from slumbering again. When Beth offered her more laudanum in water, Eleanor was hurting enough to readily drink it.

She slept through her wedding night, all the next day, and well into the next night. She awoke, hungry, able to eat the bread and butter Maigdlin brought her. Eleanor felt well after that, and decided to get up, only to find herself on the floor, her friends lifting her back into bed.

Fever came, and she saw the faces of Beth, Ainsley, and Isabella come and go. And Hart's. She wanted to cling to him and ask him a thousand questions—what had happened to Darragh? Were there any other assassins lurking? Had Inspector Fellows arrested Darragh's friends? But she had no strength to speak.

After what seemed a long time, Eleanor woke again, in quiet darkness. Her arm was sore, but the worst of the pain had receded, thank heavens. Eleanor stretched and yawned. Her body was damp with sweat, but she felt rested, relieved.

She was not alone, she discovered—Maigdlin lay back in a chair, snoring, an oil lamp glowing next to her. Feeling fusty, she woke Maigdlin and asked the startled maid to run a bath. Maigdlin protested, fearing Eleanor's fever would return, but Eleanor wanted to find Hart, and she did not want to go to her husband after sweating in bed for . . . who knew how long.

Maigdlin helped her bathe, being careful of her bandages. Three days she'd been asleep, Maigdlin told her, and so sick they feared they'd lose her.

Nonsense. Eleanor always threw off her fevers. She was strong as an ox.

Feeling much better after the bath, Eleanor wrapped herself in a thick dressing gown, put on warm slippers, and headed for Hart's bedchamber, three doors down from hers.

The hall was silent, the rest of the house asleep. The doors in between her chamber and his led to Hart's private library and study. Eleanor supposed she should be grateful that she had to walk only twenty feet to reach his bedroom. When she'd stayed at Kilmorgan as his fiancée, long ago, she'd been put in the guest wing, which was on the other side of the house.

Eleanor did not bother to knock on the immense double doors. She'd come prepared with a key, which she'd procured the day she'd arrived at Kilmorgan. But there was no need for it, because the door was unlocked. She saw why when she entered the enormous chamber. Hart wasn't in it.

Hart's bed, empty and neatly made, was colossal, with brocade hangings flowing to it from an oval canopy ten feet above it. The rest of the room was taken up with formal tables and chairs, a bookcase, a padded bench, and a console table holding brandy and a humidor.

In spite of the elegant furnishings, this was a cold room, even with the coal fire burning brightly on the hearth. Eleanor shivered.

Hart's windows faced the front of the house and the east side of the grounds. The curtains had not been drawn, and Eleanor walked to the east window and peered out.

"He's gone out to the mausoleum, Your Grace."

Eleanor stifled a shriek and turned to find Hart's French valet in the doorway. Marcel stood ramrod straight, looking not at all tired. The perfect servant, awake and alert to serve his master, even at three o'clock in the morning. Poor Maigdlin had succumbed to slumber.

"The mausoleum?" Eleanor asked when her breath returned. "In the middle of the night?"

"His Grace will go there sometimes when he can't sleep," Marcel said. "Is there anything I can fetch for you, Your Grace?"

"No, no. That's fine, Marcel. Thank you."

Marcel stood aside to let Eleanor leave the room, then he hastened down the hall ahead of her to open her bedchamber door. Eleanor thanked him politely and bade him go to bed. Hart would be fine without him, she said, and Marcel needed sleep. Marcel looked puzzled, but he went.

Eleanor bade Maigdlin, who was changing her bedsheets, to help her dress and to fix her arm in the sling. Maigdlin didn't want to, of course, but Eleanor was firm. She then sent Maigdlin up to her bed, hurried downstairs, and let herself out of the house through a back door.

She sped across the damp grass toward the squat, dark building on the edge of the grounds, her breath catching when she saw the wink of a lantern inside.

The Mackenzie family mausoleum was always cold. Hart's breath fogged inside it, even though the April night was almost balmy.

His grandfather had built this place in the 1840s, a Greek-looking mock temple with plenty of marble and granite. Hart's grandfather and grandmother reposed here, as did Hart's father and mother. Cameron's first wife did not, because Hart's father wouldn't hear of it. *She was a bitch, a whore, and Cameron's disgrace,* the duke had said. *She can make do with the churchyard, though I'll be surprised if the vicar lets her in.*

Hart's wife Sarah did have a tomb here, as did his son, Graham.

The marble of Sarah's tomb was black and gray, cold to the touch. The plaque on the front of the tomb was filled with flowery phrases that Hart never remembered asking for.

The smaller plaque next to Sarah's said, *Lord Hart Graham Mackenzie, Beloved Son, June 7, 1876.*

Hart traced the lettering of his son's name with gloved fingertips. Graham would have turned eight this year.

"I'm sorry," he whispered. "I am so sorry."

Silence and darkness filled the space. But Hart felt comfort from the cool marble, from the presence of the boy he'd held—only once.

If Hart had done everything right in his life, he and Eleanor would have been married long ago, and Kilmorgan would be overrun with children by now. The bodies of Sarah and Graham would not be in this cold place, with nothing but chisel marks on marble left to honor them.

But Hart had done everything wrong. This time, at least, this time, he'd gotten Eleanor to the altar. And then she'd pushed him out of the way of the pistol, trying to save him.

These last three days, while Eleanor lay in a fevered stupor, had been absolute hell. Tonight, the doctor had announced that the fever had turned, that Eleanor was resting. Hart in his relief hadn't known what to do. He'd shaken off his brothers' well-meaning offers of all the whiskey he could down and retreated here.

To assure himself that Eleanor wasn't out here, cold and alone? He didn't know.

All he knew was that he'd made a mess of his life, and he was still doing it. Hart, the arrogant, self-assured Mackenzie, could get nothing right, and these tombs were tangible evidence.

He'd always thought of his courtship and engagement with Eleanor as a farce in three acts.

Act I, Scenes: Their first dance together, followed by a kiss in the garden had awakened every need in his body. Next, the boathouse down by the river at Kilmorgan, where he'd unbuttoned Eleanor's modest dress and kissed her skin, discovering that she had a passion in her that she didn't hide, at least not from him.

Act II, Scene: The summerhouse. Hart remembered Eleanor riding beside him in her prim habit and riding hat, smiling and chattering as usual. The summerhouse, the old duke's folly, perched on a promontory, a gorge dropping away from it to a river below. From there, one could see across a vast stretch of Mackenzie lands all the way to the sea.

When Hart had led Eleanor inside, her reaction had been pure Eleanor.

"Hart, it's beautiful." The summerhouse folly had been fashioned like an ancient Greek temple, complete with overgrown ruined stone, a very un-Scottish structure. But the view was magnificent, and the summerhouse very private.

Eleanor turned in a circle, arms open. "My father would love this. So false and yet so true at the same time."

Hart had stepped to the stone balustrade and looked out over the vistas that never failed to stir his heart. The Mackenzies had come back from poverty and powerlessness after Culloden to become the wealthiest family in Scotland, and this panorama of their lands rammed it down the throats of every Englishman who came up here.

"You're proud of it, aren't you?" Eleanor said, coming to rest next to him. "In spite of you sneering that it's a ridiculous English affectation your father built, you like it. You would not have brought me here otherwise."

"I brought you for the view." Hart lifted Eleanor's riding hat from her head and set it out of the wind. "And for this."

He slid his arms around her waist from behind. Eleanor closed her eyes as he kissed her neck, wisps of red curls silken under his lips. Hart let his fingers drift to the buttons that closed her habit in front.

Eleanor only sighed as he unbuttoned her, her head resting against his cheek. Hart parted her placket and nibbled her bared neck.

"What are you doing to me, El?" he whispered into her ear. "I think you're breaking me."

"Hardly," she murmured. "Hart Mackenzie is far too wicked for the likes of me to tame."

"But I'd like to let you try."

He turned her around. His gaze roved her mussed hair, her parted red lips, the bodice gaping to show her damp throat. She was the most beautiful thing he'd ever seen.

He was not supposed to do this now. He'd planned to take her to London, to the elegant house in Grosvenor Square, to bring out the old and valuable Mackenzie jewels, and promise them to her if she'd agree to become his wife. Formally done, in the drawing room, his hand on his heart, dazzling her with diamonds so that she would not say no. Women would do anything for diamonds.

Up here in the summerhouse, with the jewels locked far away in the vault in Edinburgh, Hart had nothing to offer. Only the view—how bloody romantic and stupid.

But he had the feeling that if he didn't speak now, secure her *now*, his chance would slip away. Eleanor was twenty, an earl's daughter, and lovely. If he didn't lock her into an agreement, she would be fair game for every other lovelorn gentleman out there. Her poverty wouldn't matter to a nabob wanting to better his connections through her family. She had charm and grace to go with her lineage, the perfect wife for Hart Mackenzie. Hart Mackenzie would have her.

It was too soon. He should use the beautiful view from the folly as one more enticement in a string of enticements in this courtship, so that when he finally asked for her hand, Eleanor would have no reason to say no. Hart would have woven his web so tightly she'd not want to break free. If he asked her here, now, Eleanor could turn him down, and he'd have no more chance to convince her.

But Hart felt his mouth open, heard the words come out in a rush. "Marry me, Eleanor."

Eleanor's eyes widened, and she took a step back. "What? Why?"

The question stirred his anger. Hart seized her hands and forced a smile. "Why does a man wish to marry a woman? Does there have to be a logical reason?"

Eleanor blinked those big blue eyes at him. "I'm not much bothered about why any man wishes to marry any woman, in general. I'm sure there are dozens of theories, if one wanted to debate. What I would like to know is why *you* wish to marry *me*."

Hart clamped down on his impatience. "So that I may kiss you," he said, voice light. "I plan to kiss every inch of you, Eleanor, and if I do that, we'd better marry."

He saw a flicker of delight in her eyes, but Eleanor didn't melt. Dear God, she was stubborn.

"But I mean, why *me*? I'm not vain enough to believe that no other young lady in Scotland is good enough for the attentions of Hart Mackenzie, for kissing or otherwise. I have a pedigree, but so do others, and my family is a bit down at the heel. You could have any lady you wanted with the snap of your fingers." Eleanor snapped in demonstration, even though Hart still had hold of her wrist.

"I do not want any other lady in Scotland. I want you."

"You flatter me."

"God's balls, woman," he shouted. "I'm not asking you to marry me out of flattery." Hart's words echoed from the hills around them. "I'm asking you because I can't do this without you. I can't face my father, or the world. When I'm with *you*, all that doesn't matter. I need you, El. How the devil can I make you understand that?"

Eleanor stared up at him, lips parted. Any moment she'd laugh at him, sneer at him for being so sentimental. He sounded like a lovesick fool, God help him.

"That is all I wanted to know," she said softly.

"If you marry me, Eleanor Ramsay, I promise to give you everything you ever wanted."

Eleanor smiled suddenly, looked into his eyes, and said, "Yes."

Hart's heart pounded so hard it hurt. He gathered her into his arms, trying to remember how to breathe. She was like a rock in a raging river, and he clung to her as though she was the only thing between him and drowning.

His first kiss opened her lips, Hart tasting the woman he'd conquered. It was heady, joyous.

He'd had his valet pack a blanket for their picnic. Hart now spread the blanket on the summer-warm stones and began to undress her.

Eleanor said not a word, offered no protest. She smiled as her habit came open, shivered as Hart spread the laces of her corset. Her eyes went soft when he parted and removed the camisole beneath, helped her out of her skirts, and laid her on the blanket in the sunshine.

Hart gazed down at her, bare but for her stockings and prim riding boots, a beautiful woman he'd a moment ago made his. Triumph beat through him.

Hart stripped off his coat and waistcoat, shirt and boots, then underbreeches, saving the kilt for last. He liked how Eleanor watched him, not shy, wanting to look at him as much as he wanted to look at her.

Hart undid the kilt and let it fall, showing her how hard he was for her.

She was a virgin, Hart reminded himself. She'd never known the touch of a man—*not until mine*—and he knew he'd have to be patient with her. He was prepared to be, looked forward to it.

Eleanor blushed as Hart lay down with her. The feel of her body beneath his sent his heart racing. He could take her now, swiftly, make her understand who she belonged to. This could be quick, satisfying.

But Hart had learned how to give a woman, any woman, perfect pleasure. He did not need exotic techniques and devices—the key was the pleasure.

"I won't hurt you," he said.

Eleanor shook her head, smiling a little smile. "I know."

The trust in her eyes stung his heart. Hart kissed her, and gently, gently touched her, opening her to him very slowly. He went carefully, teaching her about arousal, making her damp enough to take him without hurt. His body shook with the effort of holding himself back, but it was very important that he didn't rush her.

Her body closed around his with heat that threatened to break his control. He wanted to thrust and thrust into her, to satisfy himself and forget about not rushing.

No. Take the time. Teach her. Later, when Eleanor was used
to him, he could show her more interesting things, but today,
this was about Eleanor's first pleasure.

Eleanor was so warm and ready that he slid in the first inch
without impediment. Hart stayed there a time, kissing her,
coaxing her, letting her get used to him.

Another inch, and again, stopping, teasing, nipping, teaching her what it felt like to have a man inside her. Then came
the barrier, which he knew would hurt. Hart took it slowly, a
fraction of an inch at a time.

This was a first for him too—he'd never been with a virgin.
He feared to break her, to mar her in some unrecoverable way.
Then again, Eleanor was resilient. She lifted her body to his,
touched his face, nodded when she was ready.

And then Hart was inside her, she squeezing him, a feeling
of glory and hot, hot joy.

"El," he said. "You are so tight. You feel beautiful."

Eleanor's body rocked against his, her arms coming around
him, her mouth finding his. Wanting, accepting, loving.

The astonishing feeling of her around him made him drop
his seed before he was ready. Hart groaned with it, amazed at
himself, then he laughed. Hart's women usually tried every
trick they could to make him do their bidding, to lose control
to them, and they never succeeded. Eleanor had conquered
him by lying there being warm and beautiful.

Hart kissed her, knowing that something exquisite had just
happened and not knowing quite what to do about it.

The rest of Act II had been heady. News of the betrothal
of Lord Hart Mackenzie and Lady Eleanor Ramsay spread
to every corner of the country, filling every newspaper and
magazine.

Glorious days. The happiest days of his life, Hart realized
now. At the time, the stupid, selfish young man he'd been had
only tasted triumph of landing the woman he'd wanted. Eleanor would bring the notorious Mackenzie family a measure of
respect, which they badly needed. Hart's horror of a father
had eroded the Mackenzie reputation, as had Ian's supposed
madness, Mac's running away to live among depraved artists
in Paris, and Cameron's very bad marriage.

But no one could say a wrong word about Eleanor. She sailed above all scandal, her talkative charm melting one and all. Eleanor was kind, generous, strong, and well liked. She'd lead Hart to glory.

Hart told her he loved her, and it was not a lie. But he never gave the whole of himself to her, never believed he needed to. Looking back, Hart realized that he'd kept himself from her out of fear.

And that had been his great mistake.

So stupid was Hart that he didn't understand what he had to lose, until Act III.

Scene: Eleanor Ramsay's ramshackle home in autumn, the trees surrounding it having turned brilliant red and gold. Their radiant glory splashed against the dark evergreens that marched across the mountains, silent reminders that the coming winter would be brutal and cold.

Hart had been as buoyant as the cool weather, looking forward to visiting his lady with hair the color of autumn leaves. Earl Ramsay received Hart in the house and told him, in a strangely quiet tone, that Eleanor was walking in the gardens and would see him there.

Hart had thanked the earl, unsuspecting, and had gone to find Eleanor.

The Ramsay gardens had long become overgrown and wild, despite the valiant efforts of their one gardener and his pruning shears. Eleanor always laughed at their unruly patch of land, but Hart liked it—a garden that blended into the Scottish countryside instead of being structured, overly clean, and shutting out true nature.

Eleanor paced the walks in a dress too light for the weather, the shawl too small to keep out the cold. Her hair had come down, the wind tearing at it. When Eleanor saw Hart walking toward her, she turned her back and strode away.

Hart caught up to her, seized her arm, and turned her to face him.

Her stare had made him drop his hold. Eleanor's eyes were red-rimmed in a face too white, but her glare was angry, an intense rage he'd never seen in her.

"El?" he asked in alarm. "What is it?"

Eleanor said nothing. When Hart reached for her again, she tore herself from his grip. Clenching her teeth, Eleanor yanked off the engagement ring and threw it at him.

The circlet thunked against Hart's frock-coated chest and fell with a *tink* to the paving stones.

Hart didn't bend down for the ring. This was something more than Eleanor's rare flashes of temper, her frequent exasperation at him, or their teasing arguments about ridiculous things.

"What is it?" he repeated, his voice quiet.

"Mrs. Palmer came to call on me today," Eleanor said.

Cold fingers snaked through his body. Those words should not come out of Eleanor's lips. Not *Mrs. Palmer*. Not with Eleanor. They were two separate beings, from separate worlds, separate parts of Hart. Never to meet.

"I know you know who I mean," Eleanor said.

"Yes, I bloody well know who you mean," Hart snapped. "She should not have come here."

Eleanor waited a beat, as though expecting Hart to say something like *My love, I can explain.*

Hart could explain, if he chose. Angelina Palmer had been his mistress for seven years. He had ceased to go to her once he'd started courting Eleanor. That had been Hart's decision, and so be it. But Angelina, it appeared, in her jealousy, had scuttled here to tell Eleanor Hart's dirty little secrets.

"She felt sorry for me," Eleanor said, answering Hart's silence. "She told me she'd followed me about when I was down in London last, and watched me. She learned all about me—remarkable, since I knew nothing at all about her. She saw me be kind to a wretched old lady in the park, she said. I remember I'd given a poor thing a coin and helped her to shelter. Mrs. Palmer decided that this made me a kind young woman, one who should be spared a life with you." Eleanor's eyes were full of anger, but not with anger at Angelina Palmer. At *him*.

"I admit that Mrs. Palmer was once my mistress," Hart said stiffly. "You deserve to know. She ceased to be my mistress the day I met you."

Eleanor's look turned deprecating. "A pleasing half-truth, the kind at which Hart Mackenzie excels. I've seen you say such things to others; I never dreamed you would to me." Her color rose. "Mrs. Palmer told me about your women, about your house, and hinted at the sorts of things you do there."

Oh, God, oh, damn, damn, damn, damn, damn. Hart saw his world falling away, the fiction that he could be anything other than a blackguard bastard crumbling to dust.

"All in the past," Hart said in a hard voice. "I have not touched another woman since I met you. I'm not that much of a monster. I gave it all up, Eleanor. For you. Angelina is a jealous and coldhearted woman. She'd say anything to keep me from marrying you."

If Hart had thought the speech would have Eleanor smiling and forgiving, he was wrong, oh, so wrong.

"For heaven's sake, spare me," she said. "You believe that hiding the truth is not the same as a lie, but it is. You have lied and lied, and you are still lying. You planned my seduction so carefully—Mrs. Palmer told me how you decided on me, how you finagled invitations to every gathering I went to, sometimes with her help. That you hunted me as a man tracks a fox, that you played upon my vanity and made me think I'd caught your eye. And I was stupid enough to let you."

"Does that matter?" Hart cut in. "Does it matter how I wanted you, or how we met? Nothing after that was a lie. I *need* you, El. I told you that in the summerhouse. I didn't lie about that. My dealings with Mrs. Palmer are over. You never need worry about her again."

Eleanor looked at him in cold fury. "If you believe *jealousy* has made me angry, you are very wrong. I was not shocked to find you'd had a mistress—many gentlemen have them, and you are so passionate, Hart. I can forgive a past mistress you have not visited since you started courting me, or even some of the risqué games you played, which she decided she should not describe in detail to a lady."

"It's bloody evident you can't forgive me, since you threw the blasted ring at me."

"That is the crux of the matter, isn't it? Everything is about *you*. The entire world revolves around Lord Hart Mackenzie. I should do as you wish, because I fit into a certain place in your schemes, and so does Mrs. Palmer. You treat us equally, each of us occupying certain niches in your cupboard of life."

"Eleanor . . ."

Eleanor held up her hand, her voluble nature taking over. "What's infuriated me is the *other* things she told me of. About your tempers and your rages. How you cycle between hot and cold, how Mrs. Palmer is never certain what you'll want from her from day to day, or what your mood will be. She told me she started bringing other ladies into the house, because his lordship was growing bored. She knew that she had to assuage your ennui by any means she could so you wouldn't leave her. You made use of her, and she scrambled to please you. And in the end, you threw her over because you no longer needed her." Eleanor stopped, her face red, her breath coming fast. "How could you be so cruel to another human being?"

Hart stepped back. "Have I got this right? You want to break our engagement because I've been rude to a *courtesan*?"

The pinched look around her mouth told Hart that this was the wrong thing to say. "More than rude. You played upon her, as you play upon everyone—as you played upon me. It should make no difference whether a person is a courtesan or a street girl or an earl or an earl's daughter."

Every word was a blow, because every word was true. They cut him, and Hart struck back. "Perhaps I am not as egalitarian as you."

Eleanor flinched, and Hart knew he was losing her. "Cruelty is cruelty, Hart," she said.

"And when have I had a chance not to be cruel?" Hart shouted. "If I am, it is because that's all I ever learned how to be. It is how I survived. You've met my father; you know what I grew up with. You know what he did to my brothers and me, what he made us into."

"Certainly, blame your father all you like—and I know how awful he is. I have experienced it firsthand. And I'm very sorry for you, believe me. But you have choices. The choices you make are your own, not your father's." Her eyes narrowed. "And don't you dare punish Mrs. Palmer for what she's told me. She is terrified of you—do you know that? She knows you'll never forgive her over this, that she's lost you forever. Yet, she found the courage to come and speak to me."

Even then, though, in his amazing foolishness, Hart convinced himself that he could still win.

"Yes, to turn you away from me," he said swiftly. "Obviously, she is succeeding. She might have come to you as a poor soul, but I assure you that Angelina Palmer is a manipulative bitch who will do anything to get what she wants."

Eleanor's eyes widened. "I'll thank you to believe I know my own mind. Of course Mrs. Palmer is cool and manipulative—she has had to be, a woman in such a position, alone in the world, with *you* as her only support. But you did not see her. She knew that by telling me, everything she had with you would be at an end. She was resigned to it. *Resigned.* You think me an unworldly young woman, brought up by a naive gentleman, but I know much about people. Enough to see that you broke her. She devoted herself to you—she would do anything in the world for you—and you broke her. Why should I not think that you will do the same to me?"

Hart could not breathe. Eleanor stood there like some avenging angel, making Hart face everything he was, everything he'd become. By his own choice.

He ran a shaking hand over his face, finding it wet with sweat. *You broke her.* Maybe he had. Angelina had soaked up his needs, his terrors, his tempers, and his frustrations like a sponge. She'd taken everything he'd thrown at her. This did not make her a saint—she'd been far from that—but she'd put up with Hart and his life.

But Hart Mackenzie could never bow, apologize, or back away for the sake of another. He'd never learned how to control his anger or his selfish desires—to have any idea that he ought to control them. His father had vented anger by terrorizing, and Hart had never learned there could be any other way.

Whatever Hart wanted, he took. Those who got in his way paid the price.

He looked at Eleanor with her quiet strength. No matter what he'd done or how hard he'd tried, he'd never truly won Eleanor. And that made him so *angry.*

"I can ruin your father," he said. "Don't think I can't. Ruin him, ruin you . . . easily."

Eleanor gave him a grim nod. "I am certain you could. You are wealthy and powerful, and everyone will say what a fool I am for turning you down."

"I'm not jesting, El. I can destroy him. Is that what you want?"

Hart waited for Eleanor's fear, for her need to say anything, do anything, to make him withdraw the threat. He waited for her desperation to put Hart back to his laughter and wicked jokes, to smooth him over, to do what he wanted. Everything Angelina had done.

Eleanor looked at him for the longest time, shadows from the overgrown garden playing across her face. She never registered fear. Only sadness.

"Please go, Hart."

Hart growled. "You agreed to marry me. We have a contract. It's too late."

Eleanor shook her head. "No. Please go."

Hart caught her arm in a hard grip. She stared at him in amazement, and he softened his hold but didn't let go.

"What will you do without me, Eleanor? You have no one to go to, and you have nothing. I can give you everything in the world. I told you that, remember?"

"Yes, but what price will I pay for it?"

Hart lost his temper. He knew, even then and all through the long years, that it was that temper that had lost him everything. He'd been too young and too sure of himself to understand that not everyone in the world could be bullied, especially not Eleanor Ramsay.

"You are *nothing*." The words came out a snarl. "You are the daughter of an impoverished earl who is too feckless to understand where his own dinner comes from. Is that what you want for the rest of your life? Poverty and idiocy? If I walk away from you, you are finished. Ruined. No one will want Hart Mackenzie's leavings."

Eleanor slapped him. He barely felt the sting, but he grabbed Eleanor's wrist again, and she glared at him, eyes blazing.

She didn't say anything. She didn't have to. She wrenched herself from his grasp, glared at him another moment, then turned and walked away. Head high, her shawl and light gown billowing in the wind, Eleanor Ramsay walked out of Hart's life.

Hart felt himself falling down, down, down, into an abyss of his own making. "El!" he'd called, his voice cracking, pathetic.

Eleanor did not stop and did not turn back. She walked on,

never looking at him, until she was lost in the shadows of the overgrown garden. Hart had put his hands on top of his head and watched her go, his heart aching until he thought it would burst.

He hadn't let it go at that, of course. Hart tried over the next weeks to make Eleanor change her mind. He'd attempted to recruit Lord Ramsay, only to find that Eleanor had told him everything . . . every embarrassing detail.

"I'm sorry, Mackenzie," Lord Ramsay had said sorrowfully when Hart approached him. "I'm afraid I must stand behind my daughter. You did play a rather bad game."

Even Hart's argument that he'd taken Eleanor's virginity brought him nothing.

"I've not started a child," Eleanor had said when he'd argued this. She'd not even blushed when Hart had laid out the fact that he'd ruined her to her father. "I know the signs. I'll likely not marry anyone else anyway, so it does not matter, does it?"

Eleanor and her father, the pair of them with their stubborn, steadfast, unyielding Scots stolidity, had defeated him.

End of Act III, Hart, the villain, exits. Never to return.

Act IV had to be Hart's life since Eleanor—his father's death, marrying Sarah, losing her on one day and his son the next. Hart, who never cried, had stretched across the floor of his bedroom and wept brokenly after he'd laid Sarah and Hart Graham Mackenzie to rest in the overdone Mackenzie mausoleum.

This then, was Act V. The heroine returns to drive the villain insane.

"Hart?"

Eleanor saw Hart blinking at the light as he jerked around to face her and the lantern she carried. His hand was on the chiseled letters of his son's name, and he was holding on to them for dear life.

Chapter 17

Hart's gaze was unfocused, his golden eyes glittering and moist. "You shouldn't be out here," he said. "It's too damp. You'll take sick again."

Eleanor walked to him. Hart kept his hands on the plaque, as though loathe to take his fingers from the letters.

"What are you doing here?" Eleanor asked. "You have a perfectly good fire in your bedchamber. I saw it."

Hart turned his face back to the tomb. "I was afraid."

"Of what?" It was cold, which made her hurt arm ache, but Eleanor did not want to leave him here. "Tell me."

"Losing you." Hart looked at her again, his eyes anguished. "I was remembering you throwing the ring at me and telling me to go away, how arrogant I was."

Eleanor shivered, thinking of that terrible day and how enraged and how proud they both had been. "That was a long time ago."

"No, I'm still fucking arrogant. I should have sent you home when you came bleating to me about a job. But, no, I coerced you into staying with me, and you almost died for it."

"Not everything in the world is your fault, Hart," Eleanor said.

"Yes, it is. I manipulate the world, and then I suffer the consequences. Others more so than me."

Eleanor's gaze went to the tomb, where lovely, shy Sarah lay, along with her tiny son, Lord Hart Graham Mackenzie, one day old.

"You blame yourself for their deaths too," she said softly.

"Of course I do."

"Sarah would have died carrying someone else's son," Eleanor said. "It sounds cruel to say it, but she wasn't strong enough to have a baby. Some women are not."

"She didn't want to have a baby at all. She hated being with child. She did it because that was what she'd been raised to do."

True enough. Perhaps if Sarah and her son had lived, Sarah would have changed her mind about wanting a baby. Perhaps she would have realized how much she could love her son, and thereby brought Hart some measure of happiness.

Hart caressed the letters of baby Graham's name. "Mac likes to say, *We're Mackenzies. We break what we touch.* But this little Mackenzie . . . he broke me."

Eleanor's heart squeezed. When she'd received the black-edged card from Hart with the formal words, *His Grace, the Duke of Kilmorgan, regrets to announce . . .* she'd cried. Cried for Hart and for Sarah, and for the child who'd never grow up. She'd cried for herself, for what hadn't been, and what could never be.

Hart finally let go of the letters. "I held him in my hands," he said, showing her his broad palms. "Graham was so tiny, and he just fit into them. I held him, and I loved him."

"I know you did."

Hart looked at her, his eyes still dark in the lantern's glare. "I never knew I could love like that. I don't know to this day where the feelings came from. But looking at him—so small, so perfect . . . I realized, that moment, that I'd never entirely be like my father. I'd feared and fought being like him all my life, but when I looked at Graham, I knew I was safe from that. Because I could never hurt this little boy."

Eleanor touched his arm, which was steely hard beneath his coat. "No."

"He was so frail. I would have done anything in the world to keep him safe. Anything. But I couldn't." The pain in his eyes cut her. "I couldn't save him, El. I should have been able to. I'm a strong man, the strongest I know. And *I couldn't save him*."

Eleanor pressed her forehead to his shoulder. "I know, Hart. I'm so, so sorry."

He laughed a little, the sound bitter. "Do you know, people tried to tell me that Graham's death was part of God's plan and that he'd gone to a better place? I nearly punched someone for telling me that. *A better place*. Rot that. I needed him *here*."

"Yes."

"When I looked at Graham, I saw what I'd become. You showed me part of the truth when you threw me over, but this tiny boy made me face myself. The blackest, deadliest part of me."

His words ran out, but Hart remained still, staring at his hands, head bowed.

Eleanor stepped in front of him and put her unhurt hand across his palms. "Come to the house," she said. "You're too cold out here. It's time to get warm."

~

Eleanor might wear the bandages, but he was the wounded one, Hart thought as he stripped back the covers on Eleanor's newly made bed.

Under Eleanor's heavy coat, she wore one of the old serge gowns she'd brought with her from Glenarden. She saw his frown as she slid off the coat and shook her head. "Did you think I'd go traipsing across your lawn in satin finery? That is the trouble with ladies' gowns, terribly impractical for a good tramp."

"Why the devil were you having a good tramp in the middle of the night?" Hart helped her extricate her arm from the sleeve. "Did you want to make yourself ill again?"

"I am perfectly fine, thank you very much, and I was looking for you."

"You found me." Sick at heart, floundering. He'd turned, and there she'd been.

Tell her everything, Ian had advised.

Sorry, Ian. I've had enough heartache for one night.

"I don't want to hurt you," Hart said.

Eleanor rose on tiptoe and kissed his lips. "You won't."

Did she say that because she trusted him, or because she was that sure of herself?

"I'll leave you to sleep."

Eleanor pressed another kiss to his lips. "No, indeed. Sleep with me."

She left him to walk to the bed. In the circle of the fire's warmth, she unbuttoned her gown and let it fall, then stripped off what little she wore under it. She hadn't bothered with a corset or layers of petticoats for her stroll. Her round backside rose as she leaned down to pick up the dress from the floor. She smiled over her shoulder at him as she straightened up.

God help me.

Hart stripped off his coat and muddy shoes at the same time, nearly tearing the coat in his hurry. He shed waistcoat and shirt, undershirt and socks as Eleanor lifted her coverlet and got into the bed. She lay back against the pillows, her bandaged arm across the quilts, and watched Hart pull off his kilt and let it drop.

Her smile widened as her gaze went unashamedly to his naked arousal. She lifted the covers. "Come in and get warm."

Hart slid in beside her, on her right side so he wouldn't touch her bandages. He drew his fingers across her sleek shoulder, and kissed her skin.

Making love to her the conventional way might hurt her injury, but Hart didn't mind being unconventional. He slid his leg across both of hers, putting them inside his bent knee. He kissed Eleanor's lips, slow, light kisses, enjoying her softness.

She tasted delightful. Firelight brushed her skin, and her warmth beneath the covers was chasing away his bone-deep chill.

"Sit up," he said.

Eleanor blinked. "Why?"

"Questions. Always the questions." Hart kissed the bridge of her nose. "Because I want you to."

Eleanor gave him a look that said he was hopeless, but she pushed back the covers and carefully leveraged herself to sit against the headboard. Her full, round breasts peeped above the quilts. Hart ran his finger over one areola, delighting to watch it tighten.

With an agility Hart didn't know he still possessed, he positioned himself before her, on his knees. He spread her legs around him, then slid his hands under her thighs and lifted her forward. Eleanor gave a startled gasp as she came to him.

"Rest your hand on my shoulder," Hart said. "Don't hurt your arm."

Eleanor laid the bandaged wrist on his big shoulder. Hart moved her legs over his thighs until she sat against him, chest to chest.

"Comfortable?" Hart asked.

"Very." Eleanor put her good arm around him and pulled him into a warm embrace.

Hart tucked his hands back under her buttocks, lifting them the slightest bit, so that his very needy arousal could find the place she opened. "You're wet for me," he said.

She laughed, which made her move against him in the nicest way. "I'm straddling the most glorious, naked Highlander."

Hart licked across her lips while he pulled her down onto him, his stiffness sliding straight into the goodness of her.

He nipped her neck, then licked to ease the bite. He wanted to suckle every part of her, could imagine the taste of her warm breasts, the skin of her throat, the heat between her thighs. He wanted to taste her and drink her and not stop.

Gently. She's hurt.

Hart knew how to be gentle. Rough play had its place, but there were times when the softest love was the best.

Perhaps one day they could . . .

Tell her everything.

Eleanor touched his face, hers soft with pleasure, skimming her fingers along his unshaven jaw. She smelled of her lavender soap, the scent that broke him open inside.

Hart pushed into her warmth, feeling her close around him, encasing him a tight embrace. *God, yes.* Eleanor's eyes slid closed, her head going back while she clutched his shoulder with her unhurt hand. Her nails creased his skin, the little moan in her throat exciting.

Hart and Eleanor were locked together, their bodies firmly

against each other's. Hart's skin prickled, and Eleanor's little sigh let him know she was feeling him.

He could stay here forever . . .

The small rocking motion formed a hot point around which Eleanor existed. It was an exquisite sensation, Hart inside her, their bodies pressed together, hips locked.

His eyes were dark in the dim light, pupils spreading as his passion took over. His face softened from its usual hard mask, his lips parting to let out an *ah* of satisfaction.

Hart's entire body embraced her, sweat trickling along his skin. His muscles were firm, a joy to feel. He exuded power, and yet, his eyes had swum with tears while he'd traced the name of the son he'd lost.

You break me, Hart Mackenzie.

At the moment, he was watching her intently. As though to warn her that he was being kind now, but he was holding back. He could turn wild at any moment.

The thought excited her. "You feel good," she whispered.

"You feel like fire, my wicked wife." Hart licked her neck. "I want to love you the rest of the night and all through tomorrow."

Yes. She wanted him inside her, wanted to hold him and have him hold her, where all was safe and warm.

He lifted a little, thrusting harder. "Don't let me hurt you," he whispered.

He'd never hurt her. Eleanor drew her good hand down his back, lightly scratching. Hart made a little noise in his throat, and when he looked at her, all traces of sorrow had gone.

"You make me glad I'm a sinner, Eleanor Ramsay."

Eleanor couldn't answer. Her arm throbbed, but she scarcely felt it as she held on to Hart, *her husband.* Every point of her awareness went to where they were joined, and she saw nothing, felt nothing, but *him.*

She was going to scream. And then her throat was hoarse as Hart laughed and called her his sweet, sweet lass.

"Eleanor, you unmake me." Hart's words were lost in his groan as he pushed up into her, holding her, and let go of his seed.

The feeling didn't end. It went on, Eleanor squeezing him, Hart rocking into her, his arms around her to keep her from falling. They were locked together, one.

Hart stayed inside her as he quieted little by little, his face at last relaxed, the tension released from his body. Eleanor knew she was one of the few able to see this, the Scottish duke letting himself be at ease.

Hart kissed her, with the warm kiss of lovers who had found their all in each other. He held her in his strong arms, licking the trail of freckles that led down her neck, and she felt the scrape of his teeth.

When he at last lowered her to the pillows, Eleanor was half asleep. He withdrew, the friction of him going out almost as heady as it had been going in.

He eased Eleanor onto her side and pulled the covers gently around her, Hart warm at her back. His thigh moved between her legs, solid strength, which both excited and comforted her. Surrounded by that comfort, Eleanor dove into a profound sleep.

Hart jumped awake to a clatter, a crash, a sigh of exasperation, and a mutter of, "Oh, blast."

He forced his eyes open. Sunlight streamed through the windows, landing on the warm indentation in the mattress where Eleanor had lain. The pillows bore her lavender scent, but Eleanor had gone.

Hart lifted his head, stifling a groan as his muscles protested. He found Eleanor at the foot of the bed in her dressing gown, trying, one-handed, to unfold something that looked like a cooking crane.

Hart rubbed his face, his hand finding deep stubble on his chin. "What the devil are you doing?"

Eleanor had mischief in her eyes. "Setting up the photographing apparatus. It's a bit difficult one-handed. Perhaps you could help?"

Hart sat up. Eleanor beamed and went back to her task, as though it was perfectly reasonable for her to be wrestling with a camera the morning after making love with her husband.

"You want to take photographs *now*?" he asked.

"In truth, I wanted to take one of you lying uncovered in the bed, with you half on your side as you were. You looked beautiful with the sunlight on you. But I had to drop the tripod and wake you."

"You were going to take photographs of me while I slept?"

She blinked, as though to say *Why not?* "Do not worry. I will show them to no one. They are for me to look at while you're away in London winning your election or stuck in Parliament all day. I know you won't be staying here much longer, so I must take opportunities as I can."

Hart came out of the bed. Eleanor, unworried, kept rattling the tripod until Hart grabbed it out of her hands. "I'd thought you'd forgotten about this."

"No, indeed. I am afraid I am going to be the sort of wife who refuses to let her husband run off to a mistress. If you see that I am adventurous enough to take nude photographs of you, perhaps you won't need to turn to a courtesan like your Mrs. Whitaker."

Hart opened the tripod with one yank and set it on the floor. "I told you, I have no interest in Mrs. Whitaker."

"You will be away in London quite often, and you are a very passionate man."

"*Passions I control very well.*" *Except when I am with you.* "Whatever you think of me, I am not a youth led by his desires. And I don't intend to plant you here while I am in London. You'll travel with me wherever I go."

"Oh." She looked surprised. "Will I?"

"Yes. It's why I married you." *To keep you by my side, no matter what.*

"I can see your point. I suppose you'll look like a steady, married man if your wife is always at your elbow."

"That is not the reason I had in mind, but believe what you wish. You can put away the camera."

Eleanor unlocked and opened the camera in its mahogany frame. "I find the handheld cameras quite nice to use when my father and I are out in the woods, but I prefer the tripod when I take a portrait, so I don't accidentally jiggle the image. Don't you agree?"

"El." Hart's hand came down on her good wrist. "I told you my terms. Only if I get photographs of you."

"You cannot possibly take photographs of me while my

arm is in a sling. I would look ridiculous. Now, the light is very good, and we must take advantage of it."

"*Eleanor.*"

"What are you afraid of, Hart? You're a beautiful man with a beautiful body, and I wish to photograph it. It is the same as when my father finds a perfect specimen of a mushroom. Nothing for it but he must record it for posterity. Or at least for his own enjoyment. Besides, he often eats the mushroom. Please, return to the bed. I have loaded the first plate, and I am ready."

How on earth Hart let her talk him into it, he never knew. He found himself lying back on the bed, his hands behind his head, while Eleanor tested light, peered through the camera, and tested the light again. She studied him a moment, lips pursed, then she picked up his kilt from the floor and draped it across his hips.

She went back to the camera and peered through. "Excellent. Please, do not move."

Hart held his breath, knowing that one motion would cause a blur as the shutter opened to let in light. The shutter closed again. Eleanor pulled out the plate, set it aside, and put in another one.

"Some out of the bed now, I think."

Hart smiled. "My wife, in dishabille, taking photographs of me in her bedroom. Decadent."

"I think I'd like a view of your back," she said, ignoring him.

Hart threw off the kilt and walked over to the window. This one was not as wide as the windows in his bedroom, but he preferred to be here, in Eleanor's chamber. So much cozier than the grand salon that he slept in. Maybe he'd move in here instead of having her come to him.

He put his hands on either side of the window frame, presenting his back to her. *Please God, don't let anyone be taking an early-morning stroll.*

"Delightful," Eleanor said. "Stay there."

He heard the click of the shutter, and Eleanor's sigh of delight. "Another, I think." More rattling as she changed the plate.

Eleanor looked through the camera's lens and nearly swallowed her tongue. Hart stood in a beam of sunshine, light almost glowing on his bare body. He was all that was strength. The well-defined muscles on his shoulders smoothed down his back to form a pleasing triangle to his hips. His buttocks were tight and slim, a prefect complement to his thighs and taut calves. Even his heels pleased her.

Hart looked over his shoulder, arms bunching with the movement, his eyes golden in the sunshine. "Hurry, blast you. I think the ghillie is coming down the walk."

"Perfect. Do not move, I beg you."

Eleanor held her breath as she clicked the shutter. Hart was a burnished god, a Highlander of old come to sweep her away. Old Malcolm Mackenzie must have looked much the same, a hard, handsome fighting man, who'd been twenty-five at Culloden field. He'd eloped before the battle with Lady Mary Lennox, stealing her out from under her English family's nose. Just like a Mackenzie—deciding what he wanted and taking it, even in the middle of war. From the stories Eleanor had heard, theirs had been a wild and passionate marriage.

Eleanor pulled the exposed plate out of the camera and picked up the next. Hart left the window in a hurry.

"That *is* the ghillie. We'll do these away from the windows, if you please."

Eleanor wanted to laugh. He sounded nervous, and she remembered how he'd voiced worry that his body would no longer please her. Poor Hart.

"Very well, then. You decide where to be."

Hart stood uncertainly, his brow drawn, his head bent a little in thought, his delectable body glistening with perspiration. Eleanor clicked the shutter.

Hart looked up swiftly. "I was not ready."

"No matter. It will make a lovely picture."

Hart started to laugh. Ah, there he was, the smiling, sinful man from the earlier photographs, the man who'd laid her down in the summerhouse and taught her not to fear passion.

"All right, minx. How about this?" Hart seated himself on the bench at the foot of her bed, folded his arms, and spread his legs.

"Oh, my."

The first photos she'd taken would have an artistic touch, a nude man in the sunshine. This one would be blatantly erotic.

Hart Mackenzie was unashamedly naked, his arousal obvious, his smile challenging. He was daring her to have a maidenly fit of the vapors, to look away, to not snap the picture. Eleanor studied the full length of his phallus and clicked the shutter.

"Another like that," she said, her body heating. "Perhaps with you leaning against the wall."

Hart rose and sauntered across the room. He leaned on a blank space of wall near the door, folding his arms again. His cock stood out, ramrod straight.

"Stay there." Eleanor moved the camera closer to him, settled it in, and took the picture. "I must have more."

Hart laughed. Eleanor caught him like that in the next shot, laughing in true mirth, his body bared for her delight.

"Excellent. Now some with the kilt, I think."

Hart let her take three more photographs. For two he stood bare-legged in his kilt; for the third, the kilt was off, Hart holding the folds to his abdomen while Eleanor photographed him in profile.

"Now another," Eleanor began.

Hart snarled. He dropped the kilt, came to her, hooked his arm around her waist, and pulled her from the camera. "No more."

"But I brought seven more plates."

"Save them."

Hart swept her from her feet, swiftly untying the tapes that held her dressing gown closed. He laid her on the bed and peeled the dressing gown from her, careful of her hurt arm. When he found her bare beneath, he smiled, and stole her breath.

Hart climbed over Eleanor, nuzzling the line of her hair, and then inhaling all the way down her body. Eleanor expected him to part her legs, to enter her, but instead, he tasted her.

He drew his tongue between her breasts and caught one of her nipples in his mouth. Fire blossomed from the point he suckled. Hart gave her other breast the same attention, then he kissed his way down her abdomen, licked her navel, and continued down to her thighs. He parted them, kissed the soft skin on the inside of either leg, then fastened his mouth over her tight little berry.

He'd never done that before. Eleanor gasped with the wild

pleasure of it. The sight of Hart suckling her, his eyes closed, his hair mussed, made her crazy with passion. His tongue was hot, driving her wild. He had to stop, but Hart wouldn't stop. He cradled her hips in his hands, opened her to him, and drank her in.

"Hart . . ."

More words left her lips, but they were incoherent. She rocked into the mattress, and his tongue went on torturing her. Eleanor tried to wriggle away, but he was too strong. She had to lie back and take him licking, suckling, making her insane with pleasure.

Just when Eleanor thought she'd die of joy, Hart lifted his beautiful mouth away, slid up her body, and entered her.

He was filling her now, her handsome, naked Highlander. He laughed at her at the same time he demonstrated how good pleasure could be.

His strokes were strong, his hand on her shoulder holding her down. But he was gentle, making sure he never hurt her, even as he neared his climax.

The combination of him being rough and careful at the same time sent Eleanor into another spiral of pleasure. Ecstasy ignited from where they joined and spread across her body. She shouted with it, and Hart's shout joined hers.

"El, my El," he crooned as they wound down. "Dear God, you make me wild."

You make me understand love, Eleanor thought, then the world went away except for her husband lying on her in the sunlight.

~~~

Hart and Eleanor developed the photographs together, in a darkroom Mac had set up when he'd experimented with photograph art. Mac had decided that, while photography had its merits, he preferred to slap paint on canvas and had gone back to that.

Hart took Eleanor and her stack of plates to the darkroom, locked the door, and watched her competently print the images from the dry plates. One by one, the photographs of Hart emerged, his body in full sunlight, or he coyly hiding behind the kilt. He looked like a perfect fool, and it made him laugh.

Eleanor ignored him and kept on developing. She finished the last plate, gazed at Hart holding his kilt over his front, and pronounced the proceedings satisfactory.

"Good," Hart said. "Now that you have new photographs for your memory book, you'll destroy the old ones."

Eleanor wiped her hands. "Mmm, perhaps. I still have not found all of them. I will continue my quest."

Hart stepped in front of her. "No."

"Why not? It was Fenians who wanted you dead, nothing to do with the photographs. I imagine Mr. Fellows is already in London, mopping them up. The Fenians, I mean, not the photographs. The photographs weren't the danger, and I am determined to find them."

For answer, Hart closed his arms around her and showed her that darkroom tables could be put to more use than for developing apparatus.

~

The real world, unfortunately, intruded on Eleanor's newfound marital bliss, and Hart went back to his study and his quest to win every politician in the land to his side.

Eleanor was busy herself. Now that she was the Duchess of Kilmorgan, her correspondence had multiplied into a mountain, piling up all the more while she'd lain ill.

She had Maigdlin and a footman cart all her letters to the little sitting room off her bedchamber, and she sat at the writing table, sorting through the pile and trying to ignore the continued soreness of her healing arm.

She received many letters of congratulations on her nuptials along with wishes for her to get well, and of course, a growing stack of invitations. In the middle of the pile, Eleanor came upon a rather thick envelope of now-familiar stationery.

Her heart beat faster as she tore open the envelope and unfolded the paper inside. Inside this was a small tissue-wrapped bundle, tied with white ribbon. Eleanor hastily undid the ribbon and folded back the paper, and five photographs of the naked Hart Mackenzie fell into her hand.

Chapter 18

Eleanor fanned out the photographs across her writing table. The letter that had been folded around them was short, to the point, and badly spelled.

Many fellations on your weding, from one as wishes you well.

The writer meant *felicitations.* Another indication that she was unpolished and only basically educated.

Eleanor now had all twenty photographs. Again, no threats, no demands for money, nothing.

She rewrapped the photographs in the letter, returned to her bedroom to shove the bundle inside her remembrance book, and went in search of Ian.

She found him on the grand terrace that spread across the back of the house. Ian sat cross-legged in the middle of its marble expanse, playing soldiers with his son. That is, Ian was setting up carved wooden soldiers, and Jamie was cheerfully knocking them down.

"I say, the Battle of Waterloo would have been over quickly had Jamie been there," Eleanor said.

Jamie picked up a French general, stuffed half of him into

his mouth, and waddled toward Eleanor. Ian very gently stopped him and plucked the wet soldier out of his son's mouth.

Eleanor sat down on the nearest marble bench. "Ian, I need you to tell me the names of all the ladies who lived in Hart's High Holborn house."

Ian wiped the soldier dry on his kilt while Jamie climbed up to sit next to Eleanor. Ian put his big hand on the boy's back so he wouldn't fall.

"Sally Tate, Lily Martin, Joanna Brown, Cassie Bingham, Helena Ferguson, Marion Phillips . . ."

"Stop." Eleanor raised the notebook she'd brought and started scribbling with a pencil. "Let me take it down."

Jamie pulling on the pencil slowed things, but Eleanor managed to start the list of names. "Go on."

Ian continued, naming every one. Further probing let Eleanor know that some were courtesans, some maids who worked in the house, one the cook. All had lived at Angelina Palmer's at one time or another, some staying only days.

"You wouldn't happen to know where they all are now, do you?" she asked, making notes.

Ian, being Ian, did. Jamie tired of tugging on Eleanor's pencil and climbed down from the bench. Ian steadied him, then kept a sharp eye on him as Jamie toddled about the terrace, picking up fallen soldiers.

Several of the ladies had died, he said. Most still lived in London, though one had married and emigrated to America. Quite a number had married, it seemed. Of the lot, three lived in Edinburgh. One was still a courtesan living with her protector, one was a maid in a big house, and one had married a former protector.

Eleanor wrote everything down, not asking Ian how he knew all this. She had no doubt that what he told her was accurate. The letters had most likely originated in Edinburgh, and to Edinburgh Eleanor would go. "Thank you," she said.

Ian, seeing that Eleanor had finished her questions, became fully absorbed in his son. Eleanor watched, content in the April sunshine, as Ian and Jamie set up the soldiers again, Ian lying on his stomach while Jamie worked his way around his large father.

When Jamie tired, Ian sat up and let Jamie climb onto his

plaid-clad lap. Ian closed his arms around his son, and Jamie dozed, Ian gazing down at him with such intense love that Eleanor quietly rose and left them alone.

~~~~~

Eleanor found it easy to get herself and Hart to Edinburgh not a few days later, into the very house in which one of the maids from High Holborn now worked. A woman called Mrs. McGuire had hired the maid, and Eleanor found that she and Hart—now the most sought-after couple in Scotland—had already been invited to Mrs. McGuire's next grand soiree.

Eleanor had met Mrs. McGuire many times. She was the wife of The McGuire—the leader of clan McGuire—though Mrs. McGuire had started life as an English viscount's daughter, raised to fine society in London. By all accounts, Mrs. McGuire adored her Highland husband, and her Edinburgh galas had become celebrated.

She was a kindhearted woman as well, a friend to Eleanor's late mother. Eleanor quite liked her. Why Mrs. McGuire had hired a maid out of a brothel remained to be seen.

Hart and Eleanor descended before Mrs. McGuire's Edinburgh home to the carpet a footman had spread from carriage step to doorstep. The entire street stopped to watch the fine carriage, the splendid horses, and the most famous man in Scotland and his new wife arrive at their first outing together.

Mrs. McGuire was buried with her guests upstairs, and a plump maid with very black hair took Eleanor's wraps in the relative quiet of the downstairs hall. When the maid passed Hart, he stopped, smiled at her, and gave her an unashamed wink. The maid blushed, but she shot him a sunny smile in return and winked back.

Eleanor opened her mouth to demand what it was all about, but Hart had already turned to greet some of his cronies, and was swept up the stairs with them. Maigdlin was herding her into a withdrawing room so she could repair any damage the short journey from Isabella's Edinburgh house might have done to Eleanor's hair and gown.

Before Eleanor could decide how she felt about Hart's bla-tant exchange with the maid, the maid herself entered the withdrawing room, came straight to Eleanor, and dropped a perfect maid's curtsey.

"Your Grace."

Maigdlin glared like a she-bear ready to defend her cub. "The cheek of you. You don't speak to a duchess without her permission, you ignorant woman. What do you want?"

"It's all right, Maigdlin," Eleanor said quickly. "It's Joanna Brown, isn't it?" *From the High Holborn house.*

The maid curtseyed again. "Yes, Your Grace." She had an English accent, from somewhere in London's darker environs, Eleanor thought. "I know it *is* bloody cheek, but might I have a word with you? Private like?"

Maigdlin gave Joanna a look of high disdain, but Eleanor held up a reassuring hand. "Of course. Maigdlin, will you stand outside so that we are not disturbed?"

Maigdlin's outrage was obvious, but she set down the brushes she'd taken from Eleanor's case, curtseyed stiffly, and glided out the door, as though determined to show Joanna that at least *one* of them had manners. Indeed, if Eleanor had been a stickler for rules, she could have Joanna sacked for deigning to approach her, let alone speak to her. But Eleanor had never been one to bother with rules, especially when they got in the way of what she wished to do.

"I'm sorry, Your Grace," Joanna said as soon as they were alone. "But I know you saw that wink, and I wanted to explain to you, so as you'd not have the wrong idea."

Eleanor looked her over. Joanna had black hair and blue eyes and was not long past her first youth, perhaps thirty at most. She had a winsome smile, and her eyes sparkled with animation.

"All right," Eleanor said. "But first, I must ask you. What do you know about photographs?"

The maid's smile deepened. "Many things, Your Grace. You got them, then?"

Eleanor stopped. "You have been sending me the photographs?" She thought of the ill-spelled missives, always with the closing, *From one as wishes you well.* The words went with the warm woman who stood before her now.

"Goodness," Eleanor said. "You did lead me on a merry chase. Why did you send them?"

Joanna curtseyed again, as though she couldn't help herself. "Because I knew they'd take you to him. And see—you're married to him now, and he looks ever so much better, doesn't he? Now about that wink, Your Grace, it don't mean nothing. He does that because he's a kindhearted man. It's sort of a signal, a joke between us, really."

"A joke." This was the first time in memory that Eleanor had heard someone refer to Hart as *a kindhearted man*. "Has it to do with the photographs?"

Had *Hart* told Joanna to send them? It would be like him, to confound and tease Eleanor with the photographs and at the same time pretend he cared nothing about them. Hart Mackenzie needed a good talking to.

"No, no," Joanna said. "Them's two separate things. If you'll listen, Your Grace, I'll explain."

Eleanor nodded, curbing her impatience. "Yes, indeed. Please do."

"Blame my forwardness on me upbringing, Your Grace. I grew up in London, in the east part of it, near St. Katherine's Docks. That was all right, but my father was a lout and a layabout and my mother didn't amount to nothing, so we were poor as dirt. I decided I'd clean up and learn my manners and become a maid in a Mayfair household, maybe even a lady's maid. Well, I didn't know nothing about training or references, I was that green. But I did my best, and I went and answered an advertisement for a position. Name of the lady what hired me was Mrs. Palmer."

"Oh, dear." Eleanor saw a glimmer of what was coming. "You didn't realize she was a procuress?"

"Naw. Where I came from, bad girls were obvious, flouncing about the streets and such, and what wicked tongues they had on them! But Mrs. Palmer spoke quiet like, and her house was large and filled with expensive things. I didn't know at the time that ladybirds could be so lofty and thought I'd landed in clover. But that went away as soon as she took me upstairs, where she and another lady were in a bedroom. The things they told me they wanted me to do would make you faint, Your Grace. I might have grown up rough, but I was at least taught good from bad. So I said I wouldn't, no matter how much they slapped me, and then Ma Palmer grabbed me and locked me in a room."

Eleanor's hands closed to fists, the pity she'd held for Mrs. Palmer, which had diminished over what the woman had done to Beth, diminished further. "I am sorry. Go on."

"Well, Ma Palmer let me out again later that night. She said she had to get me cleaned up, because the master of the house was coming. I thought she meant her husband, and I couldn't imagine what sort of man would marry someone like her. So there I was, washed and brushed, with a brand-new frock and cap, told I needed to bring the tea things into the parlor. Well, that didn't sound so bad, and maybe Mrs. Palmer would behave herself in front of her husband. Cook put together the tea tray, and I made sure it was all pretty and carried it into the parlor. And *he* was there."

Eleanor didn't need to ask who *he* was. Hart Mackenzie, devastatingly handsome, arrogant, compelling.

"He were the most handsome gent I'd ever seen, and obviously so very rich. I stood there in the doorway, gaping at him like a fool. He gives me such a look, like he can see me inside and out, and gents like him aren't supposed to even notice servants. At least that's what I'd been told. I should be invisible, but he takes a long time to look at me. Then he sits down on the sofa, and Mrs. Palmer puts herself next to him, fluttering and cooing like a lovesick schoolgirl. She tells me to set down the tray on the table in front of them, and I tell you I was that nervous. I was sure I'd drop all the crockery, and then I'd be out on my ear.

"Ma Palmer laughs and says to him, *Look what I've brought you.* At first, I thought she meant the tea, then I caught on that she meant *me*."

Eleanor remembered Mrs. Palmer confessing, her handsome face anguished, that she'd hired other women for Hart when she feared he'd grown tired of her. But Joanna hadn't been a game girl, only a naive young woman trying to better her life. Eleanor's pity for the late Mrs. Palmer diminished still more.

"I mean to tell you, Your Grace, I almost did drop all the tea things," Joanna said. "It hit me like a blow that Mrs. Palmer had hired me to be a whore for her husband. I still thought he were her husband at that point, you see. I wanted to cry, or run back home, or even go for a constable. But Ma Palmer grabs me and whispers into my ear, *He's a duke. You do whatever he says, or he can make things very bad for you.*

"I was that terrified. I believed her, because aristocrats, they do anything they like, don't they? I knew a lad who used to be footman to one, and the lad got a beating whenever the lord was out of temper, didn't matter that he wasn't angry at the footman at all. I was sure Mrs. Palmer was right, and I was shaking in me boots, I can tell you.

"And then His Grace, he looked me over again and told Mrs. Palmer to get out of the room. She went, not looking pleased about it, but I realized, even then, that when this gent snapped his fingers, Ma Palmer jumped.

"Anyway, she left and closed the door. And there was His Grace, a'sitting on the sofa, looking at me. You know how he does. Steady like, as though he knows everything about you, every secret you ever had, and ones you didn't even know about."

Eleanor did know. The penetrating golden stare, the stillness, Hart's conviction that he commanded everyone in his sight. "Indeed."

"So, there I was. *Well, Joanna, you're in for it now*, I was thinking. I'd be a ruined girl and never get a good place again. I'd be a whore the rest of me life, and that would be the end of it.

"His Grace just looks at me, and then he asks my name. I told him—weren't no use in lying. Then he asks where I came from, and was this my first place, and what possessed me take a job with Mrs. Palmer? I told him I hadn't known about Ma Palmer until I was already in the house. He looked angry, very angry, but I somehow knew he weren't angry at me. His Grace told me to stay where I was, and he goes to the desk and pulls out some paper. He sits down and starts writing something, me standing there with my hands empty, having no idea what to do.

"He finishes up and comes back to me, handing me the folded letter. *You take this to a lady I know in South Audley Street*, he says. *I've written the directions on the front. You walk out of this house and find a hansom and tell him to take you there. Tell the housekeeper in South Audley Street to give the letter to the lady of the house, and do not let her turn you away.* Then he hands me shillings. I didn't want to take them, but he said they were for the hansom. He told me not even to go back upstairs and get my things—such as they were.

"I was a little worried about where such a man as him would send me, but he gives me a stern look and says, *She's a lady, is Mrs. McGuire, a true lady with a tender heart. She'll look after you.*

"I started to cry and say thank you, and that he was being so kind. He put his finger to his lips and smiled at me. You've seen His Grace smile. It's like sunshine after a wet day. And he says—I'll never forget his exact words—*Don't ever say to anyone that I am kind. It will ruin my reputation. Only I will know, and you. It will be our secret.* Then he winked, like he did when he came in tonight.

"I weren't sure, even then, because I'd never heard of this Mrs. McGuire. It might be all a strange game he was playing with me. But I did what he said. He even walked me out into the hall and down to the front door. I should have gone out the back, being a servant, but he said he didn't want me walking through the kitchens.

"Mrs. Palmer comes out while he's taking me down the stairs. He gives me a little shove toward the front door, and then he turned on her. Right enraged he was. He shouted something terrible, asking Ma Palmer what was the matter with her, and *Why would you think me depraved enough to want to deflower an innocent?* Mrs. Palmer was crying and shouting back at him, and telling him she didn't know I was an innocent, which was a lie, because she'd asked me. I ran right out of that house and let the door bang behind me, so I didn't hear any more.

"Now, I could have taken the shillings and gone anywhere I wanted to, but I decided to take the hansom to South Audley Street and give the letter to Mrs. McGuire on the off chance." Joanna spread her hands. "And here I am."

The story sounded like Hart—he had an amazing sensibility about what people were like and who needed a hand up and who needed to be kept in check. That was how he'd risen so far, she thought, from a lad beaten by his father to a man knowing who to be gentle with and when.

"I still haven't told you all of it," Joanna said. "The next time

I saw His Grace, he was paying a call on Mrs. McGuire, who is a good lady, just as he told me. When I took his coat, I made to say something to him, but he puts his finger to his lips again and tips me a wink. I winked back at him, and he went away. It's become our signal, like, for me saying thank you, and for him keeping his good deeds secret. No one's ever caught the signal, except you, tonight. Stands to reason you would, since you're his wife. I wanted to tell you all about it, in case you misunderstood. And I'm married meself now," Joanna finished proudly. "I have a son, five years old and he's such trouble."

Eleanor sat still after Joanna finished, thinking the story through. "You haven't explained about the photographs. How did you get them? Did Hart himself give them to you?"

"His Grace? No. He knows nothing about them. They came my way about four months ago, around Christmas."

"Came your way how?"

"In the post. A little packet of them, and I must tell you, I blushed when I opened them. It came with a note that told me to send them on to you."

Eleanor's eyes narrowed. "A note from whom?"

"Didn't say. But I was told to send them to you one or two at a time, starting in February. I knew who you were, everyone does, and I thought it couldn't do no harm. His Grace always looks sad, and it tickled me to think you'd maybe go and see him, and show him the piccies and make him smile. And you see? You married him."

"But what about the others?" Eleanor said, her curiosity not abated. "Why were they sold to a shop in the Strand?"

Joanna blinked. "Others? I don't know about any others. I was sent the eight, which I started sending on to you."

"I see." Eleanor thought about the sequence of events. Hart had proclaimed his intention of taking a wife to his family at Ascot last year in June. Joanna was sent the photographs at Christmastime, told to start sending them to Eleanor in February. Eleanor rushes to London to see Hart, Hart begins his game of seduction, and Eleanor now was his wife.

Planned by Hart from beginning to end? He was devious enough to do it.

"How do you know His Grace himself didn't send you the photographs?"

Joanna shrugged. "Handwriting was different. I'd seen the letter he wrote to Mrs. McGuire."

Hart might be canny enough to know that, perhaps get someone else to pen the note, not telling that person what it was all about. Eleanor might have to interrogate Wilfred.

"How did you know I'd gone to London?" she asked. "The second photograph reached me there, in his house."

"Mrs. McGuire," Joanna said. "She knows everyone. Her friends in London wrote her that you were in London, you and your father guests of His Grace in Grosvenor Square. I was serving tea one afternoon when Mrs. McGuire read the letter out to her husband."

Whoever had sent Joanna the photographs remained a mystery, though perhaps not such a mystery. Hart might be perfectly innocent of it, but he loved to guide a situation to the conclusion he wanted, so much that Eleanor could not help but suspect him. The man would drive her insane. But then, Hart excelled at driving people insane.

"Thank you, Joanna." Eleanor got to her feet, took Joanna's hands, and kissed the startled woman's cheek. She reached into her reticule and pulled out a few gold coins.

Joanna held up her hands. "No, Your Grace, you don't need to give me nothing. I was doing it for *him*. And you. He needs someone to look after him, don't he?"

"Don't be silly. You have a little boy now." Eleanor took the maid's hand and pressed the coins into it, then she kissed Joanna's cheek again. "Bless you."

She hurried away and out of the room, leaving both Maigdlin and Joanna behind as she went in search of her husband.

～

Hart broke from a clump of men arguing against Irish Home Rule, they saying that the Irish were too stupid to make decisions for themselves, and headed for the card room. His blood was up. The card tables, with their games of numbers and odds would soothe him. He understood why Ian liked to immerse himself in mathematical sequences—there was a purity about numbers that eased the mind.

He heard Eleanor's light step behind him, then her clear voice.

"You're a fraud, Hart Mackenzie."

Hart turned. He and Eleanor were alone in the little hall. Laughter, masculine voices, and smoke drifted from the card room at one end, and feminine exclamations came from the drawing room at the other.

"Fraud? What are you talking about this time, minx?"

Eleanor came to him, her steps slow, her hips swaying under her bustle dress. Her color was high, and her eyes sparkled. "A complete and utter fraud."

Hart frowned, but her hot little smile, the way she stepped close to him, stirred his desire.

Stirred? It had never gone away.

"I know how Joanna came to work in this house," Eleanor said. "She told me everything."

Hart remembered the maid, so many years ago now, standing before Hart, trembling and terrified. She'd been incoherent with fear. Angelina had been trying to tempt his appetite, as usual, but she'd miscalculated with Joanna.

Hart made himself shrug. "She didn't belong there, she was an innocent, and I couldn't throw her out into the street. How does this make me a fraud?"

"The hard-hearted Duke of Kilmorgan. All must tremble before him."

"How much sherry have you drunk, El?" He wanted to draw his finger across her lips, down her throat to her bosom bared by her evening dress.

"You do an act of kindness, then beg her to tell no one, in case people discover you have a heart."

"*Beg* is going a bit far." He'd told Joanna to keep quiet to spare her reputation. The world was hard on young women tainted by the demimonde, even if they fell into it by no fault of their own. Once the line was crossed, there was no going back. Mrs. McGuire was the kindhearted one. She'd taken Joanna on Hart's word and asked no questions.

Several men started coming out of the card room. Hart grasped Eleanor's arm and steered her quickly up the stairs to the next floor. The gentlemen did not notice them, and went on to the drawing room, greeting the ladies there.

Hart opened the door nearest the top of the stairs and towed Eleanor inside. It was a little sitting room, lit by one gaslight, and Mrs. McGuire's staff were apparently storing guests' coats there.

"Say nothing about Joanna," Hart said. "For her sake."

Eleanor withdrew from his grasp. "I had no intention of saying anything. You had no need to drag me up here to tell me that. You could have whispered it into my ear."

"I did need to."

"Running from the pompous gentlemen already?" she asked, smile in place. "We've not been here above half an hour yet."

Avoiding more tiresome arguments had only been part of it. Hart had had the sudden and overwhelming urge to be alone with Eleanor, and Mac's town house, where they were staying the night, was too far away.

"Now that I do have you alone," Eleanor said, "I will tell you that it was Joanna who sent me the photographs."

Hart stopped, surprised. "Did she? Where did she get them? Stolen from Mrs. Palmer?" If Joanna had somehow found those ridiculous photographs while staying with Mrs. Palmer, would she have looked at Hart in such terror?

Eleanor's eyes narrowed. "Did *you* give them to Joanna?"

"No. Why the devil would I?"

"Playing some game of your own?"

He shook his head. "Not this time."

"Hmm." Eleanor folded her arms and regarded him skeptically.

"Now, what are you doing?" Hart asked.

"Deciding whether or not to believe you."

"Believe whatever you want." Hart could wait no longer. He snaked one arm around her waist and pulled her with him across the room to an armchair, which had given him an interesting idea. He swept the coats that had been carefully folded over the chair to the floor.

"Hart, you should not . . ."

"I should. How is your arm?"

"Much better. But you know that. You ask me three times a day."

"I am the reason you were hurt," Hart said. "I'd ask five times a day if I saw you that often. Now, come here."

"Why? What are you going to do?"

Hart seized her hand before she could back away and pulled her smack against him. "It was very dangerous for you to smile at me like you did downstairs."

As though she loved him. As though she wanted him. He touched her lips.

Eleanor pulled away the slightest bit. "What if someone comes in?"

Hart smiled his excitement. "What if someone does?"

"Oh." He saw her passion rise. "I see."

"Turn around," he said.

Hart swiftly found the fasteners that held her skirts to her bodice and undid them. He lifted the skirt off, and the petticoats as well, then untied the tapes that held her bustle in place. Under that, she wore fine lawn drawers, no more worn fabric for his wife. He had her out of those quickly too.

He sat down on the armchair, faced Eleanor away from him, unswathed the kilt from his hips, and pulled Eleanor down to his lap. Eleanor gasped in surprise, but she was so slick that Hart slid right into her.

Yes. Hart tilted her head to the side, baring her neck and shoulder to him, she still in her bodice. The satin rode low across her bosom, delphinium blue fabric to match her eyes. He suckled a little, tasting her skin and the fragrance she'd dabbed on.

Eleanor wriggled, seemingly pleased at the way that drove him inside her. Hart let her play while he fingered her curls and kissed her neck.

He'd positioned the chair so that the standing mirror across the room would reflect them. Eleanor had her eyes closed, but Hart drank in the sight of her bare legs wrapped around his browner ones, her head resting on his shoulder, trickles of her hair snaking across his chest, and the place where they joined.

He could watch as he pleasured her, see her every rise of chest and twist of mouth, every flutter of her hands as she pushed against his thighs. She was a beautiful, beautiful sight.

It did not take long, and Hart hadn't thought it would, before Eleanor found her deepest pleasure. Hart reached to the join of her legs and gently stroked her.

Eleanor's eyes opened wide, and she cried out her joy. Hart's shout joined hers, the syllables of her name a delight on his lips.

Eleanor sank back onto him with a sigh, and Hart wrapped his arms around her and held her close. He would never let her go. She was too precious to him.

He touched the bandage on her arm, a smaller dressing now, thank God, and vowed that he'd never let anything hurt her again.

~~~~~

The halcyon first days of Eleanor's marriage ended when Hart had to return to London. A telegram from David Fleming arrived at Kilmorgan, and off Hart went. It was time for him to work, and Eleanor knew that from now on, she'd see little of him.

True to his word, Hart did have Wilfred make arrangements to move Eleanor to town as soon as possible. Hart's lingering kiss promised he'd do much more when she arrived at the Grosvenor Square house, and then he was gone.

Eleanor had too much to do to wallow in missing him, and the day or so between his departure and hers flew by. She was excited not only to see Hart again, but to make a start on redecorating the house. The Grosvenor Square mansion had been left much as when Hart's father had lived in it, and Eleanor was determined to give it a new life. She'd be hosting balls, soirees, and garden parties of her own there, and she'd need to make a hurried start.

Eleanor traveled to London with Ian and Beth and their two children, plus Ainsley and her baby daughter, Gavina. Mac and Isabella had already gone, their three children in tow, back to Isabella's London social whirl. Cameron had returned south to his horses, and Daniel remained in Edinburgh at university.

Hart had a private car that was hooked to the back of the train in Edinburgh, Hart, of course, always traveling in luxury. The parlor car helped keep the three busy children contained, at least. Eleanor helped with them, enjoying the task.

She watched them with a secret hope in her heart. Her cycle was late, which could mean a child starting or could mean nothing. Eleanor hadn't conceived when she'd been Hart's lover years ago, and she was much older now.

Euston station in London was crowded when they arrived,

so many people traveling up and down the country. The train glided into its empty platform, Hart's car being the last in the line.

Eleanor was happy to alight, the overcushioned comfort starting to wear on her. Perhaps she should redecorate the car as well.

Hart was to come to the station to meet her, and her heart beat faster as she stepped down to the platform. He'd scoop her up for a kiss—Hart wouldn't care that all of London watched. She'd let him know, when she could whisper it to him, that her arm felt *much* better.

Beth and Ainsley lingered with the children's nannies to put everyone to rights, Ian protectively with them. Eleanor couldn't wait. She excused herself, eager to find Hart and go home.

Eleanor lifted her small valise and started walking down the platform, ignoring the porters and the duke's footmen, who looked shocked that she was actually carrying a bag *by herself.* She spied Mac's tall bulk in the crowd in the main part of the station, Aimee on his shoulders, Isabella beside him. No babies, so they must have been left in the charge of Nanny Westlock at home. Aimee would have insisted on coming along.

But no Hart. Eleanor tried not to let her heart sink. Her husband had many things to do now, and some crisis had likely prevented him from leaving Whitehall. That was probably why Mac had come instead.

Eleanor waved across the platforms and crowd to Isabella, and Isabella and Aimee waved back. She walked quickly onward, making her way to the main platform. She could almost feel Isabella's hug and kiss, and see Mac's huge smile and hear the booming baritone of his voice in greeting.

How splendid to be part of such a family—a large, unpredictable family with her husband at its head. Eleanor walked faster, feet light.

When she neared them, Eleanor saw, at the far end of the platform, entering the station, the unmistakable form of Hart Mackenzie. With him was the tall David Fleming, he and Hart debating something as usual. The pugilist bodyguards trailed behind them.

Eleanor resisted the urge to run straight to Hart and stopped to hug Isabella and Mac.

"There's Ian," Mac said, looking across the platforms. He shaded his eyes. "What is he doing?"

Ian was standing at the edge of the platform, two over, where their train had pulled in. His gaze was fixed on something near the waiting room, but Eleanor, glancing that way, couldn't discern what had caught his eye.

Her gaze was drawn back to Hart, and Isabella laughed. "Go on. He needs someone to be glad to see him."

Mac snatched Eleanor's valise out of her hand, and Eleanor thanked him and started pushing through the crowd toward Hart. So many people, so many bonnets and tall hats, so many bustles and folded parasols and umbrellas to wade through. Did they all have to be here *today*?

Hart loomed through the crowd, Fleming having dropped back. Across the space between them, Hart's gaze met Eleanor's. She felt warmed, happy.

She saw Hart stop, turn, scowl, then lift his hands to his mouth and shout Ian's name. Eleanor turned to look, and her mouth went slack as Ian dropped from the platform to the tracks, sprinted across them, climbed the next platform, and dropped onto the next set of tracks, never minding the giant steam engine chugging into the station toward him.

Beth saw, and screamed. Hart kept shouting. Ian cleared the tracks and leapt onto the platform with seconds to spare, his kilt flying as he ran for Hart.

A loud noise sounded to Eleanor's left, nearly drowned by the groaning breaks of the approaching train. Eleanor turned her head, heard a *boom!* then saw a giant cloud of smoke, rubble, and glass expand and rise to cover the entire platform and all the people on it.

Eleanor felt her body pushed backward. She fell against a man in a long wool coat and then slapped onto the surface of the platform. Then she was rolling toward the edge, the iron face of the engine coming at her, and she heard the horrible hiss of steam and squeal of metal on metal as the train tried to stop.

Chapter 19

At the last minute, Eleanor stopped her wild rolling and shoved herself away from the edge of the platform. The locomotive slid by, and Eleanor lay on her stomach, trying to catch her breath.

She heard screams and smelled smoke, saw bricks, stone, and glass raining like bullets onto the crowd. She dimly heard Mac swearing, and Isabella frantically calling her name.

Eleanor pushed herself up, blinking grit-stained eyes as she climbed painfully to her feet. Around her people lay groaning, crying, some trying to rise as she was. She peered through the smoke to where Hart had been standing not a yard from the explosion, and did not see him.

The train next to her was intact except for broken windows and frightened passengers looking out of them. Across the platforms, through the thick air, she glimpsed Beth and Ainsley running for her, the fearful nannies staying behind with the babies.

Eleanor shoved her way forward, ignoring Mac and Isabella, her heart constricting as she searched for any sign of her husband.

"Hart!" she shouted. She cupped her hands around her mouth, tears and smoke stinging her eyes. *"Hart!"*

She kept moving forward, gaining strength as she went, until she was running. "Hart!" She heard Beth's voice shrill behind her, *"Ian!"* because Ian had vanished too.

Eleanor saw Hart's bodyguards frantically shoving through the mob. They were searching, turning every which way, not finding him.

Eleanor's limbs turned icy with fear. "Where is he? Where is he?" she screamed at the nearest bodyguard.

The man shook his head. "He was right there. He was right *there.*" He pointed a thick finger to a patch of platform that did not exist anymore. The wall of the station house was gone as well, and remains of vendors' carts were scattered across the rubble.

Eleanor ran to the heap and started pulling away stones. Her hands were too small, her gloves too thin. The leather ripped, and her hands bled. The bodyguard started helping her, and others around caught on, reaching for stones.

A hand came into view, one groping for life. Eleanor clutched it. The bodyguard shifted a stone, then reached in and pulled the person out. An older woman, one of the vendors. She clung to Eleanor, and Eleanor held her, stroking her back.

Mac reached her, bellowing into the smoke and dust. "Where is Hart? Where is Ian?"

Eleanor could only shake her head. Tears fell, hot, to her face, and she held on to the woman at her side, having no comfort to give.

Mac started pulling away the rubble. He shouted orders in a harsh voice, and people hurried to obey. Isabella was suddenly beside Eleanor, and then Beth. Beth was crying and trying not to.

"He saw something wrong," Beth said. "He ran to warn Hart. He ran to help him."

Ainsley came to them, her capable arm around Beth's waist. "El, Beth, you should come away. The danger might not be over."

Eleanor shook her head. "Inspector Fellows was supposed to arrest them all. He was supposed to find them."

"He did," Isabella said. "The newspapers were full of it.

But there are always others." Her eyes held tears as well as rage.

"I can't go," Eleanor said. "I can't run for shelter while people are hurt. I have to help them. You take Beth and the children home." She had to stay. She had to know that Hart was all right.

She kept expecting him to rise like a giant from the ashes, shouting orders and taking charge. And Ian with him, Ian who was the most resilient man she knew. But—nothing.

People were coming, women with white pinafores, men in dark clothes, rushing to help. Eleanor gave over the woman she'd helped rescue to one of the nurses and turned to other unfortunates lying in the rubble. Mac and the bodyguards kept lifting stones, joined by workers and others in the station.

Ainsley at last persuaded Beth to leave with her, the nannies having gotten the children safely out through the other end of the station. Isabella carried Aimee, following the two ladies as they went, arms around each other. Eleanor, left alone, helped the nurses—lifted stones, held people, comforted them, bandaged the hurt.

At one point she saw a man rush in who had Hart's build and look, and her heart nearly stopped. But it wasn't Hart; the man was Inspector Fellows. Mac went to him and both stood back to survey the mess and the crowd.

Eleanor kept working, helping, trying to calm people and reassure them. The station was clearing, the injured being taken away, others gone or helping search the rubble. They found more people buried inside, all still breathing when they came out, thank God.

But no Hart, no Ian. As the station darkened with night, the platform was cleared to reveal a great, gaping hole. A noisome smell came out of the hole, which was half filled with rubble. Mac, with Inspector Fellows, bullied men to bring in equipment, and they dug down into the hole and the sewers beyond.

But they never found Hart or Ian, not a trace of them.

Hart couldn't breathe. He was choking, drowning, and someone was beating him, blows crushing his back and ribs.

Don't cry out. Don't let him know how much it hurts.

It was very important that Hart never let his father see him break down, never let his father win. The duke wanted Hart to be his slave, to obey his every wish, no matter how trivial or how vicious.

Never. Though he beats me until I die, I will never belong to him.

The old duke had never tried to drown Hart before, though. Only beating, usually with a birch cane or a leather strap—or if they were outdoors, any stray branch that looked sturdy enough.

Through the pain and fog in his mind, Hart knew there was something—something good—that he needed to remember. Something he could hang on to, which would see him through. Something that made his heart warm despite the dank chill surrounding him.

Hart opened his eyes. Or thought he did. He saw only inky darkness.

The beating went on. Dimly Hart remembered looking down the barrel of a shotgun into his father's purple and enraged face, then the explosion of sound as the gun went off. It rang in Hart's ears still. Was his father dead? He couldn't remember.

Something roiled in Hart's gut, and he rose on his hands and knees to vomit it out. He remained there, gasping and retching, but at least his father had stopped beating him.

The roaring in his ears wouldn't cease. Hart had no memory of how he came to be in this dark place, but he was certain his father had something to do with it. *I'll bury you alive, boy. Maybe that will make you respectful.*

He smelled something sharp under his nose, felt a cold, smooth edge on his lips, and then burning liquid in his mouth. Hart coughed and swallowed. The liquid seared his throat and slid to his stomach, and he felt a bit better.

The taste was familiar. "Mackenzie single malt," he croaked.

The hand that held it could not belong to Hart's father. The old man would never have given Hart a healing swig of whiskey, especially none this good. This was the reserve stock, which only Mackenzies got to drink.

"Where the hell am I?"

"Underground," a baritone voice said next to him. "In one of the middle-level interceptor sewers."

"One of the *what*?"

"Middle-level interceptor . . ."

"I heard you the first time, Ian." Hart knew it was his youngest brother with him in the dark. No other man would explain their precise location with such patience, prepared to repeat it until Hart understood.

Hart rubbed his aching head, finding something wet, which, judging from the pain, was blood. "The sewers, eh? Two Scotsmen left to die in the midst of English filth. I spent my first years as an MP on various committees on sewage. The Dung Committees, I always called them."

Silence. Ian would have no idea what Hart was talking about, nor would he care.

"We need to get out of this place." Hart reached out in the dark, found the warm solidity of his brother's arm. "Before Father finds us."

More silence. Ian touched Hart's hand. "Father is dead."

In a rush, Hart saw the shotgun again, heard the roar of it, saw his father crumple to the ground.

I shot him. I killed him.

Relief made his body light. "Thank God," he said. "Thank God."

More memories came at him, especially that good, warm one that pushed its way up and spread through his heart. But with remembering came fear.

"Eleanor. Is she safe? Did you see? Ian, *is she safe*?"

"I don't know." Hart heard anguish in Ian's usual monotone. "I saw the man put down the bomb. I tried to reach you to push you out of the way, then there was the hole, and we fell and fell. Beth was too far from the center of the blast, and so were Ainsley and Mac and Isabella. I think Eleanor was too."

"You *think* she was?"

"You were closest. I had to reach you."

Hart heard his panic. Ian could go into what he called *muddles*, where he'd either lash out or start to do one thing over and over, unable to stop. Even now, Hart felt Ian rocking back and forth as he tried to deal with his distress.

Hart reached up the best he could and put his hand on Ian's shoulder. "Ian, it's all right. I'm alive. You're alive. You were right. If you say Eleanor was too far back, she likely was." He barked a laugh. "I wager you could calculate the exact trajectory and spread of the blast."

"I'd need to know the weight and type of explosive." Ian still rocked but it slowed. "From the smell, dynamite, a few sticks. The package he had was small."

"We need to go back and get the bastard," Hart said. "In case he has another stick."

"He died," Ian said. "He did not walk away from the bomb. He lit it and stayed with it."

"Dear God, save us from madmen." Hart scrambled to his hands and knees again and tried to get to his feet, swallowing a curse when his head cracked on a low, stone ceiling. He fell, his head spinning. It wouldn't stop spinning.

Ian pushed Hart back down. "Five feet of clearance until we reach the storm platform."

"How the devil do you know that?" Hart asked.

"I learned the schematics of the tunnels under London. Water pipes, storm drains, rivers, gas lines, the London Metropolitan . . ."

"Yes, yes, of course you did. The question is why."

There was more silence as Ian considered. "To pass the time."

He meant the time before he'd met Beth, when Ian's life had been tedious.

"I'll put myself into your hands, Ian. Where is this storm platform?"

Ian took Hart's hand and pulled it in front of him to indicate direction. "That way."

Hart rubbed his head where he'd smashed it against bricks. He still couldn't make this dark world stop spinning. "All right. Lead me."

They had to crawl. As soon as Hart began to move, bile rose in his throat, and dizziness threatened to cripple him.

Thankfully, after about ten yards or so, the tunnel rose a bit, and they could stand. Hart and Ian still had to bend their backs, the round ceiling low above them, but no more going on hands and knees.

Ian led Hart onward, Hart hanging on to the back of Ian's

coat as they splashed through icy water. Hart's hands were cut and bleeding, and his head pounded like fury.

The only thing that kept Hart going was the image of Eleanor disappearing behind a cloud of rubble and dust. He had to find her, to make sure she was all right. That burning need propelled him onward.

Ian straightened to his full height in front of Hart, and a step later, Hart could too.

The echoes broadened, meaning that the ceiling had vaulted upward, and the air smelled almost fresh. A light, so faint as to be barely a light, came from Hart's right. After the complete darkness of the tunnel, it seemed bright.

"Storm drain," Ian said, gesturing to the light. "This one empties into the Fleet."

The Fleet River had been covered, partly or completely, for centuries. It was mostly a sewer now, pouring into the Thames after heavy rains via drains like this one.

"How do we get out?" Hart asked. "The hell I'm going to float myself down the filthy Fleet and get stuck halfway in a storm grating."

"Shafts go up to the streets," Ian said. "But not here."

Of course not. "Where, then?"

"Through the tunnels," Ian said. "A mile, maybe more."

Hart swallowed on dryness. Ian's face was a pale smudge in the darkness, but Hart could see little beyond that. "Give me the flask again."

Wordlessly Ian put the flask of whiskey into Hart's hand, and Hart upended more single malt into his mouth. It was ambrosia, though he'd love a clear glass of water.

Hart gave the flask back to Ian, and Ian pocketed it without drinking. "This way," he said.

Hart took two steps to follow him, then his legs buckled. He found himself on bare floor, retching again. His head was spinning like a gyroscope.

Ian was next to him. "In the explosion, something hit you in the head," Ian said.

Hart gasped for breath. "Very perceptive of you, Ian."

Ian went quiet, but Hart knew him well enough to know that thoughts were moving through Ian's head at lightning speed while he tried to decide what to do.

"If we go slowly, I can make it," Hart said.

"If we are too slow, we can't outrun the water. Or the gasses."

"I don't see that we have a bloody choice." Hart hung on to Ian as his younger brother leveraged Hart to his feet. The dizziness made everything go black for a moment. "Wait."

Hart felt his feet leave the ground as Ian hoisted Hart onto his back. Without a word, they started moving, slowly, Hart hanging on as Ian carried him out.

He knew he'd never convince Ian to leave him behind and go for help. When Ian fixed on a course, all the reasoning in the world couldn't move him. Just as well. Hart did not want to be down here alone, in any case.

The sudden echoing roar was their only warning. Rains north of the city had raised the level of the water, and now it poured into the round pipes, rising over the weirs, to flow through the storm drains and down into the rivers.

Ian yelled, his words incoherent, as he lifted Hart up and shoved him onto a tall slab of stone next to the weir. The rocks were slippery, and Hart scrambled to hold on and stay awake at the same time.

Water poured into the tunnel. In the faint light, soon obliterated by water, Hart saw his brother be swept from his feet and carried at breakneck speed away from him.

"Ian!" Hart screamed. *"Ian!"*

His words were lost in the water. For an age it pulsed through swirling waters in the darkness. Ian had been swept the other way, caught in a surge that went back into the round tunnels. But the tunnels were full to the top.

"Ian!" Hart shouted.

After a long, heartbreakingly long time, the waters receded. When it had reduced to a foot flowing on the floor below him, Hart slid down from his perch. His head pounded, and he fell, landing in the freezing cold water.

He would die in here. Ian could already be dead.

The light vanished. Hart had no way of knowing if debris in the water had blocked the drain or whether the sun was going down outside. Or maybe it was his eyes closing.

The next thing Hart knew, someone kicked him.

"This 'ere's my patch," a man said. "What you doing on it?"

Hart peeled open his eyes. A lantern swung in front of his face, blinding him, and the pounding in his head soared to sickening levels.

"You know the way out?" Hart asked. His voice came out a croak, barely audible.

"Lost, are ye? That's what ye get for being on my patch. What did ye take?"

"Show me the way out. I'll pay you."

The man thrust his hand inside Hart's coat and came out again, empty. "Seems like you don't have nothing."

Between the blast, the fall, the desperate crawling, and the flood, Hart was surprised his clothes hadn't shredded. His money pouch must have fallen out somewhere along the way.

"When you get me out, I'll pay."

"Right," the man said.

Hart saw his boot draw back, tried to grab it as it came down, but his dizziness made him clumsy. The boot struck Hart's face, and then everything went dark again.

Eleanor was back at the Grosvenor Square house with the rest of the family by the time darkness fell. Mr. Fellows and all the police in London had searched, but they'd found no sign of either Hart or Ian.

Cameron was there, summoned from Berkshire by telegram, and Daniel telegraphed to say he was on his way. Mac and Cameron were about to tear the city apart. Eleanor paced the front rooms, unable to sit down. Beth perched on the edge of a chair, just as jumpy as Eleanor.

"We have to do *something*," Beth was saying.

Eleanor couldn't answer. She wanted to rush through the streets, turning over every stone until she found Hart. Inspector Fellows and his men had explored the service tunnels under Euston station, but had found nothing. Fellows was here now, in the dining room with Cam and Mac.

Eleanor glanced out the window, but not much could be seen in the heavy fog, barely penetrated by the gaslights on the square. She felt numb, sickeningly so. *This can't be real. He'll come striding home, deriding us all for worrying.*

Beth joined her at the window, her arm around Eleanor's

waist. Two women, watching and waiting for their beloved men who might never come home again.

Beth stiffened suddenly, a small gasp emitting from her mouth. She was staring straight into the fog, intense and alert. Eleanor tried to see what she did, but the fog remained dense.

"What is it?"

Beth didn't answer. She broke away from Eleanor and rushed out of the room and down the stairs.

Beth flung open the front door and ran straight into the night, Eleanor after her, Ainsley and Isabella and the men following to see what was the matter. With a cry of joy, Beth launched herself at the giant of a man who materialized out of the fog and opened his arms to sweep her into them.

"Ian!" Eleanor shouted. "It's Ian!" she called back to the others.

Ian looked terrible. He was covered from head to foot in mud and slime, his face coated with it, but his eyes shone like golden fire. Beth held on to him, tears streaming down her face.

Eleanor reached them. "Dear heavens, Ian," she asked breathlessly. "What happened to you? Where is Hart?"

Ian kept his arms around Beth, but he looked at Eleanor. "Come with me," he said. "Come with me."

He started off, Beth at his side. Eleanor did not bother to ask questions. She hurried after him, calling for the others to come.

Fellows and Mac caught up to them as they reached Grosvenor Street. "Ian, what are you doing?" Mac demanded.

"He's taking us to Hart," Eleanor said. Ian hadn't said so, but she knew. "Where, Ian?"

Ian pointed, vaguely north and east.

"At least wait for a coach," Mac said. "Cameron's bringing it."

Ian did let them get the coach. They piled into it, Ian holding Beth on his lap, she not minding that her husband was filthy and stank to high heaven.

They rode toward Euston station but went beyond it, to Chalton Street. Ian jumped down from the coach as soon as it stopped, opened a grating, and said. "He's here. By the storm weir. I will show you."

Fellows rounded up constables and Hart's men still searching the area, as well as the work gang who'd been helping them search the tunnels. Fellows poured them all down through the street, Ian leading the way.

Eleanor waited on the pavement above, refusing to return to the coach. She paced here as she had in the drawing room, but now hope had come back, and fear, with a vengeance.

An hour later, her hopes were still there, she waiting at any moment to hear a shout that they'd found him, followed by Hart's growl that he wanted to be pulled out of the shit hole. She could imagine it so strongly that she was certain, so certain it would happen.

After an hour and a quarter, Fellows's constables and the pipe men started coming up, dirty and defeated.

Fellows spoke to the head of the gang and returned to Eleanor, followed by Ian. Fellows's brows were drawn, though Ian's jaw was tight with determination.

"He's not there, ma'am," Fellows said. "Ian led us right to the place, but it's flooded down there, and he is gone." He looked at Eleanor with eyes so like Hart's. "They're going to keep looking once the water has receded, but they're afraid he's washed into one of the rivers and is on his way to the Thames." Fellows's voice went quiet. "No one survives that journey, Your Grace."

Ian, still dirty, shook his head. "I'll find him." He looked at Eleanor, holding her gaze for once, his eyes even more like Hart's than Fellows's. "I can always find him."

Chapter 20

Eleanor.

Hart swam out of dreams to a gentle rocking. He opened his eyes, his head still pounding—sleep hadn't helped.

He stared for a moment at the board ceiling a few inches above his eyes before he realized that he lay on a pallet with a quilt over him. A threadbare, dirty quilt, but a quilt nonetheless.

The space that held the pallet was narrow, cramped, and filled with oars, ropes, and a tangled net. A crawl space, really, one someone had decided to tuck him into as well.

Hart ran his hand over his face, feeling the scratch of a deep beard. How long had he lain here? One day? Two?

Eleanor. Ian.

He tried to sit up in alarm, and cracked his head on the low beam above his head. He dropped back to the thin pillow, head spinning again.

Hart made himself lie still. He needed to find out where he was, what had happened, how much time had passed, and what he could do. And most of all, he needed to get rid of this be-damned headache.

Taking stock, Hart realized that his coat was gone and so were his waistcoat and shirt. He could feel the warm folds of his kilt around his legs, but the only thing covering his torso was the thin linen shirt he wore under his garments. He wriggled his toes and found woolen socks, boots gone.

Whoever had robbed him were fools. The handspun wool of the kilt was more valuable than the cashmere coat and lawn shirt put together. Tartans, at least for his branch of the Mackenzie clan, were spun in the mountains near Kilmorgan by a family who allowed no one else to get their hands on the wool, not even other Mackenzies. A true Mackenzie tartan was a rare and valuable thing.

At this moment, though, if shrewish old Teasag Mackenzie had crawled in here, scolding Hart for getting her plaid dirty, Hart would kiss her.

He carefully got himself off the pallet and crawled toward the square of light at the wider end of the space. He looked out at the rain, a narrow, rocking boat, and the River Thames.

The light was gray, foggy, like a film over a window. Through it he saw the dome of St. Paul's Cathedral, the line of buildings to its right that was the city, and to its left, the Strand and the Temples. The river surrounded the boat, and the south bank was shrouded in mist.

Eleanor was out there in that city somewhere. Safe at home in Grosvenor Square? Or lying hurt, or dead? He had to know. He had to leave. He had to find her.

A child sat on the gunwale of the boat, picking through a net. Not mending it, Hart saw after a moment, but pulling things out of it. The lad would study what he'd found and either toss it behind him on the boat or throw it back into the river.

Hart moved, and stopped. His head still hurt like fury, and he couldn't suppress a groan.

The lad saw him, tossed down the net, and scampered to the front of the boat and the cabin there. He returned in a moment with a man in a long coat and boots, with a lined face covered by a two-day beard.

The man casually pulled back his coat to show Hart a foot-long knife sheathed in his belt. The lad went back to the net, unconcerned.

"Awake are ye?"

Hart remembered the voice from his underground tomb. "You kicked the hell out of me," Hart said. "Bastard."

The man shrugged. "Easier to move you if you were out. Water was coming back."

"That, and I offered you money."

Another shrug. "Didn't hurt. I could see you were rich, in spite of you not having any money on you. Me wife thinks you have plenty more at home."

Home. I need to get there.

"You think I'll pay you after you stripped me and sold my clothes?" Hart asked in a casual tone.

"Clothes were in tatters. Got a couple shillings for them from the rag and bone man. That pays for your passage on the boat. For saving your life, I'll ask a bit more."

Hart pulled himself all the way out of the hole. That effort took his strength, and he sat down hard on a chest shoved against the cabin's outer wall. "You have amazing compassion." Hart rubbed his temples. "Do you also have water? Or better still, coffee?"

"The wife is brewing some now. You let her have a look at that head of yours, then you'll tell us all about who you are and where you want to be dropped off."

Home. Home. Eleanor. But caution stopped his tongue. The bomb in Euston station had been planted when someone had known he would be there, meeting his wife. Ian had said that the man who'd set the bomb had died with it, but there would be others. The attempt coming after Darragh's failure at Kilmorgan could mean more Fenians Inspector Fellows had missed, or another group deciding the Fenians had a good idea. If whoever it was discovered that the bomb had failed to kill Hart, they'd try again, or perhaps go after his family to flush Hart out of hiding. That could not happen. He would not let it.

The bank of the Thames was tantalizingly close. Hart rubbed his whiskered face again as he looked at it. His chances of reaching it if he swam for it, especially with the dent in his head, weren't good. Plus, he could not be sure that the denizens who trolled the water's edge for valuable flotsam wouldn't simply shove a knife through his ribs as he lay recovering from the swim. His rescuer might be eager to stick him too.

Men who ran up and down the river and combed the tunnels under London for treasure were a law unto themselves, standing firm against those who tried to come between them and their livelihood. Hart needed to wait, to watch, to plan.

A look at the man's unconcerned face as he disappeared into the forward cabin told Hart that his rescuer had no idea who he was—a wealthy man, that was all. Hart would need to make certain he never did find out.

Hart watched the child a little longer, then he reached down and picked up part of the net. He extracted a copper coin from the thin rope and tossed it to the boy's growing heap. "You missed this."

The boy snatched up the penny, peered at it, nodded, and let it drop. He'd collected coins, links of chains, a tin box, a necklace of shells, and a tin soldier. Hart picked up the soldier.

"Highland regiment," he said, tossing it back down. He continued looking through the net, and the lad didn't object.

"You're a Scot?" the boy asked.

"Obviously, lad." Hart played up his accent. "Who else would be lost in the sewers in a tartan?"

"Dad says they shouldn't come down here if they don't understand the streets of London."

"I agree w' ye."

By the time Dad returned with a mug of coffee, a handkerchief over it to keep the rain out, Hart had added another shell, a ha'penny piece, and a broken earring to the boy's pile.

The wife came out with him, a sturdy woman in a bulky sweater with black hair under a fisherman's cap. She sat down with a bowl of water and a cloth and started dabbing Hart's head.

It hurt, but his skull throbbed less now than it had underground. Hart gritted his teeth and got through it.

"Now, then," the man said. "Who are you?"

Hart had decided what to tell them—exactly nothing. At least for now.

He exaggerated a flinch as the wife probed the wound at the base of his skull. "That's th' trouble," he said in a careful voice. "I don't remember."

The man's eyes narrowed. "You don't remember nothing?"

Hart shrugged. "It's a blank. Perhaps I was robbed, hit on

the head, and shoved down a shaft. You said I didn't have money with me."

"That be true."

"Then that's likely what happened." Hart fixed his gaze on the man, telling him without words that it would be to his benefit not to question the story.

The man looked back at him for a long time, his hand on the hilt of his knife. Finally he nodded. "Aye," the man said. "That's what happened."

The wife stopped dabbing. "But if he don't remember who he is, how is he going to pay us?"

"He'll remember, sooner or later." The man took a pipe from his coat and shoved it into his mouth, showing missing teeth. "And the longer it takes, the more he pays."

"But we ain't got room," the wife said in worry.

"We'll manage." The man took his pipe from his mouth and pointed the stem at Hart. "You stay, but you earn your keep. Don't care if you're a lord. Or a laird, I guess the Scottish call them."

"Not the same thing," Hart said. "A lord has been given a title by a monarch. A laird is a landholder. A caretaker of his people."

"That so?" The man brought out a pouch of tobacco and stepped under the cabin's eave to fill his pipe without rain dropping in it. "How do you remember that but not your name?"

Hart shrugged again. "It came to me. Maybe my name will too."

The man slowly filled the pipe, then put the pipe into his mouth. He took out a box of matches, struck a match against the cabin wall, and touched the spurting flame to the bowl. He sucked and puffed, sucked and puffed until smoke rolled from the pipe, pungent against the smell of the river.

"Got another pipe somewhere," the man said, seeing Hart's gaze.

"Coffee is fine for now." Hart took a sip of it. Very bitter, but thick enough to cut the haze in his head.

The man pulled out a dented flask, put a drop of brandy in his cup of coffee, and added some to Hart's. "The name's Reeve. The lad there is Lewis."

Hart took another sip of coffee, fortified now with the brandy.

"I got something he can do," Mrs. Reeve said to Hart. She pointed at the cabin. "Two buckets of night soil need emptying."

Hart laid down the net. "Night soil."

"Aye." Mrs. Reeve's dark blue eyes met his, daring him. Lewis didn't register an expression. Reeve said nothing but looked on in amusement.

Earning his keep.

Hart let out his breath and got to his feet. He ducked into the cabin, removed the indicated buckets from the rear, and came back out with them. While Reeve watched with obvious enjoyment, the Duke of Kilmorgan, one of the wealthiest and most powerful men in the empire, trudged down the deck of the boat to empty buckets full of English shit.

The search for Hart Mackenzie, Duke of Kilmorgan, went on for a while longer, but the police, and the journalists with them, soon concluded that he was dead. He'd been left down in the tunnels, which the rain had washed clear. Sooner or later his body would turn up floating in the Thames.

Only Ian Mackenzie did not give up. He went out every morning at first light, often not returning until the wee hours of the morning. He'd eat in silence, with Beth watching him worriedly, sleep a few hours, and then go out again. When asked about his progress, Ian would repeat his mantra that he would find Hart, and nothing more.

David Fleming, Hart's second-in-command, stepped in to lead the coalition party. Election campaigns went on, and even without Hart, the coalition had strength. Mr. Fleming was certain of a majority, the newspapers said. Unfortunate that the duke would miss the victory he'd spent years preparing for, but that was the way of the world.

The newspapers also reported that the duke's wife staunchly refused to wear black until she had proof of her husband's death. Brave, beautiful lady.

Eleanor also refused to stay home and wring her hands. Each day she walked through the park in the center of Grosvenor Square, the key to its gates in her pocket. She'd make for the tree nearest the center of the park where the curving walkways came together. Her heart fell every afternoon when she found no flower waiting for her in the appointed spot.

Her common sense told her that if Hart had been able to come to the little park and leave their signal that he was well, he'd have simply come home. But Eleanor looked, every morning. Every afternoon, she pulled on gloves and hat and rode to Hyde Park in Hart's landau. She'd descend and stroll along the walks to the crossing paths in the middle, but again, she found nothing, no sign that Hart had been there.

She would find nothing, she knew. Hart might have forgotten all about the silly signal, in any case.

But she took comfort in the ritual, in the hope that the next time she walked to any of their agreed-upon places, she'd find Hart's sign that he was all right. She clung to the hope. She needed it.

Meanwhile, the tragic death of the duke and the grief of his family moved to the back pages of the newspaper, while dire news about General Gordon and the Sudan took the front. The journalists didn't care about Hart, Eleanor thought in disgust. They only wanted a juicy story.

The rest of the family decided to return to Kilmorgan, and asked that Eleanor come with them. Cameron was especially grim.

"Dad might have to be duke now," Daniel whispered to Eleanor as they held a family conference in Hart's drawing room. "He doesn't want to be."

"He won't," Eleanor said. "I'm going to have a baby."

The room went silent. The Mackenzies stopped jabbering among themselves and turned eyes to her—green, dark blue, and shades of gold. They were all there—Cam and Ainsley, Mac and Isabella, Daniel and Beth. Only Ian was absent, on his ever-vigilant search for Hart.

"For God's sake, tell me it's a boy," Cameron said. "Hart wouldn't be that cruel, to disappear and *not* leave behind a boy."

"Leave her be, Cam," Ainsley said. "How can she possibly know?"

"I'm certain it is a boy," Eleanor said. "I sense it. My father would say that was ridiculous, of course, but . . ."

She faltered. Eleanor had kept up her resolution that Hart

had survived—he was so strong, how could he not? She'd kept it even knowing she hadn't told him about the baby. She hadn't been certain at Kilmorgan, but every day that passed brought more certainty, as did her sicknesses in the mornings, of late. Eleanor was never sick.

She'd been looking forward to telling him. She'd imagined Hart's joy, his hope. He'd have Wilfred send the formal announcement to the newspapers, and Eleanor and Hart could celebrate privately . . .

I will not break down. I will not give up hope. If I give up, then that means he is truly gone.

Daniel, next to Eleanor on the sofa, heaved himself at her and enclosed her in a warm hug. "Ian will find him, and so will the tenacious Fellows. You'll see."

Eleanor fought back her tears. If one tear came, then a flood would.

Beth said, "It's doubly important that you come with us to Scotland, El. We'll keep Hart's baby safe at Kilmorgan."

"No." Eleanor shook her head. "If he's found, I want to be here, to go to him right away. He'll need me." And if he were found near to death, she'd never forgive herself if she weren't there to say good-bye.

Cam and Mac watched her, they looking so like Hart and yet so different. Hart's nephew, again similar and yet different, had left school in Edinburgh to hurry to help her. Their wives—her closest friends—knew what they'd feel were it their Mackenzie lost and gone. Eleanor's heart swelled with the love of this family.

On the other hand, she would not let them herd her off to Scotland and seclude her. They ought to know her better than that, by now.

At last, they stopped trying to convince her, even Beth realizing it was useless.

Later, after the family had gone, Eleanor retreated to her bedchamber, retrieved her memory book from her drawer, and opened it to the photographs of Hart. She'd pasted the ones she'd taken at Kilmorgan onto the pages following the older ones.

Eleanor studied them all, first those of Hart young and such a devil, his body beautiful. In the photograph of him in his kilt, Hart laughed out of the picture, his hand out to stop the photographer.

She turned from that to the photographs she'd taken of him in his kilt at Kilmorgan. She traced the one of him holding his kilt over himself, hiding little. The next one was of him leaning, bare, against the wall, laughing.

The flash of vision came to her of Hart over her in the dark, his body against hers, whispering, *I need you, El. I* need *you.*

Eleanor's resolution cracked, and she lay across the book and sobbed.

Eleanor loved him. She'd lost Hart, and she loved him so much.

She thought about how she'd found Hart at the tomb of his son, tracing the letters of the lad's name. Remembered him with head bowed, his hand on the cold stone—proud, proud Hart—anguished that he hadn't been strong enough to save little Graham.

Eleanor put her hand to her abdomen, where life had begun to stir. Her child. Hart's son. Tears flowed faster.

She heard someone enter the room, but she couldn't lift her head. Maigdlin, she thought, but the tread was wrong, as was the scent of cigars and wool.

The chair next to her creaked and then a broad hand touched her arm. Eleanor pried open her eyes to see Ian next to her, his hand unmoving. Ian, who rarely touched anyone but Beth.

Eleanor sat up and snatched up her handkerchief. Ian smelled of the outdoors, of coal smoke and rain. "I'm sorry, Ian. This is not me giving up hope." She drew a long breath. "It's me feeling sorry for myself."

Ian didn't answer. He was staring at the book, still open to the page with Hart naked, his kilt on the floor.

Face heating, Eleanor closed the book. "Those are . . ."

"The photographs Mrs. Palmer took of Hart. Good. She gave them to you."

Eleanor sat back, her lips parting. Joanna had said that an unknown someone had sent the photographs to her with instructions to post them to Eleanor at intervals.

Not Hart. *Ian.*

"Ian Mackenzie," she said.

Ian met her gaze for a fleeting moment, then studied the patterns on the cover of the memory book.

"You sent the photographs to the maid Joanna," Eleanor said. "You did, didn't you?"

"Yes."

"Good heavens, Ian. Why?"

Ian traced the gold curlicues that lapped and overlapped and twisted back along themselves across the book's cover. He said, without glancing up, "Mrs. Palmer had others. I couldn't find them. I was afraid they'd end up in a newspaper, so when Mrs. Palmer died, I searched the house for them. But someone had gotten there before me, and I only found the eight, stashed behind a brick in a chimney. I kept them a while, then decided to send them to Joanna."

"And told her to send them on to me?"

"Yes."

He went back to tracing the pattern. Over and over, staring at it without blinking, his body still except for the tracing finger.

"Why?" Eleanor asked, a little more sharply than she meant to.

Ian shrugged. "So you'd go to Hart."

"I mean, why now? Why not when you first found the pictures after Mrs. Palmer died? And why use Joanna as the go-between?"

"Joanna likes Hart. She'd want to help him."

He fell silent, and Eleanor regarded him impatiently. "You didn't answer my first question."

Ian sometimes did that. He'd answer what he wanted to and ignore the rest. He used that method to get around his inability to lie.

But this time, he said, "I did not send the pictures when I found them, because Hart was too busy then. He would not have paid enough attention, and he would have lost you again."

"Well, you cannot tell me he is less busy now. He is about to become prime minister."

Ian shook his head. "I waited until he finished all his plotting. Now it's almost over. Hart won't be prime minister long. He'll fall." Ian wrenched his gaze from the pattern and fixed it directly on Eleanor. "And he'll need you."

Eleanor, caught by the golden depths of Ian's eyes, could not look away. "What are you talking about? His coalition is strong, the newspapers are full of it. Even without Hart here, they'll win the majority. His party will rule."

"Hart will be a bad leader. He wants everything his way, all the time. All must obey."

"He's bad at compromise, you mean." Eleanor had to agree with Ian, there. The word *compromise* hadn't been invented for the likes of Hart Mackenzie.

"I know what you mean, Ian," she said. "Hart has large ideas and doesn't notice the smaller problems of ordinary people. Not until it's too late, anyway. Like he didn't notice the Fenians until they tried to kill him. And then he had the gall to be surprised."

Ian continued to gaze at her, unblinking, as though mesmerized by her eyes. Eleanor waved her hand in front of his face.

"Ian."

Ian jumped and looked away.

Eleanor pushed the memory book aside. "You sound very certain that you will find Hart. Almost as though you already have found him. Do you know where he is?"

Ian went silent again, his gaze moving past her to the window and the darkening fog beyond. He studied it for so long that Eleanor began to believe he *did* know and was trying to decide whether to tell her.

Then Ian rose. "No," he said and walked out of the room.

Chapter 21

The pipe-smoking Reeve rented a small boathouse near Black-friars Bridge on the south side of the Thames, but he and his wife and son spent most of their time either on the river or on the boat wedged up onshore.

Reeve roamed far and wide looking for treasure in the sewers, the river, the water and gas tunnels, under the bridges, and inside the railway tunnels. He claimed that anything along the buried Fleet River was his, though his rivals contested him from time to time. Hence the knife.

Mrs. Reeve provided her family with fresh water every day from a public pump—one of the new wells that tapped fresh water far from the river. She brought enough for all of them, even enough for Hart to wash and clean his teeth. He'd never before realized the simple joy of the tooth powder he had the lad Lewis purchase for him from a chemist.

The Reeves did not tumble to who Hart was, nor did they seem to care. Hart proved willing enough to help—he and Reeve hauled the boat in and out, Hart knew how to cast a net, and he helped Lewis go through the "catch" every night.

The only thing Reeve refused to let Hart do was go with

him into the tunnels—it took a special knack, Reeve said, and he didn't want to be hunting for Hart in them again. Hart agreed, never wanting to see the bloody sewers again. Hart knew too that Reeve didn't want to take the chance that Hart would disappear and not give Reeve his reward money.

As for Hart, he was not yet ready to leave. He wanted more than anything to get back to Eleanor—he dreamed of her every night. But once he'd discovered, through the discarded newspapers Reeve brought to the boat, that Eleanor was alive and well, and so was Ian, he made himself resist the frantic urge to rush to her. Scotland Yard and others were still hunting those trying to kill Hart, and Hart could protect Eleanor and his family better by lying low. He needed to get a message to Eleanor, however, to reassure her he was all right.

For that, he'd have to recruit help. Hart watched the Reeves, assessing them, working on winning their trust as he decided whether to trust them in return.

Hart never tried to take command of Reeve's boat or tell him what to do. He made requests instead, reasonable ones, offhand. For boots that fit so he could better help carry the boat over the shingle. A fisherman's sweater to wear over his thin shirt so he didn't have to borrow Reeve's extra coat. He'd had Mrs. Reeve find him some trousers before he'd been there a day, converting his plaid into a cover for his pallet. He also let his beard grow in, rough and red, prickly stubble. From a distance, and perhaps even up close too, he now looked like just another fisherman.

Hart started suggesting where they might take the boat and cast the nets for a better haul. He began standing guard at night so the boy and Reeve could get more sleep. Gradually Reeve began asking for Hart's opinions, and then, when Hart's ideas found them more valuable flotsam and jetsam, Reeve started waiting to be told what to do. Hart was a natural leader, and Reeve, though not a mindless follower, began to acknowledge Hart's casual command.

He decided that he should not use Reeve as his messenger to Eleanor, however. Reeve would do anything for money, and he might decide that selling information about a rich stranger leaving a message in an odd place would fetch more than what

Hart could give him. Mrs. Reeve was stoutly loyal to her husband, though she let her opinion be known when she disagreed with him. Loudly.

The lad, now. Hart had won Lewis's respect by helping with the nets and letting Lewis instruct him what to look for. Hart learned much about which bits of trash could be turned into money and which bits were worthless. Lewis was loyal to his father but also his own man, young as he was. Lads grew up fast on the river.

"Lewis," Hart said to him when he felt the time ripe. "I need you to run an errand for me."

Lewis looked up at him, neither interested nor uninterested. Hart rubbed his face, feeling that his beard had softened from stiff bristles to wiry hair.

"I need you to go to Mayfair for me," Hart said. "And not tell your father. It's a simple task, nothing dangerous to you, and I promise I am not trying to cheat your father out of what I owe him."

"How much?" Lewis asked.

He was his father's son. "How much do you want?"

Lewis contemplated. "Twenty shillings. Ten for doing it, ten for not telling my father."

The boy was a shark. "Done." Hart held out his hand, and Lewis shook it in a firm grip. "Now, then, lad, how good are you at climbing fences?"

Eleanor opened the gate of Grosvenor Square and walked into the little park. It was early by Mayfair standards, about eleven o'clock in the morning. Nannies in gray with white starched aprons pushed prams or held the hands of small children, or sat on benches while their charges played on the grass. They watched Eleanor, used by now to seeing the famous duke's wife take her morning amble. Such a brave woman, trying to bear up.

Eleanor walked past them as usual, keeping her pace unhurried. No sense rushing to the middle of the gardens, no sense drawing attention to herself. She strolled along, a parasol raised against the sunshine. Yesterday, it had been an umbrella against the rain. She came here every day, rain or bloody shine.

Eleanor counted her steps, the mantra keeping her pace even. Perhaps today. Perhaps today . . . *forty-two, forty-three, forty-four* . . .

When she reached the center of the garden, she kept walking, off the path and onto the green. Seventeen more steps. Around the base of the wide-trunked tree . . .

Eleanor stopped. A little violet, the kind men purchased from flower girls to wear on their lapels, rested at the base of the tree. Not a hothouse rose, no, but the sort of thing a man who was hiding for his life might be able to obtain and leave for her.

She closed her eyes. Someone must have dropped the flower. She wanted so much for Hart to have left it that she was inventing things.

Eleanor opened her eyes again. The flower remained, sitting in the exact place Hart had left the others for her years before.

The flower will mean that I cannot come to you as promised, but I will when I can, he'd told her when he'd come up with the idea. *And that you are in my thoughts.* He'd missed a walk with her, she'd been angry, and Hart had invented the scheme to charm her out of her bad temper. It had worked.

Eleanor picked up the violet and pressed it to her nose. Hart was alive. This had to mean that Hart was alive. She lowered the flower to her chest, to her heart, and drew in a shuddering breath, forcing back tears.

Maigdlin came around the tree. "You all right, Your Grace?"

Eleanor wiped her eyes and thrust the violet into her pocket. "Yes, yes. I'm fine. Go on. I want to sit by myself a moment."

Maigdlin peered suspiciously at Eleanor's eyes, but she nodded. "Yes, Your Grace," she said, and faded discreetly away.

You are in my thoughts.

"But *where* are you, Hart Mackenzie?" Eleanor whispered. No one knew the signal but the two of them. Why had Hart chosen to leave it but not come to the house or write a note? Did he believe himself still in danger? Or was this some new machination of his?

Eleanor doubted he'd left the flower himself. But who had he sent? She'd suspected Wilfred in the past, but Wilfred wore a black band around his arm and never left the house these days. If Hart wanted to be entirely secret, he'd need someone who'd not be suspected to be connected with him. But that someone would need a way into the gardens. Eleanor doubted that Hart had taken his key with him.

Then again, she might be entirely mistaken that Hart had left the flower. Her first thought had been that someone had dropped it, and this might be true.

Well, she would not sit here staring into the distance and being maudlin. She stood up, brushed off her skirt, and started asking those in and around the gardens—discreetly—whether they'd seen anyone odd coming into or out of the gardens in the middle of Grosvenor Square.

The evening after Hart had sent Lewis to leave the signal to Eleanor, Reeve, down on the shingle, leaned against the boat's hull and lit his pipe. Hart sat above him on the deck, eating bread dunked into the soup Mrs. Reeve had left for him. Mrs. Reeve and Lewis had gone, tired, to their beds, Lewis having earned Hart's praise—and promise of shillings—for a job well done.

Reeve had been in the tunnels all day, Mrs. Reeve taking the opportunity to visit her sister, so Lewis had had plenty of time to purchase and drop the flower in place and then linger to watch Eleanor find it. Hart listened hungrily to Lewis's description of her lifting the flower to her nose, her face flushed in happiness, how she'd pressed the violet to her heart. Then with alarm when Lewis told him how she'd walked about the square, questioning people. Of course, Eleanor would not simply pick up the flower and quietly return home.

He longed for her with a sharpness that hurt. Every night Hart dreamed of Eleanor's fiery hair, her blue eyes, the sweet sounds she made when he was deepest inside her. His darker fantasies returned, and in his dreams, Eleanor surrendered to every one of them. He'd wake hard and sweating, his body aching.

Hart pulled his thoughts from his frustrating dreams when Reeve's words caught his attention.

"I heard tell in the pub that the duke everyone said would be prime minister won't be now," Reeve said. "Seeing as how they can't find him."

He said it too easily, too lightly. Hart kept chewing bread, letting nothing show on his face.

"What do ye think of that?" Reeve asked.

Hart finished his bread. "I'm not English. Not interested."

"This duke, they say, was a Scotsman," Reeve went on as though he'd not spoken. "What you might call an eccentric. Always wore one of them Scottish skirts, like you had when I found you."

"Kilts," Hart said.

"He went missing when the bomb went off in Euston station. Some thought he might have a-fallen into the tunnels, and most think he was washed, dead, into the Thames." Reeve stopped to tamp the tobacco into his pipe and relight it. "Seems like I would have found him, had the man been trapped down in the interceptors."

Hart said nothing. Reeve studied him with his keen dark eyes as he tamped his pipe again.

"People disappear all the time," Hart said. "Sometimes never to be found again."

Reeve shrugged. "Happens that some men disappear for their own reasons."

"They do. They're found when they're ready to be found."

"This man were rich as anything, by all accounts. I'd think he'd want to go home to his palace, sleep in a soft bed, and eat off silver plates."

Hart rubbed his chin, feeling the unfamiliar beard. He'd glimpsed himself in the small, foggy mirror in the cabin earlier today, and he'd nearly recoiled, thinking he'd seen the ghost of his father. A hairy man with glittering eyes had looked out at Hart from the mirror—a fiery-tempered, arrogant man who'd believed in himself too much.

Or had he? Perhaps Hart's father had hated himself with the same self-loathing Hart sometimes felt, the man lashing out instead of turning his anger inward. The old duke was dead and gone now, and so Hart was never to know.

Reeve puffed on his pipe. "Might be worth this duke's while to not be found, eh?"

Hart held Reeve's gaze. "It might be. If he's that rich, he can do what he likes. Just as a man who feeds his family by picking through other men's trash instead of looking for a job in a factory."

Reeve snorted. "Factories. Backbreaking work all hours of the day and night, shut away and never watching your boy grow up. Freedom, that's worth all them plates of silver and a fine palace."

"I agree."

They exchanged another look. "Then we're the same, are we?" Reeve asked.

"I believe so."

Reeve made another elaborate shrug, leaned back, and sucked heavily on his pipe. "Well, I hope they find the bugger. The pipes under London can be deadly."

"So I understand."

Reeve went back to smoking quietly, and Hart gazed across the river, making his plans.

After a time, Reeve stirred. "Pub?"

Hart gave him a silent nod, and the two men left the boat to cross the shingle and mount the stairs to the streets.

The inhabitants of the pub had grown used to seeing Hart come in with Reeve, accepting Reeve's story that Hart was an itinerant worker, down on his luck, helping Reeve in return for a bed and food. Reeve talked to his cronies, and they all ignored Hart, who accepted a pint from the landlord and kept his head down while he read through a newspaper cover to cover.

David Fleming had taken over the coalition, he saw. Good. David would know what to do. The coalition was popular, because Gladstone, to most people, smacked of radicalism and revolution, and the Tories favored the large landholders. Hart's party was somewhere in between, something for everyone. Hart had planned it that way.

The elections, the newspapers said, were sure to return the men in the coalition, and Fleming, as the new head, would lead the government. The queen was not overly fond of Fleming— or Hart, for that matter—but she liked Gladstone still less.

The papers were more full of worries about Khartoum and Gordon and the Germans slowly taking over southern Africa than the missing Duke of Kilmorgan. A small story in one newspaper reported that Hart's body had not been found, but the Thames was deep and never-stopping. A sad end for so proud a man as Hart Mackenzie. Scotland was in mourning for him, but England wasn't. *Bloody good riddance,* the English paper did not say but might as well have.

He found a story on the last pages that the Mackenzie family was leaving the city to retire to Scotland. *Good,* Hart thought. *Eleanor will be well taken care of there.* Eleanor was like wild Scottish heather, happy when rippling free on Scottish hills, constrained when cut and shoved into a confining vase.

The same story said that Lord Cameron Mackenzie would be taking the coronet as duke once his oldest brother was proclaimed officially dead.

Hart touched Cameron's name and stifled his laughter. Cameron must be boiling with rage. His brother's greatest fear in life had been that Hart would peg it early and leave the dukedom to him. Hart imagined all the colorful names Cameron was calling him. But Hart knew that Cameron would take care of everyone very well. Cam's greatest strength was his ability to protect those he loved.

He turned the page and froze. His eyes fell upon the story—rather buried—that the pocket of Fenians who had set the bomb in Euston station had been discovered, their house raided by the police, headed by one Inspector Fellows. Many arrests had been made, and people rejoiced that the streets might once again be safe.

This was the morning edition of the paper, and the event had taken place the night before. So important a thing, and Hart had known nothing until he read it now.

Living on the river erased the rest of the world. It had moved on. *Without him.*

And he didn't care.

Hart touched the feeling, examining it. His frantic need his entire life had been to control the world around him, to shape it, and everyone in it, into what he wanted. He'd learned through mistakes—most notably with Eleanor—that he could not shape the people who mattered most to him. But too many people had let him, giving him the illusion that he could.

The boy who'd tried so hard to make a world that had nothing of his father in it had succeeded. Too bloody well, perhaps.

Hart had become very like the man he hated—expecting everyone to bend to his will. He'd congratulated himself for not being physically cruel, but he'd been as cruel as his father with his words and deeds.

Eleanor had been right about how he'd treated Mrs. Palmer, right to fear he'd do the same to her. He might well have, had she not thrown cold water over him and brought him to his senses.

And now the world he'd struggled to control was going on its merry way, assuming Hart was floating facedown in the Thames. He was just another body on the earth, another man, like Reeve, trying to get by and find happiness as he could.

Hart *had* found happiness. With Eleanor. But he'd decided to go on serving his obsessive ambition, setting her to one side, and assuming he'd have plenty of time for her when he finished.

Fool. Reeve had the right of it. *Backbreaking work all hours of the day and night, shut away and never watching your boy grow up. Freedom, that's worth all them plates of silver and a fine palace.*

A factory or the Houses of Parliament—it was all the same.

He needed to see Eleanor. He needed to bury himself in her softness and beg her forgiveness. He knew well and good that he'd sent the flower to her for another reason—he feared that if she believed him dead, she'd turn to another, David Fleming, perhaps, for comfort. Eleanor was beautiful, young, and now a very, very rich widow. The predators would be coming out of the woodwork.

It was time to go home.

Hart looked up from the newspaper, his world changed. The denizens of the pub went on talking and laughing with their friends, some quietly, some loudly. The Duke of Kilmorgan, the entirety of the British peerage, were nonentities here. For the first time in his life, Hart had no power at all.

Thank God.

Hart remained at the pub with Reeve, sitting quietly while his mind spun with plans for getting himself back home—Kilmorgan would be the best place for staging his resurrection—until the publican closed up for the night. Reeve said good-bye to his mates, and he and Hart turned in the darkness toward Blackfriars Bridge. Reeve walked unsteadily.

A hand reached out of a dark passage and landed on Hart's shoulder. Hart spun around, fist swinging in a perfect pugilist's right hook. The punch was caught with equal skill in a hand that was as big as his own. Eyes the color of Mackenzie singlemalt regarded Hart in the dim light of Reeve's lantern.

Hart looked back at Ian Mackenzie, face smudged and bearing lines of exhaustion. Ian put both hands on Hart's shoulders, and his fingers dug through Hart's coat.

"I found you," Ian said, his voice low and fierce. "I found you." He put his arms around Hart, and Hart for a moment sank into the strength that was his youngest brother. "I can always find you," Ian whispered.

～

"Come with me."

Eleanor looked up from the desk in the main study in the Grosvenor Square mansion, the house quiet, since the rest of the family, excepting herself, Ian, and Beth, had departed for Scotland. It was very late, and Beth and her children were asleep.

"Good heavens," she said. "Are you still up and about, Ian?"

Ian, being Ian, did not bother to answer the question. He held out his hand. "Come with me."

He was breathing hard, his eyes alight. Ian didn't smile, but Eleanor sensed his excitement, even joy, behind his still face.

"Where is he?" Eleanor asked, rising.

"Come *with* me."

That was enough for Eleanor. She snatched up her shawl, took Ian's hand, and let him lead her out.

～

Hart waited in the noisome darkness by Reeve's boathouse, listening to the Thames lap the bank not far away. Too many people lingered near Reeve's boat down the Strand—a few of Reeve's mates from the pub had come to visit, even this late— but the boathouse was deserted. Rats and thieves, those were the only things to be found on the shore of the Thames tonight. And Hart.

Hart saw them come. Swiftly and silently, the bulk of his

brother came across the littered Strand, pulling a woman in a dark shawl with him.

"Do slow down a *tiny* bit," Eleanor's voice came to him. "These rocks are slippery, and I'm certain I've stepped in something nasty. I understand why we can't have a light, but, gracious, can we pretend that we need to go carefully?"

Ian never responded or looked around at her. He kept propelling her onward, and Hart stepped out of the shadow of the boathouse.

Eleanor dropped Ian's hand. She froze, a slender upright against what light drifted down to the river, then she was running toward him, skirts swirling. Hart knew he should stay hidden, but he couldn't stop himself going to meet her—four steps, five, six, seven.

Then she was in front of him. Hart caught and lifted her, spinning her around with him. He buried his face in her neck, inhaling her goodness, feeling her warm against him. *Safe. I'm safe.* Hart's body shuddered once with a great, wrenching sob.

Eleanor was crying, her hands coming up to cup his face. She stroked his beard, staring at him in wonder.

"What happened, Hart? What happened to you? My goodness, but you look awful."

Eleanor's heart flooded with happiness. He was here, whole, with her. The flower had told her he was all right, but she needed to touch him to believe it.

She caressed his face and the strange beard, Hart looking so different and yet the same. His eyes still blazed like golden fire, even though his clothes were rough, and he smelled of the river. She put her arms around him and held on, so happy she couldn't speak.

"El," he whispered. "My El."

He turned her face up to his and kissed her. The taste of him, so familiar, so much a part of her, broke her heart.

She squirmed out of his arms and thumped her fists to his chest. "Why the devil didn't you send word? I was sick with worry, waiting and waiting . . ."

He had the gall to look surprised—so like him. "I sent the signal. I know you saw it."

"Oh, do you? You were watching me?"

"Had someone watching you," he said.

"Of course you did. Then why did you not let me send a message back? I scoured the square for any sign of who had left the flower, but no one noticed anything. Useless of them."

"I heard that too. I did not want you to find him, or me, because it was dangerous."

"Well, yes, I understand why you wanted no one to follow him to your hiding place. But you might have trusted me to be covert."

"I mean, it was dangerous for *you*!" Hart's usual shouting growl broke free. "What would have happened if an enemy knew I was still alive and you were communicating with me? He might have tried to use you to bring me out of hiding, might have tried to hurt you until you told him where I was."

"I never would have," Eleanor said. "Not even under torture."

"Damn it, I didn't want you to be tortured!"

Eleanor cupped his cheek. "Oh. That's sweet."

Ian came tramping toward them, boots grating on the gravel. "You are making too much noise."

Hart caught Eleanor's hand in his hard grip. "You are right, Ian. As usual. Come with me, El. I want to show you something."

"Can you show me at home? It's so very cold out here. It is all right now, you know. Inspector Fellows found all the assassins. At last. Do you know, I believe he is sweet on Isabella's sister. We will have to make sure they are both at Kilmorgan for the summer—"

She found his blunt fingers on her lips, his hands now rough and calloused. "Eleanor, please stop talking for a fleeting instant, and come with me. It will be warm; I promise."

Eleanor kissed his fingers. "What are you going to show me?"

He gave her a familiar, exasperated look. "Can you come along without asking questions?"

"Hmm, I can see that living rough hasn't dampened your arrogance. All right, then. Show me. And *then*, we go home."

Hart's expression changed to the triumphant one. Oh, dear.

Hart started walking up the shingle, his arm around Eleanor. She liked being so warm against him, in the protective circle of his strong arm. She babbled because the release from her sickening fear wouldn't let her do otherwise, but her heart sang.

"Ian," Hart said as they walked. "Stop at the boat there, and tell Reeve he'll get his money tomorrow morning. The publican by the bridge lets rooms—El and I will spend the night there. Then send word to Kilmorgan—discreetly—that I will be there soon."

Ian nodded. He sank his fingers into Hart's shoulder, then jogged away toward Reeve's boat, disappearing into the darkness. Ian would do it, and not betray them.

The publican and his wife had already gone to bed, but Eleanor put several crowns into the publican's hand. The man and his wife opened a room and started a fire in its stove, then shook out sheets for the bed while Eleanor stood by the shuttered window, out of the way.

Hart asked for a bath. The publican's wife gave him a dark look, but another crown later, they brought a hip bath and some towels and filled the bath with cans of steaming water.

The publican asked no questions, but both he and his wife gave Hart and Eleanor curious stares before they left them alone.

"They believe I am a courtesan," Eleanor said. "How amusing."

Hart stripped off his soiled clothing. "Do you care what they think?"

"Not really," Eleanor said. "But as happy as I am to be out of the wind, I will point out that your London house is warmer, and your bathtub larger. *And* you have running water."

Hart fished a folded newspaper out of his coat pocket and tossed it on the bed. "That is why."

Eleanor didn't glance at the paper. Instead, she watched Hart peel off his trousers and the flannels he wore underneath, and then step, naked, into the bath.

Hart lowered himself into the heat, letting out a sigh of satisfaction. Eleanor's gaze riveted to him, her large, handsome husband, now soaking wet, skin gleaming with water.

"Read the newspaper, El," Hart said. He picked up the cake of soap and lavished it over himself.

Eleanor glanced at the bed. "I've read that one. The news about the elections is in it."

"I know." He let out a breath, collapsing against the end of the small tub. He had to raise his knees to fit. "That is what I want to show you, El. The coalition, the elections, the government . . . the world. They have moved on." He spread his arms, letting water drip to the floor. "And I am still here."

"True," Eleanor said, her gaze back on Hart. "Some of your colleagues have scarcely stopped to mourn you. It's rather disgusting."

"Not what I mean. While I've been living on that boat, El, the world has passed me by. I always thought that, without me, it wouldn't. Everything would crumble and fall, unable to get on without me managing it. But I was wrong."

She watched him with a worried look. "And this pleases you?"

"Yes." Hart vigorously rubbed his hair, droplets flying. "Because, love, watching the world from afar brought it home to me. I don't *have* to run it. I have set things in motion and given Fleming his push. And now—I can *stop*."

He heaved a sigh and slid down into the water, the suds closing over him like a blanket.

Eleanor had never seen him like this. He was relaxed in the ridiculously small tub, uncaring, his grin full of true mirth. Laughing at himself. Though Hart had teased and laughed when he'd courted her long ago, he'd been, in truth, propelling himself toward a goal. Always, Hart Mackenzie had an underlying drive that made anything on the surface just that—on the surface. Right now, he was . . . himself.

"Are you certain you are feeling quite well?" Eleanor asked. "Ian told me you'd taken a blow on the head from the explosion."

Hart laughed out loud. He was delectable all wet, his hair slicked with water, his big limbs hanging out of the tub. And the beard. It had startled Eleanor when he'd first stepped into the light, but the softness of it against her lips hadn't been unpleasant at all.

"I've been mad my entire life," Hart said. "Driven. To take care of my brothers, to make sure we survived, then to take care of the nation, the world if I could. I've been terrified that if I stopped, if something happened to me, everything would go to hell. But it hasn't, has it? It's wonderful. And I am so bloody tired."

"But what about the elections? Your party will win. Everyone thinks so."

"Fleming can lead them. He'll be good at it, and he's not a trumped-up aristocrat no one will listen to. He will give Gladstone a run for his money."

"But if you come back, you can win. I know this."

"No. I am finished."

His laughter died into a relieved sigh. The mad light perpetually in Hart's eyes was absent. At the moment, he was an ordinary man enjoying the simple pleasure of a bath.

"But what about Scotland?" Eleanor asked. "Returning the Stone of Destiny?"

"A stupid dream. The queen adores Scotland, and she'll never let it go. The days of Highland might and Bonnie Prince Charlie are over, thank God. The strength of Scotland will return one day, but it will take time. I wanted to force it, but I might have made it worse. Look at the mess in Ireland." Hart splashed more water over his body and rocked up out of the tub, water crashing back into it. "The Stone of Destiny will return to Scotland—someday. I feel it in my bones." He grinned. "But not today."

Chapter 22

Eleanor cared nothing at the moment about the elections, the Stone of Destiny, and Scottish pride. She saw only Hart, tall and wet and naked, rising from his bath.

Water darkened the hair on his head and his legs, and on that between his thighs. He was hard with wanting, his smile telling her he knew she liked what she saw. Hart might have said the world would go on without him, but his conceit certainly hadn't diminished.

The days of worry, fear, hope, and dread washed over Eleanor in a great wave, and her bravado deserted her. She pressed her hand to her mouth as she ran at Hart and flung her arms around him.

Hart swept her up and into his wet embrace. Her dress got soaked, and she didn't care.

"I thought you were dead," she sobbed. "I didn't want you to be dead."

"I hurt every minute I was away from you, El. Every bloody minute."

Hart carried her to the bed, coming down on it with her.

He got her out of her clothes, tearing buttons from holes, hooks from fabric. Eleanor helped him, throwing off the last of her clothes, needing to be bare against him.

Hart entered her with a gasp of desperation, and then he stilled. They lay together, face-to-face on the high bed, Eleanor's sobs quieting.

"Eleanor," he whispered. "I love you so much."

"I love you too." Eleanor touched his hair. "I'm going to have a baby."

Hart stared. "What?"

"A child. A boy, I'm fairly sure. Your son."

"A baby?"

Eleanor nodded. "I hope you don't mind."

"Mind?" He shouted the word, and at the same time, the golden eyes of Hart Mackenzie flooded with tears. "Why the devil should I mind? I love you, El, *love you.*"

He laughed as he said it, then he came into her. Eleanor wound her arms around him, laughing with him as he started to frantically love her.

<p style="text-align:center">~~~</p>

When Eleanor woke, hours later, Hart was asleep facedown beside her, hugging a pillow, blissfully calm.

She loved this—the quiet of the room, the snap of the fire in the stove, she and her husband in a little nest shut away from the world. Only Ian Mackenzie knew where they were, and Ian would never tell.

Would this last? Eleanor wondered. When Hart went home to Kilmorgan, when the world realized he was still in it, would Hart remember his declaration tonight? Or would the world and his ambition swallow him again?

She wouldn't let it. Ambition was all very well, but now Hart would have a family. She would make sure he never forgot that.

A warm touch on her abdomen made her jump. Eleanor looked down to see Hart's hand on her belly, he watching her. His leg was twined with hers, a fine position.

"What are you thinking, El?"

Eleanor rearranged her expression. "I was wondering . . ."

"Yes, minx? What were you wondering?"

"What we did in Mrs. McGuire's upstairs chamber. Do you remember?"

Hart's growing smile told her he did. "It is burned on my brain. I could see you in the mirror. It was heaven."

Eleanor's face heated. "Is that the sort of thing you did at the High Holborn house?"

He lost his smile. "No."

"Well, then, what did you do?"

Hart turned onto his back and scrubbed his hand over his face. "El, I do not want to talk about the house and what I did there. Especially not *now*."

"Now is as good a time as any."

"I was much younger then. The first time I lived there, I did not know you; the second time, I was consoling myself for loss. I was a different man."

"You misunderstand me. I have no interest in what you did with other ladies. None at all. But I want to know what you *did*. What are these *dark proclivities* everyone, including you, hints at? I want to know, specifically."

When he looked at her, she was surprised to see that what was in Hart's eyes was fear. "I don't want to tell you," he said.

"But it is part of you. You are an unconventional man, and I am not exactly a conventional woman. Secluded, yes; conventional, no. I do not want to live with you knowing you suppress your desires or tame yourself for me, or whatever you are thinking you ought to do. Banish the idea, Hart. I am not afraid."

"I don't want you to *be* afraid. That is the point."

"Then tell me. If you don't, I will imagine all kinds of bizarre things, put together from whispers and sniggers and peeks into erotic books."

"*Eleanor.*"

"Has it to do with riding crops? Or manacles? There is a lot of jesting about manacles. Though why people would want to shackle each other, I cannot imagine."

"Eleanor, *what* are you talking about?"

"Am I wrong?" What joy it was to tease him again. "Then perhaps you ought to tell me precisely, and ease my worries in my innocence."

"Eleanor Ramsay, whatever man thinks you innocent is a complete idiot." Hart locked his hand around her wrist. His touch was gentle, but his fingers were strong.

"It's nothing to do with pain, or shackles," he said. "It's about trust. Complete trust. Absolute surrender."

She could not release herself from his grip. "Surrender?"

His eyes were dark. "To place yourself in my hands, to trust me to read your desires and lead you into experiencing them. To let me do as I please without question, to trust me to know what to do. The reward for your trust, exquisite pleasure."

"Oh," she said.

"Anything I ask." Hart kissed the inside of her wrist. "You would give me your faith that I'd never hurt you, that my only goal is your pleasure."

Eleanor's heart beat faster. *Exquisite pleasure.* "That sounds . . . interesting."

Hart rose on hands and knees over her, the movement so practiced she scarcely saw the effort of it. "Could you do it? Could you put yourself into my hands and not ask any confounded questions?"

"No questions at all? I am not certain . . ."

"I will have to go easy on you at first. You are Eleanor Ramsay. You cannot but help asking questions."

"I could try."

"Hmm. I don't believe you, but never mind."

Hart got up from the bed, again the movement effortless. He rummaged in the clothes he'd left on the floor and brought out his cravat. It was a makeshift cravat, a long, narrow piece of linen he'd wrapped around his neck to shield his throat from the wind of the Thames.

He wound the ends of the linen in his hands and came back to the bed. Eleanor knelt there, waiting for him, excited and worried at the same time.

Hart climbed up onto the big bed, his head almost touching the beams as he knelt behind her. "Give me your hands."

Eleanor's mouth formed the *wh* of *why*, and Hart bit her cheek. "No questions. Give me your hands."

Eleanor lifted them. Quickly Hart wound the linen strip around her torso, under her breasts, crossing it in a complicated twist and catching her wrists together at the end of it. He pulled her wrapped hands upward, his movements gentle but firm.

"We'll start with this." Hart nuzzled her ear. "I won't hurt you. Do you believe me?"

"I . . ."

Another nip, this time to her shoulder. "I said, do you believe me?"

"Yes," she whispered.

Surrender.

That was what Hart Mackenzie always wanted, she realized. For others to surrender to him, to let him be their master. Not because he wanted to punish them, or to have his own way, but for their own good, because he wanted to take care of them. Those who didn't understand that dashed themselves to bits on him.

"Yes," she repeated.

It was not in Eleanor's nature to surrender to anything, but with Hart's strong body behind her, his hands holding hers, she opened her heart, opened her body, and gave herself to him.

"Yes," she said a third time.

Still on his knees behind her, again with the effortlessness, he pulled her upright so that she knelt back onto his lap, her knees parted, his thighs sliding between hers. This opened her to him, she realized, his body around her making her relaxed and warm. Hart snaked one arm around her, the other still holding the bond around her wrists.

She was completely vulnerable to him. His body was solid behind hers. The only way to get away would be to crawl across the bed, but he held her bound wrists.

She should panic, she should fight . . . and yet, she knew he would not hurt her. If a stranger had done this, then, yes, terror. But she knew Hart, had shared a bed with him, had woken in his arms, curled against his side. She'd seen his face soften in sleep, had seen him weep for his child.

Passion and pleasure. That was what Hart Mackenzie wanted to give her, not fear and pain.

Surrender.

Eleanor sighed, relaxing back against him, and the thickness of him slid straight inside.

Pure pleasure blossomed where they joined. No tightness, no pain, just Hart gliding his way in. She groaned.

"Yes, that's it," Hart whispered. "You see?"

"Hart."

"Shh."

Hart smoothed her hair, and she felt his lips, the enticing brush of hair that was his new beard. He did nothing with her bound hands, only held the end of the cloth. Eleanor's wrists were pressed against her chest, Hart behind her and surrounding her.

Another cry escaped her lips. Hart responded with a groan, not immune to what he was doing.

"My sweet El. How does that feel?"

"Beautiful. You are beautiful. Oh, Hart, I don't think I can stand this!"

"Yes, you can." Hart licked her ear, the beard again tickling her. "You can stand it, my beautiful Scottish lassie. You are strong, like your kin who pushed the Sassenach soldier off th' roof."

Eleanor laughed, and the movement moved sweet bliss through her. Even Hart's jests were calculated to bring out the finest feelings.

Passion and pleasure, bodies hot where they joined. Hart held her thus for a long time, moving very little. He simply filled her, giving her the joy of feeling him inside her, of being one with him.

Hart's lips at her ear. "Do you want more?"

"Yes. Yes, please, Hart."

Eleanor heard the begging words come from her mouth, but she could not stop them. Hart chuckled, the vibration of his body wonderful.

Eleanor found herself rocking forward to her hands and knees, Hart never coming out of her. He surrounded her with arms and legs, releasing the cravat enough so that she could brace herself on the bed. But he held her, never letting her fall, never letting her go.

Their bodies grew slick with sweat, droplets trickling between Eleanor's breasts to be caught by the cravat. Where Hart joined with her was nothing but heat.

"My El," he groaned. "Don't ever leave me again. Do you understand me? I *need* you."

Eleanor shook her head. "No. I'll stay. Always, always, Hart."

"I won't let you go. Not Fenians, not my stupid pride, not my past will get between us. I'm finished."

She wasn't sure exactly what he was talking about, but she loved his words rumbling over her. "Good. Good."

"You and me, El. We're meant to be. And the world can go hang."

"Yes, Hart. *Yes.*"

"El, lass, ye are so beautiful." His Highland Scots erased every bit of English schooling pounded into him. "Stay w' me forever."

"Yes. Oh, Hart, I love you."

Without realizing he'd moved her, Eleanor found herself flat on her belly, Hart positioning her hands so that they stretched out in front of her. He was on top of her, the full weight and length of him on her body, still joined with her. She couldn't go on with this, and at the same time, she couldn't get enough of it. Hart had to stop—no, he had to *never* stop.

His words trailed into groans. His loving rubbed her against the coverlet beneath her, the friction of that driving her wild. She was trapped beneath him, and yet, the fire of him inside her made her feel powerful. She could do anything, anything, because Hart shared with her his strength.

The moment of joy went on, Hart finally surrendering to his. He shuddered, his skin damp, his breath warming her. "My El," he said as he kissed and kissed her. "My sweet, wicked lass."

He slid out of her and rolled her over, stretching on top of her and loosening her hands.

"Are you all right?"

Eleanor nodded, breathless. "Perfectly fine, my dear Hart. That was . . ." She grinned. "Perfectly fine."

Hart unwound the strip of linen from her and let it flutter to the coverlet. He lowered his head to the pillows beside her. "Thank you."

He had given her that beautiful pleasure, and he was thanking *her*? "What for?"

"The gift of your trust."

She shrugged, pretending indifference. "You are not so bad."

The sinful twinkle returned to his eyes. "Oh, no? I will have to convince you otherwise."

Eleanor touched the linen strip. "Is this the kind of thing you like to do?"

"Part of it."

"There's more?"

His wide smile sent a hot shiver through her. "Much more, El. Much, much more."

"And you will teach me all of it?"

Hart's eyes flickered as he considered. He brushed a warm lover's kiss over her lips. "Yes."

Another shiver, excitement deepening. "I look forward to it."

He lost his smile, a frown pinching his brows. "When I thought I'd lost you . . . When all I could see was the explosion and you disappearing behind it . . ."

He was shaking. Eleanor cupped his face, smoothing her thumb through the beard she was beginning to like. "Don't think on it. We came through, both of us safe. Thanks to Ian."

"Ian, yes. He's lived through terrible things, and he deserves . . . so much."

"Don't worry. He's happy now. He has Beth and his children. I've never seen him so happy."

"I know. Thank God for Beth." Hart caught her wrist, kissed it. "And thank God for you. I love you, El. I can never explain how much I love you."

His heart was in his voice, the gruff tones he used only when emotion got the better of him. That happened so rarely that Eleanor treasured it.

"I love you too, Hart. Forever."

Hart nodded. "Forever, El." He let out his breath, body shuddering as he relaxed beside her. He pulled a crumpled quilt over their bodies, and Eleanor snuggled down with him in the comfortable nest. The room grew quiet, peaceful.

"I hope you're happy, Ian," Hart muttered.

"What?" Eleanor blinked open her eyes. When Hart did not respond, she poked him. "What did you say?"

Hart chuckled, the maddening man. "Nothing. Go to sleep."
Eleanor kissed him again, and did.

⁓

Hart lay in the stillness of the room, watching Eleanor sleep,
his mind full of what had just happened.

Eleanor had sweetly surrendered to him, and he'd experienced something beyond price. The two of them had become
one, whole, complete. Hart had never felt that with any other
person in his life.

Always Hart was alone, seeking to dominate so that his
loneliness would not be used against him. Eleanor had smiled
at him tonight in surprise and delight, completely trusting.
Not seeking mindless pleasure for her own sake, but believing
he would guide and protect her through their journey together.

Looking at her now, her face so serene, one curl snaking
across her cheek, Hart knew he'd found peace. He'd just now
let his dark needs fill him without check, without fear. Because Eleanor had been there to guide him.

With her help, he'd let his needs surge into the joy they were
meant to be. Not Hart desperately seeking to forget in numbing
pleasure, or Hart taking charge to remind everyone, including
himself, who was master.

Hart had been loving a woman, showing her what joy
could be. He'd been loving Eleanor.

He'd moved from the hell of the tunnels to the purgatory of
the boat, where he'd come face-to-face with the realization
of what was the most important thing in his life. Not power,
not money or might, not controlling everything around him.

Eleanor.

He remembered how the warm thoughts of her, even when
he couldn't quite form them, had sustained him in the tunnels.
His first thoughts when he'd woken again, free of the darkness, had been of her.

All that mattered was Eleanor, and the child she now carried inside her.

Hart spread his hand over her warm abdomen. She never
moved, sleeping on.

Hart's body loosened, and he dropped into profound sleep,
curled into her warmth.

The return of Hart Mackenzie was greeted with dismay in some quarters and relief in others. England read of Hart's survival in their morning newspapers, shook heads, and said, *That family is quite unbalanced.*

Reeve got his money, more than he'd dreamed. So much that Reeve decided to quit London and take his family to live in a cottage on the southern coast.

At Kilmorgan, Hart rejoined his family to great joy, and also to scolding. The ladies were the worst. Hart barely escaped from them, taking refuge in fishing with Ian.

David Fleming came to Kilmorgan, eager to have Hart take the reins of power again. They couldn't lose, David said. Hart could hold the nation in the palm of his hand, make it do whatever he wished.

Everything he'd always wanted.

"It's up to you, old man," David said, lounging back in a chair, a cheroot in one hand, a flask in the other. "I don't mind stepping aside. I'd prefer it. What do you want to do?"

Hart looked up at the Mackenzie ancestors that marched along the walls of his huge study, from Old Malcolm Mackenzie, with the sneer that had put the fear of God into the English, to his own father, who glared at all who crossed the threshold.

Hart looked into the eyes above the beard, at the mean glitter that the painter had managed to capture. Behind those eyes was a man who'd plotted to kill his own son.

Except that this time when Hart looked at the picture, he saw that the painted eyes were just that, paint.

The old duke was gone.

Hart pressed his hands flat on the desk and closed his eyes. *I have defeated you. I no longer need to prove to you that I am not weak.*

Upstairs, in their bedchamber, Eleanor was knitting booties.

He opened his eyes. "No," he said.

David stopped, his flask halfway to his mouth. "What did you say?"

"I said no. I am resigning. You lead the party to victory."

David paled. "But I need you. *We* need you."

"No, you don't. You kept the coalition together when it looked as though I was dead. You could not have done that if I was the only thing that held the party together. I look forward to many nights sharing whiskey with you and listening to your stories of your days as prime minister. I will continue to support the party and advise you if necessary. But I no longer want the post of prime minister."

David stared at him. "You *are* joking."

Hart sat back, breathing the waft of cool Scottish air that floated through the open windows. "The fish are biting in the river down the hill. The Mackenzie distillery needs my help. Ian does fine with it, but his heart's not in brewing the finest malt whiskey known to man. I'm going to take over the running of it while he enjoys himself with the accounts. I am going to stop trying to run the world and start trying to run my life. I've neglected it."

"I see, so you'll become a proper Scottish laird, and walk about your estate in stout boots with a walking stick. I know you, Mackenzie. You'll grow bored soon enough."

"I doubt it. My wife is growing heavy with my child, and I intend not to miss a moment of his life."

"Eleanor's increasing?" David gaped. "Good Lord. Has she run mad?"

"Not yet." Hart stared comfortably out at the room that had ceased to intimidate him. Maybe he'd let Eleanor take down all these bloody pictures and redecorate the place.

David laughed a little, but he shook his head. "Ah, well. We could have been great together, Mackenzie. Tell Eleanor she has my congratulations. And my sympathies."

"I will. Now get out. I want to be alone with my wife."

David chuckled. He took a drink from his flask and dropped it in his pocket. "Don't blame you, old man. Don't blame you one whit." David shook Hart's hand one last time, clapped him on the shoulder, and finally went away.

Hart stood up. He walked to his father's portrait, a copy of the one that hung in the great stairwell down the hall. Tradition had it that the current duke hung on the first landing, the former duke on the second, and so on to the top of the house. When Beth had first moved in with Ian, she suggesting consigning the lot of them—including Hart, no doubt—to the attic.

Hart had thought Beth too full of her own opinion at the time, but now, he agreed with her. Changes would be made at Kilmorgan forthwith.

Hart gazed up at his hated father, His Grace of Kilmorgan, Daniel Fergus Mackenzie. And stopped. Clouds outside had parted, and a beam of sunshine slanted onto the portrait to show Hart something he hadn't been able to see from his desk.

Hart stared at it for some time. Then he started to laugh.

Still laughing, he tugged the bellpull, and when a footman answered, he sent him to fetch Eleanor.

Eleanor found Hart sitting at his desk, leaning his chair back on two legs, his booted feet crossed on the desk's surface. His kilt slid up to reveal his strong thighs, and he had a grin of delight on his face.

"Eleanor," he said pointing. "Did you do that?"

Eleanor turned to look at what he indicated. "Yes," she said. "I did."

"That's a valuable painting."

"You have another by the same artist hanging in the hall. Not to mention the Manet in London."

"Tell me why."

Eleanor glanced up at the old duke. She'd come in here with Hart when they'd arrived back at Kilmorgan a few days ago, and she'd seen Hart flinch under the scrutiny of those eyes.

Later, Eleanor had marched upstairs and gotten a drawing pencil, come back down, climbed up on a chair, and in a fit of pique, did her damage. The old duke now sported devil horns and round spectacles.

Hart's grin warmed his face. "Come clean, El. Tell me."

Eleanor clenched her hands. "I was so angry with him. You have always been so afraid you'd become like him, and he *made* you fear that. But you're not a bit like him at all. You have a temper, yes, but you're generous and strong and protective. So very protective. Your father was none of that. I got tired of him upsetting you." She looked at Hart, who had his hands behind his head. He'd shaved the beard, now her clean-shaven, hard-faced man again, but she might try to persuade him to grow the beard back. She'd rather liked the feel of it against any part of her he kissed.

She went on. "I've always thought you much more like your great-great-grandfather, Old Malcolm. He must have been a terror, and yet, his lady loved him. She described him well in her diaries—I read them. The things she says of him remind me of you."

Hart looked thoughtful. "Old Malcolm? I thought he was a ruthless bastard."

"Can you blame him? His four brothers and father dead at Culloden? Poor man. At least he found Mary and eloped with her. Very romantic."

"Mackenzies were romantic in those days."

"Mackenzies still are."

Hart came out of the chair with the same controlled precision he gave everything else. "Are we, now, lass?"

"I think so." Eleanor thought about the exciting things Hart had been teaching her in bed the last few days, things that made her blush, but gave her a little shiver of pleasure to think on. Hart certainly knew exotic things, but he was patient, never rushing her, always making certain she was unafraid before he proceeded. He was a wicked, wicked man, but one with a heart so full, and now he belonged to her.

She slid her hand into his and gave it a squeeze. "Of course you're romantic. Look at how pleased you are that your brothers are happily married off."

"I am." Hart made an exasperated noise. "But now I have the whole confounded lot of them here. No privacy in this house."

"They've gone fishing," Eleanor said. "With the children. They won't be back for some time. Perhaps we can take the opportunity for you to show me more of your . . . unconventional passions."

"Mmm." Hart ran his hands down her arms to move his thumbs over the insides of her wrists. "I have a few new things to play with. I got them just for you."

Her heart beat faster. "Oh?"

"No more makeshift tethers. I have real ones now."

"Do you? How splendid. I look forward to seeing you in them."

Hart started, eyes widening. "What?"

Eleanor wanted to laugh. "Yes, indeed. My bonny, braw

Scotsman, perhaps in only his kilt, with his wrists bound together, waiting for me?"

Hart stared at her for a long moment, then his sinful smile spread across his face. "Bold minx. You've been learning your lessons well."

"I believe that would make a good photograph, do you not?"

Hart opened his mouth to answer. Then he closed it. Then he growled.

Her bonny, braw Scotsman jerked her up to him, and his kiss took her breath away. "My Eleanor," he said. "I love you."

"I love you too, Hart Mackenzie."

His grin returned. "You should know better than to challenge me. I'll answer with a challenge of my own."

"Well, I should hope so," Eleanor said.

Hart growled again, then he lifted her in his arms, kicked open the door, and ran with her out of the room.

Epilogue

Hart had no interest in more official portraits of him, but Eleanor insisted. "Not just you," she'd said. "The entire family."

And so, on a fine day when Hart would have preferred to be fishing with Ian, he traipsed out onto the terrace with his brothers and their families to have their portraits taken. A photographer who'd come from Edinburgh busied himself readying the camera, his tripod, and his collection of glass plates.

First to be photographed was the Cameron Mackenzie family, only because Cameron marshaled his troops the fastest. Cameron sat on a chair, and Ainsley stood on his right, her hand on his shoulder. Daniel was on his left, and Gavina, nearly two years old now, sat on Cameron's lap. Something dribbled out of Gavina's mouth, and Cameron swiftly caught the drool on his handkerchief, wiping her clean before the camera's shutter closed.

Next came Ian and Beth. Ian sat in the chair, his kilt draped over his knees. Beth stood regally beside him in her dress of Mackenzie plaid. She held Belle in her arms, while three-year-old Jamie perched on Ian's lap. The camera caught Ian looking, not at the lens, but up at his wife, his face soft with happiness. Beth was looking back down at him, his fingers on her hand. A beautiful portrait.

Ian and Beth took the children down to the lawn to play while Mac at last got his brood chivied into place. Mac took his place in the chair, with six-year-old Aimee on his left, and Isabella standing at his right shoulder. Eileen, three now, stood leaning back against her mother, Isabella holding her hand. Two-year-old Robert, in a kilt, sat on his father's lap.

The camera caught them laughing. Sun shone on Isabella's red hair and her smile, but Mac was out and out laughing. *"Papa,"* Aimee said. "You'll spoil it."

They took another, more dignified photograph this time, but smiles underlay all expressions.

Eleanor bounced baby Hart Alec Graham Mackenzie in her arms, and Hart said, "Enough. Let us finish this."

Mac herded his three children away, Eileen running screaming after her cousin Jamie. Aimee hurried behind, having appointed herself guardian to impetuous Eileen.

Hart sat in the chair and reached for baby Alec. Alec still wore long gowns, but Eleanor had fastened a piece of Mackenzie plaid around his sturdy waist. Eleanor stood at Hart's right, and Lord Ramsay, who now called himself Grandfather Alec, took a place on Hart's left.

Hart lifted his head and stared at the camera. He imagined how the finished photo would look: himself in the middle, straight and arrogant; Lord Ramsay looking almost comically regal; Eleanor, beautiful, her face softened with good humor; and baby Alec sitting up on Hart's lap, Hart's hands around him.

Alec. The miracle of a child that Eleanor had presented to Hart on a cold December evening, one of the longest nights of Hart's life. Ian had plied him with drink, but Hart had paced and sweated, terrified that he'd relive the night that Sarah had died, and then the day that Graham had.

But Eleanor, resilient, had pulled through, and small Alec had greeted Hart with robust wails. Hart had lifted his son, small enough to hold in his cradled hands, his heart overflowing with so much joy and relief that he'd wept.

Hart thought of that night now as he looked down at Alec.

Alec stared back up at his father, his gaze perfectly steady. Going on six months old, Alec had already perfected the Mackenzie glare.

"Mind your manners, now," Hart said to him.

Alec loved Hart's rumbling voice. Even now, his eyes softened. He gave his father a grin and reached up to touch his face. The camera caught it, father and son sharing a glance, the little hand on Hart's jaw, Hart laughing down at Alec.

Hart made the photographer do another exposure, this one stiffly dignified, as portraits were supposed to be. But ever after, Eleanor would treasure the first one. She had it framed and hung it in a place of honor in the family's private drawing room.

The afternoon of photographs wasn't finished yet. Eleanor insisted they end with one of the entire family: Hart, Cameron, Mac, and Ian and their collective families, and—God help them—all the dogs.

They stood in a row, the four Mackenzies, with Ainsley and Daniel, Eleanor and Lord Ramsay, Beth and Isabella, the seven children, and the five dogs grouped around them. The portrait was difficult to pose, because no sooner were the younger children seated in front than two-year-old Robert decided that he'd much rather run after the butterfly that had landed on a flower on the edge of the terrace. Ruby and McNab decided to go after *him*.

Ben, smart animal, lay his great head between his paws and fell asleep in the sunshine, his snores sounding even over the children's cries. Aimee chased Robert, Jamie went to see what the fuss was about, and Gavina demanded to be set down so she could crawl about, or at least play with the dogs.

Daniel loped off and lifted both Jamie and Robert into his big arms, carrying them, protesting, back to the terrace. The dogs followed.

Much arguing and cajoling followed. In the midst of it, Hart gave Eleanor a squeeze and leaned down to her. "I bought you a present."

Eleanor's eyes lit. "I adore presents. What is it?"

"A surprise, minx. You'll have to wait. Your punishment for putting me through the torture of having our portrait taken."

Eleanor handed Alec to him, turned swiftly, and started

chivying the others into position as only Eleanor could chivy. They finally got settled, and the photographer said, "Still now. And . . . *done*."

The portrait of the entire Mackenzie family, seventeen of them, with five dogs, was printed on a large sheet, framed, and hung in the foyer of Kilmorgan Castle.

But that was to come. Today, the children, released from the restriction of having to stand still, now ran about the garden, screaming and shouting, in a game of tag that seemed to have no rules. Mac and Daniel dodged after them to make sure no one was hurt in the fray.

The ladies served tea and talked. And talked and talked. Cameron, Ian, and Hart exchanged a glance, went inside to discard their finery, and took out their fishing poles.

As it was, Hart did not have the chance to give Eleanor her present until late that night, which was fine with him.

Eleanor, in her silk dressing gown, gave Hart a curious look as she opened the wrappings of the square box he presented her. They were in the bedchamber Eleanor had been given when she'd become Hart's wife, which Hart had adopted as *their* bedchamber. No longer would he sleep in that mausoleum of a room when he could curl up cozily with Eleanor.

"Oh, Hart, it's lovely."

It was a small camera, so small as to fit into Eleanor's hand. She turned it around and around, examining the lens, the leather case, and the brass fittings that would let glass plates slide across its back.

"You said you liked handheld cameras."

"But this one is so tiny." Eleanor smiled at it. "How very clever. I can carry it about in my pocket."

"There is a box of dry plates in the drawer of the table behind you."

Eleanor went to it and pulled out the box. She withdrew a plate and quickly worked out how to slide it onto the back of her little camera. "Now," she said. "What on earth can I take a picture of?"

She smiled at Hart, her eyes sparkling. Hart unfastened his dressing gown and let it fall. "Let us think."

Eleanor laughed. "Do hold still."

Hart drew himself up and gave her his best portrait glare, a Mackenzie in all his dignity. Except that he wasn't wearing a stitch.

Eleanor took photo after photo, until Hart took the camera from her. "Your turn."

She hadn't paid her dues yet. Eleanor had begged off any photos while she carried Alec, as much as Hart argued that he'd never seen her so beautiful. She'd only given him the look women reserved for men they thought hopeless.

After that, they'd been busy—with Alec, with the estate, with Hart working with Ian at the distillery, with the fêtes and balls Hart still hosted as duke and supporter of his party. Never mind that the party had gone down in defeat, and Gladstone had once more returned to the fold. David Fleming vowed to carry on.

"I'm not sure I can," Eleanor said. "I'm rather shy, you know."

Hart set down the camera, came to Eleanor, and ripped open her dressing gown. She fended him off and undid the buttons herself of the nightgown she wore beneath.

Hart stood back and waited while Eleanor came into view. Her hips had grown a little more curved since she'd had Alec, her breasts more full. Her hair was a fall of red gold glory, her eyes sweetly blue. Freckles spread across her face and onto her forehead, and across her chest, dipping to her breasts.

Beautiful. Hart snapped the first photograph of her from the waist up, Eleanor with her thick hair falling across one breast.

Next, Eleanor lay on the bed, rolling onto her side, coyly shielding herself with her thigh, her arm over her bare breasts.

Nudity, not quite revealed, was even more beautiful than if she'd spread herself out for him.

Hart leaned down to kiss her. He dropped more kisses to her bare side, and then he forgot about the camera. It tumbled to the mattress while he gently lowered her onto her back, and then he climbed over her, body surrounding hers. Where he belonged. Thoughts of his past, his mistakes, his anger, and his misery, were gone. Hart looked into Eleanor's eyes, felt her arms around him, and knew he'd found home.

Author's Note

One of the most contentious debates in England in the 1880s was the question of Irish Home Rule. There were those, like William Gladstone, prime minister during the time in which the Mackenzies' series is based, who wanted to give Ireland some independence from England. In 1885, Gladstone began campaigning for his Home Rule bill, which would allow Ireland to set up a separate parliament in Dublin to contend with Irish affairs, though it would still answer to English rule. The question was a touchy one, and Gladstone had many opponents, including the queen.

Gladstone returned to power in 1886 after a temporary defeat, and was able to get the Home Rule bill passed in the House of Commons, but it was defeated by the House of Lords. The bill was once more brought to the vote in 1889 and once again passed in Commons, but again defeated in the House of Lords.

I borrowed Gladstone's struggles with Irish Home Rule for this story and moved them a few years earlier. Hart, no lover of the English, wished to put forth Home Rule for Ireland, but he wanted his version, not Gladstone's. Hart's idea was to give

Ireland *complete* independence from England, and from that victory, propose the same for Scotland. Hart's scheme was to draw followers from both Gladstone's Liberals and the Tory party, defeat Gladstone by calling a vote of no confidence, and step in to rule with a coalition.

Gladstone served as prime minister four times, resigning from office for the last time in 1894.

Turn the page for a preview of the next
historical romance by Jennifer Ashley

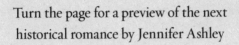

The Seduction of
Elliot McBride

Coming soon from Berkley Sensation!

Chapter 1

Juliana St. John's fiancé was an hour late to his own wedding. While Juliana sat waiting, resplendent in satin and yellow roses, her hands growing colder as the minutes ticked by, various friends and family members were dispatched through rainy Edinburgh to find out what was the matter.

Juliana's stepmother, Gemma St. John, and the matron of honor, Ainsley Mackenzie, tried to keep her spirits up, but Juliana knew in her heart that something was terribly wrong. When Grant's friends returned, embarrassed and empty-handed, Ainsley asked her husband, a tall brute of a Scotsman, to go. The result was different.

Cameron Mackenzie opened the vestry door enough to stick his head around it, never mind the group of ladies fluttering about like nervous moths. "Ainsley," he said, then shut the door again.

Ainsley pressed Juliana's hands, which by now were like ice. "Never you mind, Juliana. I'll discover what has happened."

Juliana's stepmother, only ten years older than Juliana herself, was angry. She said nothing, but Juliana saw rage in every movement Gemma made. Gemma had never liked Grant Barclay and liked Grant's mother still less.

Ainsley returned in a short time. "Juliana," she said, her voice gentle. She held out her hand. "Come with me."

When a person spoke in that tone, terrible news was certain to follow. Juliana rose in a swish of skirts. Gemma tried to follow, but Ainsley held out her hand. "Juliana alone, I think."

Gemma, of the volatile temper, started to protest, but Gemma was also intelligent. She gave Juliana a nod. "I will be here, dear."

Juliana had a temper of her own, but as she stepped out into the gusty rain of the church's courtyard, she felt nothing. No anger, no fear, nothing but a curious numbness. She'd been engaged to Grant for years now. The wedding had always been so comfortably far away that it had come as a shock to reach the day. And now . . .

Was Grant ill? Dead?

It was a rainy Edinburgh day, mist cloaking the city, the sky obscured. Ainsley led Juliana in her finery out and through a tiny yard, mud soaking Juliana's new white high-heeled boots. They reached an arched breezeway, and Ainsley started down this, away from the main church. Thank heavens, because all the guests were in the church, waiting and watching, now speculating about what had gone wrong.

Under an arcade, but still in the chill, Cameron waited alone. When Ainsley dragged Juliana over, Cameron looked down at her with flint-hard eyes. "I found him."

Still Juliana felt nothing but numbness. None of this seemed real, not the tall Scotsman in Mackenzie plaid, a silver flask in his hand, not the lowering skies outside the church, not Juliana's wedding finery.

"Where is he?" Juliana asked.

"In a carriage behind the church," Cameron said. "Do you want to speak to him?"

"Of course I want to speak to him. I am going to marry him . . ."

She noticed the look Ainsley and Cameron exchanged,

caught the glimpse of anger in Ainsley's eyes, the annoyance in Cameron's.

"What is it?" Juliana squeezed Ainsley's hand. "Tell me before I go mad."

Cameron answered for her. "He eloped," he said. "He's married."

The arches and the courtyard, solid Edinburgh stone, spun around and around her, but no, she was standing upright, staring at Cameron Mackenzie, Ainsley's warmth at her side.

"Married," she repeated. "But he's marrying me."

She knew that the last thing in the world Lord Cameron wanted to do this day was hunt down Juliana's groom and then tell Juliana what he'd discovered about the despicable man. But she kept staring at Cameron, as though if she glared hard enough, he'd change the story and tell her a different one.

"He married yesterday afternoon," Cameron said. "To a woman who was teaching him the piano."

This was mad. It had to be a joke. "Mrs. Mackinnon," Juliana said without inflection. She remembered the woman with dark hair and plain dresses who had sometimes been at Grant's mother's when Juliana arrived. "She is a widow." A strange laugh escaped her lips. "Not anymore, I suppose."

Cameron's steady gaze seemed to hold Juliana upright. "I told him he needed to have the decency to tell you himself. So I brought him. Do you want to talk with him?"

Cam was giving Juliana the choice—to face Grant while he shamefacedly confessed that he'd betrayed and abandoned Juliana, or to walk away.

"No," she said. "No."

Cameron pressed his flask into Juliana's hand. "Get that inside you, lass. It will lessen the blow."

A very proper lady did not drink spirits, and Juliana had been raised to be so very proper. But the turn of events made this a highly unproper occasion.

Juliana tipped back the flask and trickled a bit of burning Scots whiskey into her mouth. She coughed, swallowed, coughed again, and dabbed at her lips as Cameron rescued the flask.

Perhaps she should not have drunk. What Cameron had

told her was starting to seem real. Two hundred people waited
in the church for Juliana St. John and Grant Barclay to wed,
two hundred people who would have to be told to go home.
Two hundred gifts to be returned, two hundred apologies to
be penned. And the newspapers would certainly enjoy themselves.

Juliana pressed her cold hands to her face. She'd never
been in love with Grant, but she had thought they'd at least
formed a mutual respect for each other. But even that . . .
Grant hadn't given her even that.

"Ainsley, what am I going to do?"

Cameron tucked the flask inside his greatcoat. "We'll take
you home. I'll have my carriage pull up in the passage at the
end of this walk. None need to see you."

They were kind, Ainsley and Cameron—they were being
kind. Juliana didn't want kindness. She wanted to kick and
rage, not only at Grant, but at herself. She had been so secure
in her engagement, rather smug that she was no longer in danger of being left on the shelf.

Her future had just crumbled to dust, her safe choice ripped
from beneath her feet. Shock still rendered her numb, but she
sensed regret coming hard on its heels.

Juliana rubbed her arms, suddenly freezing. "Not yet. Please,
give me a moment. I need to be alone for just a moment."

Ainsley glanced into the courtyard, into which people
were now emerging from the church proper. "Not that way.
There's a chapel down here. We'll keep them out."

"Bless you, Ainsley." Juliana could not unclench herself
enough to give Ainsley the hug she deserved.

She let Ainsley guide her to the door of the chapel, which
Cameron opened. Cameron and Ainsley stepped back, and
Juliana went in alone, the door clicking closed.

The chapel was chilly but dim and peaceful. Juliana stood
for a moment in front of the bare altar, looking up at the plain
cross hanging above it, alone and unadorned.

Grant, married. To Mrs. Mackinnon. Juliana now realized
things she'd seen in the past few months but paid no mind to at
the time—Grant and Mrs. Mackinnon side by side at Grant's
mother's piano, their exchanged smiles, the looks between
them. Grant gazing pensively at Juliana as though he wanted

to speak to her about something important, and then making some joke or inane remark instead.

She knew what he meant to say, now. *Miss St. John, I've fallen in love with my piano teacher and wish to marry her, not you.*

Scandal. Humiliation.

Juliana balled her fists, wanting to shout at Providence for being so aggravating. But, even in her agitation, blasphemy in a chapel seemed wrong, so she settled for storming into a pew, her ivory skirts billowing around her.

"Blast!" she said and slammed herself into the seat.

On top of something that moved. A human something, a man with long legs under a woolen kilt, a broad body that heaved up onto strong elbows. A man coming awake to find a hundred and twenty pounds of young woman in wedding garb sitting on his thighs.

"What the devil?" Gray eyes the same color as Ainsley's flashed in a face that was too tanned to have been in Scotland long. "Juliana?"

Elliot McBride obviously had no compunction about blaspheming in a church. Or sleeping in one.

Juliana swiftly rose, but she couldn't move out of the pew. She stared back down at Elliot as he heaved himself partway up and lounged against the side of the pew, his booted feet still on the bench.

"Elliot?" Juliana said, her voice a gasp. "What are you doing here?"

"Trying to find some quiet. Too bloody many people about."

"I mean, here in Scotland. I thought you were in India. Ainsley said you were in India."

Elliot McBride was one of Ainsley's many brothers, a young man the young Juliana had fallen madly in love with about a hundred years ago. He'd disappeared to India to make his fortune, and she hadn't seen him since.

Elliot rubbed a hand over his stubbled face, though he smelled of soap and water, as though he'd recently bathed. "Decided to come home."

Laconic, that was the way to describe Elliot, the untamed McBride. Also large and strong, with a presence that knocked the breath out of her. It had been so when she was a child and he was the wild older brother of Ainsley, again when she'd been a proud debutante, and he'd attended her coming-out ball in his army regimentals.

Juliana sank to the pew again, at the end of it, beyond his feet. High in the tower of the main church, bells rang, striking the hour.

"Aren't you supposed to be in there, lass?" Elliot asked. He removed a flask from his coat and sipped from it, but unlike Cameron, he didn't offer her any. "Getting married to whatever his name is?"

"Grant Barclay. I was to have been Mrs. Grant Barclay."

His brows rose. "*Was to have been?* Did you jilt the whey-faced bastard, then?"

"No," Juliana said. "Apparently, yesterday, he eloped with his piano teacher."

It was all too much. Strange laughter welled up inside her and came pealing out of her mouth. Not quite hysterics, but a hearty laugh she couldn't stop.

Elliot lay still, like an animal deciding whether to attack or run. Poor Elliot. What must he make of a woman who'd jolted him out of his sleep by plopping down on him and then laughing uncontrollably because her fiancé had abandoned her?

Juliana's laughter eased off, and she wiped her eyes with her fingertips. Her dark red hair was tumbling down, one of the yellow roses Ainsley had tied in it falling to her lap. "Stupid flowers."

Elliot sat frozen, his hand gripping the back of the pew so hard he was surprised the wood didn't splinter. He watched as Juliana laughed, as her glorious auburn hair fell to her bared shoulders. She smiled though her blue eyes were wet, and the hands that plucked the flower from her lap were long-fingered and trembling.

Elliot wanted to put his arms around her and cradle her close. "There now," he'd say. "You're better off without the idiot." An even stronger instinct made him want to go find Grant Barclay and shoot him for the bastard he was.

But he knew that if he made the mistake of touching Juliana, he wouldn't stop at comfort. He'd tilt her head back and kiss her lips, as he'd done at her debut ball, the night she'd permitted the one kiss.

They'd both been eighteen. Before Elliot had gone to hell and back, that chaste kiss would have been enough for him. This time, it would not be enough, not by a long way.

He'd kiss his way down her pretty throat to her bosom, nuzzle her gown's satin neckline, and feather kisses to her shoulders. Then he'd lick his way back up to her ripe lips, seam them with his tongue, coax her to let him inside. He'd kiss her with long, careful kisses, tasting the goodness of her mouth while he held her and did not let her go.

Elliot would want to take everything, because Lord only knew when he'd have the chance again. A broken man learned to savor what he could when he had the time.

"It will stay with me forever," Juliana was saying. *"Poor Juliana St. John. Don't you remember? She'd already put on her wedding clothes and gone to the church, poor darling."*

What did a man say to a woman in this situation? Elliot wished for the eloquence of his barrister brother, who stood up in court and made elegant speeches for a living. Elliot could only ever speak the truth.

"Let them say it, and to the devil with them," he said.

Juliana gave him a sad smile. "The world is very much about what *they* say, my dear Elliot. Perhaps it's different in India."

Dear God, how could anyone think that? "The rules there are damn strict," he said. "You can die—or get someone else killed—by not knowing them."

"Oh." Juliana blinked. "Very well, then, I concede that such a thing sounds worse than the people expecting me to hide in shame and knit socks for the rest of my life."

"Why the devil should you knit socks? Do what you like."

"Very optimistic of you. Not fair to me, but I'm afraid I will be talked about for a long while now. *And* I am now on the shelf. Thirty years old, and no longer an ingénue. Most of the gentlemen I know are now married, and besides, many of them are Grant's friends. I know that women do all sorts of things these days besides marry, but I am too old to attend university, and even if I did, my father would die of shame that I was such a bluestocking. I was raised to pour tea, organize fetes, say the correct things to the vicar's wife."

Her words slid over Elliot without him registering them,

her musical voice soothing, whatever she might be saying. He lay back and let her talk, realizing he'd not felt so at ease in a long while.

If I could listen to her forever, if I could drift into the night hearing her voice, I might get well again.

No, nothing would be well, never again, not after the things he'd done. He'd thought that once he took refuge in Scotland, it would stop. The dreams, the waking terrors, the knowledge that a man he'd wronged was dead, gone before Elliot could make amends.

Juliana was studying him, her blue eyes like a clear summer lake. The beauty of her, the memory of those eyes, had sustained him for a long time in the dark.

Sometimes he'd dreamed she was with him, trying to wake him, her dulcet voice filling his senses. *Come on, now, Elliot. You must wake up. My kite's tangled in a tree, and you're the only one tall enough to get it down.*

He remembered the day when he'd first realized what he felt for her—they must have both been about sixteen. She'd been flying a kite for children of her father's friends, and Elliot had come to watch. He'd retrieved the kite from a tree for her and earned a red-lipped smile, a soft kiss on his cheek. From that day forward, he'd been lost.

"Elliot, are you awake?"

His eyes had drifted closed on memories, and now Juliana's voice blended with the remembered dream. He pried his eyes open. "I think so."

"You did not hear me, did you?" Her face was pink—with anger, he thought.

"Sorry, lass. I'm a bit drunk."

"Good. Not that you're drunk, but that you didn't hear me. Never mind. It was a foolish idea."

He opened his eyes wider, his brain coming alert. What the hell had he missed?

The darkness occasionally did that to him. Elliot, at times, would slide through large portions of conversation without noticing he had. He'd come back to himself realizing that people were waiting for his response and wondering what was the matter with him. Elliot had decided that avoiding people and conversation was the best solution.

With Juliana, he wanted to know. "Tell me again," Elliot said.

"I don't think I ought. If it were a cracking-good idea, you'd have leapt on it at once. As it is . . ."

He'd offended her. "Juliana, I swear to you . . . I drift in and out. I want to hear your cracking-good idea."

"No, you don't."

Females. Even ones he'd been secretly in love with for years could drive him insane.

Elliot sat up and stretched his arm along the back of the pew. He didn't touch her but let his arm rest close enough to her to feel her warmth. "Juliana, tell me, or I'll tickle you."

"I'm not eight years old anymore, Elliot McBride."

"Neither am I. When I say *tickle*, I no longer mean what I did then." He touched her bare shoulder with one finger.

A mistake. The contact shot heat up his arm and dove straight into his heart. Elliot should lift his hand away, get out of this chapel, and race back across the city to the safety of his brother's house. Back to cowering in the bedroom, having his patient manservant feed him cups of weak tea. *I am so tired of all this.*

Elliot brushed her shoulder again, and Juliana looked up at him. Her lips were close to his, lush and ripe. She had faint freckles across her nose, ten of them. She'd always had them, had always tried to rid herself of them, but to Elliot, every one was kissable.

Her eyes went still, and her voice was a whisper of breath. "What I asked, Elliot, was whether *you* would marry me."